A PLANET FOR THE PRESIDENT

A PLANET FOR ★ THE PRESIDENT

A PLANET FOR ★ THE PRESIDENT

ALISTAIR BEATON

Weidenfeld & Nicolson

LONDON

First published in Great Britain in 2004
by Weidenfeld & Nicolson

© 2004 Alistair Beaton

A CIP catalogue record for this book
is available from the British Library.

ISBN 0 297 84776 7

Typeset, printed and bound in Great Britain
by Butler and Tanner Ltd, Frome and London

Weidenfeld & Nicholson
The Orion Publishing Group Ltd
Orion House
5 Upper Saint Martin's Lane
London, WC2H 9EA

For Kate, Daniel & Helen

My thanks go to Barry Pilton for his winnowing of the words, to Max Glaskin for his remorseless research, to Nick Webb for his encouragement, to Alan Samson for his enthusiasm, to Berlin Associates for their hard work, and to Kate, whose insights, criticisms and suggestions contributed so much to this book.

Alistair Beaton

WASHINGTON:
THE NEAR FUTURE

PART ★ ONE

1

'But Mr President, I was asked to think the unthinkable.' The fat guy's tone was politely defiant. The Oval Office fell silent. Everyone else in the room knew that the President didn't like being answered back. They also knew that he didn't like fat guys. The fat guy didn't know either of these things. The fat guy just sat there with a smile on his face, staring expectantly at the President. Everyone else was staring at the carpet.

The President of the United States reached into his jacket pocket, took out a little silver box, opened it, extracted a toothpick, and began probing the gaps between his molars. It was a technique he'd acquired since coming to the White House six years before. He knew it intimidated people. It also gave him time to think. Fifteen seconds passed in silence. The President paused in his dental assault.

'It's not that it's unthinkable,' said the President. 'It's just that I don't know what the fuck you're talking about.'

The foul language was at odds with the President's pious public image. People who hadn't met him before were normally shocked and scared when he talked like this. This time it didn't work. The fat guy didn't even blink. 'I don't think it's that difficult to understand,' he said provocatively.

Jesus, thought Vince, this guy takes risks.

'Maybe you're not being very clear,' growled the President.

'Would it help if I gave you a case study?' asked the fat guy.

'Not sure we have time for a case study, Mr Boyd.'

Vince was grateful. He'd completely forgotten the name of the fat guy. President Ritchie never forgot a name.

'It won't take long,' said Boyd. 'But I need a volunteer.'

'Okay. Do it,' growled the President.

Shit, thought Vince. As the junior member of the team he knew what was next.

'Vince, I'm volunteering you,' said the President, and briefly flashed his famous smile.

'No problem, sir,' said Vince.

'Just give me a couple of seconds,' said Boyd.

Vince hated these Oval Office meetings – something to do with the spurious informality created by the two long sofas. Not that the President ever joined them on the sofas. He preferred to perch on one of the green-and-cream striped chairs. This gave him about a foot and a half height advantage over everyone else. When the President was in a *really* difficult mood, he'd make everyone sit on the sofas while he sat at the other end of the room behind his big desk, his jaw muscles twitching with tension, his big hands balled in repressed rage.

Vince looked at the sofa opposite. Defense Secretary Skidelski was burrowing into his left ear. He extracted a small lump of wax and examined it. Jesus, thought Vince, Skidelski's ear, Ritchie's mouth, this is one choice gathering of human beings.

Alongside Skidelski, the much younger Vice President was hunched down in the sofa, his suit crumpled, his shirt coming out from his trousers. Vince knew the VP wore $2,000 suits, yet somehow he always managed to look like he'd just slept in the back of his car. He provided a dramatic contrast to the only woman in the room, Dolores Delgado, Head of Homeland Futures. Delgado was perched on the arm of the same sofa, looking poised and elegant, her tanned skin set off to perfection by a cobalt-blue suit she'd bought the previous weekend from Saks Fifth Avenue. Tall and slender, with strikingly high cheekbones, dreamy brown eyes and a carefully contrived confusion of black hair, Delgado looked more like a model than a senior member of the administration. Most men assumed that a woman this good-looking had to be dumb. Most men lived to regret the assumption.

Sitting next to Vince was Jimmy Lombok, the President's National Security Adviser and fervent born-again Christian. There was always something panicky in Lombok's eyes, as if he expected the Final Judgement at any moment and wasn't 100 per cent sure of being saved. Today he merely looked preoccupied, his massive bald cranium showing a light sheen of sweat. Vince had heard rumours that Lombok's wife liked to pick up young Latinos and bring them back to her house for afternoon sex. Maybe this was one of those afternoons. Maybe Lombok *knew* this was one of those afternoons.

On the sofa opposite, Vince could see the fat guy struggling to get something out of his ugly plaid jacket. Hell, the guy was so obese he could hardly reach his inside pocket. When it came to obesity, Vince had the self-righteousness of a slim 34-year-old who never put on weight no matter what he ate or drank. With his dark, understated good looks, he regularly got the attention of young (and not so young) women around the White House, all of whom found him frustratingly loyal to his wife. This didn't make them give up. The strains of White House life routinely put paid to the most committed of relationships.

The fat guy sniffed and wiped his nose with his finger. Vince averted his gaze and found himself looking up at the huge colour photograph hanging on the east wall. Astride the planet, riding it like a bucking bronco, was President Ritchie L. Ritchie, dressed in cowboy chaps and waving a lasso. His campaign manager had handed the picture to the new President on the day of the inauguration, assuming that Ritchie would hang the memento somewhere in his private quarters, maybe in one of the green marble bathrooms in his Idaho ranch. But no, Ritchie had hung it on the east wall of the Oval Office for all to see. In the room where Harry Truman used to be photographed standing statesmanlike by a giant globe of the world, President Ritchie would routinely receive foreign heads of state right under that goddamn planet picture. Ritchie routinely enjoyed watching his visitors' eyes creep up towards it; he relished the flicker of shock in their faces, took pleasure in knowing that not one of them would have the balls to say anything about it. How could they? They knew this was the essential truth: that Ritchie L. Ritchie ruled the globe. And Ritchie L. Ritchie didn't mind who knew it.

'Okay,' said Boyd, now with a pocket computer in his hand. He tapped the metal stylus against the screen. 'I just need to ask you a few questions, Vince.'

'Sure,' said Vince, pissed at the fat guy for using his first name like that.

'How often do you eat meat?'

'Four times or five times a week.'

'Okay. Four point five . . .' Boyd tapped the answer into his PDA.

Actually, Vince was a vegetarian, but it wasn't something to admit to around the White House. Real men ate meat.

'Would you say your calorie intake is heavy, average, or low?' asked Boyd.

7

A lot less than yours, thought Vince, and answered, 'Average.'

'When you're shopping, do you buy local in-season produce?'

'Hell, no.' Vince laughed, remembering the times Lucy used to stagger home from the supermarket with bags of exotica from every continent.

'How many people in your household?'

'Two.'

'How many cars?'

'Three.' Vince was starting to feel uncomfortable. 'One of them we don't really use much.' Most days Vince used the Buick to drive to the White House, leaving his beloved BMW in its garage. He knew which he preferred, but these days you had to be careful about driving a foreign car. Only last week a friend of his had been refused service at a gas station because he was driving a foreign car. That's how things were nowadays. It didn't do his career any harm to turn up at the White House each morning in a good ol' American car.

'How many of your three vehicles give you more than twenty miles to the gallon?'

'Um ... none of them.'

'The average American drives about two hundred miles a week. How's that compare with you?'

Vince considered his daily journey into Washington from Annapolis. Then he ought to add Lucy's research trips. 'Well, I'd say that together, me and my wife drive about, well, I guess it must average about eight hundred miles a week, maybe nine hundred.'

'Okay,' murmured Boyd, using the stylus to tap more info into the PDA. 'Do any ride-sharing?'

'No way.'

'How often do you use public transport?'

'Never.'

'How many hours a year you spend flying?'

'Oh, that's a tough one.' Vince thought about the hours spent in Air Force One with the President, his twice-a-year trips to Europe with Lucy. 'I don't know ... a helluva lot. Say, fifteen hours a month? No, better make that twenty.'

'Two hundred and forty hours a year. Okay, just a couple more questions and we're through.'

'Good,' said the President, glancing at his watch.

'Yeah, we don't have all day,' boomed the VP.

'How big is your home, in square feet? Happen to know?'

Vince knew exactly. When they'd bought it a year ago the realtor had made a point of emphasising the amount of space. 'Six thousand square feet.'

The Defense Secretary whistled. 'You earn more than I thought, Vince.'

'It needed a lot of work,' said Vince. It hadn't needed *that* much work. He'd been able to pay for it with the money he'd made during his six-year stint working in Hollywood.

'How many bathrooms?' asked Boyd.

'Two,' lied Vince. Why the hell had they bought a house with four bathrooms? 'It'll be useful when we have kids,' Lucy had argued.

'Okay. Hold on . . .' Boyd tapped a few digits into the PDA. 'This is a very rough calculation, okay? Right . . . What I got here is your approximate eco-footprint.'

'What the hell's that?' growled the President.

'Ecological footprint,' explained Boyd. 'It's the amount of productive land you need to maintain one person at their current level of consumption. The average eco-footprint of an American citizen is twenty-four acres. That's about four times the global average, by the way. Now yours, Vince, is . . . let me see . . . it's approximately seventy-one acres.'

'Hey,' said the Vice President ponderously, 'that's a lot of acres.'

'How true,' said Boyd.

The VP turned pink. He didn't like sarcasm. His smooth jowls trembled. He was used to being listened to. He was used to being respected. He was the Vice President, goddamnit. True, he had nothing too original to say, but his vacuous pronouncements were delivered in tones of such suave and sonorous authority that people often took him seriously.

The fat guy appeared to be fearless. He looked the VP straight in the eye. 'If Vince's standard of living were the global norm, we would need . . .' He glanced at the screen of the PDA. 'We would need 15.2 planet Earths to support everyone.'

Vince had to admit he was kind of impressed. He'd never given his personal lifestyle much thought before.

The VP sat back in the sofa and stared malevolently at Boyd.

It was Jimmy Lombok who spoke first. Holding the big red kerchief with which he'd been mopping his brow, he said, 'That's just plain

9

stupid. No way is everyone on the planet ever going to be as rich as Vince.'

'Maybe we pay Vince too much,' said Skidelski, with a thin smile. The Defense Secretary made no secret of his dislike for Vince. He thought Vince had too much influence over the President; he thought Vince lily-livered and liable to weaken the President's resolve on crucial issues.

'Okay,' said Boyd, 'Forget Vince. Let's take the average American instead. Assuming we wanted everyone in the world to have the same standard of living as the average American, then—'

'Why would we want that?' asked the President.

'Yeah, what kind of dumb idea is that?' said the Vice President, never one to miss the opportunity of lining up with power. Together both men broke into guffawing laughter. The Head of Homeland Futures gave them a patronising smile. She had long ago got used to being the only girl in a boys' club, but that didn't mean she thought men together were a pretty sight.

Boyd frowned. 'You guys just don't get it, do you?'

Vince saw that the President was getting mad.

'Better make your points more clearly then, Mr Boyd,' said the President.

'You want it bite-sized? Fine. That's how I'll serve it up.'

Vince began to pity the fat guy. He was insulting some very powerful people. People who bore a grudge. People who found it worthwhile taking steps to end another person's career.

'Okay,' said Boyd, 'here's how it goes. Globally, the average eco-footprint is 5.6 acres per person. A fraction of the footprint produced by our friend Vince here, right? But here's the thing: *it's still too much.* The only reason the human race is still around is there's an accumulated bank of resources. But we're using them up fast.'

'Does that matter?' asked Dolores Delgado. 'Provided we got enough for ourselves?'

'Yes,' said Boyd. 'It matters.'

'Why?' asked the VP.

'Because having enough for ourselves won't work for much longer. The planet is warming up. The sea-level's rising. The ozone layer is thinning. The rainforests are disappearing.'

'Aw, not all that climate-change shit,' the President groaned.

'It's not shit. Within the foreseeable future the planet will be unable to support the present population. Not to mention a much bigger one.'

Vince glanced at the President, marvelling that Ritchie was listening to this kind of stuff. It was a reflection of how serious recent events had been.

'Think of it as a kids' party with not enough cake to go around,' said Boyd, struggling to find simple metaphors. 'The world population's now reached 6.2 billion, and they all want a slice of cake. Only the cake's much, much smaller than anyone realises. Oh, and most of it's poisoned and polluted and getting close to being uneatable. And nobody's broken the bad news to the kids yet.'

Boyd looked around. The cake metaphor hadn't made much of an impression. He tried a different tack. 'What we have is an ecological overshoot. We're borrowing our resources from the future. It's like getting a big loan from the bank. You've borrowed massive amounts at a high rate of interest, you've had a ball for a few years, spending money like there's no tomorrow, buying everything you can lay your hands on, dumping all your shit in the yard – or someone else's yard – and not worrying about how to clear it up, but now the loan's gone and the guy from the bank is at the door wanting his money. And you don't have any left.'

Vince realised that inadvertently, Boyd had just described Ritchie's economic policy.

'So what do you suggest we do, Mr Boyd?' said the President, with growing irritation.

'Well ... You could take measures to reduce the eco-footprint of the average American citizen.'

'Whoa! Stop right there!' said the President.

'Yeah, stop right there,' said the Vice President dutifully.

'I know you're hostile to green issues,' said Boyd.

'I'm hostile to dumb suggestions,' Ritchie retorted. 'How popular you think that's going to make me?' Ritchie leaned forward as if he were making a Presidential broadcast. 'My fellow Americans. I want you all to be poorer. Thank you. Goodnight. And God bless America. Forget it, Mr Boyd.' He turned to his Defense Secretary. 'I thought you said he was worth listening to?'

Right, thought Vince. End of meeting. Great. Today was Lucy's birthday. Now he'd definitely make it to the restaurant on time, thank God.

Might even be able to get home first and pick her up from there. Yeah, that would be best of all.

Boyd was not deterred by the President's caustic remarks. 'I'm not saying you should make Americans poorer.'

'So what the hell are you saying?' The President was near the end of his tether now.

'Look, Mr President. Our Census Bureau projects a US population of 403 million by the middle of the century. That's an extra 115 million people.'

'More Americans is a good thing.' Ritchie stood up. 'Sorry I can't go green for you, Mr Boyd. Thank you for coming.'

Amazingly, Boyd ignored him. He just sat there. Who did he think he was? 'I'm not suggesting you go green, Mr President. I'm suggesting you think the unthinkable. Like I was asked to do.'

Ritchie's face grew grim. 'The meeting's over.'

Defense Secretary Skidelski waved a withered hand. 'Just hang on, Ritchie, just hang on. I want to hear what the man has to say.' At sixty-three, Skidelski was the oldest person in the room, and looked it. His skeletal appearance was reinforced by the long, thin nose, which sat in a long, thin, scrawny face surmounting a long thin, scrawny neck.

'Yeah, but I *don't* want to hear what he has to say,' said Ritchie.

'Yeah, well I do,' Skidelski replied.

'Who's the fucking President, you or me?' snarled Ritchie.

Vince was amazed that Ritchie still dared to talk to the Defense Secretary like that. Joe Skidelski had become almost as powerful as the President. Maybe more. The man had spent years assiduously cultivating key figures inside and outside government. Now he had supporters at every level in the Pentagon, some who believed in him, some who were simply smart enough to see which way the wind was blowing. He also had supporters on the Hill, Senators and Congressman desperate to support the arms procurements that brought jobs and prosperity to their home towns. And he had supporters on the boards of the big electronics manufacturers who stood to make fortunes from the latest generation of smart weapons. He even had supporters in academia, especially amongst the young and the personable, those bright clean-cut ideologues who were steadily moving out of the universities and into the television studios where they boosted sales of their latest books by dripping acid on outmoded concepts such as international cooperation and the rule of law. As a result, the State Department had been sidelined and foreign policy was now effectively in the hands of the Defense Department. Now they had really important strategic discussions – like this one – without the Secretary of State even being present.

Boyd struggled to his feet, slowly heaving his vast bulk out of the sofa. Skidelski and the President were glaring spitefully at one another.

Dolores Delgado stood up. 'Mr President, I'd also like to hear more.'

'Me too,' said Jimmy Lombok, stuffing his red kerchief into his top pocket.

The VP said nothing. He was waiting to see which way the argument would go.

Before Ritchie could stop him, Skidelski had turned to the fat guy. 'Tell us what you understand by thinking the unthinkable, Mr Boyd.'

'Solving the world's problems by reducing the world's population.'

'Everybody wants to do that,' said Skidelski.

'Not in the way I want to do it.'

'How do you want to do it?'

'Drastically.'

'What's drastically mean?'

'Getting rid of a lot of people very quickly.'

'How many?'

'A lot.'

'How many's that?'

'As many as you want.'

'You're not proposing to get rid of Americans?'

'Of course not.'

'Is this . . . this solution . . . is it a practical possibility?'

'It will be soon.'

Vince looked at Skidelski, then back at Boyd. He had an odd feeling he'd just heard a routine that had been rehearsed.

'Let me get this straight,' said the President. 'Are you suggesting we wipe out millions of people?'

'No, more than that. I'm suggesting we wipe out everyone except Americans. Overnight.'

The Oval Office went silent. The President stared at the fat guy. It was like nobody dared to break the silence. Shit, thought Vince, I'm in a room with a bunch of people who're listening to a guy who wants to wipe out six billion people. He waited for the President to tell Boyd to get the hell out.

'Sit down, Mr Boyd,' said the President.

'Yes,' said the Vice President, 'sit down.'

2

A Few Months Earlier

'The bald eagle?'

   'Yes.'

   'In danger of extinction?'

   'Yes.'

   'You're kidding me.'

   'I'm afraid not, sir. Take a look at this.' Vince Lennox laid a graph on the desk. 'As you see, it's more or less disappeared from everywhere but Alaska.'

   The President peered at the graph. 'Shit.' This was bad. This was very bad.

   It wasn't that President Ritchie L. Ritchie had suddenly become ecologically aware. He still found the whole environment issue a pain in the ass. So the planet was heading down the toilet? Hey, he'd be long gone before it became a problem. Some things were just too big to deal with. And he was well into his second term, so he didn't have to worry about being re-elected. But over the last few months his aides and speechwriters had started putting pressure on him. They were warning him he could go down in history as the President who'd screwed the planet. Ritchie didn't like the thought of that. He wanted to be remembered as a great president, a heroic president, the president who'd led the fight against terrorism, the president who'd secured American power across the globe for generations to come. That's why the bald eagle thing worried him a lot. No way did he want to be the president who'd permitted the extinction of America's national symbol.

   Ritchie's finger traced the shapes of the graph. 'And now they're disappearing in Alaska too, right?'

'That's how it looks, sir. The best estimate is six hundred nesting pairs left.'

'What's causing it?'

'Probably PCBs.'

The President looked blank.

'Polychlorinated biphenyls,' said Vince.

'What the hell are *they*?' That was the great thing about his morning briefings with Vince. He didn't have to front up. Six mornings a week, President Ritchie would get up at 7.25 am, shower and shave, dress, and take the two-minute walk from the White House residence to the Oval Office, to arrive there at 8 am. For the leader of the most powerful nation on earth it wasn't the toughest of starts to the day, but Ritchie firmly believed that a relaxed president was an efficient president. Each morning as he sat down at his desk, the door would open and a steward would bring in a pot of black coffee and a bowl of oat bran with sliced apples and yogurt. Ritchie didn't really like this kind of breakfast; he'd have been much happier with crispy bacon and two eggs sunny-side-up, but the President was allergic to eggs, and bacon without the eggs hardly seemed worth it. Each morning he comforted himself with the thought that the oat bran breakfast helped keep him slim and healthy. Ritchie hated the idea of putting on weight; apart from the occasional burger he stuck to a pretty healthy diet.

Ritchie always ate his breakfast alone, reading the forty-page news summary prepared overnight by staffers. Actually, he skimmed it, rather than read it, because at 08.30 sharp Vince would arrive and brief him. For Ritchie, this was the most valuable part of the day. Vince was a genius at separating the big issues from the small. In any age, Vince would have been useful; in the age of information overload, he was indispensable. Vince could take a complex event and reduce it to its essential components. He could, basically, take a pile of incidents and make a story out of them. Ritchie could relate to that so much better than all those theoretical ramblings that other people threw at him. And he knew Vince well enough and trusted him enough to ask him basic questions that other people might think were dumb. If Ritchie needed to know what the hell PCBs were, or what was the capital of Nigeria, or where Burkina Faso was, he could ask Vince without embarrassment. He trusted Vince. This meant that by the time Ritchie started his daily meeting of the National Security Council at 09.30, he felt on top of the job.

'Polychlorinated biphenyls are a kind of toxin,' said Vince. 'They accumulate in the food chain. Heavy PCB residues are found in salmon. The bald eagle loves salmon. Or so I'm told.'

'Hey, I love salmon! Does that mean there are heavy residues of Polly-wolly-doodle-eniols in me too?'

'Probably, sir.'

'Well hey, it ain't killin' me. I feel just fine.'

'In the case of the bald eagles I guess there are other factors at work.'

'Yeah, right,' said Ritchie vaguely, staring at his schedule. For a moment all that could be heard in the Oval Office was the hum of the air conditioning. This was turning out to be the hottest September in quite some time.

Ritchie's main duty that day was hosting a State Arrival Ceremony on the South Lawn for the president of an obscure nation somewhere in the Balkans. Apparently this nation was of potential strategic import-ance, though Ritchie couldn't imagine why. No problem; Vince would brief him. Vince was the son of his one-time best friend. The poor boy was only eighteen when his dad had gone overnight from Wall Street high-flyer to bankrupt, thanks to a juicy development deal in Wisconsin that went belly-up. Vince had just started college at the time and Ritchie had helped out with the fees, even giving the boy a monthly allowance. Well, it was the least he could do: ten years before that, Vince's father had given Ritchie an investment tip that had brought Ritchie a cool twenty million dollars in the space of a week. Technically it had been insider trading, but hey, what are friends for?

The boy was smart; he burned his way through Princeton, astounding faculty members with the brilliance and originality of his intellect. Aware that he had to keep well in with his only source of funds, Vince accepted the many invitations to go stay with Ritchie and Darlene in their mansion outside Boise, back in the days before Ritchie had rebran-ded himself as a rancher. Mind you, it wasn't that big a sacrifice. Not every student could spend vacations by the pool ordering cold beers from obsequious men in white jackets.

Vince then disappointed everyone by going off to Hollywood to work in one of the big studios. His professors said it was a waste of one of the best minds of his generation, but Vince didn't care. He made money in Hollywood, and became known as one of the canniest guys around. He was respected for his extraordinary ability to read a script and assess what was good and what was bad about it. He was brilliant at reducing a whole screenplay to a single paragraph, which he would print out and place in front of the top guys. They appreciated this, especially since Vince's development recommendations were incredibly good. Vince enjoyed his work, but he wasn't exactly using every last neuron of his brain, so when the call came from the White House, he didn't hesitate.

The President had gone back to staring at the bald eagle graph. Suddenly, he had an idea. Ritchie narrowed his eyes and looked at Vince. 'How much longer does this bird have?'

'Unless we take action? A few years.'

'Five years? Ten years?'

'Nobody knows for sure.'

'But definitely more than say, two or three years, right?'

'According to the experts, yes.'

Ritchie brightened. The bald-headed eagle was going to become extinct under some other president. *He didn't have to do anything.*

Vince saw the look of relief in Ritchie's face. 'This is a serious issue, Mr President. I think maybe we need to take action.'

'I think maybe we don't.'

Vince didn't fight it.

Before getting ready for the State Arrival Ceremony on the South Lawn, President Ritchie had to make a pile of calls to European leaders. The bastards were trying to jerk him around again. They were complaining that America was wrecking Third-World economies by exporting heavily subsidised cotton. They said that Third-World farmers couldn't compete. This shit got Ritchie really mad. Like it was America's job to help Third-World farmers? Please. But he knew how to deal with those hypocrites in Europe.

Holding a laminated card listing the key points (thank you, Vince!), he gave the leaders four minutes each on the phone. After two minutes of joshing and casual chat and generally making them feel that they counted for something in the world, which they sure as hell didn't, they got two more minutes in which he made clear that if they didn't shut the fuck up he would a) slap import duties on European goods and b) tell the world about Europe's secret dumping of toxic chemicals in the Third World. That had a result.

The only leader he was nice to was James Halstead, the British Prime Minister. Halstead was Conservative, or so Ritchie's advisers told him. Ritchie had dealt with a Labour guy before, and couldn't really tell the difference. They both seemed very keen to please him. Ritchie was nice to British leaders because for some reason they were still taken seriously in the world. More importantly, they were still taken seriously by the American electorate. Ritchie couldn't really understand why. But if his advisers told him it was good politics to give a joint press conference on the White House lawn with the British Prime Minister, then hell, he'd do it every now and then. And the current one wasn't that bad. The handshake was a bit clammy and the breath wasn't too sweet, but he was friendly and relaxed and easier to talk to than most of the real Europeans.

Ritchie didn't like Europeans. They always acted so goddamn superior. Ritchie enjoyed putting them in their place. Occasionally, just to show who was boss, Ritchie would put through a call around 8 pm Eastern Standard Time, which made it 2 am in most of Europe. Ritchie liked making some European dickhead rush half-asleep out of his bedroom, terrified that an international crisis had broken, only to find that Ritchie just wanted a little chat about banana subsidies or some such thing. He could almost hear them shit their pyjamas with fear. It was great. Just about the only European leader he hadn't done that to was the British Prime Minister. The only real problem Ritchie had with James Halstead was the man's need to keep phoning *him*. He seemed to think he could influence policy in Washington. But Ritchie took as many of his calls as he could, because these days Britain was pretty much America's only ally.

There was a small problem about the State Arrival Ceremony: the temperature. From coast to coast, America was baking. By early afternoon in Washington, it had reached 108 degrees Fahrenheit, or as the visitor from the Balkans would know it, 42 degrees Celsius. Washington in summer could be a pretty hot and sticky place, with temperatures in the high eighties or low nineties. But even in July or August, 108° F would have been remarkable. In mid-September it was just plain freaky. None of this bothered the President too much. Like many of his fellow Americans, when it got too hot, he simply upped the aircon a notch or two. If anyone mentioned global warming, the President had learned to act relaxed and to point out that the highest temperature ever reached in North America was in 1913, when Death Valley hit 134° F. Not that he directly rubbished the concept of climate change. Not any more. The official line now was 'the jury's out'. This made him sound responsible and thoughtful while simultaneously doing nothing at all to deal with the problem.

On the South Lawn, everything was ready for the arrival of the Obscure Balkan President. The soldiers of the three branches of the armed forces who formed the guard of honour were all determined to put on a good show. Hanging around for hours in the grounds of the White House might be boring, but it was better than being given a transfer to a shithole base abroad where you stood a good chance of being blown up by some homicidal raghead in search of a shortcut to Paradise.

A security alert near the hotel of the Obscure Balkan President had caused a delay. The guard of honour had been standing to attention for a full forty-five minutes in temperatures now approaching 110° F. As the sound of sirens heralded the approach of the visitor's motorcade, a soldier crumpled to the ground in a dead faint. A moment later, another followed. The chiefs with the ceremonial swords stared straight ahead.

The US Armed Forces Military Band prepared to play. A long black limousine came into view. The President of the United States emerged through the doors of the Diplomatic Reception Room on to the South Lawn just as two more soldiers dropped from heat exhaustion. Ritchie saw it. He was furious. Pretending not to notice the inert figures of the soldiers, he moved towards the limo as it came to a halt. A white-gloved marine opened the passenger door, and out stepped the Obscure Balkan President. Ritchie was appalled to discover that the Obscure Balkan President was only 5 foot 2 inches tall and was actually the Small Balkan President. Ritchie felt he ought to have been warned. He was just over six foot himself and didn't think people that small should be President of anywhere, not even of an obscure Balkan state.

Having exchanged a few diplomatic banalities, the two men walked over to inspect the guard of honour. To Ritchie's relief, the wimps who'd fainted had been cleared away. The ranks had closed up, so you couldn't tell anything had gone wrong. Ritchie just hoped that no more losers would bite the dust in front of them.

As they walked down the lines of soldiers, Ritchie sensed that he and his visitor looked ridiculous together. If he'd known the guy was a midget, Ritchie would have avoided the ceremony altogether, sent the

VP or something. Ritchie didn't think it looked good, him paying attention to a guy that small.

Later, on the dais, Ritchie made a speech. 'We have common values,' Ritchie told the Small Balkan President. 'We share a belief in freedom, a love of family, and a faith in God. I am proud to call you friend.' Unaware that he was the third head of state within a week that Ritchie was proud to call friend, the Small Balkan President was deeply moved. As Ritchie concluded his remarks, the Small Balkan President turned towards him with tears in his eyes. Ritchie realised what was coming and tried to avoid it by stretching out his hand. Too late. The Small Balkan President was embracing him. Ritchie knew this would look ridiculous on television. The top of the man's head only just reached Ritchie's chest. Any smaller and the guy would look like he was trying to give Ritchie a blowjob.

Later, having gotten rid of his diminutive visitor, Ritchie watched CNN and saw his worst fears realised. That embrace was just plain embarrassing. He dreaded to think what they'd do with it on Letterman. Ritchie chewed out his media people about the Balkan midget thing on his way through to the East Room. There Ritchie signed the Alaskan Wilderness (Stage Two) Protection Act, which opened up most of the remaining Alaskan wilderness to mining and logging. He then spent thirty minutes in the Yellow Oval Room meeting Inspirational Moms and Dads. This was part of the administration's *Strong Families* initiative, and offered a much better photo-op than all that shit out on the South Lawn. Ritchie moved skilfully among the families, shaking hands and chatting with parents who'd been nominated by their kids as Inspirational Moms and Dads. He particularly took to Chuck and Geraldine from Great Falls, Montana. Chuck told him he worked an eighty-hour week running his one-man windshield replacement business, so Geraldine could stay home and look after their four kids, two of whom were diabetic. Ritchie was genuinely interested in their story. He liked meeting straightforward, decent Americans who embodied straightforward, decent American values. So much easier than all those foreigners. He spent nearly three minutes chatting and joking with Chuck and Geraldine before moving on to the other Inspirational Moms and Dads. Anna Prascilowicz, his media chief, looked relieved; this would play well on the evening bulletins, might even make up for the Small Balkan President incident.

3

Nobody in California could remember it being this hot in September. Around LA the heat was buckling the blacktops. On Hollywood Boulevard the terrazzo stonework of the famous sidewalk stars was cracking and turning lumpy. In Santa Barbara a new record high of 119 F was being recorded. In central California's San Joaquin Valley, a rancher was spraying his dairy herd with sprinklers to cool them off. In downtown San Jose the Cuban who ran the shoeshine stand at the corner of San Carlos and First was telling all his customers, 'It's hotter than Cuba.' In Escondido the third senior citizen to die that day in the Sunnyside Care and Rehabilitation Home was still sitting bolt upright in his chair in the day room. Staff were too hot and tired to notice he was dead. (The Sunnyside Care and Rehabilitation nursing home couldn't afford air conditioning.) In San Diego, so many old people were dying from heat stress that the city had run out of mortuary space. By 2 pm the dead of San Diego were being stored in refrigerated meat trucks. At 4 pm the Governor of California went on television to assure Californians that the situation was under control and that as long as people showed restraint in the use of air conditioning there would be no power outages. At 4.30 pm the first power outages began.

Cheech Lingaard wasn't bothered by the heat. His Malibu house was fitted with a reverse-cycle modulated air conditioning system that maintained the temperature at precisely the desired level without switching on and off. Cheech hated the noise made by cheap air conditioning systems switching on and off. The state-of-the-art scroll compressors that powered his aircon were 80 per cent quieter than normal systems. It was definitely worth the forty thousand dollars he'd paid to have them installed. Or was it sixty thousand? Cheech couldn't remember. Not that it mattered. Cheech could command twelve million dollars a movie. He'd even got himself a back-up generator so that he didn't have to put up with the power blackouts. The generator was programmed to kick in automatically if the power failed.

Cheech looked up from the new screenplay he was reading, picked up a little brass bell, and tinkled it. He actually relied on his agent to tell him whether a screenplay was any good or not, but he felt obliged to at least read the thing. This one bore a strong resemblance to *Dawn Raider*, his biggest box office success, but then every movie that Cheech had been in for the last ten years bore a strong resemblance to *Dawn Raider*. He rang the bell again and made a note in the margin of page 18, where the hero at the wheel of his car shouted angrily at an old lady crossing the street. They'd have to change that. Cheech Lingaard did not play heroes who shouted angrily at old ladies crossing the street.

Maria finally padded through from the kitchen. It always annoyed him the way she dragged her crummy slippers across his Tasmanian oak timber floors. Those Tasmanian oak timber floors had cost a helluva lot of money.

'Si?' said Maria.

'Glass of cold water with a slice of lime.'

'Sure.' Maria trudged off.

'No ice!' he shouted after her.

'Sure no ice,' she muttered and disappeared.

Cheech grimaced. 'Sure' wasn't the right way to handle a request from your employer. He'd tried to get her to say 'Right away, Mr Lingaard', but it never lasted more than a day before she was back to 'Sure'. It was just too embarrassing to have a shuffling maid who only ever said 'Sure'. Recently he'd taken to sending her home when he had guests coming. That was crazy. What was the point in having a maid who wasn't around when you needed her most? Trouble was, he couldn't fire her, not really. Not since the incident.

It had happened on a Friday. Maria had gone home at the usual time but returned two hours later because she'd left her house keys behind. She walked straight in on Cheech watching a pornographic film. That might not have been so bad, but Cheech was *in* the pornographic film. Cheech really liked filming himself in action. He preferred threesomes. Sometimes he did it with two beautiful girls, but what he really liked best was getting it on with a beautiful girl and a good-looking young man. They sometimes took a bit of persuading to let him film them, but Cheech Lingaard was very rich and very famous, and once he'd set up

23

the locked-off camera in the corner they pretty soon got used to it. Cheech had quite a collection of DVDs stashed away in his bedroom, all of them of a highly personal nature.

Thanks to Maria's damned soft-shoe shuffle, he hadn't heard her come in. Well, to be honest, he was pretty absorbed in the action. Watching the guy screw the girl was very, very hot. Watching himself watching the guy screw the girl was even hotter. He had to admit, he'd kept himself in very good shape. The eyelid job, the tummy tuck and the deep lift had been worth every cent. It wasn't easy looking this good when you were fifty-five. Not that it was all cosmetic. His piercing blue eyes were as piercing as ever, even when he didn't have his coloured lenses in; his hair was all his own; those beautiful tapered fingers that had been seen in a thousand close-ups, those were all his own; and his astonishingly large member, spoken of in awed whispers throughout Hollywood, was completely and utterly all his own.

As the DVD reached the point where he shot his load over the couple, he'd freeze-framed it. That's when he'd realised Maria was standing in the room. Her eyes travelled from the screen to Cheech and back to the screen. Cheech had finally leapt up and screamed, 'Get out of here!' She went, all right. He assumed she wouldn't come back. He'd sent a courier over that night with an envelope containing a thousand dollars. The next morning she turned up as if nothing had happened. He didn't know what to do. Hollywood stars had survived worse sex scandals than this one, of course. The problem was, Cheech Lingaard was a prominent member of Acting for Jesus, a loose federation of actors and actresses who made strong religious stands on major public issues of decency and morality. Cheech had also gained a reputation as an actor who would not play in any movie containing nudity or profanity. His movies contained plenty of violence, of course, but that was different. Acting for Jesus supported Ritchie L. Ritchie, and had given financial and moral support to Ritchie's re-election campaign. In fact, over on a side table in Cheech's sitting room was a photograph of Cheech in the Rose Garden, shaking hands with the President shortly after Ritchie had won his second term. Cheech had also lent his support to the President's *Strong Families* initiative, and often wished he hadn't, because it meant having to pretend that he and his wife still lived together.

A couple of weeks after the porno incident, Maria had asked him shyly if he could help with a dental bill for her eleven-year-old daughter.

As a single mother she just couldn't scrape the cash together. Cheech had given her two hundred bucks. Since then, there had been several other requests for money, always with a good story to back them up. Cheech had paid each time. The amounts were escalating. Cheech just couldn't be sure whether or not he was being blackmailed. He could have called her bluff and just fired her; after all, it would have been his word against hers. But he'd discovered that one of his secret DVDs was missing. He'd searched everywhere for it. The thought that a Mexican maid was running around with a pornographic home movie starring Cheech Lingaard brought him out in a cold sweat.

Maria finally brought the glass of iced water. 'Eez very hot outside.'

'So I've heard. Thank you, Maria.'

'Mister Lingaard. Is about Pablo. He's not well in the heat.'

'Pablo? Who the hell's Pablo?'

'Is your gardener. Please he may come in and seat in the cool?'

This was too much. He didn't pay gardeners to sit inside his house enjoying the air conditioning. Anyhow, the gardener was from Mexico too, wasn't he, or Colombia or El Salvador or some place like that? Those guys were designed to withstand the heat. 'Just tell him to get on with the gardening, Maria, okay?'

Maria stared at him for a moment. 'Sure.'

He watched her tramp back to the kitchen, her slippers slapping softly on the polished wood.

Twenty minutes later, Cheech Lingaard's gardener collapsed from severe heat stroke and dehydration. He was rushed to hospital but pronounced dead on arrival.

4

Two disasters were about to engulf the world. One would take the lives of 62,000 people; the other would take the lives of 38 people. One would be in Nepal; the other would be in California. One would get a few articles and a couple of pictures on the inside pages of America's more serious papers; the other would dominate American newspapers and television for weeks. One would scarcely get noticed in the White House; the other would seriously undermine the President's belief that he didn't need to worry all that much about climate change.

In Nepal, there was a lake that ought not to exist. It was 6,000 metres above sea level, 2 kilometres long and 150 metres deep. Thirty years ago, it had been a glacier. Now it was millions of cubic metres of water. The water was held back by a terminal moraine of frozen rock. The ice that held this wall together was melting. A few hundred metres below this wall was a densely populated valley. The people who inhabited the valley had known for years that where they lived was dangerous. They had petitioned the government to do something about the dangerous lake, but theirs was a poor country, and as global temperatures rose, glaciers all over the Himalayas were in retreat, creating hundreds, maybe thousands of dangerous new lakes, and there simply weren't the resources to do very much about them. Nevertheless, the local people were persistent, and a team of scientists finally arrived. The scientists took measurements and made observations and muttered darkly about the possibility of a GLOF, which apparently meant a Glacial Lake Outburst Flood. They finally decreed that water should be drained from the lake in order to stabilise it. This seemed like a good plan. The local people were relieved. The director of the nearby national park was also relieved: his national park was a popular trekking destination, bringing much-needed income to the area.

A few months later, the work began. A team of forty engineers gingerly drilled a series of channels through the moraine. They didn't have much experience of draining glacial lakes, but they knew it was important that the pressure in the channels shouldn't be so high that it would break up the surrounding moraine. So they started near the top of the moraine, drilling a series of small tunnels that could draw off the water in a controlled manner. It worked. The level of water in the lake began to drop. But as it dropped, it left an enormous tongue of glacial ice suspended in mid-air, several metres above the water. While the engineers were wondering whether it might break off and fall, it broke off and fell. A giant wave swept across the lake, bursting the moraine. Within seconds, a hundred and fifty million tonnes of water was rushing down the constricted valley, taking all before it. Some boulders from the moraine were later found forty kilometres away. The water engulfed fifty-seven villages and a hydroelectric plant, plunging much of Nepal into darkness. In the space of half an hour, around 62,000 Nepalese lost their lives, as well as a bunch of British backpackers who'd been trekking in the national park. 'Eight Brits feared dead in Nepal flood disaster' wrote London's *Daily Mail*. Other papers quoted a Senator who said the disaster was the result of 'human stupidity', by which he meant the mistakes made by the Nepalese engineers in trying to deal with the melting glacier, not the global warming that was melting the glacier in the first place.

The other disaster, the one in California, the one that would create shrieking headlines all around the world, was also caused by human stupidity.

Cheech Lingaard had been upset to learn that his gardener was dead. He didn't feel it was his fault or anything like that, but obviously it was awkward and unfortunate and so he'd sent a large wreath to the man's funeral and a small cheque to the man's widow, who apparently was called Graciela.

Cheech wasn't there when Graciela came to call late one evening. Her decision to go see him was a spur-of-the-moment thing. Graciela's grief at the loss of her husband had tuned to anger when she learned that her ill husband had been refused entry to Cheech Lingaard's home. Maybe if Lingaard had behaved like a decent human being her husband would still be alive. A bitter Graciela had ordered Lingaard's vast wreath to be removed from the funeral proceedings, though she'd kept the cheque; Graciela was a proud woman but she had children to feed. She also had a sister back in El Salvador to whom she sent small but regular payments.

Although the night was warm, the gardener's widow shivered slightly as she approached the house. She hadn't given much thought to what she would say to Cheech Lingaard, she just knew she needed to tell him to his face that he had killed her beloved Pablo. Graciela had never been to the place where her husband worked. She stood outside the gates and stared through to the house beyond. Silence. She pressed the intercom button on the gatepost. Nothing. She thought about breaking in and trashing the place. Stupid idea. The whole house was surrounded by a high wall. Winking red lights announced the presence of security cameras. On the stone pillar beside the eight-foot-high metal gates was a sign saying 'This property protected by Cobra Security Enforcement Inc.' and the logo of a cobra about to strike. On the other side of the gates she could make out the dull gleam of polished copper lamps along the side of the house. She realised they would be linked up to movement sensors in the yard. Even if she got over the perimeter fence, she would certainly trigger the lights, maybe set off alarms at the same time.

Graciela pressed the intercom buzzer again, this time keeping her finger on it for several seconds. Again nothing. Frustrated, she turned and took a few steps back down the dirt road. She stopped and rummaged in her handbag, taking out a pack of Marlboro. She lit her cigarette and drew deeply on it. For a few minutes she just stood there, looking at the house and the garden where Pablo had died. She finished her cigarette and threw it into the dry brush by the side of the road. Graciela knew this was exactly what she ought not to do. The long hot summer and the equally hot autumn had made everything tinder-dry. There had already been several wildfires in the area. Only a few days earlier, mandatory evacuation notices had been served on the nearby Encinal and Decker canyons, as a five-hundred-acre fire raged in the Santa Monica Mountains. That fire had now been brought under control, but the situation was still alarming. For the forty-ninth day running, the California Department of Forestry had called a 'high fire danger day'.

Graciela watched abstractedly as a few blades of wild grass by the roadside began to smoulder. Seconds later, they burst into flame. It was remarkable how fast the flames spread. The Santa Ana winds had started early this year. They dried out the brush and then, once a fire had started somewhere, fanned the flames with horrible efficiency. Graciela took a step back. The flames were spreading along the bank of brushwood now. She saw that the wind was taking the fire towards the house. She hadn't planned anything like this. There might still be time to put it out. On the other hand, there was nobody in the house. If it burned down, nobody would die. Cheech Lingaard would get a shock, though. In all conscience, it was a modest revenge for the death of a man. Graciela turned and walked crisply away from the house.

Cheech Lingaard's Malibu house might have survived the fire if the gardener had removed the dry leaf clutter from the space beneath the decking and swept up all the leaves, dead limbs and twigs that the Santa Ana winds had scattered around the house. But of course Cheech's gardener was dead, and Cheech hadn't yet got around to finding a new one.

There's something relentlessly democratic about a wildfire. A wildfire loves dry brush. A wildfire loves dead pine trees. A wildfire loves a patch of dried grass. But a wildfire, once it's up and running, will cheerfully consume a fine Tasmanian oak timber floor, no questions asked. Within ten minutes of Graciela's cigarette end hitting the ground, Cheech Lingaard's house was ablaze from end to end. Hopscotching around a few lucky homes in the area, the wildfire roared onwards, fanned by fierce gusts of wind.

At Dave Bruder's thirtieth birthday party in his very cool Malibu beach house, the celebrities weren't thinking about wildfires. When there's enough charlie on the table to wire a regiment, people are above banalities such as wildfires. Dave Bruder had recently smashed all box office records with *Blood and Water*, a daring mix of terrorism and the occult, set on an American cruise liner in the Arabian Gulf. Of all the parties to be seen at, this was *the* party. Dave Bruder was hot. The idea of being directed by Dave Bruder was hot. Just to be in the same room as Dave Bruder was hot. So hot that nobody noticed the red glow in the distance. It even took the two hunky security guys outside the main gate a very long time to notice the acrid smell in the air. That's because they were both behind a eucalyptus tree servicing a gorgeous blonde starlet. Almost half a gram of coke had led her to believe that a brief session with two real men would enliven the evening.

It was the starlet who first noticed that something was wrong. It still took her quite some time to focus on the danger, because one security man was tonguing her gloriously erect nipples while another was penetrating her from behind with a vigour that she had rarely experienced before. When she started screaming, the security men assumed she was having a good time, and went to their tasks with renewed energy. By the time they realised what was really happening, a police helicopter was overhead. From a loudspeaker a voice was screaming at them to evacuate the house.

Flash fuels such as dry grasses and light brush burn hot and fast. In the dry conditions of late summer or autumn, a field of uncut grass can produce a ten-foot-high wall of flames travelling at 20 mph. That's faster than a celebrity can jog. To add to the challenge, the trees around Dave Bruder's house were mainly pine and eucalyptus. Wildfires just love pine and eucalyptus trees, because the resin burns at incredibly high temperatures.

The wail of sirens announced the approach of police cars and fire trucks. Out of the house poured the guests, none of them in a fit state to make life-or-death decisions, at least not the right life-or-death decisions. Among them was Cheech Lingaard. He ran towards his car, just in time to see it erupt into flame.

Convected air currents caused by the fire were now lifting blazing twigs and branches into the air. Driven by the wind, these were being deposited well ahead of the main fire, starting off new fires wherever they landed. Fire-fighters call this 'spotting', and it scares them. What scares them worse is when it turns, as it easily can, into a full-scale firestorm. Tonight, a full-scale firestorm was only minutes away.

Amidst the panicking celebrities, Cheech caught sight of creepy old Anastasia Baker, the doyenne of Hollywood agents. She had her car key in her hand and was struggling to open the driver's door. Lucky Anastasia, her car seemed to be the only one that was safe from the fire. A blast of hot air hit the back of Cheech's neck as an SUV went up in flames behind him. Panting with fear, he ran towards Anastasia and tried to grab the key. She wouldn't let go, so he tore the key from her grasp, giving her a shove that sent her flying to the ground. The heat was intense. He was afraid his lacquered hair might burst into flames. He opened the car door, put the key in the ignition, turned the engine, and drove off.

When dawn broke the next day, twenty-two Hollywood stars and one

Hollywood agent were dead. The toll was terrible: fourteen Academy Award winners, eleven Academy Nominations and seven holders of a Golden Globe. (That still only came to twenty-two, because some of the dead were of course holders of Oscars *and* Golden Globes.) Two security guys were also dead, but nobody counted them. All over the world, radio and television programmes were interrupted to break the awful news to a stunned world. Many of them ran interviews with a dishevelled Cheech Lingaard, who told of his close encounter with death. Lip quivering, he recounted how he had tried in vain to rescue the aged Anastasia Baker, but had been beaten back by the ferocity of the fire. It was the finest performance of his career.

The blanket coverage of this mass cull of celebrities was so overwhelming that people not directly affected hardly noticed the extent of the fires still raging throughout huge areas of California. With more than 1,200 fire-fighters on the lines in Malibu, the state ordered in another sixty-five engines from as far away as Sacramento and San Francisco Bay. But the Santa Ana winds continued to roar into Southern California, in places gusting to 90 mph. In one blaze near Norco, east of Los Angeles, at least a dozen people were killed, none of them at all famous, not even in death. By the time most of the fires had been brought under control some three days and nights later, a total of 38 people had died, 7,000 homes had been destroyed and 95,000 acres of land reduced to a smoking, blackened wilderness.

5

The American people were traumatised by the loss of so many celebrities. It was agreed that a live presidential address to the nation was the only appropriate response.

A live presidential address was an event that always provoked extreme stress in the White House team. They all knew Ritchie wasn't great at this kind of formal television stuff. Whenever possible, they preferred to get him out in front of a live audience, where Ritchie could strut his stuff and do the kind of folksy joshing he was good at. Live on television from the White House was meant to be about gravitas, and Ritchie didn't do gravitas. The nearest he could get was a kind of scrunched-up earnest expression on his face that made people wonder whether he needed to go to the bathroom. But given the horrific events in California, there really was no choice.

At the insistence of the President, it had been decided to broadcast from the White House Treaty Room on the second floor, the room where President McKinley had supervised the signing of the treaty that ended the Spanish-American war in 1898. Ritchie wasn't that interested in history, but he knew about the Spanish-American War. It had culminated in the Battle of Santiago Bay, which marked the end of Spanish naval power. One thousand eight hundred Spanish sailors had died in that battle, with one American dead and one wounded. That was the kind of result that Ritchie liked. For most of the twentieth century, Americans had died in their hundreds of thousands in foreign wars. Now, thanks to modern weaponry and massive American technological superiority, it was possible to get back to the healthy precedent set by the Battle of Santiago Bay. The only cloud on the horizon was guerrilla warfare. Nobody in the White House or the Pentagon knew what the hell to do about guerrilla warfare, so they called it 'asymmetrical conflict' instead, because that sounded better. Sometimes, though, they called it 'terrorism' so that people could understand it was a bad thing.

As Ritchie entered the room, the television people were checking out the TelePrompTer that held the President's speech. By way of back-up, the speech was also printed out on a series of white cards. This speech, which was six minutes long, had been written by a total of forty-one people and had gone through seventeen drafts. One faction, led by Vince, believed that this was an opportunity finally to address the real issue, which to their minds was the incredibly hot dry weather that had made the fire possible. Seen this way, it could be linked to the disaster in Nepal, and the President would be perceived as a man of global stature, concerned about the environment. The other faction believed climate change was bullshit and wanted to focus instead on the terrible losses to America's iconic entertainment business. Unfortunately for Vince, this faction was led by Anna Prascilowicz, the White House's powerful Head of Communications, a woman who did not take kindly to losing an argument.

'We don't do climate change, okay?' she'd shouted at Vince. 'Forget climate change. This speech is about loss. Personal loss and national loss. Got it?'

Vince had shrugged and walked away. He tried to avoid confrontations with her. It was just too wearing. Anna Prascilowicz was a tall, angular woman in her early forties who believed that each story could only spin one way. Other people made suggestions, Anna Prascilowicz gave commands. Or rather, she barked commands. Around the White House they liked to say that her bark was as bad as her bite. A bully with her colleagues, she could be charming and witty with the media. She knew it was the relationship with the media that counted. The White House Press Corps liked her and that was all she cared about. Most everyone else was scared of her and that was fine. It meant they all made sure they spelled her name right. Anna Prascilowicz did not like it if anyone failed to spell her name right.

In the middle of these two factions stood 28-year-old Larry Dodge, the President's chief speechwriter. Larry didn't really have any beliefs other than a belief in the efficacy of the spoken word. If Hell were to offer Larry the post of Satan's personal speechwriter, Larry would take it, as long as the pay was right. Larry was the ultimate amoral craftsman, a lexicological whore, his brilliance equalled only by his sense of self-importance. It was Larry Dodge who had coined such famous phrases as 'the war against darkness'. Larry was equally adept with what Vince called 'aw shucks' stuff, like the President's call for families to eat together ('broken families who never broke bread') or small acts of kindness as a means of radically transforming society. ('What succeeds is little deeds for big needs.') Vince and Larry did not get on. Maybe their closeness in age made them natural rivals. At thirty-four, Vince was the second-youngest of the inner circle around the President. Their mutual dislike was visceral. Vince disliked the pallor of Larry's skin and the hastily combed red hair. Vince took the trouble to come into the White House each day looking groomed and unobtrusively well-dressed. He was proud of his jet-black hair and spent good money on getting it cut and styled in a Georgetown salon and spa, where he also took advantage of their other 'services for the modern man', from manicures to full-body exfoliation. Lucy often teased him about how much money he spent on grooming, suggesting he was vain. Vince didn't see it that way. He just liked to look good.

Today President Ritchie L. Ritchie was jumpy and nervous. He hated having to deal with national disasters. Suddenly everyone wanted you to be their wise father. And this national disaster had really rattled him. As a fan of the movies, he'd been as shocked as any other American by the deaths of so many stars. Like any other American, he had sat open-mouthed in front of his television, gawping at the dreadful images coming in from California. Like any other American, he'd wept as he watched workmen swathe the Hollywood sign in black cloth. Unlike most of his compatriots, though, he'd lost people he regarded as his personal friends. He didn't realise that the whole point of stardom was that *everyone* regarded stars as personal friends.

Ritchie's misery had been compounded by a phone call from his nineteen-year-old son Edward, who was doing an MBA at Harvard. They'd started off sharing shocked reactions to the Hollywood disaster but ended up having a huge argument. Edward (who to his father's discomfort insisted on calling himself Eddie) hated Harvard and blamed his father for making him go there. The call had ended with the boy calling his father an asshole and a bigot and putting the phone down. This felt like the last straw. Thank heavens for his daughter, Janie. Janie had never given him any trouble. And thank heavens that his friend and supporter Cheech Lingaard had escaped the inferno. He'd called Cheech only a few hours before to congratulate him on his courage, and to commiserate with him on the loss of friends. They'd finished by reassuring one another that this was nothing to do with global warming. It had just been a hot summer, that was all.

The Treaty Room was a mass of cables. Ritchie picked his way gingerly across the room, reading half-aloud from his white cards while aides scurried all around him and technicians ran final checks on the equipment and made sure the timing was precise. They didn't want a repeat of a recent presidential broadcast where the networks had cut live to Ritchie fifteen seconds too early, and the world had seen lipstick being applied to the President of the United States.

Vince looked on anxiously as Anna Prascilowicz took the President aside. Vince hoped there weren't going to be any more changes to the speech. He'd managed to sneak in two telling sentences about the environment. That maybe didn't sound like much, but it was a big deal. White House staffers could be on a high for a week if they got even just one phrase through to the final draft of a presidential speech.

Prascilowicz called Larry Dodge over. Shit, thought Vince. Larry was in there like lightning. Prascilowicz asked him something about the environment. Larry stuck his weasel-like face close to Ritchie's and stabbed a finger at one of the cards. He seemed to be exhorting the President to change something. Vince hurried over. 'Something the matter, Larry?'

'No,' said the weaselly redhead.

Ritchie sniffed. 'Anna wants me to take out the bit about the environment, you know, where I say some stuff about the lessons learnt from the tragedy. She thinks I should keep it personal.'

'And I agree,' said Larry.

'Personal's good, sir,' said Vince, 'but it needs a wider perspective. Otherwise there's no statesmanlike.'

'There's plenty of statesmanlike,' Larry retorted with a tone of contempt.

Vince looked at the outbreak of virulent little red and yellow spots on the side of Larry Dodge's nose and felt a sense of revulsion. Couldn't he *do* something about that for Chrissake?

'Fifteen minutes!' shouted the senior technician. Two makeup artists fluttered around the President. He snarled at them for getting in his way.

'Larry's right,' snapped Anna Prascilowicz, putting a line through two sentences and handing the card to an assistant, who hurried off to give it to the TeleprompTer operator. Larry Dodge smirked at Vince. Vince sighed and moved away.

Ritchie waved his hands in the air. 'Everyone quiet! Close those doors! Close them goddamnit! I want to run through this.'

They'd decided to go for brief and dignified. The whole speech might only be six minutes long, but that made getting it right even more important. For the run-through Ritchie crossed to the big oak lectern that he liked to stand behind when he spoke to the world. Occasionally he did speeches from behind his desk in the Oval Office, because people kind of expected that, but he much preferred the lectern. This was because the lectern had an extra built-in prompt screen, hidden behind a high rim and completely undetectable to anyone else. In an emergency, say during a press conference, if Ritchie was hit with a question he couldn't answer, he was adept at stalling with a few generalised homilies while a trusted aide in a neighbouring room rapidly typed in an answer for him. So successful was this system that Ritchie had ordered up three more of the lecterns. One was now kept permanently at the White House and one at Camp David, while two others were kept on board each of the two identical planes that the public thought of as Air Force One.

Ritchie spoke slowly and movingly. Vince made notes. The senior engineer looked anxiously at his watch. When Ritchie came to the bit about 'a loss as deep as the ocean, a grief as dark as night', he began to look tearful. Vince grimaced. Ritchie's tendency to weep in public was a liability. The President stopped reading from the prompter and looked over at Vince. 'What's the matter?'

'I think you should keep the emotion at bay here, sir.

Larry Dodge intervened. 'But it's a very emotional moment.'

'I didn't ask you, Larry,' Ritchie snarled. Chewing out someone who had just won an argument was one of Ritchie's favourite techniques. It meant nobody could ever be sure who was in favour and who wasn't. Ritchie knew a thing or two about people management. He looked at Vince again.

'What if I'm, like, dewy-eyed?'

'I think it would be a mistake, sir.'

Prascilowicz intervened. 'How about a tremor in the voice?'

'That's good. Thanks, Anna. I'll go for the tremor.'

The President waved a hand at the prompt operator. 'Page six. Tremor. Okay?'

'Very good, Mr President.'

The senior engineer stuck a hand in the air. 'Ten minutes!'

Ritchie reached the end of the run-through and beckoned Vince to come over. 'How was it?'

'It was good, sir. Just a bit more weight.'

'More weight? Whaddya mean, more weight?'

'You're hit by this tragedy, but it's important to show it hasn't touched your authority.'

'Oh, right.'

'The subtext is: America is strong. America will overcome.'

'Gotcha. That's good. Thanks, Vince.'

Vince was aware that Prascilowicz was hovering nearby. He tried to ignore her. 'Oh, and Mr President,' he added. 'Where you talk about talent...' He pointed out the sentence. 'Here. You say "the grievous loss of talent". I think that sounds too cold. I think it ought to be, more personal. I suggest "the grievous loss of so many fine and talented human beings". What do you think?' From the corner of his eye, he could see Larry about to intervene. That clunky talent line had been his.

'I like that, Vince,' said the President. 'Much better.'

'Yes,' said Prascilowicz. 'More personal. Much better.'

Vince caught sight of the sour look on Larry Dodge's face and felt fucking great.

'One minute, Mr President,' shouted the engineer.

6

Later that evening, Ritchie withdrew to the presidential study just behind the Oval Office. The live address to the nation had not gone well. He'd stumbled over several phrases. And he shouldn't have waved away that makeup girl just before he went on air. A little powder would have hidden the sweat that had formed on his brow halfway through his speech. Sweat wasn't good. Sweat suggested panic. The American people liked their presidents dry.

The presidential study has been built after Eisenhower's heart attack, so that the President could have naps without straying too far from the Oval Office. It was also the spot often chosen by Clinton to have sex with Monica Lewinsky. Ritchie didn't approve of that sort of thing. He was a happily married man. Well, he was a married man. And anyhow, to Ritchie's mind, power was a lot more fun than sex. How a President could risk losing power for the sake of an orgasm was beyond him.

The presidential study was Ritchie's favourite room in the whole White House. Staffers didn't dare disturb him there. They knew this was the place where Ritchie withdrew 'to be alone with his God'. They didn't know that today this was also the place where Ritchie had withdrawn to be alone with his bottle.

Ritchie gently closed the door behind him, unlocked the small cherrywood cabinet containing his grandmother's bible and his father's World War Two pistol, and removed a bottle of Wild Turkey bourbon. It was unopened. He'd secretly stashed it there on the day of the Malibu fire. He wasn't sure why, maybe some desperate need of comfort. The Malibu fire had disturbed him deeply. For Ritchie, a blow to the heart of the American movie industry was like a blow of the heart of America itself. He felt uneasy, frightened. He stared at the bottle for a long time, but didn't open it.

Driven by political ambition from an early age, Ritchie had correctly deduced that the strong puritanical streak among American voters made them more likely to support a candidate who steered clear of the demon drink. Ritchie had only ever fallen off the wagon once. It was more than twenty years ago now, when he'd been running for governor of Idaho. Ritchie had spent the evening in a back room of the Red Rooster Roadhouse in Boise, talking to a small group of crooked businessmen, or as they preferred to be known, leaders of the local business community. There had been some heavy drinking; they were celebrating a downtown development deal that left the businessmen a lot richer while adding half a million dollars to Ritchie's campaign funds. Ritchie was so happy that he'd let them talk him into knocking back a few glasses of bourbon; he didn't recall exactly how many. As they ambled through the bar on their way to their waiting cars, Ritchie recognised a journalist sitting at a table in the corner, a little guy with a squint. It was Bob Bloom, who'd just done a vicious profile of him in the local rag, calling Ritchie 'a danger to democracy'. Before anyone could stop him, Ritchie had lurched over. Bob Bloom looked up to see the candidate for the governorship of Idaho taking out his penis.

'Suck my dick, faggot!' screamed Ritchie as he waved his meat in Bob Bloom's face. Nearby drinkers stared in astonishment. Five desperate businessmen leapt on Ritchie and bundled him out to his car. They then had to move fast to stop the story getting out. 'Candidate exposes himself in public bar' was not a story calculated to propel Ritchie into the Governor's office. It was a close-run thing. Ritchie's friends pulled out all the stops to close the story down. The next day poor Bob Bloom paid the price for having witnessed Ritchie's manhood at close quarters: he was made redundant by an editor who refused to look him in the eye, even in the eye that didn't have the squint. Attempts by the journalist to find witnesses to the event drew a blank: mysteriously, nobody could remember seeing anything. Shocked at how close he'd come to disaster, Ritchie had never touched another drop. Until now.

He took no more than one swig before putting the bottle of Wild Turkey back in the cherrywood cabinet. Nobody would ever know. He then got down on his knees and bowed his head. For a whole ten minutes he prayed to his God, like he did every day. At least, that's what he told himself. In fact, quite a few of those ten minutes were normally spent thinking about what to have for dinner or whether he ought to have his teeth whitened again or when he might be able to get away to his ranch for a long weekend. Ritchie was devout, but he found it hard to keep focused on a conversation with God. God didn't give much feedback.

But today was different. Today Ritchie prayed with a kind of desperate determination. It felt like big things were happening in the world. Big, confusing things. Not the disaster in Nepal, that didn't bother him too much. The world was overpopulated anyhow. He'd sent the Nepalese president or king or whatever the hell it was they had there a message of concern and a couple of planeloads of blankets and that was fine. No, what got to him was the feeling that something terrible was happening in the heart of America. Something new. Something he couldn't control. Something he didn't understand. When he held press conferences now, there were more and more questions about pressure on the environment and climate change and disappearing fish and unexpected floods and God knows what else, and he had to spend hours beforehand being briefed by aides. In the previous twelve months an endless catalogue of floods and mudslides and storms had forced him to declare six emergencies, eight disasters and eleven major disasters. These categories weren't arbitrary. The choice of classification decided how much extra funding would be released to the Federal Emergency Management Agency. The bill for all this emergency aid was starting to be a sizeable item on the federal budget. Only last week he'd had to sign emergency assistance orders for Ohio, North Carolina and Maryland. What a pain in the ass.

When he'd been elected first time around, none of this shit had been on the agenda. He was willing to learn new stuff, always had been, but heck, he was in his second term, it hardly seemed worth it. Dumb system, of course. Two terms, that wasn't enough for a man to leave his stamp on history. Roosevelt had managed to wangle himself a third *and* fourth term. And no way could anyone argue that FDR was a greater President than Ritchie. But the fucking 22nd Amendment had put the kibosh on all that. Sometimes – not often, but sometimes – Ritchie wondered whether a grateful Congress might offer to get rid of that amendment, though he'd never dared mention it to anyone. But wouldn't it be neat if somebody suggested it?

Opening his eyes, Ritchie took the bottle back out of the cherrywood cabinet. Maybe he'd have just one more. A small one. Still on his knees, he took a couple of sips and put the bottle back. That was better. He slowly got to his feet. It had been a tough few days. Foreign leaders had been calling him all week, offering their commiserations for the Malibu fire disaster and pledging their support. Ritchie didn't need either their commiserations or their support, but his foreign policy advisers kept telling him that shit like that was important. The British guy, Halstead, had been on the phone for about half an hour, proposing a new Anglo-American summit on climate change. Halstead said he was willing to come over to talk about it, but Ritchie didn't warm to the idea. He strongly suspected that half the leaders calling him were fishing for invites to one of the celebrity funerals. The Canadians had even had the nerve to offer men and equipment to help fight the fires in California. Fuck them. No way was the United States going to depend on Canadians to put out fires. *Canadians* for Chrissake!

Sometimes Ritchie got resentful at having to spend so much time dealing with the rest of the world. Oh sure, they rang up to weep their crocodile tears, but most of the time the rest of the world was just plain ungrateful. Here was America sending guns and planes and soldiers to defend freedom in just about every part of the globe, and never a word of thanks. Worse than that, Americans everywhere were being shot at or bombed or kidnapped, when all they wanted to do was help make the world safe for democracy. And it wasn't all that easy at home, either. There were liberals coming out of the woodwork all over, and eco-nuts who wanted to close down American industry so that their little feathered friends could be happy. Fucking tree-huggers and duck-squeezers.

Nobody out there realised what it was like to be President. You had to make decisions all day long. It exhausted Ritchie. He'd delegated as many decisions as possible to other people, but that still left about two dozen a day. What Ritchie liked about power wasn't making decisions, it was being out on the stump, meeting people, getting adulation. He particularly enjoyed going to military bases, where he could be the people's Commander-in-Chief, the top gun who knew how to josh with the grunts. He knew he was good at working a room, knew he could be funny and spontaneous. He knew how to flatter people, too. President Ritchie L. Ritchie might have only the vaguest grasp of history, economics and geography, but he had a prodigious memory for names. Ritchie could run into someone he hadn't seen in ten years and have immediate recall of the name. This was a major asset.

Ritchie's other great skill was paying attention to people. Maybe you only got thirty seconds with the President, but in those thirty seconds you just knew that President Ritchie thought you were the most important, the most interesting person on the planet. After meeting other successful politicians, people came out feeling good about the politician; after meeting Ritchie, people came out feeling good about *themselves*. This was a precious gift, and one of the reasons that the powerful forces behind Ritchie had chosen him to be their man.

Ritchie finished praying, got up, and went over to the telephones beside the single bed. He wondered which of the three phone systems to use. There was the command and control system, run by the White House Communications Agency. There was a secure cell phone frequency. And there was a network of lines run by the local telephone company. He opted for the command and control system, the most secure. It was intended for calls of strategic or military importance. Ritchie liked to use it for ordering pizza takeaways from downtown stores. It kind of gave him a kick, though it drove the Secret Service crazy, because they had to hotfoot it down to the restaurant to supervise the preparation of the food in case somebody tried to poison the President. Sometimes Ritchie ordered up cheeseburgers and fries from Hamburger Heaven, a cheap downtown burger joint. A guy on a motorbike (closely followed by two carloads of Secret Service men) would rush it over to the White House. Everyone at Hamburger Heaven was sworn to secrecy, but Ritchie knew it would leak eventually. He didn't mind. It would add to his reputation as a man in touch with ordinary folks. Anyway, he didn't do it very often. He liked to keep in shape – worked out four or five times a week, and always went jogging when he was at Camp David. He couldn't bear the idea of getting fat. Fat people were gross. Fat people really disgusted him. Only he had to keep that quiet, seeing as an awful lot of fat people had voted for him.

Ritchie felt a pang of hunger, but he didn't want to eat alone. There was too much on his mind. He needed company. He needed someone he could talk to. That ruled out Mrs Ritchie. He loved his wife, but she wasn't what you'd call a good listener. And you couldn't exactly say she had a grasp of politics. He picked up the phone and put it down again. Maybe he'd have just one more shot of bourbon – a small one.

The fierce liquor revived his spirits. He couldn't decide who to call. Maybe he'd call Vince. He trusted Vince. To bring Vince into the White House, Ritchie had created a completely new post. He hadn't known what to call it, till Vince suggested the simple title of 'Special Assistant to the President', which was what he became. Unofficially, he was known around the White House as Head of Story Development. People laughed at first. They joked about Ritchie needing a guy who took Hollywood movies into development. But smart people knew that hiring Vince was a good move. For a President like Ritchie, the world needed interpreting in ways he could make sense of. The arc of presidential power needed to be experienced and retold to the public as a story, a Hollywood story of good versus evil, a satisfying, old-fashioned story with a beginning a middle and an end.

Yeah. Probably he'd call Vince. But first he'd have one last shot of bourbon. Jus a small one. Then he'd never touch the stuff again. He opened the cherrywood cabinet.

7

Vince Lennox looked in vain for a jar of Périgord truffles. He finally had to ask a sales assistant.

'You'll find Oregon white truffles second aisle on your left,' she replied briskly.

'No, I want the Périgord black winter truffles.'

'Oh *those*. Are you sure you want those?'

'Yes.'

'They're expensive.'

This struck Vince as a dumb thing to say. Just in Thyme was a late-night gourmet store on Dupont Circle that attracted a well-heeled Washington crowd. People like Vince didn't think twice about paying good money for luxury items.

'I know they're expensive. But I want them.'

'They're in the security cabinet. Hold on while I get a key.'

Security cabinet? What was this about a security cabinet? Vince waited, shivering slightly in the fierce cold of the air conditioning. He was wearing a light summer suit. He looked down at his basket of shopping. He had everything except the wine. His plan was to hurry home and prepare tagliatelle with butter and shaved black winter truffles, accompanied by a rocket and watercress salad. He'd be home in fifty minutes and be able to throw the whole thing together in no time. It was Lucy's favourite meal, and they hadn't had it in a year. Making it for her now would be his way of saying he realised he'd been neglecting her, and was sorry. He'd called her up and left a message telling her he was making supper and not to eat till he got there. He glanced at his watch. Shit, he'd promised to be there by nine-thirty latest and now it was nearly ten. He looked around for the sales assistant. Where the hell was she?

She was behind him, a tiny glass jar in her hand. 'We only carry the two-ounce size.'

'The two-ounce will do.'

'It's two hundred and sixty dollars.'

'WHAT?!'

'That's why we keep them in a security cabinet.'

'Two hundred and sixty dollars?! Are you serious?'

'Actually, it's only two hundred and fifty-nine fifty,' she said, pointing to the price sticker.

'Last time I paid about forty. For a bigger jar than this.'

'Oh, that would be last year's supplies. This year I heard the harvest failed. Bad weather in Italy or something.'

'Périgord truffles only grow in France.'

'Well, in France, then. There were floods. Or drought, or something.'

Vince held the jar in his hand and stared at it. Two hundred and sixty dollars. Jesus Christ. 'I'll take it.'

'Okay.'

'Thanks for your help.'

'You're welcome.' The sales assistant moved off. She earned $6.90 an hour. She was used to seeing customers come in to Just in Thyme and in ten minutes spend what she earned in a month. She didn't resent it. She was a fully paid-up subscriber to the American dream. She had plans. A few years from now, *she* would be the one spending big money on small jars of weird little black things.

Vince felt a bit queasy about spending that kind of money on a jar of truffles. What the hell. Maybe he'd casually let slip to Lucy how much they'd cost. Two hundred and sixty bucks for a pasta supper at home. Plus wine. Yes, that's how much he loved her.

Vince glanced at his watch and hurried over to the wine department. He'd hoped to get away from the White House by eight-thirty, right after the live broadcast, but he'd been sucked into an emergency huddle on the President's wish to attend at least one of the celebrity funerals in Hollywood. The presidential team were split on the issue. Some thought it would be a major publicity coup. Others, including Vince, thought the whole thing would turn Tinseltown-tacky and end up making the President look cheap. In the end, Vince's side had won.

Vince reached the wine department. He stopped in front of the French section and looked around cautiously. It wouldn't be good if he were seen with a basket full of French produce. Mind you, he'd never actually come across any White House staffers shopping at Just in Thyme. It wasn't their kind of place. It wasn't actually Vince's kind of place either; he hated the false folksiness of it all: the rustic charcuterie stall with its strings of garlic bulbs, the bakery counter with its 'home-baked farm bread' (which Vince heard was made from frozen dough shipped from New York), and the free bunches of fresh thyme that the sales staff added to your shopping at the checkout. But Just in Thyme stayed open till midnight and was located usefully near Dupont Circle, allowing Vince to call in on his way home after working late. Recently he'd been there a lot. Lucy had more or less given up on making evening meals. He couldn't blame her. His working hours were getting longer. The President was depending on him more and more. This gave Vince influence. He believed he used this influence responsibly. In fact, sometimes he felt he was the voice of reason in an unpredictable White House. Vince also happened to like Ritchie. In some odd way, everybody liked Ritchie. But he didn't want to be Ritchie's best buddy. And he desperately needed to spend more time with his wife. Though there were times he thought maybe she didn't want to spend more time with *him*.

When he'd accepted the job, she'd implied he had an unhealthy relationship to power. Maybe she was right. There had always been some lack of purpose to Vince's successes. He'd drifted into Hollywood without caring all that much about the industry. Or even knowing that much. But within three years of arriving in Hollywood Vince could safely say he was already a player. He relished the sense of awe around him as he carved his way upwards at breathtaking speed. Power was fun. That was the bottom line. Power made you feel good about yourself. Even if there were times when you had to be more ruthless than you really wanted to be.

He'd first met Lucy at a party in Beverly Hills. He'd been in a room where he and Lucy were the only ones not doing coke. This produced a natural solidarity. They'd drifted out to the pool together. The chemistry was immediate. He felt his throat go dry as Lucy talked. What a voice: dark, throaty, husky. And the English accent turned him on. She wasn't beautiful in any obvious way: an elfin face, spiky dark hair, a sassy grin and an outrageously loud laugh. She laughed a lot, at a party where most people were too concerned about their careers to actually enjoy themselves. That's why parties like this depended on copious amounts of coke. Vince hated the cocaine fashion in Hollywood. The drug was meant to free you up from your inhibitions, but in Vince's experience it just led to people delivering incredibly boring monologues at you. And the loss of sexual control bothered him. The only time he'd snorted coke, he'd ended up in bed with a very cute girl from Pittsburgh and been completely unable to get it up. She'd stomped off home muttering about Hollywood fags.

Vince had been gazing into Lucy's eyes as a tubby blond guy in his fifties came by. The tubby blond guy casually slid his hand along Lucy's ass as he passed, something that Vince was very much wanting to do himself. 'Nice ass, baby,' he said.

While Vince was still wondering how to react, Lucy handed him her glass of champagne. 'Hold this, will you?' Vince took the glass.

Lucy hurried after the tubby blond guy. 'Excuse me,' she said.

The blond guy turned. 'Hey,' he said, his eyes running up and down Lucy's body.

'Hey,' said Lucy, as with one smooth motion she grabbed his hairpiece and threw it into the pool. The tubby blond guy, now the tubby bald guy, could not believe what had happened.

Lucy walked back to Vince, and reclaimed her glass. 'Thanks,' she said.

'Do you know who that was?' asked Vince.

'Sure. Norman Stark.'

Norman Stark was the enormously rich, enormously powerful producer of the *Teen Terror* movies. The latest one, *Teen Terror 3*, had grossed just over one billion dollars. Sensible girls goosed by the producer of *Teen Terror 3* did not throw his hairpiece into the pool. Vince stared at Lucy and decided he was in love.

Just in Thyme was famous for its selection of wines. Vince gazed at the Burgundies. Again he looked around to make sure there was nobody he knew in the store. The cheese-eating surrender monkeys thing had more or less gone, but many people hadn't entirely forgiven France for refusing to support America's military incursions in the Middle East. If it wasn't any longer a hanging offence to be seen buying French wine, it wasn't exactly a career boost either. Not that Spanish wine was much better these days. Buying foreign wine had become a nightmare. Come to think of it, given the evangelical earnestness that permeated this administration, being seen buying *any* kind of wine was a bad move.

Vince selected a Meursault. Expensive, but what the hell. And cheap compared to the truffles. Really, he'd have preferred a red, but Lucy only ever drank white.

As he emerged from the store, some three hundred dollars poorer, Vince flicked away the sprig of thyme sitting on top of his bag of groceries and walked up the street to where he'd found a parking space. Jesus, late evening, late September, and it was still unbearably hot. He couldn't wait to get into the car and get the aircon running. He was just opening the trunk when his cell phone rang. Struggling with the paper bags, he managed to flip his cell open to see who was calling.

'Yes, Mr President?' he said.

'Vince, I need to talk to you.'

'Go right ahead, sir.'

'I mean, in person.'

Vince knew he meant in person. He'd been hoping he might get away with a quick phone call. He glanced at his watch. It was five after ten.

'Where are you?' demanded the President.

'I can be back there in ten minutes, sir.'

'Great.' The President rang off.

Shit, thought Vince. Shit, shit, shit. He rang Lucy again. Still no reply. He wasn't worried. Since starting the research for her new book she'd been driving off to all kinds of strange places at all hours of the day and night. He just wished she'd let him know, that was all.

8

'Hi, Vince. Come on in.' The President of the United States was lying full-length on one of the big sofas in the Oval Office with his boots still on. He was watching the late news. The networks were still majoring on the celebrity deaths in Malibu.

Vince's heart sank when he saw that Rascal was lying on one of the sofas. Rascal was an American water spaniel belonging to Ritchie and Darlene. For some considerable time, Vince had wanted Rascal dead. Rascal was allowed into every room in the White House. You could be in the middle of a discussion about a nuclear stand-off between India and Pakistan and suddenly Rascal would be bounding into the room and leaping up on the President's lap. After that, what spark of attention the President might have been giving to the subject in hand was reduced to an occasional grunt of assent as he concentrated on tickling Rascal's big floppy ears. Fortunately, on this occasion, Rascal appeared to be asleep.

'Good of you to stop by,' said the President. Ritchie never forgot those little courtesies, meaningless as they were. Both men knew that when the President of the United States asked you to stop by, you stopped by. 'You want some coffee or something?'

'No thank you, sir.' Vince thought for a moment he caught the smell of bourbon, but dismissed the thought almost immediately. He knew Ritchie didn't drink. Next he noticed a strong smell of peppermint. The President was chewing gum. That was unusual.

He waved Vince towards the other sofa. 'I've ordered burgers. They'll be here soon.'

Vince the vegetarian sat down. 'Great,' he said.

'I know you like burgers.'

'Love 'em.' Vince cursed the moment when the President had first ordered up burgers in his presence. Still new to the job, Vince had decided it would be prudent not to mention he was vegetarian. From there on in, there was no way back. Sometimes Vince hated himself for the compromises he'd made to keep in with Ritchie. A couple of times after eating a burger he'd had to go to the bathroom and be sick. Now these late-night chats with the President were becoming more frequent. He ought to be flattered, but he wasn't. It was ruining his marriage. And probably his health. Vince was working crazy hours. He normally got up at four and was in his office by five, gutting the latest news and looking ahead to the President's day to make sure there were no nasty surprises. He could make do with five or six hours sleep a night, but recently he'd been lucky to get four. Often it wasn't worth going home and he just bedded down on a mattress in his office.

A big movie star appeared on the news. She looked angry. Ritchie upped the volume. The big movie star was telling people that Hollywood was finished. Ritchie frowned. The big movie star said that the celebrity deaths were just the beginning. She said that nobody felt safe in California any more. She listed five or six other stars who'd told her personally that they were moving away. It wasn't just the fire risk, it was the pollution, the water problems, the traffic. The big movie star then blamed the President for allowing the local environment to be destroyed. She said it was time the President faced up to climate change.

Ritchie leapt up from the sofa. 'You fucking traitor!' he screamed. Ritchie turned to Vince. 'She's on the board of *Acting for Jesus* for Chrissake! That woman is one of my biggest supporters.'

'Was,' thought Vince.

'I kissed her, I kissed her on both cheeks right out there on the White House lawn. In front of the fucking cameras. You bitch!'

The TV report cut to footage of a blackened landscape and the shells of houses. In front of the shells of houses, former owners were being interviewed, many of them weeping. They'd been showing this stuff for days now, nobody seemed to tire of it. The only real news was the outbreak of fire in the Sequoia National Park. Thousands of giant redwoods were apparently under threat. Ritchie turned off the sound in disgust. Changing gear with the skill of a racing car driver, he suddenly gave Vince his personal attention.

'How's Lucy?'

Ritchie had the unnerving ability to recall the names of wives and partners. Even those he hadn't met. Vince knew that the only answer to the question was a tremendously positive one. 'Terrific. Happy, busy.'

'That's good. A man's marriage is the rock upon which all his achievements rest.'

Vince nodded. He was relieved that so far he'd managed to prevent Lucy meeting the President. He was scared that if Ritchie came out with that kind of cornball stuff about love and marriage Lucy might just tell him he was talking nonsense. She was like that.

The President chewed his gum and fell silent. Vince knew better than to say anything. He'd know soon enough what the President wanted to talk about. Sometimes it was a war. Sometimes it was a problem with Congress. Sometimes it was baseball. You rarely knew in advance.

'The live broadcast was lousy. I was lousy.'

Ah, so that was it. 'It wasn't great, sir.'

Ritchie gave him a wry grin. 'Thanks, Vince. Thanks for telling me the truth. That's what I like about you.'

Vince knew that Ritchie saw him as a truth-teller. Ritchie was smart enough to know that every President needed a truth-teller. but the gratitude made Vince feel bad. Vince knew that really he was a half-truth-teller. For a start, he lied about burgers. He also lied about Jesus. The whole religious ethos of the White House gave Vince the creeps. Ritchie wasn't too bad; there was a welcome hint of tokenism about Ritchie's faith, but Jimmy Lombok really freaked Vince out. Vince didn't think it was healthy to have a National Security Adviser who had a positive attitude to the end of the world. But Vince kept his anxieties to himself. Vince reckoned a little hypocrisy was a small price to pay for having influence over the most powerful man on Earth. Leastways, that was how he squared it with his conscience.

'The Malibu fire . . . I guess it'll turn out to be arson, right?'

'They're still checking it out, sir.'

'I hope it's going to be arson.'

'Why?' Vince knew why, but it seemed rude not to ask.

'If it's arson, it's harder to present it as an eco thing.'

'Might be arson *and* an eco thing.'

'Do you think it's an eco thing?'

'Of course it's an eco thing, sir. Sure, looks better if it's arson, but it doesn't matter a damn in the end. No way would the fire have spread the way it did if it hadn't been for the freaky weather we've been having.'

The President stared morosely into space, his jaws working away rhythmically. Then he took the wad of gum from his mouth and stuck it under the sofa. 'It's scary, Vince, that's what it is.'

'What's scary, Mr President?'

'Well, if you're not safe in Malibu, where are you safe? I mean, it's one thing if there's a flood in Asia or something, they're forever having floods, they're used to it, right? I mean, for them life is cheap, right? And if it's a bit worse for them now than how it used to be, well, hell, it wasn't that good to start with, so it's no big deal. But California, that's another story. And now they're blaming me.'

Vince thought he saw an opportunity to push his case. 'Mr President, I'm worried. You're looking out of step with the times. You can't just keep on pretending that the green agenda's all bullshit. It's a question of how you'll be seen in history, sir.' Vince knew that the your-place-in-history factor was the one big argument that still carried weight with Ritchie. True, the mid-term Congressional elections were still to come, but the supportive majority in Congress that Ritchie could command looked pretty impregnable.

There was a discreet knock at the door.

'Yeah?' shouted Ritchie.

'Your burgers have arrived, sir,' came a soothing voice from behind the door.

'Well, heck, bring 'em in, then!'

The door opened and a senior White House steward entered, carrying two big polystyrene containers on a silver tray. Ritchie used to have the delivery boy bring the burgers in personally, it kind of gave him the feeling of being in touch with ordinary people, but his security people wouldn't let him do it any more.

The senior steward, a straight-backed silver-haired man in his mid-fifties, struggled to conceal his disapproval as he carefully placed the burgers on the low table between the sofas. Trained to serve exquisite cuisine to the planet's most important people, it grieved him to be laying junk food before the President of the United States. For a few weeks after Ritchie's arrival in the White House the man had tried to insinuate plates, silver cutlery and linen napkins into the arrangement, to lend at least a modicum of respectability to the event, but had been sternly told off by the President. Now all he was allowed to do was serve the burgers in their delivery containers bearing the garish logo of Hamburger Heaven. He then opened two bottles of Coca-Cola and put them down beside the burgers. Ritchie grabbed one of the bottles and raised it to his lips.

'Thanks, Ted. Cheers.'

'Sir,' said the senior steward, suffering grievously at the sight of the chief drinking Coke – *and* straight from the bottle. He gave the merest hint of a bow and withdrew, closing the door carefully behind him.

'Ain't he the greatest?' said Ritchie. 'First day here, I thought of getting rid of him, but he's served four Presidents, there's nothing he doesn't know, and I can trust him one hundred and one per cent. What more could you want? Come on, Vince, get going on that burger.' The President had already removed his burger from the polystyrene box and was biting down on it.

'I'm there,' said Vince, looking at the enormous slab of ground beef jammed between two slabs of carbohydrate. About half a pound of cheese had been melted over the top. Vince took a deep breath and bit down on his cheeseburger.

'Oh boy, this is real good,' said Ritchie. 'Yours too?'

'Terrific,' said Vince, struggling not to gag. Occasionally he wondered whether Ritchie knew he was vegetarian and had turned the whole thing into some kind of grotesque test of loyalty.

'You can't beat a good 'old cheeseburger, right? A big, gooey, five-napkin cheeseburger. Has to be well done of course. A rare cheeseburger, that is one disgusting item. Not to mention those abominations they serve up in the fancy places. Darlene told me there's a place in Georgetown serves a Greekburger. That's right, a Greekburger. Ground beef served with feta cheese and olives. Can you believe that?'

Vince thought it sounded marginally better than what he was eating right now. 'Yuck,' said Vince.

'Right,' said the President. 'Yuck. Yuck is right.'

They munched in silence for a few minutes. Vince swigged from his bottle of Coke, thinking regretfully of the bottle of Meursault in the boot of his car. He'd bought it chilled. Now it would be warming up, damnit. He didn't know whether Lucy had called back, but he couldn't check his messages in the presence of the President. Most of the time, Ritchie came on all friendly and casual to him, but that was only when he felt like it. Vince knew from experience that the man had a very short fuse. The slightest irritation and Ritchie would make clear who was boss.

The 'breaking news' caption flashed red on the TV screen. Vince wasn't bothered. Breaking news didn't mean anything any more. Breaking news could be announcing a new zit on some pop star's face. But Ritchie had already tuned on the sound. The network was revealing the results of its new poll about the Malibu disaster. People had been asked who was to blame. Fifty-two per cent said they blamed the President. Ritchie swallowed a huge chunk of ground beef and nearly choked. Vince had to slap him on the back. A pink-faced Ritchie finally recovered his breath. 'Why's it my fault? Did I light the fire? Jesus ... What did they want me to do? Go out there and piss on it?'

Vince felt a rush of optimism. This really was a chance to move the President on to a new agenda, to make him face the realities of climate change. Vince pondered his next move. Too late. The President had stood up.

'Thanks for coming,' Ritchie said.

Vince jumped to his feet. 'You're welcome, sir.'

The President placed an avuncular hand on Vince's shoulders and guided him towards the door. 'This whole planet thing is an awful big issue, Vince. I'm in the Lord's hands on this one.'

Vince didn't know what to say. He hesitated. 'Me too.' He closed his eyes for a moment, thinking he would never, ever tell a soul what he had just said. Vince knew he made these compromises so as to be a restraining influence on Ritchie. Vince knew he was the voice of sanity in a White House full of fruitcakes. Vince just *knew* he hadn't been corrupted by power. 'That was a great burger, sir,' he said.

'Glad you enjoyed it, Vince.' The President's eyes suddenly swivelled back to the television. He rushed to the sofa, grabbed the remote and stabbed at the sound button. His face was horribly contorted. Vince followed his gaze and saw a Californian redwood swathed in flames. Slowly, majestically, it toppled. 'Live from Sequoia National Park' read the caption. Ritchie was making strange choking noises. For a moment, Vince didn't get it. So everybody loved giant redwoods, but still ... Then he registered the hysterical voice of the reporter. The falling tree was the General Sherman, all 275 feet of it. It was the oldest and the tallest and the most famous living thing on earth. Despite desperate attempts by hundreds of fire-fighters and thousands of volunteers, the fire raging through the National Park had finally engulfed America's favourite tree. In a huge, majestic arc, it fell.

Vince briefly reflected that during the Civil War, General Sherman had torched Atlanta, so there was a kind of glorious symmetry about the tree named after him going up in flames. This frivolous thought was instantly gone as the great tree finally hit the ground, bounced majestically once, then came to rest in an enormous cloud of smoke and glowing embers.

'Fuck me,' said the President.

9

Vince took a gulp of the Meursault and pulled a face. It didn't taste good this warm. He crossed to the fridge, pushed his glass against the ice dispenser and allowed three cubes to fall into it. No way to treat a good wine, he thought, but he didn't care. There was plenty of cheap white in the fridge, he could have saved the Meursault till Lucy turned up, but he wanted to punish her. He'd got back from the White House after midnight and amidst the mess of newspapers and books and dirty plates on the kitchen table had found a note saying 'Out, back soon.' He'd immediately called her. It took him a moment or two to register that her cell phone was ringing somewhere upstairs. He'd found it on the floor of her bathroom under a towel. Lucy was forever doing stuff like that. Once she'd left her passport in a restroom at JFK and they'd missed their flight to Paris.

Flicking on the small TV next to the microwave, Vince saw that the destruction of the General Sherman Tree was turning into the big story of the night. He made a half-hearted attempt to clear up the mess in the kitchen while keeping one eye on the television. He felt dog-tired, but he couldn't bring himself to go to bed till he knew that Lucy was safe. He was actually more irritated than concerned. She was pretty good at looking after herself. Since throwing in her job as a reporter in LA so as to come East with him, Lucy had been writing books. Her first, a detective novel, had done reasonably well, but not well enough. She'd been researching her second for about a year now, and Vince wished she'd get on with it. He'd married a journalist, not a writer. He was jealous of the amount of attention she gave to her writing. A shitload more than Vince got nowadays. And the research for this second book seemed to go on and on. He poured another glass of wine, dropped more ice cubes into it, and broke open a pack of chocolate chip cookies. He sat down and munched disconsolately on those. Naturally, he wondered whether Lucy was having an affair. He was alarmed to realise that he really had no idea whether that was likely or not. He hardly had any evidence to go on, since they'd seen so little of each other recently.

He'd just decided to go to bed when he heard her car in the drive. As he came downstairs the phone was ringing. Lucy got to it first, which irritated him because he assumed it would be for him.

'Hello,' said Lucy. 'White House 24-hour helpline.'

The duty press officer wasn't thrown. He'd had Lucy answer the phone before. He apologised for calling at this time of night, but it was important. 'Let me guess,' said Lucy. 'The President's peed his pants.'

Vince grabbed the phone from her. 'Hi. It's Vince. Sorry about that. What's happening?' He shot Lucy a furious glance. He looked at his watch. it was 3.30.

Lucy left the room and went upstairs.

'Do you remember Chuck and Geraldine?' said the press officer.

'Chuck and Geraldine . . . who the hell are Chuck and Geraldine?'

'Chuck and Geraldine from Great Falls, Montana. You know, the Inspirational Moms and Dads? They met Ritchie in the White House. It got a lot of coverage.'

'Oh yeah, yeah . . . I remember.'

'Well, Chuck's just been arrested for murdering Geraldine – and their four kids.'

'Oh Jesus.'

'The guy had a Smith and Wesson 500 at home. It's normally used for big-game hunting. Five bullets in the chamber – one for each of them.'

'Oh Jesus Christ, that's horrible.'

'Yeah. Inspirational dads, who needs 'em? It'll be on the wires within an hour. The networks will keep running those pictures of Ritchie meeting them. It'll be damaging. Anna's on the case. She's talking to Skidelski right now.'

'Why to Skidelski? What's this got to do with the Defense Department?'

'No idea. Anyhow, I thought you needed to know about Chuck and Geraldine before you brief the President. I guess he'll be upset.'

Lucy re-entered the room, stark naked. Vince's eyes followed as she went to get herself a glass of iced water.

Lucy drained the glass of water, walked over to Vince, kissed him full on the mouth and pulled the phone lead from the wall. He thought of protesting, but he was already getting aroused.

She lifted his arm to look at his wristwatch. He murmured, 'We have time,' and pulled her towards him.

Vince was late for work that morning, not arriving till ten after five. He was tired but feeling good about the world.

Anna Prascilowicz as at her desk by six, easily an hour earlier than normal. She called Vince, asking him to come to her office.

Vince hated being interrupted at this time of day. He had to be ready to brief the President by 08.30. 'Is it important?' he asked.

'Yes,' she snapped. 'Otherwise I wouldn't be calling you, would I?'

When Vince entered her office, she was on the phone to the Defense Secretary. 'Okay,' she said., 'we'll press-release at nine.' She put the phone down. 'Vince. We're about to bomb Haiti. Should we wake the President?'

'Why are we bombing Haiti?'

'We have evidence of terrorist groupings planning an attack on the United States.'

'You mean that sad little bunch of leftist guerrillas? The ones we've known about for ages?'

'Terrorist groupings, Vince.'

'Oh, I get it. We need to deflect attention from Chuck and Geraldine.'

'That's one way of looking at it. I'd say it was Chuck and Geraldine *and* the celebs *and* General Sherman.'

'Anna. Are you really sure about this?'

'It's not my decision. Talk to Joe Skidelski.'

'People will be killed.'

Anna Prascilowicz gave Vince a long hard look. 'You know, Vince, sometimes I worry about you.'

Four hours later the airstrike on Haiti went ahead. In the depths of the Haitian mangrove swamps, one guerrilla, eleven fishermen and twenty-two villagers were killed in the space of seven minutes. The President went live on television that night to praise the nation's vigilance in saving America from a ruthless terrorist attack.

For the next forty-eight hours of television Chuck and Geraldine hardly got a look in. But General Sherman and the celebs were made of sterner stuff and still made second and third place in most bulletins.

10

Braced between the edge of a seat and a leather-clad bulwark, Anna Prascilowicz remained standing as Air Force One climbed away from Andrews Air Force base at a 45-degree angle, engines screaming with the strain. This angle of take-off was standard procedure; it reduced to a minimum the time the plane was within range of the surface-to-air missiles of any potential assassin. The descent for landing would be equally steep and, to anyone who hadn't experienced it before, equally terrifying. There were no rules about seatbelts on Air Force One. Most of the younger staffers liked to show how cool they were by refusing to sit down during take-off and landing, usually standing wedged in some favourite corner where they could brace themselves against the G-forces. The *really* cool ones got on with mundane tasks such as photocopying.

Anna Prascilowicz might not be young any more, but she was determined not to be upstaged by callow youth. More important, she liked to show the press that she had more balls than they did. Lined up in front of her, near the rear of the plane, were the dozen or so journalists of the White House Press Pool who'd been invited to accompany the President on his flight to Toledo, Ohio, where Ritchie was to spend two hours visiting a school and opening a big new pharmaceuticals plant that would bring jobs to a depressed area. Twenty-four hours earlier, two C-5 Galaxy heavy transport aircraft had taken off from Andrews, carrying the President's armoured limousine, a stand-by limo, a fully equipped ambulance, and several limos for use as decoys.

Unlike Anna, all the press pool had opted for the traditional wimp approach to take-off, which was to sit well back in the seat, wait for the plane to gain height, and not think about it. They all avoided Anna's eye. She liked that.

*

Much further forward in the plane, President Ritchie was sitting in the plush leather armchairs of the stateroom with his son Edward and the hero of the Malibu fire, Cheech Lingaard. This wouldn't be the first time Ritchie had invited personal guests along for a ride on Air Force One. It gave Ritchie a warm feeling inside to be able to offer such a gift. Even the sophisticated and the blasé were thrilled at the thought of being allowed to travel on the plane of the most powerful man in the world. Ritchie often used it to awe some foreign leader into compliance. Once he'd used it to bounce the British Prime Minister into supporting the illegal invasion of a troublesome small country. Right now, Ritchie was using it for a more ambitious purpose: to repair his relationship with his son. Edward had been on board only twice before, and had loved it. The idea of inviting Cheech Lingaard along had come to Ritchie at the last minute. He knew Edward had seen most of Lingaard's movies, and now Lingaard was more than just a movie star; he was a national hero, a man who'd shown courage in the face of terrible danger. And as a supporter of the *Strong Families* initiative, Lingaard could be useful to the President. The more Ritchie was battered by complex problems like global warming and terrorism, the more he warmed to simple, downhome moral issues, such as the importance of family life. Inviting Lingaard along was a way of combining the personal with the political.

The only problem so far was that Lingaard had gone very, very pale and quiet during take-off.

Ritchie tried to reassure him. 'The take-off's kinda steep. People find it a bit scary the first time.'

'Hey, not me.'

The minute Air Force One reached cruising altitude, Anna Prascilowicz launched into her press briefing. Her piercing voice could easily be heard above the dull roar of the engines. First she outlined the schedule for the day, then she took questions.

After a couple of dutiful but half-hearted enquiries about economic policy, the press pool got going on the stuff that really interested them. Prascilowicz gave crisp, clear answers, some of them true.

'Is the President drinking tea or coffee on this flight?'

'He normally starts with a Diet Coke.'

'Is the President in the conference room or the stateroom?'

'He's in the conference room with his advisers, discussing economic issues affecting the Mid-West.'

'Will the President be using the on-board gym during this flight?'

'No.'

'What's the President having for lunch?'

'Turkey sandwiches.'

'Is it true that the President has two private guests on board?'

Prascilowicz hadn't realised that they knew this, but she didn't miss a beat.

'Yes. His son. The President believes in strong families. That's why he's also invited Cheech Lingaard along, who as you know is a campaigner for the President's *Strong Families* initiative. I'll take one more question.'

'What colour tie is the President wearing today?'

'No fucking idea.'

The press pool collapsed in laughter.

In the stateroom, Ritchie and Cheech were drinking Diet Coke, while Edward was drinking a black coffee and hanging on to every word that Cheech uttered. Cheech Lingaard, who had now regained his colour, had a vast stock of Hollywood stories and knew how to tell them. Ritchie was pleased. His plan was working. This trip would bring him closer to Edward, heal a few wounds. He looked at his son and thought what a good-looking boy he was. Tall and slim, with his mother's almond-shaped eyes and his father's luxuriant dark hair, he was every inch the son that Ritchie had hoped for. Maybe he needed to fill out a bit, build some muscle, but that would come in time.

Ritchie knew that by rights he ought to be in the conference room, getting briefed about economic conditions in the Mid-West, but hell, family was important too, right? His wife had even wanted to come along, but he'd talked her out of it. He'd explained to Darlene that what the boy needed was a bit of male bonding.

As the steward brought them turkey sandwiches, Cheech finally paused in his cascade of anecdotes. They all sat back and relaxed and gazed idly out of the window.

Quite casually, Edward suddenly said, 'Dad, this is the last time I'll come on Air Force One.'

Ritchie hoped this was some kind of joke. 'Why's that, son?'

'Because it's polluting the planet.'

Oh shit, thought Ritchie. 'Hell, son, all planes cause a bit of pollution. No way around that.'

'Yes, there is. We could all stop flying.'

Ritchie laughed and spread his hands, appealing to Lingaard. 'See what a father's up against these days?'

To his horror, Lingaard replied, 'I kinda see what Eddie means.'

'Whaddya mean, you see what he means?' You dumb fuck, thought Ritchie, I didn't bring you along to support my son's idiotic rebellions. Who's called Edward, by the way, not Eddie.

Before Lingaard could answer, Edward leapt in excitedly. 'I knew Cheech would understand. He's been through it. He *knows* what climate change means. He's been through it. It nearly cost him his life.'

'It damned near did, Eddie. It damned near did.'

Ritchie balled his fists, realised it, and forced himself to relax his hands. He tried to sound unruffled. 'Climate change had nothing to do with it. It was a wildfire, that's all. Right, Cheech?'

Cheech turned his cold blue eyes on him. 'Yeah,' he said. 'Most probably.'

Ritchie leaned forward, balling his fists again. 'Most probably?! What's most probably got to do with it? I thought you were on my side?'

'I *am* on your side,' said Cheech. 'But it's important that we keep an open mind on these issues.'

'I got an open mind, goddamnit!' said Ritchie.

'Bullshit, Dad!' shouted Edward. 'No way do you have an open mind!'

There was a knock at the door of the stateroom and a young staffer appeared. 'Sorry to disturb you, Mr President. There's a call from the British Prime Minister. Do you want to take it?'

Ritchie didn't really want to take it, but he was relieved to escape the looming confrontation with his son.

'Sure.'

'Oh and Larry says he really needs to go through that speech you're making in the school today, sir.'

Ritchie stood up. 'Yeah, yeah, fine. I'll be right there.' He turned to Cheech. 'You tell Edward more of your funny tales from Hollywood. No more climate-change shit, okay?' He gave Cheech a friendly punch on the shoulder and left the stateroom.

'Hi James,' said Ritchie into the phone as he flopped into the Chief's chair in the conference room. 'What can I do for you?'

'Ritchie, splendid to hear your voice.'

Ritchie rolled his eyes at a couple of staffers who, as was routine, were listening in to the call on their own handsets and taking notes. The staffers grinned.

'Great to hear yours, James,' said Ritchie.

'Ritchie, I just wanted to say you have the full support of Britain.'

Ritchie grunted. He always had the full support of Britain.

'We believe the bombing of Haiti was fully justified.'

Oh, so that's what he's referring to, thought Ritchie. 'I'm grateful for that, James.' Ritchie frowned. He could have sworn that Halstead had phoned to express his support about half an hour after the bombing was announced.

'I know I've called you about this already, but you know, what I wanted to say was, well, I've had a chat with the Chief of Defence Staff and we just wanted to say that if you decide to send peace-keeping forces in, we'd be proud to contribute.'

Yeah, thought Ritchie, about fifty grunts and two old trucks. 'Thanks, James, I'll certainly keep that in mind.' He glanced at his watch. 'It's been good to talk to you.' He could hear the note of disappointment in the other man's voice, but he had more important things to do than chat with Halstead.

'Right. Goodbye, Ritchie. Talk to you soon.'

'You bet. Bye, James.'

Ritchie put down the phone and sighed.

Larry Dodge was lingering palely by his side, with a sheaf of papers in his hand. 'The school speech, sir?'

Ritchie got up. 'We got plenty of time.'

As Ritchie re-entered the stateroom, the conversation between Cheech and Edward ceased.

'Hey, don't stop talking on my account,' said the President. 'Anyone want something more to eat? Or drink?'

Cheech Lingaard said, 'Ritchie. Eddie has something to tell you.'

'Edward. His name's Edward.'

'Yeah, well he still has something to tell you. Right, Eddie?'

Edward hesitated for a moment. 'Dad, I want to quit Harvard. I want to go to UCLA and do film studies.'

Ritchie turned to Lingaard. 'Did *you* put him up to this?'

'Nobody put me up to it, Dad! I'm not a kid any more. I make up my own mind, okay?!'

There was a perfunctory knock and the door opened. Larry Dodge said, 'Mr President, we really need to go through the Toledo speech soon, sir.'

'Fuck you, Larry!' said the President. 'Can't you see I'm spending quality time with my son?!'

11

Vince didn't often find himself in the office of the Vice President, but having managed to avoid the trip to Ohio, he was taking the opportunity to talk to Murdo Robertson in private. Strictly speaking, this was a breach of protocol. As Special Assistant to the President, Vince wasn't meant to break the chain of command like this.

Murdo Robertson, today's expensive suit as crumpled as any of the others, was ensconced behind the vice-presidential desk in his huge office in the Eisenhower Executive Office Building next to the West Wing. For the previous twenty-five years, Vice Presidents had been content with a modest office in the West Wing itself, retaining the grand ceremonial office for major meetings and press interviews. But this wasn't good enough for Murdo Robertson. Murdo Robertson wanted to show everyone just how important the job of Vice President was. Vince had to admit that in some ways the move was appropriate. There was a hollow grandeur to the VP's ceremonial office that suited the hollow grandeur of most of Murdo Robertson's pronouncements.

The job of Vice President was a curious mixture of power and irrelevance. The power came mainly from everyone's awareness that if the President were to die, the Vice President would instantly become the world's most powerful person. The irrelevance came from everyone's awareness that as long as the President was alive, the Vice President didn't matter very much. He did matter a bit, though, and that was why Vince was there. Murdo Robertson fulfilled one small but vital function in the Ritchie administration: he was articulate and he exuded confidence. If troublesome Congressmen had to be soothed, or anxious business leaders placated, Ritchie would frequently plead pressure of work and send Robertson along instead. Robertson had the plausibility of the successful salesman without any of the effort. His plump, smooth cheeks, his generous belly, his rich authoritative voice, all suggested a man who had put the world to rights or could effortlessly do so. Even the crumpled suit and the shirt coming out of the trousers suggested an insouciance bred of worldly confidence.

'I don't really see what you're asking me to do,' said Robertson, as Vince paced up and down in front of him.

Vince hesitated. This was a tricky call. Murdo Robertson would never line up with any faction until he knew he'd be on the winning side. Until very recently, the balance of power within the White House had been on the side of the people who saw global warming as at best a diversion from what really counted, at worst some kind of liberal conspiracy to reduce the living standards of the American people. But the great Malibu fire and the destruction of General Sherman – together these two events had changed something. They'd rattled Ritchie for a start. This was an opportunity to push for a change in administration policy.

To get the VP on board Vince would have to plant the idea that the new thinking was in the ascendancy. But he realised he hadn't properly worked out how to do it. He bought a few seconds' thinking time by staring at a large framed photograph of Murdo Robertson in full Highland dress, standing on the battlements of Edinburgh Castle. It was a grim spectacle. But Vince knew that Robertson was proud of his Scottish heritage, so he said, 'Terrific photograph, sir.'

'Yes, I like it very much,' boomed Robertson. 'Can you tell me what tartan that is, Vince? Can you?'

'Let me see . . . The Robertson tartan?'

'Ahhh.' Robertson wagged a plump finger at him. 'That's what everyone thinks. But there are several different Robertson tartans. There's Hunting Modern, there's Hunting Ancient, there's Hunting Muted, there's Hunting Weathered, there's Red Modern, there's Red Ancient, and there's Red Weathered. Seven in all.'

'Who'd have thought it?' said Vince, in what he hoped was a tone of wonderment.

'Yep, seven in all. I'm a Hunting Ancient man myself. Neatest tartan in the world.'

'It's fascinating.'

'The entire history of tartan is fascinating, Vince. A man could devote his whole life to it.'

'I bet he could.'

'Did you know the Robertsons are descended from Crinan, Lord of Atholl?'

'No, sir, I didn't know that.'

'And the Lords of Atholl were the forebears of Duncan, King of the Scots.'

'Does this mean you have royal blood, sir?'

'I believe it does, Vince. Not that I like to boast about it too much. After all, we live in a Republic, right?' Robertson thought this was very funny, and broke into loud peals of laughter.

Vince laughed along as heartily as he could. They both stopped laughing at the same moment and Vince said, 'Sir. Climate change.'

The big office fell silent.

'What about it?'

'I believe that the President is moving on the issue, sir.'

'Do you, now?'

'Yes, sir. I think the weight of scientific evidence is growing. And I believe that the American people are ready to face up to the big issues.'

'And what makes you think that?'

'The various floods and natural disasters we've been experiencing for the last couple of years. And more recently, the Malibu fire disaster and the loss of General Sherman. I think they've all made a profound impact.'

'And you think the President is changing his view?'

'Yes, sir, I think so.'

Robertson leaned back in his big leather chair and laid his hands across his ample stomach. 'Well do you know, something, Vince? I'm going to wait till the President tells me that in person. Because I didn't know it was your job to make policy. And now if you'll excuse me, I have a meeting in five minutes.'

'Sir.'

'Goodbye, Vince.'

'Goodbye, sir. Thank you for your time.'

The Vice President grunted and turned his attention to some papers on his desk.

Shit, thought Vince as he left the vice-presidential office, shit, shit, shit.

Vince got back to his desk to find a message from Toledo, Ohio. The visit hadn't gone well. A series of mishaps had culminated in Ritchie making a speech to the citizens of Toledo in which he said how happy he was to be in Denver. Vince grinned. The Denver visit was scheduled for the following week. Somebody must have screwed up on the Tele-PrompTer. Vince hoped Larry Dodge would be the fall guy.

PART ★ TWO

12

The camera scanned the licence plates on Al Boyd's SUV. A moment later the red-and-white striped pole rose to let him into the parking lot. Al Boyd did not like the new American Way building. For a start, it was ten miles outside Washington in McLean, Virginia. The old building had been just eight blocks from the White House. But fear of suicide bombings had made the directors decide to move to a safer location. Boyd thought this sucked. People got scared too easily. Also, The American Way was a think tank. What kind of terrorist was going to want to take out a *think tank* for Chrissake? And anyhow, since the destruction of General Sherman people had become more afraid of being immolated by wildfires than being bombed by terrorists. The power of the image, thought Boyd. It had been the same with the Twin Towers, or those photographs of Iraqi prisoners being tortured by the good guys. Those were all pictures that changed the way people felt about the world. Sometimes that was good. Boyd needed people to be scared, and not just of terrorists. Boyd reckoned maybe his moment had come. Especially if today's meeting came up with the goods.

He parked as near to the building as he could, which was not near enough. He grunted as he descended from his dark-green Lincoln Navigator. Boyd could easily have had a car with chauffeur, or updated to a newer model, but he liked driving his good ol' SUV, with its automatic dual-zone climate control, heated and cooled front seats, Sirius Satellite Radio, in-dash six-disc changer, and, not least, its throaty DOHC 32-valve V8 engine. But what he liked most was the stately comfort of his Lincoln 'Gator, its soft leather seats, its Audiophile stereo (with tweeters) and its cool flat-screen nav system. It was an awesome ride.

Leaning into the wind, he made his way across the parking lot. It felt like they could be in for a tropical storm. What the hell, anything that made a change from the blanketing, stifling heat they'd been having for the last three months. As he moved, banks of CCTV cameras on tall poles tracked his lumbering progress. These were no ordinary surveillance cameras. A computer in the basement of the building was analysing his movements. Using statistical modelling, it compared his way of walking with stored data about the gaits of authorised personnel. If they didn't match, an alarm went off. It was called gait recognition. The idea was to stop any unauthorised person long before they got near enough the building to cause any serious damage with a bomb. This was cutting-edge technology, and had cost fourteen million dollars to install. Like most cutting-edge technology, it didn't work properly. Three times already – *three times!* – Boyd had had to lie face down on the grimy asphalt of the parking lot while a loudspeaker warned him that lethal force would be used if he attempted to move. This made Boyd's daily journey across the parking lot a test of nerves and endurance. Nobody else had been wrongly identified three times. Boyd put it down to his 260-pound bulk. Jesus, even computers hated fat people. What a fucking world. He'd compensate by ordering cream donuts with his morning coffee, that's what he'd do. Maybe he'd have a powdered blueberry-filled. Or should he go for a cinnamon twist? So he was putting on even more weight. Who cared?

To his relief, he reached the building without incident. Just as well. He had an important meeting that day with a scientist from England. It was going to need his focused attention. He enjoyed the rush of chilled air in the lobby; the aircon still seemed to be set for the blazing heat of a few days before. Okay by him. He nodded to the four security guards as he reached into his wallet for his ID. 'Hi, guys,' he said, swiping his card through the scanner.

'Morning, Mr Boyd,' they replied in a cheerful chorus.

Boyd thought they were cheerful because they liked him. In fact, they were cheerful because for the last six months the security teams had all been betting on when Boyd would become too fat to get through the revolving security gate. The total stood at nearly two hundred dollars. The team that happened to be on duty when Boyd got stuck stood to hit the jackpot. Boyd breathed in and managed to squeeze through. The security guys hid their disappointment. Two hundred bucks split four ways was not to be sneezed at. They might be working for some big-time think tank (or policy research institute, as the management preferred to call it), but that didn't mean they were paid much above the minimum wage. The American Way Institute had better things to do with its money.

Generously bankrolled by a dozen of the world's biggest corporations, openly backed by several right-wing charitable foundations, and covertly encouraged by the administration, The American Way employed almost 550 full-time staff. About half of these worked in the media-monitoring unit, pouring a withering fire of moral outrage on any newspaper owner, editor, producer, reporter or DJ suspected of liberal bias (such as presenting both sides of an argument). Another hundred or so ran the American Way Website and the influential weekly journal *Freedom First*. Seventy or eighty concentrated on academia, organising grants to help young right-wing thinkers publish insightful rants, or funding academic research for any social scientist who seemed likely to come up with politically useful conclusions.

That left about 150 for the Blue Skies Unit, which was where Boyd worked. Everybody knew the Blue Skies people were the elite, and had by far the biggest budget, even if nobody quite knew what they were up to. That was the idea. Their job was to dream up fresh stuff, to think outside the envelope, to push out the parameters, in other words, to make the unacceptable acceptable. This didn't mean ignoring electoral considerations. The big money behind the President knew that if the only people Ritchie L. Ritchie could count on for support were the people whose interests he represented, then he'd get about 3 per cent of the vote. So the guys in the Blue Skies Unit made sure they appeared to share the decent, humane instincts of ordinary Americans while in reality they were fighting for quite different outcomes. These were the guys who came up with bright ideas like removing pollution controls from American factories and calling it the Clear Air Initiative, or streamlining consumer protection laws by purging them of outmoded concepts such as the protection of consumers.

Their triumphs weren't just legislative. Some of their work was about changing mindsets. For example, the Blue Skies Unit had played a big role in making SUVs acceptable (a subject close to Boyd's heart). The basic appeal was to those millions of Americans whose position was 'If I want to drive a nine-mile-to-the-gallon gas-guzzling monster then, hey, I'll fucking do it and fuck you and fuck the planet.' Sadly, it was becoming harder to say this openly, and so The American Way had concentrated on researching the supposed safety aspects of SUVs. Hundreds of press releases and well-placed magazine articles in the space of a year and pretty soon half of America believed that SUV drivers were people who cared about their kids. Only heartless, monstrous, uncaring parents would cram their offspring into crappy little Japanese thirty-miles-to-the-gallon cars where they could so easily be killed or maimed in an accident. Especially an accident with an SUV.

The Blue Skies people also had a few foreign policy successes under their belts. Last year they'd helped launch an international court case against the Secretary-General of the UN for blocking the development of GM crops in the Third World. Lawyers for The American Way had argued that twenty-five million people a year were dying of starvation because of the UN's unreasonable insistence on allowing people to know what they were eating. The court case got nowhere, of course, but the publicity was terrific. The biotech companies had almost doubled their funding to Boyd's think tank.

Boyd made his way across the marble-floored lobby, past the bamboo grove that graced the atrium. He caught a glimpse of the giant panda that had recently been installed there to prove that The American Way cared about the natural world. Boyd didn't much like the look of the panda. It struck him as passive and defiantly stupid. No wonder the fucking things were an endangered species.

In a building this elegant, a building where nearly everyone dressed with a studied Ivy League casualness, Boyd stood out. His vast bulk was accentuated by the shapeless sweatshirts and the billowing jeans. He looked like a slob from Middle America. He knew he looked like a slob. He was proud that he looked like a slob. He reckoned looking like a slob helped you think like a slob, helped you understand how a slob felt. The biscotti-and-latte people might run America, but come election time, the people who counted were the biscuits-and-gravy crowd. Everyone in that building was there to look after the long-term interests of America, right? And in Boyd's opinion, fat slobs from Middle America knew a damn sight more about the long-term interests of the nation than a bunch of gym-toned preppies. This attitude didn't make Boyd popular, of course. He knew that a lot of the top people in the organisation would like to get rid of him. They couldn't, though. He was too good at what he did.

74

He stepped heavily into an elevator. Eight people got in with him. A few others hung back, eyeing the fat guy nervously and checking the sign that said 'max. capacity twelve persons'. They didn't want to push their luck.

13

Dolores Delgado was happy. As Head of Homeland Futures she'd had some difficult times, but she just knew that today was going to be a good day. The sassy, stylish 38-year-old was the first holder of the post, which had been created only three years earlier to supplement the work of Homeland Security. The plan was to keep one step ahead of America's enemies. While Homeland Security was busy dealing with today's threats, Homeland Futures was meant to identify tomorrow's threats and come up with strategies for dealing with them.

Dolores Delgado was pretty sure that tomorrow's threats included global warming, but she wasn't planning to do anything about it. Not unless the balance of power in the White House shifted dramatically, and she didn't think that had happened yet. Dolores cared about the planet, but not quite as much as she cared about her job.

As she looked out of the window of the presidential limousine she felt pretty pleased with herself. For a start, it was an honour to be sitting next to the Chief. And she could tell that the Chief felt pretty good about it too. Every time Delgado crossed and uncrossed her legs, he noticed. She made sure he noticed. God didn't give her legs like that just for walking with. She turned to Ritchie and gave him the full power of her dreamy brown eyes. 'You know something, Mr President? This is one of the proudest days of my life.'

'I'm pleased to hear that, Dolores.'

'Don't you want to know why, sir?'

'Okay, Dolores, tell me why.'

She moved a fraction closer to him. 'Because I am sitting beside the man who's done more than any other to make America safe. And now, together, we're about to make it even safer.' For a moment she wondered if she'd gone too far. She sometimes found it hard to calibrate the degree of flattery that worked with Ritchie.

Ritchie nodded, turned to her, and smiled. 'I'm glad to have you on board, Dolores.'

'Thank you, Mr President,' she murmured. She could tell that he meant it.

Ritchie did mean it, though not exactly in the way Delgado thought. He was delighted to have her on board because he was sick and tired of making speeches, especially since that Toledo–Denver fuck-up. Ritchie just hated the idea of people laughing at him behind his back, and he was pretty sure several million Americans had done just that. No, Ritchie was very happy indeed with the plan for the day: Dolores Delgado would make the big speech and he'd say a couple of words and press the button that would light up a new system of electronic signs all over Washington DC and then they'd ride back to the White House in his limo and Dolores would give him another little leg display, which he quite enjoyed but which he would never allow to interfere with his judgements.

Today's ceremony would mark the opening of the first of many similar systems to be rolled out across all of America's cities over the following eighteen months, at a cost of $7.5 billion. Known as the ACT system ('America Combats Terror'), its purpose was to provide citizens with a flow of constantly updated information about security, through a network of huge electronic road signs sited at key intersections. Not only would the signs display a coloured panel showing the current terror alert level (green, blue, yellow, orange or red), they would also provide local information in the event of an attack, so that concerned citizens could take appropriate action.

Sitting in a van three vehicles behind the President (the two in between were laden with heavily armed Secret Service teams), Vince was unable to muster much enthusiasm for the event. In fact, he thought the whole ACT system was a terrific waste of money. Nobody had successfully explained to Vince what concerned citizens were actually meant to *do* in response to a heightened terror alert level. And as for local information, how the hell was that meant to work? Vince had visions of flashing signs saying stuff like 'Al Qaeda attacking Smithsonian. Long tailbacks. Avoid area.'

Of course, nothing that morning would have pleased Vince. He was still feeling very low. Lucy was holed up with her crime novel and extremely crabby, claiming to be even busier than he was. And ever since the Toledo incident the President had been crabby with him too, as if it had been Vince's fault. Nor had the Haiti bombing worked for more than a few days. General Sherman was still on everyone's mind. A discreet call from the White House had ensured that the director of the Sequoia National Park was made to take the rap for the big tree fiasco. He'd duly resigned, but got his revenge by issuing a statement in which he said that President Ritchie's contempt for the environment was responsible for the loss of America's oldest tree. The national mood was not exactly frothy and the damage quickly showed in the President's personal ratings. He was forced to receive a delegation of Congressmen suddenly anxious about their prospects in the mid-term elections. They urged him to take initiatives to show the electorate that he took environmental concerns seriously. They suggested he fly out to California. That wasn't how his advisers saw it. They feared demonstrations and more bad publicity if he went anywhere near. They urged him to put distance between himself and the disasters in California, to be the leader who had to choose priorities in the national interest. Which is why Ritchie was now preparing to declare the new ACT system well and truly open.

Ritchie looked out at the trees bending in the gusts of wind that were whipping through Washington. Getting out and about always made him feel better. He liked the idea of the ACT system. This was something he could relate to. It showed Americans that Ritchie was on the case. And it said to the world, 'Don't fuck with America.'

The motorcade swung onto the Arlington Memorial Bridge that crosses the Potomac and links Arlington National Cemetery with the Lincoln Memorial. This bridge had been chosen because of its closeness to those two potent symbols of American freedom. And because it would look good on television. A dais swathed in red, white and blue had been erected in the middle of the bridge. The bridge had naturally been closed to traffic, so all over Washington there was gridlock.

As the motorcade reached its destination, a military policeman stepped forward to open the five-inch-thick armoured door of the President's limousine. Fifty yards away, the world's press were corralled behind low metal barriers. Ritchie graciously allowed Dolores Delgado to get out first. The gusting wind played havoc with her clouds of black hair, but somehow it rendered her even more attractive, giving her a dangerous, wild quality. Ritchie stepped out and gave a cheerful wave to the cameras. Behind him, Vince and other staffers gathered discreetly a short distance away. The Mayor of Washington was waiting on the dais to greet Delgado and the President. Directly above them was one of the huge new electronic signs, spanning the whole of the bridge. The idea was to let the photographers get the President and the new sign into the same shot. As soon as Ritchie pressed the button, the sign above him would flash 'ACT: AMERICA COMBATS TERROR' in giant electronic letters.

Well, at least that was the plan.

14

'What are you earning right now?'

Dr Robin Fawcett shifted uncomfortably in his chair. In England, you didn't ask questions like that. Especially not twenty minutes after meeting somebody for the first time. 'I earn a reasonable amount, I suppose.'

'How much is that?'

'It's ... well, one doesn't like to complain ...'

Jesus, thought Boyd. What was it with the Brits? They had to dance a fucking minuet around every question before sidling cautiously towards an answer. Having a conversation with them was so fucking *exhausting*.

'Are you satisfied with what you earn in England?'

'It could be better, I suppose. But you know, most academics in England accept that they're not going to make a great deal of money. One isn't really in it for the money.'

Yeah, right, thought Boyd. And that's why you accepted a first-class return airfare across the Atlantic, a suite in the Hay-Adams at $1,400 a night and the services of a limo with driver.

Fawcett ran a hand through his wiry grey hair. At fifty-three he was still slim and elegant. He had a charming wife and two lovely children. He headed up a distinguished research team at Cranbrooke College, London. He had published some extremely well-received papers in a number of academic journals. He was recognised as one of Britain's leading experts on T-cell-mediated immunopathology during lung viral infection, or in plain English, he was an expert on flu. All in all, a creditable career path. But not exactly glittering. He was constantly hampered by lack of funding, by red tape, by institutional caution. And it wasn't as if he was rich. Two children at boarding school accounted for more than a quarter of his income. His wife suffered from ME and could do very little around the house, far less hold down a paying job.

Their annual holidays were modest affairs: normally three weeks in a cottage in Devon. Meanwhile, two of his younger colleagues had gone off to plum jobs in industry.

Then, six months ago, he'd made a breakthrough in an area he'd been quietly working on for years, a new development that he felt sure could revolutionise the world's understanding of the influenza virus. But to take it further would require extra funding. He published a paper and waited for the reaction. At first, there was nothing. Then the attacks started. Colleagues sallied into print, questioning his results, rubbishing his research methods. He began to feel bitter. He pondered the possibility of taking early retirement. And then had come the call from The American Way. It was an invitation to come to Washington to 'discuss a number of options'. Fawcett had heard of The American Way. He knew they had vast resources at their disposal. He knew they put money into all kinds of unlikely projects. He was vaguely aware they had a political agenda, but he didn't want to think about that. An expenses-paid trip to Washington to discuss options, well, as he'd told his wife, there was really nothing to lose, was there?

Fawcett shivered slightly, Boyd's office was cold, even by Washington standards, but to a visiting Englishman unused to American air conditioning it was close to arctic. Boyd noticed the shiver and ignored it. This was his kind of temperature. And anyhow, he wanted to win back the advantage. He realised that talking early on about money had been the wrong tack for an uptight English guy with an odd name. Did Fawcett know what his name meant in America? What was it they called it in England again? A tap, yeah, that was it, a tap. Well this tap wasn't flowing yet.

'More coffee?' Boyd asked.

'Yes, thank you. That would be lovely.'

No it wouldn't, thought Boyd, it'd just be a fucking coffee. He struggled to get out of his chair to refill Fawcett's cup from the vast vacuum flask of coffee that always sat on his desk, but the Englishman had already skipped forward and was holding out his cup. Boyd filled it. The Englishman sat down again and stared dubiously at the thin American coffee.

'Donut?' asked Boyd, holding out the plate of Krispy Kreme Donuts that he'd ordered up specially.

'Thank you, I'd rather not,' said the Englishman.

'You don't know what you're missing,' said the American, reaching out to the plate. He rammed a whole cinnamon twist into his mouth and worked on it. Fawcett looked away. Fawcett was a fastidious man. He wished he didn't have to deal with Boyd. But he had no choice. Judging by his size, Boyd was a slob. But judging by the size of his office, Boyd was an important slob.

'Let's talk about the science of this thing,' said Boyd eventually, licking the last of the cream from his fingers.

'Fine,' Fawcett said, clasping his hands primly on his lap. He felt relieved to get off the subject of money. 'Do you know anything about the Spanish flu epidemic of 1918?'

'Nope,' Boyd lied.

'Well, actually, to be precise, the Spanish flu epidemic of 1918 and 1919.'

Boyd thought, just fucking get on with it.

'It killed at least thirty million people worldwide. Maybe as many as fifty million. It spread with extraordinary speed. Effectively, to every inhabited place on earth. Virologists have always been puzzled as to why it was so lethal. There have been many competing theories, but no evidence. Until now.'

Boyd knew some of this. He'd gone into the background of Fawcett's work pretty thoroughly. But he wanted to hear it directly. He needed to assess how far Fawcett had gone. More important, he needed to assess how far Fawcett would go.

15

Deep in the windowless basement of the CIA headquarters in Langley, Virginia, are the hundred or so rooms that comprise the Counter-terrorism Center. In the very smallest and stuffiest of these rooms, 23-year-old Jay Positano was sitting alone, thumbing through the latest edition of *Paintball World*. Jay was bored. He was bored and he was hot. In theory, the entire building was air-conditioned, but down in Jay's grim little bunker the air was heavy and thick. That's how they treat me, thought Jay. Those assholes don't care about the little people, the people who do the real work.

He paused at the advertisements for paintball guns, staring longingly at a colour picture of the Dragon Intimidator. At $1,200 it was way beyond what he could afford. Add on a few accessories, like a trigger upgrade, a hopper, maybe also a hopper agitator (because higher-end paintball guns like the Dragon Intimidator fired so fast you had to ensure a smooth rapid flow of paintballs), and there would be no change from $1,500. Man, what would he give to own a cool weapon like a Timmy. Hell, he'd just have to make do with his Raptor Extreme, which wasn't bad as semi-automatics go, but still pretty crappy compared to a Timmy.

Trouble was, paintballing was an expensive hobby. There was the gun, of course, and then the camouflage outfit, the ammo pouch, the gloves, the JT Crossfire battle mask, the paintballs themselves, not to mention the admission charge to a decent paintball battlefield, right? Not some dumb place with mud everywhere, but a good one, with lots of wooded areas and bunkers, well, hell, that cost at least $30 just to get in.

Jay kept hoping for promotion. He'd been in the same job for two years now, doing important work, really important work dealing with homeland security. Okay, so he was on the bottom rung, recording boring conversations and checking transcripts and shit like that, but they'd made him sign one of those new Homeland Security secrecy agreements, with life imprisonment if he ever spoke to anyone about it, so it had to be important stuff, right? The pay might be lousy, but it was okay to be working for the CIA. Working for the CIA made him feel good about himself. Since the terrorist attacks on America, the role of the CIA had expanded. Nobody cared any more about the old divisions between the CIA and the FBI. It was open season for spying, wiretapping and arresting anyone you didn't like the look of. Yeah, thought Jay, it was a good time to be with the Agency. And he was only twenty-three, he had prospects. Really, he'd like to have been in the army, and done cool shit like go to some Arab country to defend freedom and kill terrorists, but his skinny physique and chronic asthma meant he hadn't even made it to the first interview.

Jay looked at his watch. It was only three in the afternoon. His shift didn't finish till five. He slipped his headphones back on and listened briefly. Two assholes going on about viruses. One of them sounded like he was English. Sounded like he was a fag and all. Christ knows why anyone wanted a transcript of *him*. As far as Jay was concerned, all fags deserved to die, even white Anglo-Saxon fags.

Jay wasn't allowed to know the names of the people whose conversations he was recording, which was okay by him. He didn't even have to listen much to what was said, because at the same time as he recorded, the speech-recognition system was converting it into a transcript. Nowadays so many people were under surveillance it just wasn't possible to cover them all without using automated recording and transcribing systems. Problem was, the system didn't always get it right, so in the case of selected suspects it would be Jay's job to go over the transcript and where it was all muddled go back to the recordings, check what was actually said, and correct the text. That sounded easy, but it wasn't. Sometimes it took for ever. The people you were recording muttered, and mumbled and coughed and switched on radios and shit like that and sometimes you just couldn't make out what they were saying. What Jay was meant to do then was type in '[indecipherable]' like that, in square brackets. But his boss was a fat-assed woman who always chewed him out for not listening hard enough when he typed in '[indecipherable]' and wouldn't even let him type in '[unclear]' which was easier to spell, so Jay would mostly make something up that felt like it fitted, and just type it in anyhow. Fuck her with her fat black ass and her big fat salary that by rights ought to be going to a white person who knew how to do things right.

Not that Jay was the only one she mouthed off at. He'd once witnessed her giving the finger to her head of department. How could she get away with that? Maybe she was screwing some white guy high up in the CIA. Yeah, that would be it.

He turned the pages of his magazine and came to a full-page ad for that year's Texas Throwdown. This was a three-day, three-night paintball extravaganza in Houston. With piloted ultralight aircraft for paintball strafing runs and grenade bombing. Cool. A twenty-minute flight was only $65. Maybe he could afford that. But shit, no, the Throwdown was before his next payday, and all his credit cads were maxed out, and by the time he'd paid for the gas to drive down there and the admission fee and all the other shit. . . . If only he hadn't spent two hundred dollars on that hooker last month, he hated her anyhow, after he was gone he just knew she laughed about what he'd asked her to do. But hell, he was paying her, wasn't he? If that's what he liked, that's what he got, right? He'd like to have that whore in his sights when he finally got himself a Dragon Intimidator.

Footsteps in the corridor. He thrust *Paintball World* into the bottom drawer and slammed the drawer shut. Just in time.

His boss walked in. 'Jay. Soon as that meeting's over, I need the transcript.'

'I finish at five, Ms Greene.' Jay knew that even with a few creative shortcuts it could still take hours of work to produce a full transcript.

'You stay on till it's finished, okay?' What was it with young people today?

'Oh. Till what time?'

'Till it's finished.' With that she turned and left the room, closing the door noisily behind her.

He hated her. It was all right for her to sit on her fat ass in that big office of hers and tell other people to work late. She was paid stacks of money, you could tell she was by the amount she spent on clothes and hair, whereas Jay didn't even have enough to buy a Dragon Intimidator. It was an unfair world. Sometimes Jay felt like doing something about it. Maybe one day he would.

16

The President was pleased he'd asked Dolores Delgado to make the main speech on the bridge. Not only because he was fed up with speech-making, but because he knew Delgado nearly always got a good press. And letting her be seen in public gave people the impression that there were plenty of opportunities for female advancement in Ritchie's administration, which was decidedly not the case. Maybe her speech had been a tad long, but she was near the end now, so what the hell.

'And so it is my very great pleasure,' concluded Delgado, whose words kept being whipped away by gusts of wind, 'to ask the President of the United States to switch on the new system.' She turned to Ritchie with a heart-melting smile. 'Mr President – it's all yours.'

'Thank you,' said the President, moving to the microphone. 'I'm mighty proud to be here today. And I want to thank all those people who made this new system possible. Above all, the Secretary of State for Homeland Futures, Dolores Delgado. For your hard work and your commitment to the safety of Americans everywhere, I want to thank you, Dolores.'

Ritchie led the applause, let it run for maybe fifteen seconds and then turned to the big red button that he was about to press. 'Okay,' he roared. 'Let's roll!'

He'd decided it would be more masculine to punch the button with the side of his fist rather than the flat of his hand. Wham, down it came. With a big smile on his face, Ritchie turned so that the cameras could get a good shot. The excitement among the press was enormous, better than anything he could have hoped for. Hundreds of them were fighting to get a good angle.

From where he stood, Ritchie couldn't see what was written on the sign directly above him, which was maybe just as well, because instead of flashing 'ACT: AMERICA COMBATS TERROR' like it was meant to, it was flashing 'WHO KILLED GENERAL SHERMAN?'

Oh shit, thought Vince, condemned at this moment to be an onlooker. It was going to be another bad week in the White House.

'WHO KILLED GENERAL SHERMAN?' was meanwhile coming up on 118 other new signs all across Washington DC. Around thirty thousand gridlocked drivers had plenty of time to read it.

17

'Global pandemic?'

'Yes.'

'And what causes a global pandemic?' Boyd's eyes flickered towards the plate with the remaining Krispy Kremes. He wondered whether he could take another without interrupting the English guy's train of thought. Probably not.

'Well, three times in recent history the flu virus has evolved from a minor ailment – you know, coughs and sneezes and so on – into a disease that has the potential to kill millions. Most people don't appreciate what a deadly virus it is. The "flu". It sounds so innocuous, doesn't it?'

'That's right,' said Boyd, feeling a flicker of excitement.

'Whereas the truth is, the flu virus is an absolute genius at evading the human immune response.'

'So how come we haven't all been killed off by it?'

Fawcett sipped at his coffee. He didn't much like the taste, but it gave him a moment's time to think about how to put the information in terms that the fat American would understand. Fawcett always found it hard explaining virology to a layman. 'You need to understand a bit more about the flu virus,' he finally said. 'I'll try to put it in simple terms.'

'You do that.' What was it with the English? Boyd asked himself. They were always so fucking patronising.

'There are three types of flu virus: A, B and C,' Fawcett explained.

'Which is the one that killed people off in 1918?'

'That was the "A" virus.'

'Is it more lethal than the others?'

'Oh, yes.'

'Why?'

'Because of the way its genomes evolve.'

88

'What's that in English?'

Fawcett bristled slightly. He hated the fat man's brusque manner. But he wasn't going to be thrown by this lout with his ugly clothes and his big steel-and-glass desk. He took a deep breath. 'The "A" type is dangerous because it readily undergoes gene swapping. Also known as reassortment. What this means is, two strains of the virus are capable of infecting the same cell and swapping genetic information. They then hybridise to create a new strain. It's this process of gene swapping that's linked to the emergence of most global pandemics. Now ...' Fawcett paused. 'Now, that's pretty basic stuff. Any virologist could tell you that. But I followed a different route. I decided I would actually go out and *find* the 1918 virus.'

'You mean it's still around?'

'Yes.'

'Where?'

'In the permafrost.'

'I don't get it.'

'We went to Yakutsk, in Siberia. Near Saskylakh we dug up seventeen victims of the 1918 pandemic. They were in an almost perfect state of preservation. I succeeded in recovering fragments of the virus from one of them.'

Boyd stared at this weedy, pink-faced Englishman with surprise. 'You mean ... you went out to Siberia and actually, you know, dug up the corpses yourself?'

'Oh yes. It was actually a rather fun outing. One gets tired of being cooped up in the lab day in day out.'

'Yes. Yes, I can see that.' Boyd found it hard to imagine this skinny theorist plodding across the Siberian wasteland with a shovel over his shoulder, ready to dig up frozen stiffs. Maybe there was more to the English creep than he'd assumed.

'Of course, we had a couple of locals, helping us with the digging. It's all really rather basic: pickaxes and spades. Though you have to switch to trowels as you get near the cadavers.'

'Right. So you took the virus from the bodies and—?'

'It's not quite that simple. We took samples of lung tissue. Later, these allowed me to reconstruct the viral genes. And that's when I realised that there was something special about the 1918 virus, something that made it uniquely lethal.'

At this point, Boyd farted. He often did this when he was excited. It was a habit that he tried to control, but just couldn't.

Fawcett politely pretended not to have heard. 'I came to the conclusion that the 1918 virus wasn't a reassortment at all. It was a recombination.' The Englishman sat back in his chair, waiting for the American to be astonished.

The American just looked puzzled. 'What's the difference?'

'In a recombination, a new gene is created. This is a very rare event in nature. When faced with a completely new viral gene, the immune system can't cope. In fact, it is likely to be completely overwhelmed.'

'And that's what happened in 1918?'

'That's what I believe. It's not a theory that's been accepted by the scientific community at large.'

'I don't care about them,' said Boyd. 'Let's come back to my question: how come it didn't wipe out everybody?'

'This was 1918. There were huge movements of peoples at that time. A world war had just finished. That facilitated the spread of the virus. But compared to today, it was a static world. Today there are probably more people crossing continents in a day than there were in a year back then.'

'You mean, this same virus let loose today would be . . . even more lethal?'

'It would spread much more quickly, yes.'

'Would it . . . could it kill . . . could it kill everybody?'

'Theoretically. But the human immune system is very clever. There's a good chance it would quickly find ways of fighting back, even against a new gene. Unless . . .' Fawcett wondered how much more he should say.

'Unless what?' said Boyd, his voice suddenly husky. He hoped he wasn't about to fart again.

'Some of this is . . . well, I regard it as confidential.'

'Look,' said Boyd, 'you're going to have to be frank with me. You're going to have to trust me. The American Way can be useful to you, Dr Fawcett, we have a lot of influence. But if you prefer to play your cards close to your chest, you can do that. We have plenty of other projects to invest in.'

That'll scare him, Boyd thought. He watched the response.

'I'm happy to talk about it with you, Mr Boyd.'

Bingo.

'However, I'm afraid I haven't quite grasped the exact nature of your interest with regard to this project.'

Oh Christ, thought Boyd, what a pain in the ass. 'The American Way funds a lot of projects around the globe. We're interested in seeing new ideas develop. We believe in talent. And we believe in rewarding talent. That means money to fund research. It means money to pay people well. People like you. Giving them the respect they deserve. Giving them the break they deserve. It's what America's all about.'

'And this is all entirely unclouded by self-interest?'

'You mean, what's in it for us?'

'Yes, I suppose I do.'

Boyd tried to make it sound as casual as he could. 'We'd like access to your research results before they're published, that's all.'

'I see,' Fawcett said cautiously. 'And why would you want access to my research results before they're published?'

'Security reasons.'

'It doesn't mean my results would be used for military purposes?'

Boyd had been waiting for this. 'Would that worry you?'

'Yes, I rather fear it would.'

'I respect that,' said Boyd, with a straight face. 'And I can assure you that your work would be for medical, humanitarian and scientific purposes only. You have my word on that.'

'Good. I hope you understand my position . . .'

'Of course,' said Boyd. He understood the other man's position exceedingly well. This wasn't the first time he'd seen someone feebly waving the flag of conscience. Boyd recognised empty gestures when he saw them. If Fawcett really wanted to make a moral stand against militarism, he wouldn't be sitting here right now. What Fawcett needed was a shameless lie to reassure him, and that's what he'd just been given. In his heart Fawcett would know it was a shameless lie, but he would feel better. Boyd wasn't shocked by this. This was normal. Everyone had a price. For some it was money. For some it was sex. For some it was science. Boyd had never met anyone who didn't have a price of some kind. 'For security purposes, I'd have to inform the military as to the nature of the project. That's all. You work in a sensitive area, Mr Fawcett. We wouldn't want your knowledge to fall into the hands of enemies of America. Imagine what a bio-terrorist could do with some clever little influenza virus.'

'Yes. Well, quite.'

'You were telling me about, you know ...'

'Oh, yes. Yes. Well, the next bit is rather complex ...'

'I'll try to cope.'

'Well ...'

Boyd wished the Englishman would stop saying 'Well' like that.

Fawcett sucked the air through his teeth and wondered whether he was doing the right thing by confiding in the fat American.

Boyd sighed loudly and looked at his watch.

Fawcett felt a frisson of fear. He needed access to funding. Major funding. And his suite at the Hay-Adams was awfully nice. It had real antiques.

'Well,' he said to Boyd, who'd been starting to look horribly gloomy. 'Well, there's a substance called IL-4.'

'IL-what?' asked Boyd, pen in hand.

'IL-4. Interleukin-4. It's a natural immuno-suppressant. There have been experiments – by other people, not by me – to genetically splice it into an existing virus. They managed to do it with the mousepox virus, which is a close relative of the smallpox virus.'

'What happened?'

'It made the virus so effective that it wiped out every mouse in the lab.'

Fawcett paused, coughed, stood up and stared out of the window. He though he heard the squeak of a tiny repressed fart from Boyd's direction.

Boyd shifted in his chair and waited.

Fawcett turned back to face Boyd. 'Now, it occurred to me ... what would happen if we genetically modified the 1918 flu virus to contain IL-4?'

'What *would* happen?'

'Well ... We wouldn't know till we tried it, but I imagine that what we'd have is a flu virus with one hundred per cent lethality.'

'I see. You mean, an unstoppable flu virus. A flu virus that could wipe out the human race?'

'Something rather along those lines, yes.'

Boyd swallowed hard. He was struggling to sound casual now. 'Would it be possible to develop a vaccine against this virus?'

'Oh I would think so, yes. But it would take time and money.'

'But in principle, you know, in purely theoretical terms, there could be a vaccine.'

'That's right, yes.'

'And the new virus would kill off anybody who hadn't been given the vaccine?'

'Yes. So you can see why I wouldn't want this to fall into the hands of the military. It could be so horribly abused.'

'It's a scary thought. But there's one thought even scarier, Mr Fawcett. That's the thought of this falling into the hands of terrorists.'

'I certainly wouldn't want that. But you know, I don't think I would want it to fall into the hands of the military either.'

Boyd stared at him solemnly. 'Dr Fawcett. This is the United States of America. We care about the freedom and the dignity of every individual. No way would this nation contemplate the use of a weapon that could wipe out millions of people.'

'Billons, actually,' said Fawcett.

'Right. Billions,' said Boyd, and farted very, very loudly.

18

The President was hurting. Physically and spiritually, he was hurting. It was just his bad luck that seconds after the unwelcome message had appeared on the big electronic sign above him, a flagpole on the bridge had snapped off in the wind, making a noise like a rifle shot. His Secret Service guys had gone apeshit, pulling the President down off the dais and bundling him brutally into the armoured limo as if he were a terrorist suspect.

'So what did the sign say?' spat the President, as the motorcade, sirens wailing, sped towards Constitution Gardens. He was rubbing repeatedly at his shoulder where it had caught the edge of the limo door.

The two Secret Servicemen who were crouched one on each side of the President with handguns drawn decided they'd better leave the Head of Homeland Futures to answer that one.

'I guess there was some kind of electronic failure in the ACT system,' she said. 'You know, teething troubles.'

'What did it say?!' shouted the President.

Delgado swallowed had. 'I didn't manage to read it.'

'Dolores, don't lie to me. What did it say?' Without waiting for an answer, Ritchie turned to the two security men. 'Shut the fuck up with these sirens, will you? The whole world's gonna think I've been shot or something. Jesus Christ!'

'Kill the sirens! Kill the sirens!' shouted the senior security guy into his sleeve.

Delgado realised they were approaching another of the signs. It also read 'WHO KILLED GENERAL SHERMAN?' She moved forward in her seat so as to block the view from Ritchie, hoping that he would focus on her breasts instead. But Ritchie wasn't in the mood for breasts. He pushed forward to get a better view. He finally saw the sign. Eyes popping, he fell to his knees on the floor of the limo. 'Aw, Christ Almighty,' he moaned.

'Why's the system not closed down?!' shouted Delgado. 'Cut the power to the system. I want it closed down NOW!'

'Kill the signs! Kill the signs!' shouted both security guys at once into their sleeves.

Delgado tried to pull the President back on to the seat, but he shook her off. There was a faraway look in his eyes.

At the corner of 23rd and Constitution Avenue, a group of Japanese tourists were surprised to see the President of the United States speed past, his face pressed against the window of his limo, staring upwards. He appeared to be on his knees. The Japanese tourists followed the direction of his eyes and wondered who General Sherman was and why somebody had killed him.

19

Vince came out of the Oval Office feeling tired and resentful. For twenty long minutes Ritchie had chewed him out about the screw-up on the bridge. Both men knew that Vince had nothing to do with the planning for the event and nothing to do with the security failure that had allowed someone to hack into the software, but that made no difference. Ritchie needed to vent his fury. Vince had just sat there and taken it. He'd been through this shit before. Individual punishment was how Ritchie liked to do these things. Screaming abuse at people one at a time meant they had no chance to gang up on you. And for days afterwards each of them would wonder what had been said to the others.

On this particular day, Ritchie's anger had a vicious edge to it, because he'd just had a shouting match with his son. Edward was still intent on that damnfool idea of doing film studies. As if that wasn't bad enough, the boy had reneged on his promise to come to the ranch for the weekend. On the phone, he'd sounded drunk. Ritchie had given him a little lecture about the dangers of alcohol, and the boy had gone crazy, shouting and hollering and telling him he was destroying the planet. Ritchie had slammed the phone down. He felt sick to his stomach at the idea that his own son might be turning into an environmentalist. Thank God he also had a daughter. At twenty-four, Janie ought by rights to be married and settled down, but basically she kept out of his hair, got on with her job as producer on some obscure TV station, and turned up for enough family events to make him feel like a proud father. It was hard figuring out how to deal with kids. Dealing with the idiots who worked for you was much easier. They could always be fired.

As Vince walked down the corridor away from the Oval Office he ran into Jimmy Lombok going in the opposite direction. He assumed Lombok was next for shouting at. Lombok shot Vince a resentful glance as he passed. In the hierarchy of the White House there was even a hierarchy of humiliation.

Jimmy Lombok felt vaguely piqued that he was only the seventh person to be called into the Oval Office and shouted at. Surely Lombok, as the President's National Security Adviser, ought to have been the first, or at least the second person to be called into the Oval Office and shouted at?

'It was a failure of security, and that's your responsibility, Jimmy,' the President said, balled fists on his desk as Lombok huddled miserably on one of the sofas. 'I was made to look a fool. Do you think there's now anyone in America who doesn't associate me personally with the destruction of General Sherman? Purely because you screwed up.'

'I don't think it's right to describe it in those terms.'

'Oh don't you? Well, I do. How many people have been arrested so far?'

'None, as far as I know.'

'As far as you know?! As far as you know?!'

Jimmy Lombok winced and struggled to keep calm. He knew that his enormous bald head would be beaded with sweat, but he was scared to mop it in case Ritchie made a sarcastic comment. 'Making the arrests is an FBI responsibility. I got in touch with Hickie Langshite right away, and he's on the case.'

'Oh yeah? That's convenient for you, isn't it?'

'Sorry, Mr President, but it's an FBI responsibility and that's a fact.'

Ritchie took his feet down off the desk, leaned forward, and bellowed, 'FUCK FACTS!'

'Yessir,' mumbled Lombok pointlessly. He pondered how best to retrieve the situation and, as so often in his life, opted for Jesus. 'I've spent some time praying about this, Mr President. I've asked the Good Lord for guidance, and I believe that He in His wisdom has indicated a number of options.'

Ritchie immediately calmed down. A belief in the efficacy of prayer was something that he and Jimmy Lombok shared. Nobody could say that Ritchie was deeply devout in the way that Lombok was. Ritchie's God was more of an emergency facility, a 24-hour convenience store where he could stock up on reassurance. But they prayed to the same God, and looked on Jesus as a friend. Or at least an acquaintance.

'Go on,' Ritchie said.

Lombok decided to risk mopping his head. He took out a red linen handkerchief and mopped.

'Nice handkerchief,' sneered Ritchie. 'Glad you got time to think about buying nice handkerchiefs.'

'It's my wife, she ...'

'Yeah, yeah, I know.' Ritchie waved a dismissive hand.

'Okay,' said Lombok. 'We know that somebody hacked into the central computer, right? And judging by the General Sherman message, we're talking eco-nuts, okay?'

'Brilliant. Did the good Lord give you that information directly?'

Lombok swallowed hard. He couldn't handle jokes about the Deity.

'Go on,' said the President.

'I've been liaising with the FBI. At dawn tomorrow there'll be a raid on a total of one hundred and sixty premises in the DC area. We're bringing in anyone with a record of any radical involvement in environmental protest. We're going to use the new Citizens Defense Act, so there'll be no problems about how long we hold them or when we bring charges. Just 'cause they're green don't mean they're not terrorists, right?'

'Right,' growled Ritchie.

'Right,' echoed Lombok, with relief. Obviously the President was calming down. Maybe this wouldn't be so bad after all.

'Just one question,' said Ritchie thoughtfully.

'Yes?'

'We're only arresting suspects in the DC area, is that right?'

'Initially, yes.'

Ritchie got up from behind his desk and advanced slowly on Lombok. 'And do you need to be in the DC area to hack into a computer in the DC area?'

'No, I guess not, but ...'

'You could, in fact, be anywhere, right?'

'I suppose so, but ...'

'So arresting people in the DC area makes no sense, does it?'

'Well, we got to start somewhere, right?' said Lombok hopefully. He looked up to see the President looming over him. He wondered whether to stand up or not.

'Jimmy,' said the President, 'YOU ARE A FUCKING MORON!'

'Yessir.'

20

There was a knock at the door. Desiree Greene looked up from the pool of light that spilled across her sleek mahogany desk. 'Come in.'

Jay Positano entered, a fat file in his hand. 'I finished the transcript, Ms Greene,' he said sullenly. It was after ten at night.

'Thank you, Jay. I appreciate that.' She gave him a big smile. Desiree Greene was famous for her big smile. It worked on just about everyone except Jay Positano. But then, when it came to getting a good response from Jay Positano, she had three big problems: she was black, she was a woman, and she was his boss. Also, to his mind, there were far too many 'e's in her name. Desiree Greene. How the hell was he meant to spell that correctly every time? So all she got in return for her big smile was a small scowl. She held out her hand for the file. In a minor act of insubordination, instead of giving it to her, Jay placed it on her desk. She shot a glance at him, picked up the file, and opened it. The file contained two copies of the transcript. Ms Greene always insisted on two copies. Jay made his way to the door.

'Did I say you could leave?'

'I just, um, assumed I could.'

'Is that so?' she said, in her soft drawl.

'It's five hours after the end of my shift, Ms Greene.'

'Is that right?'

Greene's eyes remained on the transcript. She left Jay standing in silence for a good three or four minutes as she skimmed through several pages. 'Looks like you did good work here, Jay.'

Jay stared at the carpet. He found being praised by her even worse than being shouted at. How could he show her that he didn't care what she thought about him?

'I said, you did some good work here.'

'Yeah, right, thank you Ms Greene,' Jay stammered. How come she always made him feel like he was back at school?

She turned to near the end of the document. 'What's the NSI on page 148? And again here on . . . on page 150?'

Jay said, 'I don't remember.' An NSI was a Non-Specific Interruption. In other words, an unidentifiable noise. Sometimes the software that controlled the automatic transcriber would get confused by an unidentifiable noise and try to make words out of it, printing out some weird shit that had nothing to do with the conversation. Then Jay had to put on his headphones, track down the right moment on the recording, and check whether it really was words or just a noise.

'You don't remember?'

'That's right.' He remembered very well, of course. It was the sound of a guy farting. He'd listened twice to be sure, because the voice-recognition software had turned one fart into the word 'trump' and the other fart (the longer, louder one) into 'coronary'. He didn't want to mention farting to Desiree Greene. It was just too gross.

'You seem to have fewer indecipherables than usual,' she commented.

'I think you'll find there are none at all, Ms Greene.'

'Oh. Well, that's just great, Jay. Well done.'

She'd fallen for it. He always knew she was dumb. 'Yeah, well, I, like, worked hard on it,' he replied. Like fuck he did. There was a whole pile of words on the auto-transcript that hadn't made sense, and when he'd listened to the recording they just weren't clear and anyhow the English guy talked strange and so Jay had invented lots of stuff.

'You did well,' said Desiree.

'Is it OK if I go home now, Ms Greene?'

'Oh, yeah, sure, Jay.'

'Goodnight, Ms Greene,' he said politely. He didn't want to blow it completely. He needed this job.

Greene ignored him.

Typical, thought Jay. You're polite to trash like her and what happens? You get treated with contempt. He closed the door loudly behind him. Not loud enough to have slammed it, just loud enough to let the bitch know what he really thought of her.

Greene looked up as the door shut and thought about calling him back into the room and giving the little punk a piece of her mind, but decided she had more important things to do. She had to read through the entire transcript highlighting what she felt was important. Then it would be passed up the CIA's chain of command. But it was the other copy that was really important. She would take that one with her when she left the building. It would be a breach of regulations, but it was something she did all the time. Desiree Greene's loyalties were to the security of the United States of America, not to some bureaucratic chain of command. And if sometimes that meant breaking the rules, then she would break the rules. She was doing this for her country, she told herself as she packed her brown leather briefcase. The money had nothing to do with it.

21

The big, bare room at home that Lucy had designated her office was covered in piles of papers, newspapers, folders, notebooks, dried apple cores, and the occasional mould-encrusted coffee mug. This room was her sacred zone, from which Vince was banned. Not that he would have wanted to be in here for long, thought Lucy, as she rummaged through some yellowing copies of the *Washington Post*. One glimpse of the mouldy mugs and he'd have run screaming from the room.

Lucy failed to find what she was looking for. This was not a new experience. But she almost enjoyed her chaos; she certainly needed her chaos. Maybe that was why, when she could access most newspapers online, she still liked to have copies of them piled on the floor. She picked up an apple from a bowl by her desk and munched on it as she stacked a pile of Maryland newspapers and journals. She was after her address book, which was pretty vital. But she lost it at least once a day and it always turned up again, so she wasn't unduly worried. Vince was always telling her to get an electronic organiser, because for some reason he assumed it would be more reliable, which struck Lucy as a very male assumption. Lucy thought she could just as easily lose an electronic organiser as she could lose a diary, and at least a diary couldn't crash and wipe out the entire contents.

As she sifted through a heap of movie reviews that she'd been planning to file away somewhere, she came across a letter from her father. Damn. She'd completely forgotten to reply to him. She peered at the date (her father's handwriting was incredibly difficult) and saw it had been written six weeks earlier. This made her feel bad. Her father, a retired professor of medieval history at Oxford, resolutely refused to enter the electronic age. She'd pleaded with him to adopt e-mail, but to no avail. She couldn't really blame him: he was in his late seventies now, as was her mother, and both were increasingly resistant to change. Lucy often regretted the double burden of being an only child born to parents old enough to have passed as her grandparents.

Lucy stared at her father's letter and decided that she'd phone him. Not today though. The phone calls tended to be very long, with her mum and dad each demanding a comprehensive update about all her news. And then of course at the end would come the question: when was she coming over to see them? And for the hundredth time she would duck the issue. And then she'd put the phone down and feel horribly guilty.

She pinned the letter on a board near her desk and sat down at her laptop. She'd never bothered to get herself a proper desktop computer. She booted up and selected the file she was working on. This was the project that Vince thought was her second crime novel. But it wasn't a crime novel. It wasn't even a novel. But she couldn't tell Vince that. Not yet, at least. She would finish it first before telling him. Because Vince wouldn't like the idea one little bit. And neither would the White House.

22

Joseph Skidelski was sixty-three, but thanks to Viagra he was half his age in bed. This was just as well, because his wife was half his age all the time. Beneath him she writhed and gasped as he drove into her. He hoped she would come soon, because he couldn't hold out much longer. She was moaning now, that was good. He needed to get this over soon anyway, because he was expecting an important message and Lianna didn't like it if he took calls in the middle of love-making. She was unreasonable like that. She just didn't get it that sometimes the Secretary of State for Defense had to take important calls. Lianna was unreasonable in lots of other ways as well. She wouldn't let him suck her toes, for example. Still, she was young and she was beautiful, frighteningly beautiful. She'd once dreamed of becoming a supermodel, in fact was so keen on becoming a supermodel that she'd had plastic surgery done to get rid of a slight imperfection in her left ear. The surgeon had screwed up and severed a facial nerve. It couldn't be repaired. As a result, she had a one-sided smile. Pretty girls with one-sided smiles didn't become top models. Still, as long as she didn't smile, she looked amazing. And since marrying Skidelski, she hadn't found reason to smile all that much anyway.

The marriage had of course stunned the nation. His reputation was for pursuing power, not pretty girls. He knew the two of them were often referred to as 'Beauty and the Beast', but he didn't care. That old goat Arthur Miller had pulled Marilyn Monroe, hadn't he? And a Secretary of State for Defense had a great deal more to offer than some fucking liberal playwright. Throughout history, power and beauty had always been attracted to one other. Yes, this was a good union, even if it sometimes involved a bit more sex than he really wanted. And a bit more conflict than he could handle. Lianna took offence at the slightest thing. If he didn't smooth it over right away she was apt to get one of her turns. This often involved throwing things at him. If he fled to another room, she would follow, still throwing things. It sometimes made him nostalgic for his first wife. It's true there hadn't been much excitement in his life then, but it was a lot less stressful. After a year together, he and the first Mrs Skidelski had decided they neither loved each other very much nor hated each other very much, and in this undemanding spirit had raised two children. Yes, those were definitely easier times. Still, when he walked into some big White House dinner nowadays with Lianna on his arm and he saw the looks she got from the men – especially the *older* men – well, then suddenly all the hassle was worth it.

Lianna's fingers were digging into his back now. She must be close. He risked a glance at the bedside clock. It was almost 11 pm. Beside the bed, three phones were off the hook, including the red one, reserved for emergencies. On the other side of the room lay two cell phones, both switched off. Sometimes Skidelski wondered what would happen if somebody launched a nuclear missile while he was screwing Lianna. He pushed hard against her. He was close now. So was she.

'Mmmmmm. Ahhhh. Ohhhh. Yeeeeeeessssssssssssss. OH GOD! OH CHRIST! YES! YES! FUCK ME, JOE, FUCK ME. YE-AHHHH.'

He liked how loud she was. Tomorrow morning he would catch a certain look of respect in the eyes of the live-in staff. They knew they were looking at a man who in the space of fifteen minutes could a) incinerate any country on the face of the earth and b) fuck the brains out of America's most beautiful woman. Yep, he was some guy.

With a grunt and a shudder, the Defense Secretary came. He thrust into her a couple more times, then paused. Would there be a message waiting?

'Honey, that was wonderful,' he told her.

'Mmmmm' she replied.

He waited for a bit, then rolled off her and kissed her on the forehead. 'Be right back.'

'Stay.'

'Got to go to the bathroom.' He got out of bed and pulled on his grey bathrobe. The cell phone he needed, the one for very private messages, was already strategically placed in the pocket. It was no ordinary cell phone. It was a Rohde & Schwartz, with a 128-bit key for voice encryption. Ostentatiously ignoring the cell phones lying on the chest of drawers, he went into the bathroom and locked the door. He took the phone from his pocket and switched it on. He waited a moment then accessed the message. It was from Desiree Greene, who also had a Rohde and Schwartz cell phone. Skidelski had made sure she had one. No way did he want the CIA to know that he had direct access to some of their surveillance operations. It wasn't that he thought the CIA guys would cheat on him – after all, the Director of the CIA had been nominated by Skidelski in person. No, the reason he had to keep tabs on the CIA was they were so fucking incompetent. You couldn't trust those assholes to get *anything* right.

The message from Greene told him that the English virologist had been with Boyd for five hours that day. Skidelski didn't like the sound of that. Five hours meant a serious meeting. Greene said she was on her way with a transcript of the conversation. Good. Greene was smart. Bringing it to his home wasn't risk-free, but it was safer than e-mailing it. E-mails left footprints. He wasn't sure what Boyd was up to. The American Way people were basically okay, but Skidelski thought there was too much empire-building going on in the Blue Skies Unit. They kept straying into areas that really belonged to the Pentagon. Skidelski had already been given a secret report on the English virologist, with an initial assessment of the possible military applications of Fawcett's work. He hadn't gotten around to doing anything about it. Now here was Boyd muscling in. Boyd wasn't the type to waste five hours chatting about the weather. Skidelski definitely needed to know what had been said in that meeting.

Skidelski finished reading the transcript, took off his glasses and walked round the polished rosewood table to the cabinet where he kept the port. He liked working late at night in his dining room. The big oval table, which could accommodate eighteen for a meal but rarely did (Lianna didn't like dinner parties at home), somehow gave him a sense of order. It offered so much surface space that he could spread his papers out on it and still enjoy the warm glow of the polished wood in the lamplight. He tilted the port decanter carefully and filled a small glass. Sipping at it, he returned to his seat at the table. He could of course intervene immediately, push Boyd out of the picture, and buy up Fawcett. But that would tell Boyd that his office was bugged, and Skidelski got an awful lot of useful information by that route. Anyhow,

Fawcett struck him as a tricky kind of guy to deal with. Judging by the transcript, Boyd was handling the English scientist pretty well. Any move towards developing a new virus would require the kind of funding and back-up that only the Pentagon could offer. So, he reflected, the best thing was to wait. Pretty soon, Boyd would come to him. Then Skidelski would have the whip-hand. And if it all went wrong, he'd have someone to blame.

The dining-room door burst open and Lianna came in, a coffee cup in her upraised hand.

'Hi, sweetheart,' he said.

The cup flew past his head and broke against the wall.

'You bastard. You'd rather spend the night reading your fucking papers than spend the night making love.'

'Honey, be reasonable, I—'

'You're old and you're ugly and I wish I hadn't married you.'

23

Four hundred miles west of Freetown, Senegal, 10 degrees north of the Equator, in one of the Atlantic Ocean's deepest troughs known as the Cape Verde Basin, an area of low pressure was heading west. The sun beating down on the sea raised the surface temperature to 27 degrees Celsius, warm enough to swim in. Wind speeds were 29 mph.

The air warmed by the sea rose quickly, taking moisture with it and leaving a centre of low pressure. The depression deepened and moved due west. The rising air cooled, creating towering cumulus and cumulonimbus clouds. Stirred by the rotation of the Earth, the wind speed at the centre of the depression rose to 40 mph. Under international agreement, every Atlantic cyclone that reaches 39 mph officially becomes a tropical storm and is given a name. Now the moving depression was not just any old moving depression; now it boasted the name of Wendy. It maybe wasn't the most distinguished of names, but at this point nobody thought Wendy would have much of a career.

Heading gently northwest across the Atlantic and roughly a thousand miles from Venezuela, Wendy deepened again and the winds rose to 52 mph.

Wendy was of course being tracked by the National Hurricane Center in Dade County, Miami. The National Hurricane Center was run by serious people. Not only did they have a mission statement, they also had a vision statement. Their vision, they said, was *to be America's calm, clear and trusted voice in the eye of the storm, and enable communities to be safe from tropical weather threats.*

It was a worthy aim, not to be sneered at.

24

The world's biggest office building squats rudely between Arlington National Cemetery and the Potamac. But though the Pentagon has seventeen and a half miles of corridors, thanks to its shape it takes only seven minutes to walk between any two points in the building. This fact might comfort some of the Pentagon's 23,000 employees, but it meant nothing to Joe Skidelski. He was the boss, and if he wanted to speak to anyone, they came to him, no matter where they were in the building. No matter where they were in the *country*. No matter where they were on the goddamn *planet*.

Al Boyd lumbered down the long Eisenhower Corridor towards the marine standing to attention outside Skidelski's office. The marine in question was having a problem. The man approaching him didn't look like the sort of person who ought to be running loose around the Pentagon. The Marine didn't know that Al Boyd had made an effort that morning, putting on a yellow plaid jacket over a clean T-shirt and forsaking the normal baggy jeans for a pair of only slightly stained grey slacks. To the marine, the guy still looked like a fat screwball. The 260-pound apparition grew closer. The marine remained rigidly at attention, not a muscle moving, but a tiny bead of sweat breaking out just above his left eye. His knowledge of the Pentagon told him that nobody could get this near the Secretary of State for Defense without going through four layers of security checks. But his training told him it was his job to protect the man who protected the world from evil.

Al Boyd was breathing heavily as he approached the door. He hated coming to the Pentagon, with its gloomy corridors and its old-fashioned water coolers and all those muscled young men in immaculate uniforms snapping their heels and saluting. He especially hated having to come here at this time of the morning, but when he'd called Skidelski's office the previous afternoon he'd been told it was the only slot available for three weeks. He was now ten minutes late and sweating heavily.

As he got to the big leather-padded door, Boyd reached into his inside jacket pocket to check that he hadn't left his pocket computer at one of the security checks. The only thing the marine registered was the movement of a hand towards a pocket that might hold a weapon. Training was training. He instantly snapped his rifle down at an angle to prevent the suspect opening the door. Boyd failed to see it in time.

'Sir!' shouted the marine, a tad late.

'Ooomph,' said Boyd, bouncing back off the rifle.

'Your ID please, SIR!' shouted the marine.

'Fuck you, asshole,' gasped Boyd, clutching his stomach where it had impacted with the rifle barrel and wondering why the world was against him. The marine looked like he was about to jump him. The door behind them flew open.

'You must be Mr Boyd,' said Lieutenant Lunt, an attractive raven-haired woman in her thirties.

'Yeah ... yeah, that's right.' Boyd gave the marine a vicious look and limped into the ante-room.

Closing the door behind her, the beautiful Lieutenant Lunt asked Boyd to take a seat and disappeared through to the main office. Typical Skidelski power game, thought Boyd. Now I have to wait.

Joseph Skidelski's vast desk was immaculate. Not a pen, not a phone, not a notepad was out of place. In a drawer in the ante-room, Lieutenant Lunt kept a scale map of the top of her boss's desk, showing the exact location of every item, and God help anyone, assistant, secretary or cleaner, who got it wrong. Skidelski looked up appreciatively as his number one secretary approached.

'Mr Boyd is here, sir,' purred Lieutenant Lunt. 'I asked him to wait'.

Skidelski twinkled up at her. 'I hope you offered him an extra strong chair, Lieutenant.' He smiled, his smile emphasising the unfortunate nose.

'I sure did, sir,' she replied.

God, she's beautiful, thought Skidelski. Maybe he'd ask her to stay behind and work late with him one night.

God, he's ugly, thought the Lieutenant. Maybe she'd ask for a transfer.

Skidelski glanced at the transcript in front of him. 'Send him through in ...' he glanced at his watch ... 'Send him through in ten minutes from now.'

'Yes, sir.'

Skidelski closed the transcript of Boyd's conversation with the English scientist and placed it carefully in a drawer. Now he'd start the meeting with a big built-in advantage. It was good when you knew stuff that the other guy didn't know you knew.

As soon as he heard the door open, Skidelski busied himself with some papers. He grunted an acknowledgement and kept his head down as Lieutenant Lunt announced Al Boyd. No harm in reminding Boyd that he was in the presence of power. He waited till Boyd had been seated for a good thirty seconds before putting down his pen, standing up, and stretching out his hand. 'Al. Good to see you.'

'Hi, Joe.' Boyd didn't bother to get up. He was used to Skidelski's power games. He found them pretty damn stupid. The two men knew each other quite well, even liked each other to some extent. But nothing could stop Skidelski's practised routines. He never stood up when some-body came into the room, always waited till they had sat down, and then unfolded his tall, angular body and extended a leathery hand. This would usually make his visitor stand up again, or at the very least feel uncomfortable as they were towered over by Skidelski, dressed in one of his immaculate grey suits.

'Looks like we're in for a storm,' said Skidelski. 'Pretty remorseless, huh? First we get three months of unbearable heat and now a storm.'

'It's global warming,' said Boyd, never one for small talk.

'Bullshit,' said the Defense Secretary.

'Joe,' insisted Boyd, 'it's global warming.'

'Joined the panic-mongers, have you?'

'You'd have to be blind not to see it's global warming.'

'Thanks.'

'Climate change is here, Joe. Better get used to it.'

Skidelski poured himself a glass of filtered water. It was all he ever drank. He held up the jug questioningly in Boyd's direction.

Boyd shook his head. He was pleased that the weather was so awful. By a stroke of luck, it made his timing look perfect.

Skidelski sipped at the water. It was important to sip water and not gulp it. A lot of people didn't understand that. He felt irritated. He always felt irritated when the climate-change thing was brought up. It didn't fit in with his vision of the world. In common with most of the

111

people close to President Ritchie, he dealt with the problem by pretending it didn't exist. True, that was getting harder to do. Last winter they'd had to deal with the heaviest snowfalls in Washington DC that anyone could remember. In the space of four days and nights, thirty-eight inches of snow had been dumped on the streets. In late March, for God's sake! The capital city of the most powerful nation in the world had ground to a halt. For several days Skidelski had been forced to go everywhere by helicopter, which was a pain, because Skidelski was afraid of helicopters. He couldn't tell anyone about it, of course. It wouldn't be good if people knew that the Defense Secretary was scared of choppers.

'So,' said Skidelski suddenly. 'What can I do for you?'

Boyd liked to come straight to the point. 'I've come across a new virus. A new virus that could have big military implications. It's called Flaxil-4. Flu type A x Interleukin-4. I think you ought to know about it.'

'A new virus, eh? You're full of surprises, Al,' Skidelski chuckled.

25

For six thousand years the mudflats, islands and natural barriers that protect the vast Louisiana wetlands from the sea have been sinking under their own weight. For six thousand years they were regularly replenished by the sediment from the Mississippi River system, deposited every year during the spring flooding. Then, in the eighteenth century, along came some European settlers, who thought it would be a neat idea to build dykes along the lower river in order to prevent flooding, and the levee system was born. It worked pretty well for a while, but in order to make the Mississippi navigable, its course had to be more and more constrained by levees. The river was unable to flood the wetlands any more, and so the mudflats and islands couldn't be replenished. As a result, for about 150 years the Louisiana wetlands have been disappearing beneath the sea at the rate of around twenty square miles a year.

A few years back, some wise people realised that if the Louisiana wetlands weren't saved, it would have catastrophic consequences for the nation. They pointed out that five of the largest ports in the United States were in Louisiana. They pointed out that every year a billion pounds of fish were landed in Louisiana. They pointed out that a quarter of all oil and gas consumed in the United Stated came across Louisiana's shore. They even pointed out that 5 million migratory waterfowl depended on the wetlands for their survival. So back in the 1990s Louisiana, with the help of the Federal government and the oil companies, made a plan to save the wetlands. They called this plan Coast 2050. At an initial cost of $14 billion it was to be the largest engineering project ever attempted in the world.

It was a pity that Ritchie never rated the project very highly. It was a pity that the oil companies lobbied the White House asking for a holiday from contributing to the scheme. (Times were hard, they explained.) It was a pity that Ritchie agreed to their request, although understandable, because after all they'd given generously to his election campaigns. It was a pity that the Federal contribution to the project was cut back. All this was a pity, because the wetlands were protecting the roads, piers, wharves, oil wells, gas tanks, pipelines and fisheries of Louisiana from storm surges coming in from the Gulf of Mexico. They were also protecting the inhabitants of New Orleans, a city below sea level, surrounded on three sides by lakes, and bisected by America's largest river.

26

Boyd completed his outline of the facts. He'd been careful not to ask Skidelski directly for the massive funding the project would need. He was sure that if the bait was good enough, Skidelski would find the money.

'Hmmm,' said Skidelski and took three careful sips of filtered water. 'I can see that we need to manufacture this virus. I mean, if we don't, an enemy will.'

'Exactly.' Boyd was familiar with this argument. It was an argument used by the Defense Department all the time, because it was still the best way of extracting money out of Congress. Having come up with the idea of some potentially useful and massively expensive weapon, you first scared the bejeezus out of a bunch of Congressmen by reporting on its supposed existence 'out there' and your belief that it could fall into the hands of nasty people who worshipped Allah. If necessary, you got the CIA to prepare a secret report suggesting that the weapon, normally described as 'a weapon of mass destruction', could already be in the hands of terrorists. Knowing that the funds would be allocated, you could then proceed to develop the weapon yourself, confident that the other guys didn't yet have it. It was that simple. Candy from a baby.

Skidelski played with a pencil. The room fell silent. Both men were being careful.

Boyd was being careful because he knew the development of Fawcett's virus was too big for him to handle on his own; but no way was he going to have the Pentagon take this thing over lock, stock and barrel and leave him sidelined. This was *his* idea, goddamnit.

Skidelski was being careful because although he'd read the transcript of the meeting between Boyd and the English scientist, he couldn't reveal how much he knew, otherwise Boyd would realise his office was bugged.

This didn't mean the two men had nothing in common. They had plenty in common: they wanted America to triumph, by any means necessary. They also shared a contempt for the CIA. They just loved it when the CIA screwed up. It gave them something to complain about. They wouldn't know how to start their day if they couldn't complain about the CIA. For Boyd, this ritual hatred was in no way diminished by the fact that the CIA centre in England had done a brilliant job in passing him a pile of useful information on Fawcett. Gratitude was not Boyd's strong point.

Skidelski sipped again at his glass of filtered water which, judging by his withered, leathery skin, didn't do a lot for him. 'Since this virus has a potential military application, then obviously the Defense Department needs to control its development.'

'I'm sure the Defense Department ought to have input.'

Skidelski smiled. 'That's not what I said.'

Boyd smiled back. 'I know.'

Both men kind of enjoyed this game of chess. They'd played it before, but never for such high stakes. Their relationship was a mix of equalities and inequalities. On paper, Skidelski was by far the more powerful of the two. Not only did he run a military budget bigger than the military budget of every other country in the world put together, he had access to the President whenever he wanted it. In Washington, access to the Oval Office was what it was all about. Face time with the President, that's what Boyd longed for. He'd tried just about everything and had almost decided he was never going to get through the doors of the Oval Office. So he'd settled on befriending Skidelski instead, long before Skidelski had become as powerful as he was now. That had been the best decision of his life. He knew he impressed Skidelski. Joe Skidelski was no intellectual but he always appreciated a clear-cut, well-presented, intellectually coherent case, and that was what Boyd always gave him.

A few years back, this kind of cooperation between the Pentagon and a supposedly independent think tank would have been unthinkable, but since the terrorist attacks on America the rule-book had been thrown out of the window. Skidelski had seen his chance and gone for it. With every day that passed, the distinctions between Pentagon and White House were being eroded. His aim now was nothing less than the militarisation of government. So far, he was doing pretty well, and nobody had made too much fuss about it.

Skidelski sucked in his thin lips. This always freaked Boyd out. The guy has thin enough lips to start with, thought Boyd. Once he starts sucking tem in like that, it's like he's got no fucking mouth at all, only a nose. Creepy.

Skidelski's mouth finally made a reappearance. 'This will obviously cost a lot of money. More than your people can come up with. So it has to be run by the Defense Department.'

Boyd shrugged. Or rather, he made a vague heaving motion with his upper body. Boyd was too fat to shrug like most people shrugged. 'Right,' he said, with studied casualness. So far so good: Skidelski would find the money for the development program. Boyd wanted to be sure it would be enough. 'Soon as we know it's a viable option, we'll want to move on to manufacturing the vaccine. Enough for the entire population of the United States.'

Skidelski narrowed his eyes. 'You mean, just in case an enemy also has access to this virus.'

'Right,' said Boyd.

The two men stared at one another for several seconds. Each knew that a much bigger, much nastier thought had just passed between them. Each was waiting for the other to say it.

Finally, Skidelski spoke. 'I think we need to talk to the President.'

'Let's do that,' Boyd replied casually, while thinking. 'Yeah, at last!'

'And I think we need to talk to him soon. I'll set it up. But we need to consider our approach to this thing. You and I need to put our heads together first.'

'Right.'

'It sounds to me like this new virus has got enormous potential.'

'I believe it has, Joe.'

Skidelski stared off into space for a few seconds. He was still staring into space as he said, 'Al, I think maybe it's time to think the unthinkable.'

'You know something, Joe? That's just what I was thinking.'

27

The people at the National Hurricane Center examined the satellite images and other data coming in from the Atlantic and saw that westerly winds high in the atmosphere were knocking the cloud top off the storm. Wind speeds had fallen to 46 mph while air pressure had risen to a comforting 1014 millibars. This tropical storm was obviously not going to become a hurricane. The experts concluded that the storm would blow itself out long before reaching the Carolinas, 1,800 miles to the northwest. All in all, Wendy was turning out to be a bit of a letdown.

28

Skidelski turned to the fat guy. 'Tell us what you understand by thinking the unthinkable, Mr Boyd.'

'Solving the world's problems by reducing the world's population.'

'Everybody wants to do that,' said Skidelski.

'Not in the way I want to do it.'

'How do you want to do it?'

'Drastically.'

'What's drastically mean?'

'Getting rid of a lot of people very quickly.'

'How many?'

'A lot.'

'How many's that?'

'As many as you want.'

'You're not proposing to get rid of Americans?'

'Of course not.'

'Is this . . . this solution . . . is it a practical possibility?'

'It will be soon.'

Vince looked at Skidelski, then back at Boyd. He had an odd feeling he'd just heard a routine that had been rehearsed.

'Let me get this straight,' said the President. 'Are you suggesting we wipe out millions of people?'

'No, more than that. I'm suggesting we wipe out everyone except Americans. Overnight.'

The Oval Office went silent. The President stared at the fat guy. It was like nobody dared to break the silence. Shit, thought Vince, I'm in a room with a bunch of people who're listening to a guy who wants to wipe out six billion people. He waited for the President to tell Boyd to get the hell out.

'Sit down, Mr Boyd,' said the President.

'Yes,' said the Vice President, 'sit down.'

Skidelski cracked a faint smile but otherwise concealed his feelings of elation. He was in the midst of a very high-risk strategy here. He had worked out a plan that involved Boyd being the first one to float the big idea to the President. That way, Skidelski could disown it if Ritchie pissed all over it. After all, Skidelski didn't really believe in all this global warming bullshit; his conversion to the concept of climate change was purely pragmatic, a means to an end, and a glorious end at that: the final historic triumph of America.

'Okay,' said Ritchie slowly and cautiously, as everyone reoccupied their seats. 'Okay ... Tell me more, Mr Boyd.'

'There's not a whole lot more to tell, Mr President. Give us the funds, and we can develop the means to do this.'

Jimmy Lombok sighed with frustration. He wasn't feeling very patient. He'd been a bit upset when only a few hours after the arrest of fourteen thousand environmental activists nationwide, a twelve-year-old schoolboy had owned up to hacking into the ACT system. Now the fat guy was really getting on his nerves. Lombok said, 'Can you be more specific?'

'Not at this stage, no,' Boyd replied curtly.

'We're asking you to be more specific, so be more specific,' snapped Delgado, who was currently on a very short fuse. The whole atmosphere of the White House had been edgy and difficult ever since the PR fiasco on the Arlington Memorial Bridge, and it was getting to everyone. The phrase 'Who Killed General Sherman?' had spread like wildfire and now could be seen spray-painted on walls all over America.

'You want specifics, it'll take time.'

'Maybe we should schedule another meeting,' said Skidelski. His strategy was to plant the seed of this idea and then let it germinate. He was afraid that if they went into specifics now, the plan would get shot down.

'Perhaps Mr Boyd could prepare a document with all the arguments for and against,' proclaimed the Vice President from the depths of the sofa. He was tired. He'd just returned from a long trip to foreign capitals and had come to this meeting straight from the airport. As a result, the VP's normally crumpled demeanour was even more crumpled than usual. His shirt was so far out of his trousers that the entire room could catch glimpses of his belly.

Boyd said firmly, 'No way am I putting this in writing.'

Vince smiled wryly. He could see why.

Delgado, with her perfect makeup and her immaculate pale lemon suit, gave the VP a look of quiet contempt. Dolores Delgado was always immaculate. Vince reckoned she'd been *born* immaculate. She said, 'What kind of weapon are we talking about here? I can't see how we can give this our consideration unless we have more information.'

Skidelski realised they were going to have to go into a bit of detail. 'Right. Tell us more, Mr Boyd.'

Shit, thought Vince. He'd hoped the meeting was about to end. He wasn't taking it very seriously. It was just another of those crazy proposals that got floated every so often in the White House and then got forgotten. No, Vince's main concern was not Boyd's crazy idea. Vince's main concern was getting to the restaurant on time. If he blew it on Lucy's birthday, he'd be in deep shit.

29

The people at the National Hurricane Centre had just changed their minds. Nothing amazing or discreditable about that, happened all the time. Hurricane prediction was not an exact science. The satellites had picked up worrying images. The high-level winds that had been thwarting Wendy's ambitions had melted away, allowing storm clouds to grow again at the top as more moisture was picked up from the ocean and whirled upwards. Wind speeds rose to 58 mph and the air pressure dropped to 1004 millibars. Given new heart by this development, Wendy surged onwards. As she passed a few hundred miles north of Puerto Rico, wind speeds hit 74 mph and Wendy was no longer a tropical storm. Wendy was now officially a hurricane. Admittedly, she was only a Category One hurricane, and therefore not that scary, but scary enough for people on Cat Island and Nassau in the Bahamas to start nailing stuff down, because Wendy had swung west and was coming their way. She was now heading straight for the Florida Keys and the Gulf of Mexico. She started to show up on the weather radar screens in New Orleans, which was no mean achievement for a hurricane that had started from such humble beginnings. In fact, you could say that Wendy was turning out to be a real American success story. Wendy was the comeback kid. Wendy ought to have been in a musical.

30

Ritchie decided he had time for a quick shot of bourbon before Vince arrived. Not that he'd taken up drinking or anything, but in these difficult times an occasional glass helped ease the stress, and surely there was no harm in that? He'd got hold of Vince on his cell phone just as Vince had sat down at a table in a restaurant with his wife. An anniversary or birthday or something, but really not important compared to what Ritchie was having to deal with. The bourbon made him feel better. So much better that he had another one. Then he carefully locked the bottle of Wild Turkey away in the cherrywood cabinet in the study, popped a piece of peppermint gum into his mouth, and made his way through to the Oval Office.

He lay on a sofa for a while, occasionally scratching the ears of Rascal the water spaniel, and thinking hard. Maybe the fat guy's idea wasn't so crazy ... No, no. Of course it was crazy. You couldn't start planning the annihilation of most of the human race. Could you? Even if it did solve an awful lot of problems. No, you most definitely could not. Still, a man can dream, right? Shit, this was getting out of hand. Ritchie slid off the sofa, fell to his knees, bowed his head and prayed. Ritchie prayed about a lot of stuff, but this night he prayed to be delivered from temptation. The temptation in question was bigger than any temptation ever faced by an American president. Maybe it was even the biggest temptation faced by any man in history. This was way out of his league. Ritchie had been scared of quite a few ideas in his time as President, but the idea of wiping out most of humanity, well, shit, that was definitely the scariest yet.

The President looked up as there came a respectful knock at the door. He got back up on the sofa before inviting Vince to enter. 'Come on in.'

'Good evening, Mr President.'

'Hi, Vince, good of you to come.'

'No problem, sir.'

What a fucking lie, thought Vince. Lucy had turned really difficult in the restaurant. She'd told him to choose between her and the President. He'd explained he would lose his job if he didn't turn up. She'd said, 'So lose your job. Better than losing me, isn't it?' She finally said she'd stay on her own till closing time and if he wasn't back she'd pull the waiter. Vince thought she might not be bluffing. The waiter was a very good-looking and a bit flirtatious. She'd gone through with a threat like that once before, and Vince had been devastated. Sometimes Vince thought there must have been other infidelities, never spoken of. The thought made him angry and scared at the same time.

He jumped as he realised Rascal was sniffing and snuffling at his feet. For the hundredth time, he resisted an impulse to kick the animal across the room.

'Sit down, Vince.'

Vince sat down.

'I'm gonna cut to the chase. This plan, Vince, you know, the one we heard today from the think-tank guy, Boyd?'

'Sir?'

'What's your take on it? Is the guy nuts?'

'No. He's not nuts.' If only he were.

'So what's your take on it?'

Vince thought the whole thing sucked. He thought it was somewhere between obscene and laughable. What he said was, 'I think it's a high-risk strategy.'

'Why?'

'The technology's unproven. The organisation required to set up the operation would be massive. Unprecedented in its scale. I find it hard to believe that secrecy could be maintained. If it came out, and it were linked to you, you'd be finished. We'd all be finished. You'd be impeached. We'd be in jail. The reputation of the United States would never recover. For those reasons, sir, I'm against it.'

'Well, Vince, I'm against it too.'

'I'm relieved to hear it, sir. I kind of got the impression earlier that you were interested.'

'You're right. I was. But that was before I used WWJD,' said Ritchie.

'Okay . . .' said Vince.

It was Jimmy Lombok who'd introduced WWJD into the White

House. Having a National Security Adviser who asked 'What Would Jesus Do?' before recommending a course of action that could affect the lives of millions struck Vince as worrying. Now the habit was apparently spreading to the President. This was not good news.

'I used WWJD,' repeated the President, a hit of irritation in his voice.

'Sorry, sir. And what *would* Jesus do?'

'Jesus would say, heck no, I'm not killing all those poor folks out there.'

'Well ... exactly, sir.' Vince wondered briefly what the Jesus position would be on the use of thermonuclear weapons, but quickly pushed the thought out of his head.

'I've been praying about this, Vince. In fact, I spent over an hour in prayer this evening, through there in the study. And I think to do what Boyd is suggesting would be ... well, Vince, it's my belief it would be just plain evil.'

'Sir.'

'Joe's keen on it, of course.'

'I noticed,' said Vince. In fact, Vince strongly suspected that Joe Skidelski and fatboy Boyd were in cahoots on this one.

'He spoke to me afterwards. He wants us to keep the options open. You know, investigate the possibilities. Check out if it could really be done. Push a few million dollars into researching the technology. I was thinking maybe that would be okay. I mean, it wouldn't commit us or anything. And it'd get Joe off my back.'

'It's a step on the road to greenlighting the project, sir.'

'You think so?'

'Yes, sir. It's a Skidelski technique. If he can't win outright, he side-tracks, gets a little concession here, a little agreement there. It's how he works. He ... well, he ... you know.' Vince's voice tailed off. He was never quite sure how far he could go in criticising the Defense Secretary.

'You're right,' said Ritchie. 'You're right. We ought to kill this idea off, right now, kill it stone dead.'

'I agree, sir.'

'It's an unholy idea. It makes us as low and bad as those murdering terrorists out there with their Islamic jihad shit.'

'That's right.'

'Still. It'd solve a lot of problems, right? Yessir,' he chuckled. 'It'd sure solve a whole lot of problems.'

Vince remained silent.

'Don't worry. Only kidding. Really nice to see you, Vince. How's Lucy, by the way?'

'She's doing great.'

'That's terrific. Marriage is the one true certainty in an uncertain world, do you know that?'

'Yes, sir, I surely do.'

'You be sure to give Lucy my regards.'

'Thank you, sir, I'll do that.' Was he being dismissed? He hoped so. He could be back in the restaurant within twenty minutes. He stood up.

'I ordered up some burgers for us, Vince. I know how much you love burgers.'

He sat down again. 'Burgers. Terrific.'

31

'You fucked him?'

'That's right, Vince, yes, I fucked him.'

'Jesus, Lucy . . .'

'It was my birthday.'

'You're drunk.'

'Right again, Vince. I'm drunk. It's my birthday, and I got laid and I got drunk. I would have preferred to have got laid by you and got drunk with you, but you weren't around, were you? You were hanging out with that asshole in the White House, dreaming up new ways to fuck the planet.' With a shaking hand, Lucy poured another glass of wine.

Vince strode across the kitchen, tore the glass from her hand and emptied it down the sink.

'I see,' said Lucy. She raised the bottle to her lips.

Vince went back, prised the bottle from her grip, and emptied it down the sink. 'Don't pretend it's about politics. Don't pretend it's about the morals of my job. It's about you fucking a waiter, all right? That's what it's about.' He realised he was shouting. He paused. He said, 'You're kidding me, right? About the waiter.'

'No.'

'Jesus.' Vince sat down at the kitchen table, angrily sweeping a plate on to the floor, enjoying the sound of it breaking.

Vince wanted to take her. He wanted to do it right there. In the kitchen. On the floor. Make her his own again. But his pride intervened. 'I'll sleep in the guest room tonight.' He left the room.

She called after him. 'Vince. I'm sorry.'

He came back in. 'I changed my mind. *You* sleep in the fucking guest room.'

Lucy did sleep in the guest room. Till about 2 am, when she woke to find him climbing into bed beside her. The sex was rough and not at all considerate. She didn't mind.

32

The teen abstinence rally in the ballroom of the Radisson Riverfront in Atlanta, Georgia was entitled *Keep Your Pants On!* The organisers were proud to have come up with such a cool title. Close on a thousand 7th and 8th graders sat in neat rows. Most had a bright, freshly scrubbed quality about them, a shining eagerness that suggested they had recently been in touch with Jesus. Some wore T-shirts saying *Everyone is NOT doing it*, or *It's great to wait*, though the overwhelming majority had opted for the straightforward *Abstinence is cool* or just the plain simple *I'm waiting*. A few rebels among them wore the button with the slogan: *Teen Sex Sucks*, a button not officially approved by the rally people. Crystal Prosser, Director of the Teen Abstinence Campaign, would certainly not have okayed a slogan with connotations of oral sex. Teen abstention campaigners had a bit of a thing about oral sex, even within the sanctified bond of marriage. It wasn't that they actually banned oral sex, they just felt, well, it was unhygienic. God did not make your mouth for *that*. As for homosexuality, that didn't even get mentioned. Too terrible to contemplate.

Crystal Prosser sat to one side of the platform. Her left foot tapped in time with the music and her gorgeously coiffured head nodded approvingly as Kool Soul Daddy II performed 'Get Yo' Hands off Ma Yo-Yo'. She'd gone to a lot of trouble to look right for the occasion, it not being easy for a slightly overweight 45-year-old mother of two to look cool and yet authoritative. She'd finally settled for tight blue jeans and a scarlet leather jacket with matching high-heel shoes. She was sure she must have chosen well, because she was getting so many looks from the teenagers. It felt good to know she must be a role model for them. It had been Crystal's idea to book Kool Soul Daddy II, a good-looking young man with the most dazzling smile and surprisingly neat dreadlocks. It wasn't easy to find a clean-living African-American Christian rapper who really spoke to young people, and she was very pleased she'd managed to overcome the scepticism of the other organisers. True, she'd been a bit taken aback by the fee he'd demanded, but quality, she reflected, never came cheap and anyway, thanks to Ritchie's generous federal grants, teen abstinence programmes across America were awash with money.

The kids broke into loud applause and whoops of appreciation as Kool Soul Daddy II finished his number. Crystal felt cheered by the response. She knew that most of the young people attending the rally were there from conviction, but in her experience there was always an element likely to cause trouble, students who'd tagged along simply in order to miss out on a day's schooling. Those were the kids who would snigger loudly at any hint of double entendre. Crystal had long ago learned the dangers of speaking to a youthful audience. Only a few days after becoming president of the *I'm Waiting* movement, she had given her first big speech to a high-school audience. Referring to the spiritual strength conferred by premarital virginity, she'd told a group of teens, 'You young men and women can put your hands upon a powerful weapon.' She'd meant abstinence, of course, but thrown by the immediate outbreak of sniggering, she'd veered off her prepared text and soon found herself talking about 'coming together'. As the sniggering grew in volume, she'd launched desperately into a long anecdote about her week-long retreat in a cabin in the Rockies, where she'd been woken one morning 'by a young man delivering the wood'. At this point the whole hall dissolved into hysterics.

Puzzled and hurt, Crystal had cut short her speech. It was only later she found out that 'delivering the wood' was popular slang for sexual intercourse. Determined never to make the same mistake again, Crystal had driven straight to a 24-hour store in the poor part of town (an area she normally avoided). There she waited in the parking lot till she saw a lean, mean-looking black kid in his late teens. Taking a deep breath, Crystal went over to him and offered him $50 to write out a list of all the slang terms he knew for sexual intercourse. At first the kid thought this weirdo white bitch with her lacquered hair and expensive clothes was trying to hit on him or something, but he finally came round to believing her. He wrote the list, then demanded $100 for it. She gave it to him, tore the list from his hands, drove to her office, and typed the words and phrases into her software program. She was astounded at the number and the range of expressions, and baffled by a few of them. She could make sense of 'slapping skins' as a description of sexual intercourse (though she and her husband Gerald had never slapped skins very vigorously), but she would never in a thousand years have guessed that 'knocking boots' could mean the same thing. Heavens above, were there people who did it *without taking their shoes off?*

From that time on, every single speech Crystal gave was automatically scanned for words that could have a dangerous second meaning. The argot of youth changed fast, of course, so she updated it twice a year, with the help of one of the street kids she'd helped save from promiscuity.

Crystal wriggled a little in her jeans, which were too tight for comfort, and surreptitiously checked her watch as Kool Soul Daddy II sang 'The Longer You Wait the Better It Gets'. This was not perhaps Kool Soul Daddy II's best-ever lyric, and it didn't seem to be going down too well. She could sense a hint of restlessness in the audience, particularly in a couple of rows near the back of the hall. Today, above all, things had to go perfectly. Because today, after almost a year of lobbying, Crystal Prosser had succeeded in getting Edward Ritchie, the son of the President of the United States, to make an appearance at her teen abstinence rally. What a coup. She'd even hoped that the President might come along in person, but his people had explained that he was too busy. Still, it was a big, big event, and it was going to get a lot of media coverage.

Normally, the *I'm Waiting* rallies culminated in the showing of a short video. Sometimes this was a three-minute video, set to music, of aborted foetuses. At other times it was a longer video showing in graphic detail the physical effects of sexually transmitted disease, also set to music. Either of these was capable of reducing a teen audience to a state of stunned silence. Crystal believed there was no harm at all in using a little fear to back up the moral message. If it helped put kids off premarital sex, it was justified.

Today, though, there was to be no video. Instead, there would be a Purity Pledging Ceremony, in which several dozen students aged between fifteen and twenty, including Edward Ritchie, would come up on to the platform, make their brief purity pledge, and receive a scroll and a silver pin from the great movie star Cheech Lingaard, who was coming despite his recent bereavements. As he told Crystal on the phone, 'Our kids are our future, and I care about our future.' He did, however, stipulate that out of respect for the dead of Hollywood he would make no long speeches.

A high-school band struck up as the students moved towards the side of the stage. Crystal handed Cheech Lingaard the first of the scrolls and the silver pins. As the closing bars of 'America the Beautiful' were heard, Cheech Lingaard stepped forward to the microphone and with simple dignity said, 'Ladies and gentlemen, boys and girls. I admire you all so much. God bless you. And God bless America.'

The applause for Lingaard finally subsided, and the students made their way one by one up the little flight of stairs to where they would receive their scrolls. Each one took a few seconds to declare to the hall their commitment to complete sexual abstinence until marriage.

'Hi, I'm Teresa, and I'm waiting,' said Teresa into the microphone and went over to get her scroll and pin.

'Hi, I'm Wanda, and I'm waiting,' said Wanda.

'Hi, I'm Harvey, and I'm waiting,' said Harvey.

'Hi, I'm Emily, and I'm waiting,' said Emily.

And so it went on until there were only three students left before Edward Ritchie. The press moved closer. the cameramen checked for focus.

'Hi, I'm Scott, and I'm waiting,' said Scott.

'Hi, I'm Chantal, and I'm waiting,' said Chantal.

'Hi, I'm Otto, and I'm waiting,' said Otto.

And finally, here he was, Edward Ritchie, the son of the President of the United States. A wall of flashlights lit his face as he leaned into the microphone.

'Hi, I'm Eddie, and I'm gay.'

33

Hurricane Wendy was now causing serious anxiety all along America's eastern seaboard. With winds hitting 155 mph, it had become a Category Four. Its course, however, remained erratic. It swerved around the tip of Florida and north of Cuba and for a few hours it looked like it might leave the coast and dissipate its energy harmlessly in the Gulf of Mexico. Finally, having stalled for quite some time, Wendy suddenly veered west and headed straight for Louisiana. She'd finally made up her mind. And she was in a foul mood.

By the time Wendy hit the southern tip of Louisiana, windspeed was reaching 195 mph, meaning Wendy had achieved Category Five, the highest of them all. Air pressure plunged to 941 millibars, low enough to make your ears pop, if you could hear your ears pop above the sound of the hurricane. Having destroyed every building in the little coastal town of Grand Isle, Wendy barrelled up the Barataria Basin towards New Orleans. Lake Pontchartrain, just north of the city, filled up rapidly with raging waters. Soon it was twelve feet above its normal level. The hurricane's counterclockwise winds battered the levees on the northern shore of the city, piling up the lake waters against them until finally they poured over the top. Hundreds of millions of gallons of water rushed towards New Orleans. Within twelve hours, New Orleans was flooded to a depth of twenty-eight feet.

There had been adequate warnings, of course. Many people had fled the city long before Wendy arrived. But many others had put their faith in the elaborate system of protective dykes and levees and drainage canals. Unfortunately, these were based on climate models that pre-dated global warming and knew nothing of rising sea levels and increasingly violent storms. Even the most pessimistic projection had assumed that the strongest hurricane that could ever reach New Orleans would be a Category Four. And not only was Wendy a Category Five, she was a record-breaking Category Five, record-breaking enough for climatologists later to decide that there needed to be a Category Six.

More people would have survived if their three major evacuation routes had not been vulnerable to the same flooding as the city itself. Thousands of would-be escapers, naively assuming that an official evacuation route would remain above water, were caught and drowned on Interstate 10.

Critics later pointed out that approximately 2 per cent of what America spent annually on its War on Terror would have been enough to save the Louisiana wetlands and maybe also the 23,142 Americans who died that day in and around New Orleans. But Ritchie L. Ritchie was the President of the United States, and Ritchie L. Ritchie had other priorities.

34

'We're not making decisions here today, is that clear?' said Ritchie.

'I think we're all aware this is purely an exploratory meeting, Mr President,' said Defense Secretary Skidelski, scratching at the tip of his long, thin nose.

'Exactly,' said the President. 'Exploratory meeting. That's all this is.'

Everybody nodded. The mood was dark. Since the double disaster of 23,000 dead in New Orleans and one son gay in Atlanta, Ritchie had been unable to separate out the two events in his head. He knew that the loss of 23,000 people and the economic devastation brought on by the flooding was a much greater tragedy than having a fag for a son, but sometimes it felt like it was a tough call. Certainly the two events had had a profound effect on him. People said Ritchie was not the man he was. Bullshit. Ritchie was *more* than the man he was. Battered, humiliated, scared, resentful, Ritchie was in a mood to show the world who was boss. That's why he'd recalled the fat guy to the Oval Office. 'Take us through it, will you, Mr Boyd?' said Ritchie crisply.

'Thank you, Mr President,' said Boyd with uncharacteristic courtesy. (Skidelski had told him to be on his best behaviour.) Boyd's manner was relaxed, matter-of-fact. 'I'll get straight to the point. Mr President, you have a chance to save the planet and save humanity. To do so, it will be necessary to make some hard choices. The hardest of these will be the need to dispose of a large number of people. That choice is yours, sir, and not mine. I see my job as making the task possible, pointing out both the possibilities and the difficulties. In other words, I want to give you the big picture. So before I present the best option as I see it, I want to take us back to a few basics, okay? Okay. Now, eliminating a very large number of people in a relatively short timeframe inevitably brings us up against a series of military, logistical and to some extent presentational problems. And of course we'd be doing this thing on a scale that nobody's even thought about before, far less tried. But the limits of any large-scale operation of this nature are largely technological.'

Everybody in the Oval Office was watching Boyd intently. Except Vince. Vince's eyes were on the carpet.

Boyd was settling into a smooth and casual presentation. 'For example, you could in theory dispose of most of the world's population by a well-planned, carefully executed pre-emptive nuclear strike. But as we all know, even if nobody managed to fire a few back at us, we'd still be left with a planet polluted by long-term radiation. So we don't do it.'

The President frowned. 'Maybe we don't do it because it wouldn't be a very American thing to do.'

'If that's what you like to believe, Mr President, that's your privilege,' replied Boyd. In Boyd's terms this was polite.

Skidelski shifted in his chair and coughed pointedly. He'd taken a risk by bringing Boyd back to the Oval Office. Boyd was hard to control. But without Boyd it would look like the whole thing was Skidelski's idea, and he didn't want that. If this all went wrong, he'd need someone to blame. 'Just give us the current issues, Al, okay?'

'Sure,' said Boyd, puzzled. It wasn't as if he'd been impolite to anyone, was it?

Skidelski was thinking he ought to be careful not to use Boyd's first name like that. Nor did he want to get Boyd too excited. He knew the awful effect excitement had on Boyd's digestive tract.

Boyd went on. 'Ruling out the nuclear options leaves us with three choices. One, conventional weapons. Two, chemical weapons. Three, biological weapons. Conventional weapons we can forget. Too slow. Too inefficient. And we're outnumbered. For example, we'd never have a chance in hell in China. And if we started winning in Russia, or China, or India or Pakistan we'd pretty soon find somebody using the nuclear option against us. So we can forget conventional. Next, let's look at chemical.'

Vince's eyes were still fixed firmly on the carpet. Something very odd was happening to him; he was starting to feel nostalgic about Hollywood.

'Chemical weapons have a lot of advantages, but too many disadvantages: the chemical agent is difficult to spread, it's vulnerable to basic variables such as wind direction, and most important of all, it's hard to protect your own side. In a limited battlefield context chemical weapons have their uses, but as weapons of mass destruction they suck. In fact, chemical weapons aren't weapons of mass destruction in any real sense of the term.'

Why on earth had he left his job in the movies? Vince had met some pretty nasty people during his time in Hollywood, but none of them actually sat around planning to murder millions of people.

'That leaves biological weapons. Now, over the last few months I've learned that in discussing bio weapons you have to ask a number of key questions.' Boyd numbered them off on his fingers. 'What is the nature of the pathogen? Is it viral or bacterial? Is it easy and safe to produce? Is it hardy and easy to disperse? Does it require a vector? Does it—'

'What's the fuck's a vector?' said the President.

'It's what the virus piggy-backs on. Take typhus. Typhus makes a lousy bio-weapon because it needs an insect vector – rat fleas – for it to be spread. Whereas an effective pathogen can be carried through the air easily, like pollen, so that anyone who breathes it in becomes infected.'

Lombok leaned forward, his bald head gleaming with its usual patina of sweat. 'So, inhalation is the best transmission route.'

'Exactly so, Mr Lombok. Okay, other questions you have to ask: How long is the incubation period? How infectious is it? How do you protect your own side? Till now, the answers to all these questions have meant that no single pathogen would be suitable for MPR, at least not—'

'MPR?' enquired the President.

'Mass Population Reduction. Sorry, it's an in-house term.'

'Oh. Okay. Go on.'

Vince stared at Boyd and remembered Norman Stark, the producer of the *Teen Terror* movies. Norman Stark was a disgusting man. Small, tubby, with bulging eyes and a ridiculous blond wig, he shamelessly thrust himself upon young women at every opportunity. And yet, suddenly, compared to Al Boyd, Stark seemed like a cuddly bunny.

'Till recently, we didn't have an MPR-compatible pathogen, at least not one that would operate at the speed needed for something on the scale that we're contemplating.'

Dolores Delgado crossed her shapely legs and said, 'Why does speed matter?'

Boyd was oblivious to the legs. 'Same reason why we can't just sterilise people, like's been suggested in the past. They're going to notice we're reproducing and they aren't. It's the same for a pathogen. If it takes weeks, or months, or years, then people are going to wonder why the hell Americans aren't dying of this disease.'

'So let them wonder,' said Murdo Robertson.

Boyd stared at the Vice President. 'That's just plain dumb.'

Skidelski bit at his lip. Why the hell did Boyd always have to be so damned rude? 'Just tell them why you disagree, okay, Mr Boyd?'

'Okay. Imagine it. Hundreds of millions of people dead and dying from some previously unknown pathogen. Mass panic. And I mean panic on a scale you haven't even dreamt of. And in the midst of the panic, anger. Anger because no Americans are affected. They don't even need to find out it was deliberate, they'll just be mad because we're well and they're dying.'

Vince thought maybe he could go back to Hollywood. Go back to discussing fictional disasters instead of real ones, back to flattering airheads, brain-dead executives and neurotic screenplay writers. Not really such a bad job compared with this one.

'In those circumstances, the chances are, someone somewhere will let fly with a thermonuclear warhead. Millions of Americans dead. We naturally have to retaliate and hey, before you know it, we're back to the nuclear wasteland scenario. So that's why any pathogen has to act fast.'

'And *do* we have a pathogen that will act fast?' The President was leaning forward in his chair.

'Yes.'

'How fast?' asked Delgado.

'Let me tell you a bit more about the pathogen,' said Boyd.

Of course, Vince reflected, he could forget about Hollywood and write his memoirs instead. A shocking exposé of daily life in the White House. That would get him an advance of at least a million. And there were a few people in the Ritchie White House that Vince would really enjoy shafting.

'At one time or another, we've all had flu, right? Influenza, flu, call it what you want, it doesn't scare us. That's because we've forgotten about the flu epidemic of 1919. It killed at least thirty million people. Maybe fifty million. Imagine a pathogen that's even more deadly than that. A pathogen that kills anyone not vaccinated against it. And I mean anyone. No protection, no hope. And imagine only the United States possesses such a pathogen. And it's an airborne pathogen.' Boyd paused to let the information sink in. Silence filled the room.

On the other hand, thought Vince, the last insider to announce he was writing a memoir was dead, killed by a hit-and-run driver. The driver had never been traced.

'So airborne is the key factor?' said the Vice President, anxious to demonstrate that he was following the argument.

'Yes. Basically, if an infection is airborne, provided the agent is highly infectious, it spreads exponentially. You sneeze on the subway, you've given it to maybe twenty people. Each of them goes home and passes it on to two or three of their family, or friends or neighbours, whatever. So by the end of the day you've got maybe sixty people infected. Let's assume fifty of these go out to work or to school the next day, each of them infects maybe ten others. That's six hundred people infected. In less than twenty-four hours. From just one sneeze. Each of those six hundred goes out and does much the same, so in forty-eight hours it's 600 times 600, that's 360,000 people. And so on . . .'

Boyd paused to let this sink in. Exponential growth was always stunning to anyone who hadn't thought much about it before. He looked around the Oval Office and saw he had his audience's attention. That young Vince guy was the only one looking uninterested. Well, fuck him.

Vince was wondering whether there was really any chance of them going through with this. Probably not. It was just another crazy plan that would be discarded somewhere along the way, like dozens of other half-baked schemes he'd listened to over the last six years.

Boyd forged on. 'Let's imagine for a moment what would have happened if Aids had been airborne. Now, Aids was pretty scary. Still is scary. But it's only passed on by the exchange of blood or bodily fluids. Which basically is not that easy to do.'

'Unless you're a fag,' growled Jimmy Lombok.

'Yeah,' said Boyd. 'But you have to be a fag who wants to exchange bodily fluids.'

'All fags want to exchange bodily fluids. It's all they ever think about. That's why they're fags.'

'Jimmy!' hissed Skidelski, too late.

'Just shut the fuck up about fags, okay?' said Ritchie with sudden vehemence.

'Sorry,' said Lombok. The President's National Security Adviser was a well-known fag-hater. It was part of his Christian belief system. Now the President had a gay son he'd have to be more careful.

Boyd didn't much care how people got their jollies; there were more important things to worry about. 'What I'm trying to say is, passing on blood or bodily fluids is a deliberate act. Breathing out isn't. Sneezing isn't. Coughing isn't. Okay, now suppose a new virus were to appear, one that combined say the deadliness of smallpox with the infectivity of the 1918 flu virus . . . It would be unstoppable.'

'And there is such a virus?' asked the President.

'Yes,' said Boyd. And farted.

'Where . . . how, I mean, how do we know about it?' said the President, wondering who had dared to fart in his presence.

'It's being genetically engineered. In a lab. An American lab. We're calling it Flaxil-4.'

'Suppose we went for this,' said Skidelski, as if all this were new to him. 'Suppose we went for this, what about means of delivery?'

'There are a number of options. At this moment in time, the most promising seems to be release in aerosol form from planes. The droplets are very fine, but still heavier than air. But we're going to need a helluva lot of planes.'

Vince stared at Skidelski, as repulsed as ever by the leathery folds of skin and the long nose. He knew the man probably had no limits. Vince had been there the time Skidelski strolled casually into the Oval Office and told the President that since the ultimate enemy was China, why didn't we sneak in a nuclear strike now before the Chinese began to deploy anti-missile systems? Scarily, Ritchie had thought about it for a few moments before declaring that 'on balance' he thought it wasn't a good idea.

Delgado adjusted a misplaced wisp of beautiful hair. She gave Boyd her most piercing look. 'Where does the scenario go from there?'

'Well, like I said, a lot would depend on wind direction, and temperature, and the concentration we used, but basically, we'd expect to be able to carpet most of a country the size of . . . the size of, say, France, in about eight hours.'

Skidelski chuckled. 'France. Yeah. Nice country France. I like the architecture. I like the food. If I drank wine, I guess I'd probably like the wine. Only problem, it's full of French people, right? I should know. I gotta go there in a couple of months. Any chance we can do this thing before then, save me having to be polite to them?' Skidelski's dry laughter crackled through the room.

140

'Hell, Joe,' said Ritchie, 'there's no need to be polite to the bastards!'

The room rang with sycophantic laughter.

Oh God, Vince was thinking. I have screwed up my entire life. Instead of being rich and happy in California, I am going to end up in jail, criminal assistant to a disgraced President, who's either going to be impeached or jailed or both. Oh shit, shit, shit.

'Go on, please, Mr Boyd,' the President snapped.

'Yes,' added an increasingly eager Delgado. 'What happens once the virus reaches ground level?'

'Nothing for a few hours. Then the infection hits very fast. Chest pains, dizziness, nausea. Next the lungs start to malfunction. They fill up with fluid. Basically the victim drowns. They're normally dead within twelve hours. What's useful is that there's a window of three or four hours when the victim is asymptomatic.'

'Why's that useful?' asked the President.

'Like I said, because he's asymptomatic.'

'Because he's what?' said the Vice President.

'He doesn't have any symptoms.'

'Okay. Gotcha.'

'So he doesn't know he's infected. But he's a carrier. He's passing it on.'

Vince now told himself that if there was really a chance of this thing happening, he had a clear duty to stay on and stop it.

'So, from appearance of first symptoms to . . . to death, is about twelve hours, right?' said the Vice President.

'On average. Twenty-four hours, max. In the flu epidemic of 1919, people felt unwell in the morning and died in the afternoon.'

Again the room fell silent.

Vince knew he had influence with the President. A lot of influence. Ritchie trusted him. Ritchie listened to him. Yes, the responsible course of action was to stay in his post and try to stop him.

Jimmy Lombok had a look of intense concentration on his face. 'Uh, maybe I missed something here, but . . . well, isn't this stuff going to kill Americans as well? I mean, sure, we could close our airspace I guess, but it's going to be pretty much impossible to stop the disease from coming here, isn't it?'

'Absolutely right, Mr Lombok, vital point,' Boyd flattered.

It would mean taking on Skidelski, of course. Vince looked over at him. Christ, that was a thought.

'So how would we stop it?' asked Lombok.

'We'd vaccinate every American.'

The President's body was now tightly coiled, tense, with that wiry fighter's tension of his that so scared his opponents. 'There's already a vaccine?'

'We're working on one. It's looking good.'

'Okay, let me get this straight,' said the Vice President. 'One, there's a new virus that kills quickly. Well, at just the right pace, correct?'

'Correct. Flaxil-4.'

'Two, we have the means of dispersing this ... Flaxil-4.'

'Correct. Thousands of planes would have to be fitted with special spraying equipment, but I'd say that's a pretty straightforward procedure.'

'Three, we have a vaccine that could protect Americans from this disease.'

'In principle, but not in practice. We'll need to launch a major program to manufacture enough vaccine.'

'How long will that take?' asked Delgado.

This wasn't happening, thought Vince. The whole idea was grotesque, absurd, laughable. A bunch of reasonably civilised, reasonably courteous human beings sitting around together in a comfortable room planning mass murder ... Suddenly Vince saw an image. An old image in black and white. An image of a villa by a lake, with big cars drawn up outside.

'Now hold on, just hold on a goddamn minute,' The President had stood up and was pacing. 'There's no way we can vaccinate three hundred million Americans without the rest of the world noticing. So what are we going to tell the rest of the world? The truth? I don't think so.'

'It wouldn't be a problem, Mr President,' said Skidelski. 'Would it, Mr Boyd?'

'Right. We'd tell them there was credible evidence suggesting a massive terrorist attack upon the United States. A biological attack using a deadly new virus. We'd tell them we're going to make the vaccine available worldwide, but naturally we're going to have to look after our own citizens first.'

Vince remembered seeing a film about it. About the Wannsee Conference. Berlin, January 1942. The annihilation of European Jewry agreed in the space of a few hours, over fine wines and cigars. The unthinkable made thinkable, the monstrous made routine. The railroads, the gas, the ovens, it could be done. It could be done efficiently. Only a few years before, nobody would have thought it possible.

Skidelski sipped at a glass of water. 'We'd have to strike a balance, of course. We'd need to make the terrorist threat sound credible, so that there'd be no great resistance from Americans to the idea of a mass vaccination programme. On the other hand, we can't make the terrorist threat sound so big that half the countries in the world come banging on our door demanding the vaccine for their own citizens.'

The decision took only an hour. Afterwards, hands were shaken. Hitler salutes given. Good wishes exchanged. Give my regards to your wife and children, won't you? Be sure to come to supper sometime soon. The important people leave. The underlings clear the table and wash the crystal glasses and carefully stack the Meissen plates and close the cedarwood cigar boxes.

'I have a meeting at twelve,' said the President. 'We need to wrap this up. Like I said, there's going to be no decision on this thing here and now. It's too big and important for that.'

'Absolutely right, Mr President,' said Murdo Robertson, tucking his shirt in.

'However,' Ritchie went on, 'I want to know what you're all thinking. I'm going to go around the room and I want each of you to give me a one-sentence opinion, okay?'

Vince no longer heard a word. He was thinking how the subordinates always got on with it. Still plenty of them out there willing to do what they're told. No need to give them the whole story. The smart ones will guess, of course, but there are ways of knowing without knowing. Ways of looking the other way. It's thinkable now. The technology offers the means. Once it's possible, it's thinkable. Yes, all in all a good meeting. No time wasted. Things done well. The decencies observed. A model of good government. The only difference: now the technology's better. Then it was six million. Now it could be six billion.

'Vince? . . . Vince?'

Vince looked up abruptly. They were talking to him. The President was talking to him. Vince realised Ritchie had been going around the room doing his end-of-meeting routine.

'I said, what's your take on this, Vince?'

The President was staring at him. The whole room was staring at him. He swiftly considered how to attack the practicalities of the plan. He knew if he let loose with moral indignation he'd be quickly sidelined. 'I think the logistics mean that it's not a realistic option.'

The President turned to his National Security Adviser. 'Jimmy, you have the last word.'

Lombok adopted his most pious and thoughtful tone. 'My answer comes in the form of a question, Mr President.'

Oh no, thought, Vince, he's not really going to do the WWJD thing, is he?

But he was.

'And the question is this: What Would Jesus Do?'

Skidelski grimaced. 'Is that a yes or a no?'

'It's a yes.'

Vince knew it was stupid to be shocked. The Vatican hadn't been too troubled by the Holocaust, and Lombok's evangelicals made Popes look cuddly, so in principle there ought to be no big surprise about enlisting Jesus in a plan to wipe out several billion people. Still, Vince was shocked.

Lombok was still talking. Lombok always did that. The President would ask everyone for a one-sentence summary of their views, and Lombok would be allowed to talk for about five minutes. It felt like the President was scared to interrupt, in case Lombok really did have a direct line to God.

'Jesus was not a sentimental man,' Lombok was saying. 'He squared up to evil, same as America does. Remember the money changers in the temple? He took them on. He turned their tables over. He went in hard. This is no different. I believe that in this situation, Jesus would go in hard.'

The President nodded.

Suddenly, Vince felt scared.

PART ★ THREE

35

'What do you mean, you're having doubts?'

'Well,' said the Englishman, running a hand through his wiry hair. 'Well, actually, in a sense I'm rather pleased with how things have gone.' He paused to let a lab assistant overtake them in the corridor. There was just enough room for her to squeeze past Boyd's bulk.

'So you're having doubts *and* you're pleased?'

'Yes. Well, no. Not exactly. How can I put it? I'm pleased in a professional sense. But I'm uneasy as to the implications.'

'I'm not following you.'

'Well, I suppose in a way one wonders what one's become involved in.'

'In what way does one wonder?'

'Well, I'd say, um, I'd say, it's been a great privilege to take the work to the level I've taken it, and I'm enormously grateful for the opportunities you've given me, and yet, well, how can I put it? Um, well, one wonders a little. In the long reaches of the night, as it were.'

Suddenly Al Boyd couldn't take any more. He stopped, turned to Fawcett and moved towards him until he was very close. Fawcett tried to back off, but the corridor was narrow and Boyd virtually had him pinned against a wall. It occurred to Fawcett that Boyd was capable of crushing him to death. Boyd brought his face very close. Fawcett could smell fried onions.

'Dr Fawcett . . .'

'Yes?'

'What the fuck are you talking about?'

'Well . . . I'm having some doubts. Moral doubts.'

'I don't believe I'm hearing this.'

'I'm afraid it's true.'

Boyd stared malevolently at the nervous Englishman. Boyd had moved heaven and earth to get everything set up for Fawcett in record time. He'd fast-tracked the whole thing through The American Way and then charmed Skidelski into providing trained staff, lab facilities and two hundred million dollars for initial development. He'd even pitched to the President of the United States in person. It hadn't been easy; of late he'd bent and broken more rules than he'd bent and broken in his life.

To be fair, the Pentagon had come through with the goods. Once Skidelski wanted something, he generally got it. Which is why Dr Robin Fawcett was now installed as Program Director at the United States Army Medical Research Institute of Infectious Diseases at Fort Detrick in Maryland, with a staff of ninety and 6,000 square feet of America's biggest biological containment laboratory at his disposal. The official purpose of USAMRIID, as it was unaffectionately known, was to develop responses to new biological threats that might confront the US military. But everybody knew that in the world of biological warfare, the line between defensive and offensive was hard to draw.

Fawcett tried and failed to avoid the dreadful fumes emanating from Al Boyd's mouth. 'Perhaps if we went through to my office, where we can talk in private.'

'Let's do that.' Boyd took a step back.

Fawcett managed to produce a thin smile. 'Thank you. This way, please.'

Boyd trundled along behind Fawcett. Boyd had dropped into the labs without warning, just to see how things were going. He liked to be spontaneous; it kept other people on their toes. Fawcett hadn't been sure how to handle his important visitor. This was a laboratory operating at Biosafety Level Four, the highest of all security categories. Like any other BSL-4 laboratory, it had a series of strict controls over access by visitors. In addition, this lab carried a special security classification. Boyd had been forced to sit in the lobby for half an hour while a call was put through to Skidelski's office in the Pentagon to allow them to give him a special Class 4 clearance.

Fawcett led the way down three or four brilliantly lit corridors, all of them narrow, white and without any source of natural light. They ended up at a door looking much like any of the other doors. Fawcett pushed his thumb down on an electronic sensor and waited for his print to be read. Five seconds later, the door clicked open. Boyd reflected morosely that if it had been him, it would have malfunctioned.

Boyd stepped into a large office of pristine cleanliness. The only personal notes were a family photograph on the desk and, on the far wall, a cricket bat covered in faded signatures. Boyd recognised it as a cricket bat because as a boy he'd been taken to England by his godfather, who'd insisted they go and see a cricket match. It had been Boyd's first experience of a cricket match. It was not an experience he ever wished to repeat.

'Do please take a seat, Mr Boyd.'

Boyd surveyed the narrow tubular steel chair that he was being offered. It had arms. Boyd didn't like chairs with arms, because so often he couldn't fit into them. He looked around the room for an alternative. There was none.

'Please,' said Fawcett, flapping a hand in the direction of the useless chair as he sat down on an identical model on the other side of the desk.

Boyd said, 'I'll stand.'

'Oh. Well, if that's what you prefer . . .'

'Yeah, that's what I prefer.'

'Let me see how I can best explain the situation,' said Fawcett. 'Um, right at the beginning, I expressed some doubts as to the military applications of my work.'

Boyd immediately knew how to handle this. He held up a podgy hand. 'Maybe we haven't been giving you enough back-up. Maybe we can help you some more. Your salary. I'm sure we could look at that.'

'Oh no, my salary's fine. Generous. Very generous.'

'What about more resources? More staff?'

'Staffing levels are really very good.'

'What about senior people? People who can take the strain off you? I mean, is there anyone who has full scientific knowledge of the program, so that, say, you could take a couple of weeks' vacation with your family?'

'Oh, heavens, yes. There are at least four people here whose knowledge of this is now every bit as advanced as my own.'

'You mean, Americans?'

'Oh, yes.'

Good, thought Boyd. That's what I needed to know. That's really all I needed to know.

'No, that's not the problem at all,' said Fawcett. 'The problem is . . .

well, it's become clear to me that effectively, I'm hand in glove with the military.'

No kidding, thought Boyd. You're working at the United States Army Medical Research Institute of Infectious Diseases and you've just realised that you're hand in glove with the military. He said, 'I didn't think you had a problem with that.'

'Look, Mr Boyd, I'd be the first to admit that this is a rather tardy crisis of conscience I am having. And I cannot stand here, hand on heart, and say that I have been entirely consistent.'

You sure as fuck can't, pal, thought Boyd.

'But I do think, better late than never, don't you?'

'Oh absolutely, Dr Fawcett, I understand exactly.'

'Oh good. What a relief. I thought you might be angry about it.'

'Of course not. And Flaxil-4? That's all running to plan?'

'Oh, yes. We're virtually ready to go into full production. Though as you now know, I'd prefer we didn't do that. Because of the implications.'

'I understand. And what about the vaccine? Where do we stand on the vaccine?'

'Oh that's actually ahead of schedule. Because I do feel anxious about the implications of this deadly new virus being around without adequate supplies of vaccine available.'

'Dr Fawcett. Do you know what I'm going to do? I'm going to recommend that this program is taken away from the military. With you in charge of it. Would that please you?'

'Oh, well that would be wonderful news, Mr Boyd. I'd be very, very grateful.' The Englishman fussed towards him and took his hand. Boyd was disgusted to see tears in his eyes. 'You see, Mr Boyd, I love science. I love virology. I love my work. But I don't like the idea of killing people.'

'Nobody does, Dr Fawcett. Nobody does.'

36

The motorcycle outriders came first, blue lights flashing. In a perfect V-formation they swept up the Avenue de Paris towards the Palace of Versailles. Behind them, flanked by more police outriders in white uniforms, came three Humvees with blacked-out windows, packed with armed men and women from the American Secret Service. Next came three slightly smaller SUVs also with blacked-out windows, packed with armed men and women from the French Secret Service, all of them burning with resentment at having to travel behind the Americans. Next came a big American limo hardened to withstand anything short of a direct hit with an RPG. It had been flown in by transporter from Washington two days before, much to the fury of the French, who had wanted one of their own cars. But the use of the American limo was declared non-negotiable. In the rear seat sat the Defence Ministers of France and the United States side by side. Each wore a fixed smile. Each was determined to show the world that France and America had much in common. Neither believed this to be the case, but each waved dutifully anyhow. The tourists on the sidewalks didn't wave back; they were displeased at travelling all the way to Versailles only to find it closed for the day.

Behind the armoured limo with the Ministers came a smaller limo carrying Skidelski's personal protection team, behind that, a long, low ambulance, discreetly disguised, carrying a surgeon, a doctor, a nurse and twenty litres of Skidelski-compatible blood. After a small gap occupied by ten more police motorcycles came about fifteen minibuses, carrying junior officials, secretaries and members of the press. Ten white police vans with flashing blue lights brought up the rear. Above, a police helicopter clattered. For Skidelski, all this was nothing out of the ordinary. This was just how powerful Americans travelled abroad in the early twenty-first century.

The small group of protesters had been corralled behind metal barriers about a hundred yards from the main entrance. As Skidelski's car approached the gates of the palace, a middle-aged woman in a yellow raincoat unfurled an American flag with a skull and crossbones superimposed on it. She managed to hold it up for about half a second before three plainclothes security agents bundled her to the ground, cracking her head on the sidewalk as they did so. Skidelski caught a glimpse of the fracas but quickly looked away. He'd learned not to notice demonstrators. God knows, there were enough of them. Whenever he travelled abroad, he was stalked by weirdos who hated America. His officials had sent the French a stern warning that there were to be no incidents. These days you never knew. That innocent-looking demonstrator might suddenly step forward and detonate the explosive strapped around his body. Or her body come to that. Yes, nowadays even women did that sort of stuff. So to hell with the niceties of democratic protest, just keep the bastards at a distance, okay?

The motorcade rumbled across the rough cobbles of the courtyard and came to a halt near the equestrian statue of Louis XIV. Joséphine du Bois, the young and stylish Minister for Defence, took a deep breath. This wasn't going to be easy. In common with many French people of discernment, she found Versailles vulgar and tasteless. She also found Joseph Skidelski vulgar and tasteless. To deal with both on the same day struck her as a task bordering on the superhuman.

Uniformed flunkeys wearing white gloves lined up as the Defence Ministers emerged from the limo. The Chief Curator of the Musée National des Châteaux de Versailles et de Trianon stepped forward to greet the important guests, his elegant grey hair glinting in the morning light. Along the rooftops of the palace the police sharpshooters tightened their grips on their weapons, scanning the area with renewed vigour.

'Welcome to Versailles,' said the Curator, in accurate but heavily accented English. 'It is a great honour to receive such a distinguished guest.'

'Hi,' said Skidelski. He was vaguely aware that in the distance he could hear a faint chanting. For a moment he thought it might be *FUCK YOU, AMERICA*, but then the sounds were carried away on the wind. Maybe he'd imagined it. Surely the French wouldn't allow that? He smiled routinely at the Curator. 'Great to be here. How are you today?'

'I'm very well, thank you,' said the Curator, puzzled as to why America's Secretary of State for Defense should take an interest in his health. They shook hands. Skidelski turned to stare up at the equestrian statue that loomed above him. He put up a hand to shade his eyes from the sun. 'Who's the guy on the horse?' he asked.

'Louis XIV,' replied the Curator. '*Le Roi-Soleil.*'

'Neat bit of sculpture,' said Skidelski. 'Pity they had to go chop the poor guy's head off.' The French Defence Minister and the Curator exchanged glances. Each wondered which of them was going to tell the American that Louis XIV died before the French Revolution was thought of. Each decided to leave it to the other, so Skidelski was to be none the wiser. He was looking in the direction that Louis XIV was looking and saw Paris spread out before him in the distance. 'That Louis certainly knew how to choose a good place for a palace,' he grinned.

'Absolutely. This way please, *messieurs dames,*' said the Curator with a slight bow. As he turned, a senior official from the French Defence Ministry approached him and hurriedly whispered something. A look of consternation crossed the Curator's face.

'But the visit is always more impressive if we start *inside,*' hissed the Curator.

'Sorry, it's a security decision,' whispered the senior official.

Noticing that there was some kind of hitch, Joséphine du Bois took Skidelski by the elbow, pointing out various aspects of the equestrian statue and talking easily about some key moments in the seventeenth century.

But Skidelski had noticed something was up. There was a bit of running around and lots of people talking into cell phones. He gestured to his senior security man. 'What's going on?'

'We're making a small change in the order of the visit, sir. No big deal.'

'Oh. Okay,' Skidelski grunted. He didn't much care. This sort of thing happened all the time. He'd learned not to be bothered by it. He wondered how Lianna was getting on. She'd passed on Versailles so as to be able to go shopping and have lunch in some high-end restaurant. Skidelski was a bit embarrassed about that, but the French hadn't turned a hair. They were very keen to make a good impression. The daughter of the Foreign Minister had even volunteered to be Lianna's shopping guide.

The Curator came towards him. '*Désolé.* Please forgive me. There has been a small change of plan. If you and Madame du Bois care to follow me, we're going to start with the terrace. Since the weather is so good.'

'Sure.'

It was true that the weather was good. But it was also true that it was expected to stay good. No, the problem was the demonstration. The official published timetable for Skidelski's visit showed him arriving at Versailles three hours later than was actually planned. This dis-information was designed to make any protesters arrive about an hour after Skidelski had left. The press, of course, had to be given the true timetable, otherwise there would be no coverage. Unfortunately, an enterprising young dissident had hacked into the computer of a reporter from *Le Monde* early that morning and discovered the real timetable. Within seconds, e-mails were flying round Paris, urging protesters to get to Versailles as quickly as possible. Taken by surprise, the police had failed to seal off the RER station at Versailles Rive-Gauche. As a result, thousands of anti-American protesters were now streaming from the train station towards the Palace. Very soon, the chants of *FUCK YOU, AMERICA* would get loud enough to be heard in the gardens of Ver-sailles. Best get the outside part of Skidelski's visit over with quickly. That was the thinking.

Skidelski was quite interested in seeing Versailles. He had a bit of catching up to do. After all, he came from a country where more than 70 per cent of the population didn't have a passport, most of them proud of the fact. Skidelski hadn't even done the backpacking routine across Europe when he was young. He'd been too busy making money and forging connections. Hell, he didn't get where he was today by drifting around the world staring at old buildings. No, doing things this way round was much better. If there was something he'd missed in his youth and really wanted to see (like the old Paris opera house, for example, or Versailles, which he'd heard was pretty impressive), then he'd just tell his officials to arrange it. He could even fix for an entire building to be emptied for him. It was a neat way of seeing places.

Skidelski found himself utterly smitten by Versailles. For a start, it was so goddamn *big*! And there was the sheer confidence and splendour of the place. It exuded not just a sense of history, but a sense of *power*, the power of an absolute monarch. Standing on the terrace and looking over the gardens of Versailles, Skidelski was unaccountably moved. The scene was breathtaking. This made the gardens of the White House look about as big as a pocket handkerchief. And about as exciting. In front of him, the Grand Perspective seemed to stretch almost to the horizon. His eye went (as the designer had intended all eyes to do) from the water parterres near the Palace down to the Fountain of Latona, onwards to the long grassy stretch of the Royal Avenue then to the Fountain of Apollo with its vast esplanade before finally taking in the Grand Canal, all 1,650 metres of it, reaching, it seemed, into infinity. He stood and stared and stared and stared.

It was then that the idea came to him. It was so simple, so obvious. Why hadn't he thought of it before?

The security men finally managed to get Skidelski to move on into the interior of the Palace. He'd really wanted to stay longer in the gardens – they'd even switched the fountains on specially for him, which was terrific – but everyone was adamant that they should move on. He didn't realise it, but the sound of the fountains had masked the growing noise from the demonstrators.

Skidelski was overwhelmed by the unrestrained magnificence of the interiors. Above all, the copious amount of gold. Everything shone and glowed with a lustre he could never have imagined. He marvelled at the green and gold Genoa velvet wallpaper in the *Salon de l'Abondance*, he gawped at the red velvet walls and the sumptuous gilded coving of the *Salon de Mars*, he was utterly enchanted by the darkly suggestive Rape of Europa, painted on a gilded ground on the ceiling of the *Salon de Vénus*, and he was awestruck by the six golden statues supporting the candleholders in the *Salon d'Apollon*. It was here that he stood silently in front of Rigaud's portrait of Louis XIV, painted when the King was sixty-three years old. *Skidelski's age now.* He stared at it. The King was serene, majestic, with great achievements behind him, yet with ambition and resolution drawn on every line of his face. Here was a 63-year-old man with great achievements still to come. Yes, Skidelski felt that he and this Sun-King guy had quite a lot in common.

A gentle touch on his elbow from the Curator brought him back to everyday reality. He smiled and nodded as the clutch of politicians, art experts, historians, curating staff, interpreters and security men moved on through the *Salon de la Guerre*, with its magnificent chimney-piece dripping in gold, and into the *Galerie des Glaces*, the world-famous Hall of Mirrors. Here Skidelski's jaw almost hung open at the sheer, utter, gilded splendour of it all: the seventeen tall arched windows overlooking the gardens, each window echoed by an arched mirror on the opposite wall. He craned his neck to stare up at the vast candelabras in Bohemian glass, at the painted ceilings, the gilded cornices. The Curator explained to him that in Louis XIV's time the furnishings in the Hall of Mirrors were all solid silver: the tables, the footstools, the flowerpots for the orange trees, everything. Skidelski smiled politely and nodded, but he wasn't impressed. He was staring at the line of gilded statues down each side of the hall. Silver had nothing on gold. He heard the Curator explaining that Bismarck had mischievously chosen to declare the unification of Germany here in 1871, while Prussian troops were still putting paid to the last bit of French resistance just down the road in Paris. This struck Skidelski as very interesting. The idea he'd had on the terrace began to grow and take shape.

Ten minutes later he was staring at the gilded hangings in the King's Bedchamber. The gilded pilasters around the gilded doors, the gilded balustrade in front of the gilded bed. Skidelski feared he might swoon. He listened, rapt, as the Curator explained the ceremonies of the *Levée* and the *Couchée*, when the King rose or retired. Skidelski learned that the first valet would waken the King at eight o'clock sharp (perhaps a little early for Skidelski's tastes). A small team of valets would then perform his toilette, prior to the *Grandes Entrées*, when persons of high rank would be accorded the great honour of helping the King to don a garment – which, thought Skidelski, was a perfectly good way of doing things and maybe it was a pity that nowadays authority wasn't always granted the respect that was its due.

Skidelski learned that more junior supplicants wouldn't be allowed in until the *Secondes Entrées*, after which the King might condescend to appear in the ante-room, where a uniformed usher would strike the ground once with his halberd and shout, 'Gentlemen, the King!' Way to go, thought Skidelski, way to go! He wouldn't be able to call himself King, of course, that would go against the great republican traditions of America, but still, somebody would be needed to rule Europe, a pulsing, vibrant young Europe full of bold and maybe unruly American settlers, who would need to learn that the representative of the United States was someone who had to be treated with respect. Maybe even a degree of reverence.

Skidelski was still wrapped in dreams when he emerged from the Palace. Shaking hands with the Curator as he thanked him for the visit, Skidelski struggled to make himself heard above the roar of three helicopters hanging low in the sky above them. Jesus, did they really need *three*? Did they really need to be so goddamn low?! He could hardly hear himself think.

Around Versailles there were now some ten thousand protesters. The chant of FUCK YOU, AMERICA was incredibly loud, though not loud enough for Skidelski to hear above the roar of the three helicopters.

Throughout the visit, Joséphine du Bois had been discreetly kept in touch with the situation by her officials. She knew exactly why the helicopters were there, but was worried that Skidelski might still be able to hear the chanting as they pulled out of the gates of the Palace. She was furious. Despite the moral posturing that was routinely heard from the Elysée Palace, the French were desperate to sign a weapons deal with the Americans. They also were in desperate need of American help in reconstructing Provence, where whole towns had been destroyed and 700 people drowned in the freak floods of the previous winter. The last thing they needed was Skidelski flying back to Washington and badmouthing them. She would just have to engage him in lots of loud and animated conversation. Maybe she'd even have to flirt with him. *Mon Dieu, quelle pensée horrible!*

Anxious to obey the order to keep the protesters as far from the Palace as possible, the police had pushed them all the way down to the Avenue du Général de Gaulle, pinning them into a small area near the rail station. This would have been a good plan if only they'd remembered to stop the RER trains arriving from central Paris, each of them packed with hundreds more demonstrators. Within a very short time, the pro testers at the front, hard up against the police lines, were in danger of being crushed by the sheer pressure building up from behind. The Chief of Police belatedly ordered the suspension of all RER train services from Paris to Versailles. At Police HQ an inspector with a bad hangover misunderstood the instruction and ordered the closure of the adjacent SNCF station in Versailles.

The Chief of Police was getting worried. He couldn't understand why people were still pouring out of the station. The demonstrators at the front had no great desire to break through the police lines. They knew there was every chance of being gassed, clubbed or beaten. But they feared it was even more dangerous to remain where they were. Even then, the situation might have been contained, had not a rumour suddenly swept the crowd that a woman demonstrator had been killed. This was the woman in the yellow raincoat, briefly glimpsed by Skidelski on his way into the Palace. In fact, the woman in the yellow raincoat was at that moment drinking a *grand rouge* in a café next to the hospital where they'd examined her and put a sticking plaster on the minor contusion to her forehead. But in the crowd, she was already acquiring the status of a martyr.

'*Elle est morte!*'

'*Les flics l'ont tuée!*'

'*Assassins!*'

With a huge collective roar, the protesters burst against the police lines. Temporarily overwhelmed, the police fell back, clubs swinging. Gaps opened up in their ranks. The protesters poured through, some triumphant, some relieved, some clutching bloodied heads. Down the avenue they poured, past the Hôtel de Ville and into the Avenue de Paris. The Chief of Police desperately radioed his second-in-command at the palace, to tell him not to allow the motorcade to leave. Too late.

The gates of the palace swung open, the police outriders swung into formation and the huge cavalcade swept out of Versailles. In the back of the ministerial limo, Joséphine du Bois wondered what on earth to talk about. She needn't have worried. Skidelski was in full flow.

'Awesome, that's all I can say, awesome. I mean, I'd heard it was a neat place, but I had no idea . . .' Here he sighed and shook his head. 'Awesome. That's what it is, awesome.'

Joséphine du Bois nodded and agreed it was awesome.

The sight of several hundred protesters pouring across the Avenue de Paris had forced the police outriders into a quick decision. They wheeled the cavalcade left into Avenue de l'Europe (Versailles is like that – even the street names are grand) and then right into Avenue de Saint-Cloud. This seemed to be a good decision. The leading outrider heard a voice in his earpiece telling him to lead the motorcade down to the Place Alexandre 1e, then turn right into the Rue de Refuge, from where they could rejoin the D10 and the planned route back into Paris. With a bit of luck the Americans wouldn't even notice the small detour.

They might have gotten away with it if it hadn't been for *les rolleurs*. Roller-blades plus mobile phones had transformed the tactics of French protest. Demonstrators were now able to move large numbers of people at short notice and at great speed. Official tactics had not yet changed to deal with this new threat. Why should they? After all, the French riot police were a proud body of men. Their great-grandfathers had dealt with the arrival of barbed wire and the machine gun by sending millions of men towards certain death. It was not considered dignified to sit around a long table discussing how to *se deféndre contre les rolleurs.*

The helicopters spotted *les rolleurs*, of course. There were only about a hundred roller-bladers, but they were moving at speed towards the Place Alexandre 1e.

There was still time for the motorcade to speed up and get there before them, but unfortunately the police helicopters were on a different frequency from the police outriders. This small but potentially deadly communications gap had been much talked about but nothing had been done. Such screw-ups are not peculiar to the French. In New York on September 11, 2001, the police helicopters circling the Twin Towers discovered they had no means of communicating directly with the firefighters below them.

In the limo, Joe Skidelski was still in the throes of awe. Now he was enthusing about the gold. Joséphine du Bois wondered whether she should explain to him the difference between gold leaf and gold. She also wondered why they were going back a different way. As the motorcade came into Place Alexandre 1e it suddenly slowed.

Skidelski's eyes were gleaming as he described for the second time how his heart had skipped a beat as they'd entered the Hall of Mirrors. Joséphine du Bois smiled and nodded. *Nom de Dieu, comme il est emmerdant!* At that moment she saw the young man framed in the window behind Skidelski. He was holding on to the car and being whisked along with it. He had one finger raised in an obscene gesture. Behind him, more *rolleurs* appeared. A police motorcyclist came alongside the young man and clubbed the legs away from under him. He disappeared from sight. Joséphine thought she heard screams. The car braked sharply. Skidelski spun round in alarm.

By now dozens of roller-bladers were weaving in and out of the police outriders. Some were felled by the police, others got through. A motorcyclist trying to run down a roller-blader lost control of his bike and slid majestically into the path of the leading Humvee. The American driver of the Humvee kept on driving. Those were his orders. but the motorbike became entangled with the wheel tunnel of the Humvee, which crunched to a halt. The doors burst open and out spilled a dozen

American Secret Service people, some of them with handguns already drawn. They ran towards Skidelski's car. It was their job to protect him at all costs, if necessary by sacrificing themselves. The limo driver also had orders: in case of emergency, switch on the sirens and get the fuck out of there. He swung the wheel hard round, sending Skidelski flying into the delicious bosom of Joséphine du Bois. The Humvee in front also pulled out, narrowly missed an enterprising press photographer, and collided with a French SUV. Nervous Frenchmen toting sub-machine guns tumbled out, looking for their attackers. Blocked by entangled vehicles in front, the limo driver slammed the car viciously into reverse. Skidelski and du Bois were flung from the back seat on to the thickly carpeted floor. They thus failed to witness the moment that would next day grace the front page of most of the world's newspapers: the moment when American Secret Service men shot dead six French security men.

The next day Europe was in agreement that Skidelski's visit to France had been a diplomatic disaster. Skidelski, on the other hand, thought it had been the most fruitful trip of his life. He now knew what life held for him after Operation Deliverance. That was what he'd decided to call it, Operation Deliverance. He was pleased with that title, it had the right ring to it. He was even more pleased that night in his sumptuous hotel bedroom. Lianna was so thrilled with her time in Paris that she allowed him to suck her toes.

37

The death of Dr Fawcett devastated the staff at Fort Detrick. The quirky Englishman had been surprisingly popular. Yet it wasn't just personal affection that fuelled the grief. Everybody was shocked and surprised and a little fearful. Fawcett had always been painstakingly careful in the labs, had never knowingly taken risks. To have entered a Level Four Containment Area late at night on his own, well that was against all the rules. Even then, it was terrible luck that his positive-pressure one-piece personnel suit chose to malfunction on the very night that there was an escape of virus from one of the safety cabinets. His colleagues all agreed it was a great tragedy, and vowed to take greater care themselves in future. A few of them thought it didn't add up and were a little puzzled. Maybe they should have been more puzzled than they were, but they worked for the military, and the military did not encourage enquiring minds.

38

There were flakes of snow in the bitter wind that blew through the trees of Camp David. Dolores Delgado pulled her long woollen coat around her. After the hottest summer since records began, it was now the coldest winter that anyone could remember.

'Couldn't we discuss this in one of the cabins?' she asked Skidelski.

'No.'

'Why not?'

'Because it's private.'

'You know something, Joe? You're paranoid.'

'I probably am.' Skidelski smiled his thin smile. The length of his nose was emphasised by the enormous Russian musquash hat he wore, the flaps hanging down ridiculously like giant rabbit ears. He'd been given it during an official visit to Moscow – one of the few official gifts that he'd ever found useful. He kicked at the leaves, which were caught by the wind and sent whirling into the air. 'I want you to read this, Dolores.' He held up a slim blue cardboard folder.

'You brought me out in these temperatures to tell me I have to read something?'

'This evening, you know, later on, when it's kind of relaxed, I think maybe that's when we could clinch this thing.'

By now Dolores Delgado knew what Joe Skidelski meant when he mentioned 'this thing'.

'Okay . . .' she said cautiously.

'By the way, I think we ought to call it Operation Deliverance.'

'Okay,' said Delgado non-committally. She didn't think it much mattered what they called it.

'Dolores. It's time for the President to commit. He's stalling. I think Vince Lennox has a malign influence over him. That's why I engineered a little trip for young Vince.' In fact, Skidelski was getting increasingly anxious about Vince. Maybe it was time to put some surveillance on him. 'Without Vince around, we can clinch this thing. But to do that, I need you.'

She didn't look at him. 'I told you, I'm in favour of the plan. But we haven't given enough thought to what happens afterwards. That's typical of this country. That's how we fight our wars. We go in hard and figure out the consequences later. It's no good.' She dropped her voice and looked around. But this was as good a place as any for a private conversation. In the distance she could see a couple of security men trying hard to be inconspicuous. They wore huge padded jackets against the bitter cold. They were better prepared than she was.

Skidelski put a hand on her shoulder. She didn't like that much. There was something creepy about Skidelski. 'You think it's the right thing to do, don't you, Doe?'

She drifted away to examine some berries, so as to make him remove his hand. 'Yes. I do.'

'Then read this.' He held up the blue folder.

'What is it?'

'Al Boyd prepared it for me. It's a brilliant summary of the climate-change argument. All the key facts in one short document. I want you to hit Ritchie with it this evening.'

'Why me?'

'You've always been one of the big sceptics on the climate-change issue. It makes it all the more powerful, coming from you.'

She laughed. 'I'm not really a sceptic. Not any more. To start with, I thought that climate change was just the hook we hang this thing on. But it's all gotten too serious. Too many environmental crises for us to keep looking the other way. I've been thinking long and hard about this, Joe.'

'Yeah, I guess we all have.'

'I now believe there's a genuine moral case for Operation Deliverance.'

Skidelski was startled. Delgado didn't often use the word 'moral'.

'What I mean is,' she went on, 'long term, it may well be the only way of saving humanity.'

Skidelski's eyes gleamed. 'That's what you need to say to the President. Tonight.'

She reached out a gloved hand. 'I'll take a look at it.'

'Thanks, Doe.'

He handed her the blue folder. She put it under her arm without glancing at it. They wandered on in silence for a few moments.

Very casually, Skidelski said, 'I guess you're right. We ought to be giving some thought to how the world's going to be run after we do this thing.'

'Definitely.'

Skidelski stopped and turned to face her. His hands were thrust deep into his pockets, his shoulders hunched against the cold. 'Dolores, I want you to have Asia.'

She stared back at him. 'Sorry?'

'I want you to have Asia. You deserve it.'

'What are you talking about?'

'Ritchie hasn't managed to get his head round this one yet. But he's going to need trusted people to run the planet. You know how it is with Ritchie: if it feels too complicated he leaves it to us. I think you'd be ideal for Asia. You did your doctorate on the Tiger economies, didn't you?'

'Are you crazy?'

'No. We have to start planning now for a post-Deliverance world.'

'What exactly do you mean by "I get Asia?"'

'I mean, you rule Asia. Everybody should get somewhere. I already spoke to Murdo Robertson. He wants Scotland.'

'The VP wants Scotland?'

'Yes.'

'Scotland's small.'

'I know, but he thinks he's descended from Duncan or Macbeth or somebody. I don't care. Let him have Scotland. But you're bigger than that, Dolores, you deserve a continent. And given that we'd be administering a new frontier, I don't think democratic norms need apply.'

'Oh, so I get to be supreme ruler of Asia?'

'I don't know what you'd call it, but basically, yeah, something like that.'

'And what are you getting? If 'm getting Asia, what are you getting?'

'Europe. I was thinking I might have Europe.'

'Scotland's in Europe.'

'Yeah, but what the hell, I don't need Scotland. Let Murdo have Scotland. I'd be based at Versailles. A stone's throw from Paris. Paris is a great city. Lianna would like it in Paris. I want her to be happy.'

'You're kidding yourself there, Joe. Lianna's never going to be happy.'

'You're wrong about that.'

'Well, I wish you luck. What's she going to do about clothes? Are you going to get France's top couturiers vaccinated? And maybe a couple of top chefs?'

Secretly, Skidelski thought this wasn't a bad idea, but he wasn't about to admit that to Dolores Delgado. 'Come on, Doe, get serious. Are you in?'

'So I get Asia and you get Europe?'

'Yup. Something like that. I'd say that's a pretty good deal for you. Asia's a lot bigger than Europe.'

'Isn't this jumping the gun? I mean, the President hasn't even green-lighted the operation yet.'

'I know. I want to push for a decision very quickly now. We obviously have to do this before the end of his second term. That's not a lot of time.'

'How soon could we start producing the virus?'

'We're already producing it.'

'Oh. And what about manufacturing the vaccine?'

'I just gave the go-ahead.'

'Does Ritchie know this?'

'No. It'd only make him feel like he's being pushed.'

'You mean, he's not being pushed?'

'Of course not.'

Delgado looked at that long leathery face and thought she detected a smile.

In the distance they could hear the clatter of a helicopter patrolling the perimeter fence. There were more snowflakes now, and the light was fading.

'Would Asia include China?' asked Delgado.

'Oh yes, I think so.'

'I don't much like Beijing.'

'Rule it from some place else then. Thailand's nice. Bangkok would be a lovely city without all those Thais.'

They turned and wandered back towards the cabins.

Delgado quite liked the idea of running Asia.

President Ritchie L. Ritchie loved going to Camp David. He liked the simplicity of it. In reality, the simplicity was only made possible by the combined organisational skills of some two hundred people, but President Ritchie didn't have to worry about that. He just enjoyed getting out of a suit and tie and into plaid shirt, jeans, cowboy boots, leather flying jacket and a hunting cap. With a couple of aides in attendance and only a few dozen security men hovering at a discreet distance in the surrounding woods, he could wander freely and chat freely, knowing there was no danger of any of his words being recorded for posterity. Come evening, the menfolk would break open a few beers, grab handfuls of pretzels and talk about baseball until the wives joined them for a simple meal of T-bone steaks with freedom fries. Ritchie liked it best when the womenfolk went to bed early and he could hunker down in one of the cabins with a few of his key advisers and chew things over. It was almost like being at college again. Only problem was, there were women among his key advisers. That was one of the drawbacks of the modern world. You couldn't be seen with an all-male team, it didn't play well with the electorate. Which was a pity, because things were easier when it was just guys together. You could do guy things and make guy jokes and talk a little bit dirty and yak long into the night without worrying about being politically correct. Still, the only woman present was Dolores Delgado, and she was basically okay. She was almost as good as a guy. A little bit humourless maybe, but not really shockable. And awful nice to look at. Anyhow, she generally went to bed by midnight.

It was about eleven in the evening when Ritchie's inner circle finally gathered in Ritchie's favourite cabin. Ritchie was feeling relaxed. It was that fine time of year between Thanksgiving and Christmas when he always felt book-ended by goodwill. Around the rough-hewn wooden table sat Joe Skidelski, in a roll-neck sweater, Vice President Robertson in a crumpled tartan jacket, and National Security Adviser Jimmy Lombok in khaki chinos and a grey sweatshirt that said 'Friend of Jesus'. Dolores Delgado didn't really like dressing casual, but she knew that at Camp David dressing casual was compulsory, so she'd pulled on a pair of old Armani jeans and a pink Prada sweater.

'Okay,' said the President, opening another Bud, 'let's noodle this thing out.' That was how Ritchie generally opened a strategy meeting at Camp David. He'd found that inviting people to help him noodle it out made the big issues seem containable. Noodlin' it out meant you could be a good ol' boy *and* leader of the Free World.

The President swigged his Bud from the bottle, wiped his mouth with the back of his hand, and belched. 'Sorry, guys.'

There was laughter around the table. Delgado's laughter was maybe just a bit forced.

Ritchie didn't regard drinking beer as 'drinking' in the real sense of the word, but even so, it was only at Camp David he risked consuming any kind of alcohol in front of other people. Nobody here would leak to the press. Here he was among friends. He looked around and felt a tremendous rush of warmth. These were the good guys. He kinda wished Vince could have been present, but hey, you couldn't have everything. 'So, who's gonna kick it off?' he asked.

There was a longish pause. Everyone there knew that the later contributions to a debate had more impact on the President than the early voices. Well, it was hard for one man to remember all the details of a long discussion.

Murdo Robertson finally broke the silence. 'This is a pretty big thing we're contemplating here. Sure, there are sound arguments for. But there are sound arguments against, too.' He paused, feeling pleased with himself. He reckoned he'd delivered a pretty good summary.

Delgado didn't conceal her look of contempt. God help America if Ritchie were to drop dead one day. Ritchie might not be the brightest bulb in the firmament, but he was seven Einsteins compared with the Vice President. And at least Ritchie wasn't afraid to express a view. Unlike the VP, who spent his life working out which way the wind was blowing.

'Okay,' said Delgado. 'It's time we did some straight talking. We're thinking about killing six billion people.'

A frown crossed the President's face. 'Put like that . . .'

'Exactly,' interrupted Delgado. 'Put like that it sounds kind of brutal. Well, here's the truth, people. It is kind of brutal. But does that make it wrong? No, it does not. Want to know why? I'll tell you why. The alternative, that's why.'

'So what's the alternative?' asked Ritchie.

'The extinction of the human species.'

'That's putting it a bit strongly, isn't it?' said Ritchie.

'No,' said Delgado.

Skidelski stayed silent and watched intently. This was good. This was way better than anything he'd hoped for. And it was much stronger coming from Delgado than from him. He knew they all thought he was a bit of a warmonger. Stuff like this coming from Delgado was worth its weight in gold. Yes, that walk in the woods had definitely been a good idea. Skidelski wasn't real sure about giving Delgado the whole of Asia, but hey, tomorrow was another day.

Delgado pushed a strand of hair from her eyes. The wind had done serious damage to her styling. She hated all this outdoor stuff that went on at Camp David. She didn't see why they couldn't all stay in Washington and discuss things in civilised surroundings. She turned to face Ritchie directly. 'Ritchie. You got elected – twice – because the American people don't want to face up to the truth. And the truth is, our way of life is unsustainable.'

Ritchie blinked. 'Dolors, are you alright?'

'Yes, Ritchie, I'm fine.' Her voice was cold, forceful. Ritchie couldn't remember when she'd last been so aggressive.

She leaned across the table and tapped the President in the chest. He looked down at the finger. He didn't much like this.

'The icecaps are melting, Ritchie. The sea-level's rising. The ozone layer is thinning. The rainforests are disappearing. The planet is warming up.'

Ritchie hit straight back. 'The global warming thing, it's unproven.'

'Bullshit.'

'There's a guy in Switzerland says global warming is a myth. What's his name? Some climate expert. Young guy. Very bright.'

'Hans-Rudi Adenbecker?'

'Yeah, him.'

She turned to Skidelski. 'Tell him, Joe.'

'Adenbecker takes money from Boyd's people.'

The President waved a hand dismissively. 'The American Way gives out grants all over the place. That proves nothing.'

'Ritchie,' said Delgado, 'the American Way people are putting half a million dollars a year into a numbered bank account for his personal use.'

'They are?' Ritchie was genuinely surprised.

'They are. And for that kind of money they expect results.'

'Oh,' said the President.

Skidelski smiled. Sometimes there was a genuine naivety about the President that was quite touching. He raised an amused eyebrow in Delgado's direction.

Ritchie thought for a moment. 'He's not the only one. There's a lot of people say that global warming's bullshit.'

'Only people with an interest in saying it,' said Delgado. 'There isn't a single, respectable, authoritative, independent voice that claims global warming isn't happening.'

The President was feeling very rattled. Dolores Delgado was one of his most loyal supporters. What the hell was going on? 'Doe, have you turned into some kind of eco-nut?'

Delgado ignored him. 'Sir, in America we're building five thousand homes every day.'

Yeah, thought Skidelski, way to go! Dolores had absorbed all the key details from the blue file.

'That's American know-how,' said Ritchie. 'Makes me proud.'

'Five thousand homes a day, that's one and three-quarter million homes a year. When's the last time you looked down when you were on Air Force One? There are no suburbs out there any more, only exurbs. Travel from Washington to New York, all you see is buildings. Buildings and freeways. We now average two cars per household. *Average.* On top of that we're releasing 200 million acres of American wilderness a year for mining, drilling, logging and road-building.'

'So that Americans can be better off,' said the President fiercely. 'This nation was built upon conquering the wilderness. It's part of the frontier spirit.'

'In ten to twenty years time there won't *be* any wilderness in America,' Delgado retorted. 'And basically, the same process is going on all around the world. Unless it's stopped. That's what the environmentalists want, they want it stopped.'

'Stupid assholes,' growled the President.

'Right. Exactly. Stupid assholes. It can't be done. Signing up for Kyoto would require us to reduce our emissions to seven per cent below their 1990 levels. To do that we'd have to lay waste to the American economy. It's the dream of a madman. The green dream of a madman.'

Ritchie nodded. 'Loony tunes, that's all it is, loony tunes.'

'Okay,' said Delgado, reverting to the question-and-answer technique which was her speciality, 'can we continue to consume more? No, we can't. Why? Because we're running out of planet. Can we consume less? No, we can't. Why? Because the American people would go apeshit if we tried. So is there another option here? Yes, there is. And it's our only salvation. That's why we're calling it Operation Deliverance.'

Ritchie nodded. 'Good title.'

'But it requires courage and vision and determination. The qualities that you are known for, sir.'

Ritchie felt a lump in his throat and swallowed hard. 'Thank you, Doe, I appreciate that.' He paused, took a swig of beer. 'But I don't want to be remembered in history as the man who killed six billion people. That just ain't how a man wants to be remembered.'

'But think of the alternative,' said Delgado.

Skidelski's eyes were shining as he leant forward. 'You wouldn't be killing six billion people, Ritchie. You'd be saving three hundred million Americans.'

'You'd be saving the human race,' corrected Delgado.

'That'd certainly be quite some achievement, sir,' said the Vice President.

The room fell silent. Ritchie desperately needed time to think. He took out the little silver box from his shirt pocket, extracted a toothpick, and began probing the gaps between his molars. He felt his world was falling apart. Where were the simple certainties he'd been brought up to believe in? What had become of the downhome truths that he used to pass off as policies? Now his advisers were suddenly throwing all this eco-bullshit at him. What was going on? True, he'd noticed something pretty weird happening to the weather. True, that thing in New Orleans had been horrible. True, there were all those dead celebs in Hollywood. True, he was very, *very* worried that the American bald eagle might after all become extinct before the end of his second term. But for six years he'd been surrounded by people telling him everything was basically okay, people telling him the American way of life was not under threat, people telling him that global warming was a myth dreamed up by liberal troublemakers. Now he was suddenly expected to rethink everything. It was all very confusing.

'Oh, and another thing,' said Dolores Delgado, 'there are too many of us.'

'Too many people?' asked the President.

'Too many Americans.'

'Too many *Americans*?' said the President in disbelief.

'That's right, Ritchie. Too many Americans. In 1970 there were two hundred million of us. Now there are three hundred million. By 2040 there will be four hundred million. We need more space.'

'Couldn't we just invade Canada?' asked the Vice President. 'They've got a lot of space in Canada.'

'Yes,' said Delgado, 'we could. But will that stop the planet warming up? Will that stop the sea-levels rising? No. Sure we need extra living space for the American people, but it's got to be sustainable living space. Clean living space. We need to think long-term here, guys. Because if we don't, the planet's fucked. And you, Ritchie, you'll be remembered as the President who fucked it.'

Normally Ritchie liked it when Delgado swore. It freed him from the feeling that he had to step carefully in the presence of a woman. But being told by her that he was fucking the planet, well, hey, there were limits. 'What do you mean, the President who fucked the planet? I don't like that kind of talk.'

'Listen. We've got four per cent of the world's population and we're responsible for a quarter of the world's carbon dioxide emissions . . .'

'Wow,' said the Vice President, 'is it that much?'

'Sure it's that much. If we look at our total contribution to global warming, we find that we—'

'This is very negative stuff, Doe, I really didn't know you thought like this.'

'I didn't, Ritchie. When you were first elected I believed in what we told people. But I don't believe in it any more.'

Ritchie hunched his shoulders. His small eyes grew narrower, almost disappearing into the sockets. There was a sudden tension in the cabin. All that could be heard was the faint crackling of the log fire. Everyone in the room knew that Ritchie had a short fuse, an anger that held the potential for physical violence. He'd learnt to control the violent instincts in him, he knew that politically it could be fatal, but he couldn't stop himself *feeling* violent, could he? His voice was quiet, tight. 'If you don't believe in our policies any more, Dolores, maybe you ought to consider your position.'

Delgado's eyes flashed.

Skidelski didn't like the turn the conversation had taken. He quickly leaned across the table. 'Ritchie. We're all on the same side here. We want the same things. It's how we achieve it, that's what we're talking about. As friends. As colleagues.'

'Too many Americans!' the President snorted. he pulled a bottle of

171

Bud from the ice bucket and, staring Delgado straight in the face, took the cap off with his teeth. It was an old trick he'd learned at Harvard. He'd used it to impress the girls and scare the guys. Still staring at Delgado, he spat the metal cap into the corner of the cabin.

'Suppose it were too *few* Americans,' said Skidelski quickly.

'Uh?'

'Imagine if we needed Americans to colonise the empty spaces across the world.'

'Dolores is telling me there aren't going to be any empty spaces.'

'There will be if we put Operation Deliverance into place. The whole world will be there waiting for us. Imagine it, Mr President. A new frontier. A global frontier. Americans moving West, East, North, South, setting up new outposts, braving the hazards of new territories, bringing up kids who respect what this country stands for. And wherever you look, the Stars and Stripes. Old Glory flying proudly over every nation on earth. America no longer just a nation, America a planet. Eventually, people won't call it planet Earth any more, they'll call it planet America. Is that not a vision to set the pulse racing?'

Ritchie thought it wasn't without its attractions. But it was scary too. He was two years into his second term of office. Another two years and he could pack it in, settle down in his ranch to write his memoirs. Or better still, get some one to write them for him. It wouldn't be as much fun as running America, but it'd be okay.

It was then that Skidelski delivered his clincher. 'Mr President. I think in the context of such a serious world crisis, Congress would be open to the idea of allowing you a third term. Who knows, maybe even a fourth? It would require a constitutional amendment, of course, but I'm confident we could get it through. In such troubled times, the American people would want stability, continuity. They'd want you, Ritchie.'

Yeah. Thought Ritchie. That's right. I hadn't thought of that before. They'd want *me*.

39

President Ritchie turned the White House Christmas card over and over in his hands. Really, he ought to be going through his forty-page news summary before Vince arrived to give him his morning briefing, but he found himself unable to concentrate. The problem of the Christmas card struck Ritchie as a damned sight more pressing than some shit about terrorists or tax cuts or budget deficits, which in the end were simple issues – terrorists were bad, tax cuts were good, budget deficits didn't matter – whereas the Christmas card problem didn't appear to have any easy solution.

Ritchie was at a loss. He didn't associate Christmas with problems. He'd always liked Christmas, but since coming to the White House he'd liked Christmas *a lot*. Most people only had one tree at Christmas; Ritchie had twenty-three. And he didn't have to decorate a single one of them. From early December onwards, just about every important room in the White House had a tree in it: the Blue Room, the Green Room, the Red Room, the East Room, the Yellow Oval Room, the Family Dining Room, the Library, the West Wing Lobby, the Diplomatic Reception Room, all of them were pictures of pure Christmas joy. In addition to the Christmas trees, the White House was festooned with 825 feet of garlands, 272 wreaths, 320 bows, and a total of 71,450 lights, all put up by carefully vetted volunteers.

The one and three-quarter million Christmas cards to be sent to 'friends and family', each them bearing what looked remarkably like a genuine handwritten greeting from the President and the First Lady, were handled with equal efficiency. Having one and three-quarter million friends and family to send cards to may seem problematic, but it's not as if a President actually has to sign or address them, or stick stamps on the envelopes or any of the other things that normal people have to do at Christmas. At one point Ritchie had even considered sending a Christmas card to *every* American, until Vince pointed out that quite a lot of Americans were Jews, Muslims, Hindus, Sikhs, Buddhists, and even atheists, none of whom would particularly appreciate receiving a card celebrating the birth of the baby Jesus.

Ritchie placed the Christmas card in the centre of his desk, leaned back in his chair, and stared at it. On the front was a photograph of the President, the First Lady, their son Edward, Edward's older sister Janie, and Rascal the spaniel, all arrayed charmingly alongside the Christmas tree in the Family Dining Room. The picture had been taken back in July, because it takes time to print and send out one and three-quarter million Christmas cards. The card people had decorated the room specially, even putting up a Christmas tree, which had felt very odd in July, but that's how these things had to be done. (It hadn't occurred to anyone that it might have been easier to take the photograph the previous Christmas.) Now July seemed a very long time away. In July, Ritchie had still been the head of a normal American family. Now he was the father of a homosexual. Was it right to send one and three-quarter million families a Christmas card featuring a homosexual? What kind of message was that sending to the American people?

'What the hell is going on, Mr President?' Vince closed the door of the Oval Office behind him and strode towards the President's desk.

Ritchie looked up and stared. He wasn't used to being talked to like that. Anyhow, Vince always arrived at 08.30, and it was only 08.10. Ritchie turned the Christmas card face-down on the desk, pushed his half-eaten bowl of bran and yogurt to one side and wondered what the hell had gotten into Vince. 'How was your trip?' he enquired.

'My trip was fine,' Vince said curtly, now understanding why Skidelski had found it so important for Vince to go away for two days to attend a conference on bio-terrorism. 'Sir, I just spoke to Jimmy Lombok. He says you greenlighted the Boyd plan at Camp David yesterday.'

'Yes, Vince. That's right. I did.'

'I'm sorry, sir, I'm your special assistant. I can't do my job if I'm excluded from the decision-making process. Especially something this big.'

'Is that right?' said Ritchie. Carefully and deliberately he took out his little silver box and extracted a toothpick. He let Vince sit there in silence for a good ten or twenty seconds while he worked his molars. Eventually, he dropped the toothpick into the litter basket beside his desk and returned the little silver box to his picket. 'You're resigning, are you?'

Vince swallowed hard and stared at the President.

Ritchie chuckled, stood up, leaned across the desk and gave Vince a big, friendly squeeze on the shoulder. 'Sit down, son.'

Vince sat down.

'Coffee?'

'Um . . . Yes. Yes, please.'

Under the desk, Ritchie reached for the button that alerted the duty steward. Exactly five seconds later, the door swung open.

'Another pot of coffee, please, Sam.' Ritchie knew all the stewards by their first names.

'Yes. Mr President,' said Sam, and withdrew.

Ritchie gave Vince a big, warm smile. 'Lucy's well, I hope?'

'Yes, sir.'

'Good, good. Be sure to give her my best, won't you?'

'Yes, sir.'

'A man and a woman joined together in holy wedlock. There's nothing finer.'

'Right,' muttered Vince, fighting back his anger. Who needed this shit?

'I understand your reservations about Operation Deliverance, Vince.'

'Oh that's what it's going to be called, is it?'

'Yeah. Good name, right?' Ritchie chuckled. 'But knowing how everyone around here likes to shorten everything, it'll probably end up being known as OpDel. But tell me about your reservations.'

'They're more than reservations. I believe the whole plan is fundamentally wrong.'

'I think we pretty much covered all the arguments at Camp David over the weekend. Pity you couldn't be there. Dolores put the case very powerfully.'

'Dolores is in favour?'

'That's right. I suddenly saw things more clearly. This thing isn't about killing people, Vince. This is about saving the planet.'

'Is that what she told you?'

'One day, planet Earth could be known as planet America, have you thought about that, Vince?' Actually, since the previous day's meeting at Camp David, a better idea had occurred to Ritchie. If he was to be remembered as the saviour of humanity, wouldn't the planet eventually become known as planet Ritchie? Having a planet named after you struck Ritchie as a pretty neat idea. He hadn't shared this thought with anyone just yet, in case it was taken the wrong way.

Vince stared at the carpet. If Dolores Delgado had been won over, that meant the balance of power had swung decisively in Skidelski's direction.

Sam the steward reappeared. He was one of the youngest members of staff, and revered Ritchie beyond all imagining. He could hardly believe that the President of the United States remembered the name of a mere steward. 'Coffee, Mr President.'

'Thanks, Sam. It's for my good friend Vince, here.'

Sam dutifully poured a coffee for Vince and withdrew.

Ritchie doodled briefly on his notepad. 'I need you on board for Operation Deliverance. I rely on you. You're like a son to me, Vince, I hope you know that. That's always mattered to me. But it matters to me a whole lot more now that I don't have a son of my own.'

Vince looked up and thought he saw tears in the President's eyes. He didn't know what to say. That a homosexual son was still a son? That he no longer wanted to be part of this administration? That mass murder was still mass murder, even if you called it an 'operation' and gave it a fancy name?

'Oh, something I wanted to ask you,' said Ritchie. 'I can't make up my mind about RascalCam. How many seasonal videos should we have on the White House website this year? It's important to get it right. I'm told there were nearly ten million hits on that site last year. We got two choices: one is Rascal romping in the snow with me on the lawn. We already shot that one. The other's going to be Rascal's guided tour of the Christmas decorations inside the White House. Problem is, if we use both, which one are we going to call 'Rascal's Winter Wonderland'? I like that title, it's kind of catchy.'

'Um ... I'd say "Rascal's Winter Wonderland" is better for the snow one.'

'You're right, you're absolutely right. So what are we going to call the other one? Any ideas?'

'How about ... "Rascal's Good Cheer Tour of the White House"?'

'Rascal's Good Cheer Tour of the White House' ... That's a terrific title, Vince.'

'Thanks.'

Actually, the President thought it was a crappy title, but he wanted to keep Vince on board. He didn't want to tackle Operation Deliverance without Vince. On the other hand, nobody was indispensable . . .

Vince knew exactly what was going on. He'd seen the Ritchie technique in action only too often. Ritchie was flattering him by asking for his opinions. At the same time he'd smoothly changed the subject so that it became difficult for Vince to pursue his line of thought. Well, fuck it, thought Vince, I'm not going to be fobbed off, this is too important to be fobbed off. He stood up. 'I'm sorry, sir. I have a fundamental objection to this plan.'

'Fundamental objection noted,' said Ritchie, and turned to the computer screen on his desk where a little telephone logo had started flashing. 'Hmm,' he said, 'there's a call from the British Prime Minister. I guess I ought to take it.' He waved at Vince to sit down. 'Stay there. This won't take long.' He picked up the phone and said, 'Put James Halstead through, willya?' He smiled at Vince, who reluctantly sat down again. He then turned his attention to the call. 'Hi James!'

From where he was sitting, Vince could vaguely hear the fruity voice at the other end of the line. 'Good afternoon, Ritchie. Oh, I beg your pardon, it's still the morning there, isn't it?'

'That's right. How're ya doin' James?'

'I'm well, thank you. And yourself?'

Ritchie sighed. 'I'm great. What's on your mind, James?'

'Well, as you presumably know, as of midnight last night the entire North Sea was closed to fishing. For at least ten years.'

Ritchie didn't know. 'Why's that?'

'No fish.'

'That's too bad.'

'Well, of course there are *some* fish. But not many. A complete ban is our last hope of saving what's left.'

'I see.' Ritchie didn't really see. He gestured to Vince to pick up another handset. Other staffers would already be monitoring the call, but he wanted Vince's take on it. Vince picked up the handset.

James Halstead cleared his throat. 'I'd like to send you the last cod.'

'What?'

'As a gesture of friendship. The last cod from the North Sea for at least ten years. Actually, I suppose it could be the last North Sea cod ever. It's being air-freighted over packed in ice. I hope you enjoy it.'

'That's very kind of you, James. Sounds delicious.' Ritchie looked at Vince and pulled a face. He hated cod.

'Look, I'm most awfully sorry, Ritchie, but I'm going to be making a speech about the environment tomorrow, and you might not agree with all of it.'

'Oh?' Ritchie didn't much like the sound of this.

'Yes, well what with the recent floods in France and the loss of much of East Anglia last week . . .'

'Yes, I was real sorry to hear about that, James.'

'Yes, thank you. But you know, it means that for domestic political reasons, I may have to be a bit critical of the United States on the climate-change front.'

'Well . . . I hope it isn't too critical, James. I mean, we are allies. Shoulder to shoulder, right?'

'Oh absolutely. It'll be relatively mild. But I'm afraid my backbenchers are getting restive and, well, one has to be practical about these things.'

'Yeah, sure. I gotta go, James. Kinda busy right now.' Ritchie didn't want to sound too accommodating. It was time to exude a little authority.

'Of course,' said the Prime Minister. 'Quite understand. I do hope you enjoy the cod.'

'You bet. Bye James.'

'Goodbye, Ritchie. And thank you for your understanding.'

'No problem.' Ritchie put down the phone and looked up at Vince as he did the same.

'You and Lucy want a cod?'

'No thank you, sir.'

'He'd better not criticise me directly. Asshole.' Ritchie bit his lip and balled his fists. He knew that Halstead, as America's most loyal supporter, would get listened to around the globe if he started to criticise Washington . . .

Suddenly, it was as if a shaft of sunlight had illuminated Ritchie's face. 'Hey. How dumb am I?! I don't have to worry about Britain any more. Screw Britain! Screw Halstead! Pretty soon, there won't be any Britons around. Yeah!' His fists in the air, Ritchie rose to his feet. 'Yeah,' he screamed. 'Fuck you, Britain!!'

Vince looked on, appalled.

Ritchie shrugged, shot his cuffs, and sat down. He leaned towards Vince and dropped his voice. 'Do you think maybe we should send some vaccine to their royal family?'

Vince stared at him blankly.

Ritchie wrinkled his nose. 'No, probably not. We shouldn't make exceptions. Of course, there's Israel. It doesn't seem right to wipe Israel out, does it?' Ritchie went into deep thought.

Vince couldn't find words and wondered whether he ought just to walk out of the room.

'Can I ask you a question, Vince?'

'Go ahead, sir.' Vince hoped Ritchie was harbouring doubts. To Vince's way of thinking, Ritchie wasn't really a bad guy, just a weak guy who allowed himself to be manipulated. It seemed impossible that Ritchie could really go ahead with something as horrible as Operation Deliverance. Maybe he was about to admit that.

'What I want to ask you, Vince, is this ...' Ritchie picked up the Christmas card and stared at the photograph. 'How would I know if my daughter was a lesbian?'

Vince headed home early that day, pleading ill health. This wasn't a good career move. In the White House, ill people were either disbelieved or fired. But Vince needed to escape. He needed to think. He needed to decide what to do. He needed to talk to Lucy, needed to tell her everything.

A little over an hour later, he was home. As he pulled into the driveway, he realised he'd simply assumed his wife would be at home writing, as she had been most days recently. But her car wasn't in the drive. Damnit. Angry at himself for not having thought of calling her, he went inside.

Glancing at the kitchen clock, he decided that 5.45 wasn't really too early to mix a vodka martini. He took the drink through to his study and called Lucy on her cell phone. After a few seconds he realised it was ringing upstairs some place. She'd forgotten it again. He decided to be magnanimous, find the cell phone and put in on its charger. Lucy was forever forgetting to charge it. He followed the sound of ringing and opened the door of her office. He knew she didn't like him going in there, but hey, he was doing her a favour. The cell phone was on the desk by her open laptop, right beside the mouse. He gingerly made his way across the debris-strewn floor (how could she work in this squalor?)

and picked up the phone, inadvertently moving the mouse. The vibration was enough to rouse the laptop from sleep mode. Vince was about to turn away when he registered what was on the screen. He stopped and stared for a moment. He thought about walking away. This was an intrusion into Lucy's private space.

He stared some more. Then he sat down at the screen, made a note of the page number, and went to the top of the open document. It was entitled *Life Near the Top: the White House As You Never Saw It Before*. Underneath it was Lucy's name. He blinked. This didn't look very much like a detective novel. He read a few pages. It was an account of one woman's life with a White House insider. The autobiographical element was thinly disguised. In fact, it was hardly disguised at all.

Lucy had been lying to him. For how long? He ran a page count. Two hundred and forty-two pages, and apparently unfinished. It had to be at least six months' work, didn't it? Maybe a year. Maybe longer. Depended on how fast she wrote this kind of stuff. One thing was clear, if she published it, his job was over. He couldn't be associated with this. That's why she'd kept it secret.

He heard the door opening downstairs and quickly took the cursor back to the page it had been on. He left the document exactly as he had found it and hoped the laptop would go back to sleep mode quickly. He hurried downstairs.

They met in the kitchen, and kissed.

She looked at him. 'You're home early.'

'Yeah. I'm exhausted.'

She looked at him again. 'Is there something wrong?'

He wanted to say, 'Yes, you've been lying to me.' But he realised there was something so much bigger to talk about, so much more important. Something that rendered books and careers completely unimportant. And he couldn't do it. He couldn't fucking well do it. Because he didn't trust her any more. At least, that's what he told himself.

40

The lighting of the White House Christmas tree was a tradition that went all the way back to Calvin Coolidge. It was one of President Ritchie's favourite moments of the year. Ritchie always got a little sentimental around Christmas time. He liked nothing better than a slice of cherry yule log, even though he had to be careful that no eggs had gone into its preparation. He still remembered the time he'd had an anaphylactic allergic reaction to a chocolate cake made with eggs, and it wasn't an experience that he ever intended to repeat. For the benefit of the cameras, he'd sometimes have to take at least a dozen bites of yule log, but hey, sometimes it was fun to do stuff like that for the press.

Before crossing to the Ellipse in front of the White House, he and Mrs Ritchie each had a bowl of piping hot broth. The lighting ceremony was quite a long one, and even in the warmest clothes you could start feeling a bit of a chill creeping up your legs. The broth provided inner fortification. Especially this year. The weather was horrific. It was both cold and windy. The previous day, Ritchie's aides had begged him to postpone the ceremony, pointing out that storm-force winds were predicted. Ritchie had refused outright. No way was he going to miss out just because of some dumb wind. People would think he was a coward.

Ever since the destruction of New Orleans and the outing of his son, something had happened to Ritchie. He'd become more bitter, stubborn, difficult. His staffers found him less suggestible, less manipulable. This meant that more and more decisions were actually taken by Ritchie himself. Even the President's most ardent supporters would not argue that this was entirely a good thing.

The President and Mrs Ritchie settled down in their seats on the huge rostrum specially constructed each year for the event. The US Coastguard Band struck up 'Jingle Bells' and Ritchie felt engulfed by a great love for America. When three hundred deprived kids from the Boys and Girls Clubs of America sang 'White Christmas', he had to wipe away a tear. This was the America that he loved and revered.

The America that loved and revered Ritchie was of course also there. Just to Ritchie's left was the CEO of the missile guidance systems manufacturers who'd kindly donated the Christmas tree lights. A couple of rows behind was the chief of an important news network that ran endless feelgood stories about the President and never, ever, allowed its reporters to ask awkward questions. Just in front of Skidelski was the boss of Arkan, the giant conglomerate that was to donate a giant Christmas cake to the three hundred deprived children. In common with most of their other food products, their giant Christmas cake was of course packed with averagely carcinogenic colourings and preservatives. A little behind these heads of industry were carefully selected stars of screen, stage and television. Cheech Lingaard, hero of the Malibu celebrity fire, was there, lovingly holding hands with his wife. Well, hell, it was only a couple of hours and they wouldn't have to see each other again for several months.

A cheer went up from the deprived kids as Santa's arrival was announced. A gust of wind sent several hats flying. White House officials looked up anxiously at the Christmas tree, as it swished back and forward. They'd attached extra steel mooring cables, but it still looked a bit alarming.

Santa was exactly how a Santa ought to be: plump, cheerful, rosy-cheeked and patronising. Putting down his sack, he puffed up his cheeks and looking around said, 'My, my, my, what a gathering! It's just terrific to see you all moms and dads and grandmas and grandpas and all you little ones. I can't tell you how happy I am to be ho- ho- ho- ho- ho- hosting this great event!'

The wind gusted fiercely. Santa felt his beard coming unstuck and grabbed at it. He looked up to see the Christmas tree leaning at a worrying angle and decided maybe he'd cut short his appearance. 'Ladies and gentlemen, boys and girls, I gotta go in a moment because I left my reindeer double-parked on East Street. And you wouldn't want them to get a ticket, now would you? So let's move right on to the big moment when the President lights the tree. Come on boys and girls, let's hear it for the President!'

A ragged cheer went up. Santa tried to pick up his sack, momentarily letting go of his beard, which flew out into the audience. As Ritchie advanced towards the microphones one of the cables supporting the tree tore itself out of the ground. Somebody screamed. Ritchie looked up to see the tree falling towards him. Two Secret Service men leapt towards the President and pushed him out of the way. As it fell, the tree brought down an electric cable that snaked and thrashed for a moment till it connected with a panic-stricken Santa, who thought it must be a rope and grabbed at the end of it. He died instantly, with a choked-off scream and quite a lot of smoke.

Next day's headlines were horrific:

SANTA DEAD IN WHITE HOUSE HORROR
FESTIVE DISASTER AT THE WHITE HOUSE
SANTA'S WIDOW TO SUE PRESIDENT
RITCHIE'S XMAS MAYHEM

and, in a vicious echo of the General Sherman disaster, **WHO KILLED SANTA?**

Somebody in the White House must have leaked, because many papers suggested that Ritchie, having insisted on the ceremony going ahead despite the terrible winds, was personally responsible for Santa's death.

All this got Ritchie so mad that it made him want to kill people. It made him want to kill a lot of people.

41

'My fellow Americans,' said the President in a special television address broadcast on the evening of the 1st of January. 'We live in difficult and challenging times. All around us, the enemies of freedom are looking for new ways to attack America. Quite naturally, in this holiday season, this is not something we wish to think about. This is a time for families, a time for small, everyday pleasures, a time for Americans to rest and to relax. Yet there can be no rest, no relaxation for those who are guarding our liberty and protecting our country in the ongoing war between good and evil.

'The brave and committed men and women of our armed services are in the front line of the war against terror. Yet there are others, equally brave, equally committed, that we hear little of. These are the men and women of our intelligence services. From them we have received a warning that I, as President of the United States of America, am solemnly obliged to pass on to you, the people of America.'

At this point the camera moved in slowly to a big close-up of the President, who was grim-faced.

'The enemies of freedom have developed a new weapon. A biological weapon. A weapon of mass terror. Thanks to the vigilance and the determination of our intelligence community, we have obtained a sample of this pathogen. Our scientists confirm that if released in our great cities, there could be many deaths. Possibly millions of deaths. There is, as yet, no known means of protecting ourselves from this terrible new weapon, which takes the form of a lethal virus.

'Now, of course we do not know for sure that our enemies are planning to use this weapon against us, but we do know that our enemies are ruthless. That's why it would be foolish not to find ways of protecting ourselves against an attack that could devastate America. I am pleased to be able to tell you that American scientists – the best scientists in the world – are already working on a vaccine against this deadly pathogen, and have assured me that it can be ready within months. Preparations for a mass vaccination of Americans are already under way. As soon as I have confirmation that the vaccine is ready, every single man, woman and child in this country will be protected. That is my solemn promise to you.'

The President paused. The camera went to a wider angle. 'These are hard things to say at a time of celebration and good will. You know that I would not say them unless they had to be said. I wish you, your families and your loved ones, a very happy and prosperous New Year. May God bless you all. And may God bless America.'

'Did you write that?' said Lucy, and switched the television off.

Vince shook his head, 'No, those were mostly the golden words of Larry Dodge.'

'Is any of it true?'

Vince didn't know how to reply. They'd watched the presidential address in bed, having been to a New Year party that went on till 9 am. It had been a very good party. They'd had fun. They'd come home at 10 am, fallen into bed, somehow made love, and fallen asleep. Vince had fought hard to get the time off; Ritchie had wanted him there for the presidential address. For the second time since he'd been in the White House, Vince had refused to accede to a request from the President. The first was the invitation to spend Christmas with him and his family. Vince couldn't bear the thought, and didn't even mention it to Lucy. She'd have refused anyhow.

Ritchie was mad at him, of course, on both counts. He wasn't used to Vince being difficult like this and couldn't figure it out. Vince couldn't figure it out either.

Maybe he just wanted to spend the New year with Lucy and to hell with it, maybe it was his way of disengaging himself from Operation Deliverance. But Vince knew that disengaging from Operation Deliverance wasn't really possible. He could no longer write it off as a mad scheme that would never happen. He had to take a stance. He'd agonised about it for hours, days, weeks, and had concluded there were only two options:

1. Go public and try to stop it.
2. Work from the inside and try to stop it.

He knew he ought to have told Lucy by now, but the secret exposé she was writing didn't exactly make him want to confide in her. Anyhow, he was sure she would push for Option 1, and Vince was afraid that if he went public nobody would believe him and probably he'd have a bad accident, like that poor English scientist had. And he couldn't figure out how to get evidence that would convince anyone of the truth of such a monstrous and unimaginable plan. He strongly suspected Option 2 was the only realistic option, but he'd have to change his attitude quick, show some enthusiasm for the plan, else he'd be frozen out. Maybe worse than frozen out. Vince wasn't sure how far Skidelski would go to keep Operation Deliverance secret, and decided there would probably be no limits.

Shit, it looked like both options could be dangerous. And Lucy would not be exempt from the danger. Did he have the right to put her at risk too? Maybe he ought to just play for time, appear to be the loyal assistant, while looking for ways to wreck the project.

'Vince! I said, is any of it true?'

'There's ... there's some truth in it.'

'Better than most presidential broadcasts, then.'

'Yes.'

Lucy was surprised. She hadn't expected him to agree. 'I wish you'd communicate with me a bit. You've been completely locked inside yourself for weeks now.'

'I know. I'm sorry.'

'Why are you like this?'

'I don't know.'

'Oh, very useful,' said Lucy, getting out of bed. 'I'm going to make coffee.'

Vince wondered what was still keeping them together, apart from sex, a shared concern for big issues, and a lack of time to start looking around for anyone new. Not much, he decided.

In the windowless basement of the CIA headquarters in Langley, Jay Positano was having a very bad New Year. What bastards they were to put him on listening duty over the holiday. He'd been hoping to get to a paintball field and have some fun, instead of sitting here recording some assholes in Annapolis, some boring couple by the sound of it, who seemed to just go around arguing, unless they were fucking, which really upset Jay, because it made him feel dirty. At least they were straight. Jay was also bugging some young sicko called Edward, who seemed to be getting an awful lot of sex with other men, and why the CIA should want recordings of that, Jay couldn't imagine because it was disgusting. Jay didn't read the papers, else it might have occurred to him that this was Edward the son of the President, but that would have made no difference, it would still have been disgusting, and it made Jay want to go out and kill the pervert, or if not that pervert then the first pervert he came across. Or anyone who looked like a pervert.

42

Ritchie's broadcast made an impact, though not quite the impact he'd intended. First there were the protests from all the religious sects who believed vaccination was a mortal sin. Then there was the call from the British Prime Minister ...

'Quite frankly, Ritchie, America can't do this to us.'

'What can't we do to you, James?'

'Leave us in the lurch like this. I mean, if you think you might be attacked with this ghastly new virus, then there's a fair chance that we're going to be attacked too, isn't there? Stands to reason. As your staunchest ally, we're very much in the firing line, wouldn't you say?'

More than you know, thought Ritchie. 'We'll certainly make Britain a priority for the vaccine.'

'Yes, but when?'

'We're fast-tracking the production. We're doing everything we can. I promise you that Britain is our number one priority.'

'Hmmm. Well ...' The PM didn't sound entirely convinced. 'I'd be grateful if you could say something to that effect in public.'

Ritchie said, 'Of course.' He knew he couldn't do anything of the kind, because amidst the deluge of protesting calls, he'd already promised about seven other leaders that their countries were America's number one priority for getting the vaccine.

A grumpy Prime Minister rang off.

The White House attempted damage control by launching a day of press briefings, clarifying the policy on vaccination and assuring the world that America cared. As Anna Prascilowicz told a room packed with the world's press, 'It is the duty of any government to ensure the safety of its own citizens as its first priority. But the United States would like to make it clear that it intends to make the vaccine available on a worldwide scale just as soon as humanly possible.'

43

General Barry B. Steinberger III, Supreme Commander of the United States Air Force and Chairman of the Joint Chiefs of Staff, nodded and said, 'Sounds good to me.'

Skidelski was relieved. You couldn't be absolutely certain how somebody was going to react to the idea of killing six billion people. Even military men had their limits. 'I'm pleased you're on board, General.'

'Me too, sir. World's full of bad people. People who hate America. We been soft with them long enough. Time something was done about it. This world has become a dirty place. It needs cleaning up, no question. Yes, sir, I like it. It's a good plan. Sensible plan, Hard, but sensible. Yes, sir.' The General's megalithic jaw worked rhythmically on the wad of gum that was always in his mouth. He knew a gum-chewing general was a cliché, but he didn't care. He was proud to conform to the popular image of a general. Barrel-chested, blue-eyed, and with huge baseball-mitt hands, he was the living embodiment of what people either loved or hated about the military. By training, he was an airman, capable of piloting the world's most sophisticated warplanes. Heck, only last week those big hands of his had been at the controls of that beautiful babe, the B-2 Stealth bomber, a cool two billion dollars' worth of cutting-edge technology. But at heart he still saw himself as a simple soldier at the service of his country. 'What's our time scale on this operation, sir? Just give me the parameters.'

Now that the difficult bit was over, Skidelski felt able to come out from behind his desk and pace around his spacious office. 'Supplies of Flaxil-4 are no problem. We already have just about enough to do the job. It has to be weaponised, of course, and then your planes will have to be fitted with the spraying equipment, but I understand those are both pretty straightforward procedures. The key determinant is the vaccine. We're approximately twelve months way from having enough to inoculate every American. Assuming three months for a mass vaccination program to be completed, that makes it fifteen months from now. That enough time for you, General?'

'I reckon. Complex operation, though. Lot of detail to be worked out.'

'It's important there aren't any delays.'

'Delay isn't a word we're familiar with in the Air Force, sir.'

'General, I like your attitude.'

'Sir.'

'Pity there aren't more like you.'

'Sir.'

Skidelski stopped pacing, turned to face General Steinberger, and sucked in his thin lips the way he always did when he was wrestling with a problem.

Shit, thought the General, the Secretary of State's mouth just disappeared.

Skidelski's mouth made a sudden comeback. 'How many planes have we got at our disposal, General?'

'The United States Air Force currently has a total of 33,892 warplanes, sir. That total is presently increasing at a rate of fifteen warplanes a week. Given the threat facing our nation from terrorism, I'd like it to be more, sir, but I guess we all have to live in the real world.'

'And how many of those planes would be suitable for the actual spraying operation?'

'Let's put the question the other way round, sir. How many planes are we going to need?'

'Okay. How many planes are we going to need?'

General Steinberger's flicked the gum from one side of his mouth to the other and his chewing rate rose slightly. He didn't know for sure till he did the calculations, but he suspected there were already plenty of planes to do the job. But heck, this was a chance to increase the size of his air force. He saw no hint of personal aggrandisement in this. As the defender of freedom around the globe, America needed every warplane it could get its hands on, simple as that. There was no question of the Land of the Free having too many warplanes. All around the world, America's enemies were lying in wait, ready to strike the moment the mighty giant dropped its guard. True, if Operation Deliverance was successful, America wouldn't *have* any enemies, but years of combat experience told the General that you could never guarantee the success of any operation. You never said that to the politicians, of course, because they needed to believe in the invincibility of the military.

'We're probably going to need more planes than we got, sir.'

Skidelski flinched. His mouth briefly came and went a few times. 'You trying to tell me we can't do it?'

'Can't is not a word I recognise, sir. I will have an assessment of aircraft number needs on your desk within seventy-two hours. If we don't have enough planes – and I'm pretty sure we don't – then I'll need immediate authorisation for a big increase in my budget so we can order more.'

'Can they be built in time?'

'Not if they were new models being developed from scratch, they couldn't, no. But we're talking about existing models. The production lines are already there. They don't need retooling. They just have to up their output. I happen to know that a lot of plants are operating well below capacity. Could be a big economic boost, too. Thousands of new jobs. Yes, all in all a pretty positive prospect, yes, sir.'

'How much money are we talking about here, General?'

'Hard to say right off. Probably not a lot. Maybe ten, twenty billion?'

Skidelski frowned. Congress wouldn't like that. He ran a leathery hand through his thinning hair. 'That much could be difficult.'

General Steinberger leaned back in his chair, put his hands behind his head, and narrowed his eyes. Under the presidency of Ritchie L. Ritchie, the defense budget had almost doubled, really there was nothing to complain about. But the General was a man who knew when he held a winning hand, and right now he held a winning hand.

Skidelski took a deep breath. 'Give me your assessment soon as you can, General, and I'll see what I can do.'

The General rose smartly to his feet. 'Appreciate that, sir. There will be a dossier on your desk within seventy-two hours.'

'Thanks for coming, General.'

'Always a pleasure to be of service to my country, sir. Yes, sir, yes indeed.'

The General walked over and shook Joe Skidelski by the hand. Looking him straight in the eye, he said, 'I consider it an honour to serve under the greatest Secretary of State for Defense that this country has ever known.'

To the surprise of both men, Skidelski's eyes filled with tears. 'Oh. Oh, well, that's very kind of you, General.'

'It's only the truth, sir, yes, sir, only the truth.' He then swallowed to deal with the sudden lump in his own throat, crisply saluted, turned on his heel, and marched towards the door. There he stopped and turned.

'Oh. One other thing, sir.'

'What's that?'

'The bodies.'

'What do you mean, the bodies?'

'I seen them on the battlefield, sir. And smelt them. Dead bodies smell bad, sir. Very bad. Biggest number of dead bodies I ever smelt was around four hundred. Now admittedly, most of them were Arabs, and I don't know, sir, maybe dead Arabs smell worse than other kinds of dead, wouldn't surprise me a bit. But that was one bad smell, sir, yes sir, that battlefield smelled worse than hell on house-cleaning day.'

Skidelski gawped. He hadn't yet given much thought to minor details such as dead bodies. 'You mean … you mean, we ought to bury them, or what?'

'Can't see how it's possible to bury six billion stiffs worldwide, sir. We just ain't got the manpower for that. No, sir, I reckon, the United States of America is going to be smelling pretty damn ripe for a while. Especially along our borders. Think about it, sir. Dead Mexicans to the south of us, dead Canadians to the north of us.'

'I don't really think a bad smell is the worst of our problems, General.'

General Barry B. Steinberger III didn't believe what he was hearing. Surely any decent, civilised man knew that a bad smell was a sign of a morally backward person? He himself showered three times daily, changing his underwear each time. After missions abroad he was in the habit of having all his clothes autoclaved, so as to remove all trace of foreign bacteria. In his office, he had the windows open for at least an hour every day, regardless of the temperature outside. And in his bathroom he insisted on two bottles of bleach by the side of the toilet (one pine fragrance, one lemon fragrance), a selection of at least three air fresheners, and a bowl of dried rose petals on a side table. It was unfortunate that people had to defecate, he wished it wasn't necessary, but at least the foul odours could be dealt with.

When travelling in other countries, General Steinberger noticed that people were not always as meticulous about personal hygiene as they were in America. He'd always found the Middle East particularly malodorous and it came as no surprise to him that this was the region that nurtured international terrorism. Even in the relatively clean surroundings of Europe he'd had some terrible experiences. He still shuddered at the memory of a weekend in Paris. The people next to him in the Opera were so sweaty that the General and his wife had walked out at the interval. He'd had to leave the Louvre after ten minutes for exactly the same reason. What can you expect, he'd told his wife, what can you expect of those cowards who let the Nazis run all over them? And at least the Nazis had kept the place clean. You could say that much for fascism, it gave hygiene its due and proper place.

The General snapped out of his reverie. The Secretary of State was speaking to him.

'I said, will there be anything else, General?'

So that's how it was. Well, okay, if Joe Skidelski wasn't going to square up to the odour problem, then heck, he'd just have to solve the problem on his own. 'No, sir, no further questions, sir. I'll start work on that assessment with immediate effect, sir.'

'Thank you. Goodbye, General.'

'Goodbye, sir.'

As the door closed behind the General, Joe Skidelski made a mental note never to allow Al Boyd into the same room as General Steinberger.

44

As Secretary of State for Health and Human Services, Harriet Knibbs had only twice had face time with the President. Everybody talked about how important her job was, but it didn't feel like that to her. A trim, grey-haired 63-year-old, she did her best to ameliorate the worst effects of the budget cuts she was forced to impose, but it was a thankless task, and she was looking forward to retirement.

She had been summoned to the Oval Office to report on the plans for producing the new vaccine. She didn't know the real reason for having to produce 300 million doses of vaccine in the space of twelve months, but she did know it was a tall order and intended to say as much. A straight talker by nature, she had become more and more direct of late. The loss of political ambition, she reflected, could have a curiously liberating effect.

The door to the Oval Office was opened for her by a steward and she went in. The President was behind his desk and didn't get up.

'Good morning, Mr President,' said Harriet Knibbs crisply.

'Morning,' mumbled the President and waved a hand towards the sofas. He wasn't in the mood for a meeting. He didn't want to be here at all. He wanted to be on his ranch, roping cattle, and riding the range with his red-blooded heterosexual son, except he didn't have a red-blooded heterosexual son and there was something damned weird about the idea of riding the range with a gay son.

Knibbs wasn't surprised to see Vince Lennox sitting there, but hadn't expected to see the Defense Secretary. At least they both had the courtesy to get to their feet and greet her properly.

Skidelski said, 'Okay, Harriet. Vaccine production. Where do we stand?'

Vince glanced up at the President, who had his feet up on the desk and was gazing abstractedly into space.

194

Knibbs decided to ignore the President; after all, he was ignoring her. She opened a slim, well-organised folder. 'You want three hundred million doses of a new vaccine produced and ready for use in twelve months. You want a mass vaccination program launched and completed within another three months. I'm here to tell you it can't be done.'

'Why can't it be done?' said Skidelski.

'Are you familiar with the manufacturing process for an influenza vaccine?'

Skidelski shook his head.

'I thought not.'

Skidelski frowned.

'Let me explain. Flu vaccines are made in factories using embryonic eggs from pathogen-free hens. It's a very laborious process, and in a way, oddly old-fashioned. Each embryonic egg has a sample of the live virus injected into it. The shell is then sealed. The egg is incubated for forty-eight hours at a temperature of 33 to 35 degrees centigrade. This allows the virus to replicate itself. Somebody has to check each egg and—'

'Do we need all this technical stuff?' asked Skidelski.

'Yes,' said Knibbs crisply and went on. 'Somebody has to check each egg by shining a light through it. Eggs with dead embryos are thrown away. Each egg is then opened and the fluid inside harvested. This fluid contains the live virus. It must then go through a long and complex cleaning process to remove impurities before it is deactivated. As far as I understand it – because I'm not a scientist—'

'You could have fooled me,' said Skidelski.

Knibbs gave him the briefest and thinnest of smiles. 'As far as I understand it, this involves some kind of filtering and centrifuge action, which takes time. Only then do you have the beginnings of a vaccine. I'm telling you all this because you need to know this is long and slow and labour-intensive and there's a limit to how much it can be speeded up. Especially since you're insisting that the entire process must take place within the United States.'

'What do you reckon, Vince?' asked Skidelski, realising they weren't likely to get much out of the President. Skidelski was feeling almost warm towards Vince who, after a bad patch around Christmas, now seemed to have re-committed himself to the job. In fact, Vince had apparently become utterly devoted to Operation Deliverance, even volunteering to attend planning meetings where his presence wasn't essential.

Vince was searching desperately for something useful to say about the vaccine. He had to keep being indispensable to Ritchie and Skidelski, that was his plan, that was his only plan, until he could see some way to derail Operation Deliverance. 'Well,' he said finally, 'what precisely are the factors that are likely to cause delays?'

'The eggs. We need at least three hundred million eggs.'

Skidelski looked sceptical. 'It can't be that hard to find three hundred million eggs.'

Knibbs gave him an impatient glance. 'It's not like the eggs you have for breakfast. These have to be pathogen-free eggs. Normally, vaccine manufacturers order them eighteen months in advance, from certified pathogen-free flocks. There's no way the United States can provide three hundred million pathogen-free eggs in twelve months.'

Vince asked, 'Could we import them?'

'Yes, but I was told not to. I was told to insist on using American eggs. I don't know why.'

Knibbs looked over at the President. She couldn't work out whether he was taking this in or not.

Skidelski said, 'I guess we just wanted to ensure the quality of supply.'

This was only partly true. It had been feared that buying up pathogen-free eggs from around the globe, and therefore depriving other countries of the ability to make all kinds of other vaccines, would massively increase hostility to America.

Knibbs gazed at Skidelski over the top of her glasses. 'If you don't import some of the eggs, you won't have your vaccine ready in time.'

'Hell,' said Skidelski thinking nobody would care much about upsetting Europeans, 'so let's buy the goddamn eggs wherever we can get them.'

'Fine,' said Knibbs primly, making a note. 'That makes the task much easier.'

'Eggs,' said Ritchie quietly.

All three turned to look at the President, who was still in the same position as before, and still staring into space. He lowered his gaze. 'Eggs. I'm allergic to eggs. That means I can't have a flu shot. Because the vaccine is made from eggs.'

Vince's spirits suddenly rose. He knew about the eggs allergy, but he hadn't made the connection to the vaccine. If Ritchie couldn't be vaccinated, then Operation Deliverance obviously couldn't go ahead . . .

Ritchie slowly took his feet off the desk and stood up. Still speaking very softly, he said, 'So you're busy figuring how to protect three hundred million ordinary Americans from a deadly virus, while completely forgetting about your President, huh? That's nice. That's very nice. Well, may I suggest you find a way of solving this little problem?' He paused, then brought both hands down on the desk with an almighty thump. 'YOU FUCKING ASSHOLES!'

45

General Barry B. Steinberger III washed off the last of the Buffalo shower gel, and stepped out of the shower unit in the en suite bathroom he'd had specially installed in his office. It was exactly 11.55 am, and this was his second shower of the day. Taking a freshly laundered white towel from the pile, he rubbed himself dry, then sprayed liberal amounts of Buffalo male deodorant all over himself. He then carefully sprinkled some Buffalo talc into his clean underwear before pulling it on.

He'd discovered the Buffalo range of male toiletries some twenty years before, and was an immediate convert. Buffalo had an assertive, masculine quality about it that felt about right for a military man.

Carefully checking his uniform in the mirror, the General pronounced himself satisfied with his appearance. His magnificent barrel chest, his cropped blond hair, his strong jawline all gave him a natural air of authority that he believed was enhanced by his personal freshness.

Whistling a jaunty tune, he returned to his desk, and at precisely 11 am resumed work on the dossier that he'd promised Skidelski. It hadn't taken him long to establish that releasing a virus in aerosol form simultaneously around the globe was achievable. Sure, it would be a vast logistical operation, but in his youth he'd studied the Normandy landings of World War Two in detail, and he was confident that by comparison this operation would be a cakewalk. He had already discovered that the virus could only survive within a certain temperature range. This meant that the spraying altitude would be determined by the air temperature. In addition, predicted wind speeds would have to be taken into account, as would precipitation patterns, cloud formation and a whole pile of other data. All this information was already being collated and fed into a computer model. The General had pulled several of his brightest IT people off other projects and put them on to this instead. They'd been told that the purpose of the simulation was to establish the relative effectiveness of aerial crop spraying in different countries. They all assumed this meant that the Pentagon was developing new weapons to knock out the enemy's food supplies and starve him into submission. They thought this was a cool idea, and set to work with a will. The computer model would come up with its initial results by the end of the day. That gave the General time to deal with another vital matter. He picked up his top-security phone.

Cal Ashton, Chief Executive Officer of Persona Personal Products, manufacturers of the Buffalo range of male toiletries, had just sat down in his shabby office in San Diego and was staring gloomily at his sales returns and biting his nails when his telephone rang. He picked it up and snapped, 'Marina, I thought I told you no calls.' Cal Ashton wasn't about to go into a meeting or anything, he was just feeling too depressed to take calls. He turned to check out his new hairpiece in a mirror on the wall, and felt sure it wasn't at all convincing. He felt aggrieved that at the age of thirty-nine he'd already lost most of his hair. Life was a bitch.

'Yes, I know, sir,' she rasped, the voice that of a heavy smoker, 'but I think you'll want to take this call. It's from a General Steinberger.'

'Do we know General Steinberger?'

'I don't think so, sir, but I get the feeling he's somebody important.'

'Steinberger . . .' The name was familiar.

'He asked to speak to you personally.'

'Oh. Yeah, right. Um, okay. Better put him on.'

'Go ahead please, General.'

The crisp voice of General Steinberger came on the line. 'Steinberger here. Barry B. Steinberger III, Supreme Commander of the United States Air Force and Chairman of the Joint Chiefs of Staff. Your secretary didn't seem to know who I was. My advice is, get rid of her.'

Cal Ashton swallowed hard. 'Good morning, General. How are you?'

'I'm good. Let's cut to the chase. I'm a devoted user of Buffalo male toiletries.'

'I'm delighted to hear it, General.' Ashton's eyes drifted back to the sales chart. The General was unfortunately one of a rapidly shrinking group of people. The Buffalo image just wasn't working any more. The only part of the country where sales of Buffalo products were holding up was southern Texas.

'I have a personal request, Ashley.'

'Ashton. Cal Ashton.'

The General took no notice of the correction. 'This request has to be in the strictest confidence, is that understood?'

Ashton was pretty sure he knew where this was heading. He'd had calls like this before. Minor celebrities and the like, trying to get themselves free supplies. They were mostly a nuisance, but a four-star general wearing Buffalo deodorant, that was different, that could be good publicity.

'I can assure you, General, that this conversation will go no further.' In a little room next door, really more of a cupboard than a room, Marina smiled to herself. When bored she quite often listened in to her boss's phone calls, but this was one turning out more interesting than most.

'Good,' barked the General. 'I'll keep you to that, Ashley, yes, sir, I surely will. Now. Buffalo deodorant. You make it. I want it.'

Cal Ashton wasn't sure what to say. He assumed the General was looking for a gift. 'Suppose we send you a selection pack of our products? That would of course be with our compliments, General.'

'I need a lot.'

'I'm sure we can see our way to doing something kind of special for you. How about we send you a case?'

'I need a whole lot more than a case.'

There was a limit to how much Cal Ashford could give away for free. He wondered how to put that without offending the General. 'If it were a big order, we could maybe offer a discount.'

'How soon can you deliver half a million gallons?'

Cal grabbed at the edge of his desk. 'I . . . I'd have to get back to you on that, General. It's . . . well, you see, well, normally, we sell it in 4 oz or 8 oz bottles.'

'How much of the stuff do you normally produce per year?'

'I'd have to check that out and—'

'And how much can you produce in the next fifteen months?'

'Um, well, I guess I'd probably have to get back to you on that, too.'

'You want this order, you tell me right now.'

'Oh. Right, um . . . just give me a few seconds.'

'Make it quick, Ashley. I have freedom to defend.'

Cal Ashton put down the phone and raced through to his secretary's office. As her boss burst into the room Marina hurriedly put down the extension phone she'd been listening in on. He demanded a copy of last year's annual report to shareholders. Marina handed it to him, looking at his new hairpiece and trying not to giggle. He took the report and ran out. She immediately picked up her phone again. This was getting interesting.

'Hello? General? Are you still there? I'm really sorry to—'

'I'm here. Talk.'

Cal leafed frantically through the annual report till he came to the technical stuff at the back. Shit. It showed the production statistics all right, but in fluid ounces. 'We ... um, last year we produced ... um, in fluid ounces it would amount to ...'

'Fluid ounces mean nothing to me. Talk gallons, Ashley.'

Cal snatched his calculator off a nearby shelf. Fingers dancing over the buttons, he worked out that there would be roughly 20 standard 6 oz bottles to a gallon. So, half a million gallons would be ... Christ, it would be ten million bottles. That was more than twenty times their entire sales for last year. Could they produce that much in fifteen months? Yes, yes, they would have to. This would save the company. Cal could negotiate himself an enormous bonus. Cal would be rich. He could buy himself a better hairpiece. No, to hell with that. He could buy himself a high-quality hair implant.

'Shake it up there, Ashley. I'm a busy man.'

'Five hundred thousand gallons is ten million bottles. We can do that.'

'Forget bottles. I'm talking tankers.'

'Tankers?'

'Tankers, yes sir, tankers. You heard.'

Cal Ashton couldn't begin to figure out why the General needed tankers of deodorant, but that didn't matter. What mattered was clinching the deal. 'Obviously that will be cheaper than buying it by the bottle. I'll work out a price and get back to you.'

'I don't give a damn about the price, Ashley. What matters is, you have those tankers ready to deliver on time. One year and three months from now. Can you do that?'

'Yes, General, I can.'

'Can you guarantee it?'

'Yes, General, I can.'

'Okay. Now listen up, Ashley. You will shortly receive a formal confirmation of this order from the DLA, that's the Defense Logistics Agency. Those are also the people you will invoice. But it will all be in the strictest confidence, do you understand that?'

'Whatever suits you best, General.'

'Any of this leaks, you're finished, Ashley.'

'I can assure you General, that there's no way I would risk the professional damage that—'

'I don't mean finished as in professionally damaged. I mean finished as in dead.'

'Oh.' Cal wasn't sure what was the correct business response to a death threat, but before he could speak, the General had rung off.

For five whole minutes Cal Ashton sat silently at his desk. He'd briefly considered the possibility that the whole call was a hoax, but he'd seen the General on television, and that voice was unmistakable. No, bizarre as it all was, this looked very much like the biggest break he had ever had in his not wholly successful life as a businessman. In his head he kept hearing the General's words, 'I don't give a damn about the price.'

He stood up. It was time to celebrate. He'd go and have lunch in the best restaurant in town. Maybe he'd even order a glass of champagne. What the hell, he'd order a whole bottle. He adjusted his hairpiece in the mirror and walked through to his secretary's room to tell her he would be out at a meeting till at least three o'clock. She nodded, apparently unsurprised. He briefly considered giving her a pay rise, but decided against it.

This was a pity, because if he'd given her a rise, Marina might not have felt resentful, and if she hadn't felt resentful she might not have called her old flame Bob Bloom and given him all the details of her boss's phone call. Her affair with Bob Bloom had been over for years, but somewhere she still felt sorry for him. Poor old Bob, he'd been down on his luck ever since that time years ago when he'd lost his job in Boise at the hands of the guy who was now President. All the booze since than hadn't helped, of course. She didn't know if he had a regular job at the moment; not many editors wanted to hire a small alcoholic loser with a squint and an attitude problem. Probably he was just selling the odd article here and there. Poor bastard. She'd never been able to help him before. Now maybe she could. Maybe it was just one of those silly diary stories, but at least it was a story. She picked up the phone.

*

Back in the Pentagon, General Barry B. Steinberger III calculated exactly how many aircraft he'd need to spray deodorant along a twenty-mile-wide path on each side of the Canadian border. He then did a similar calculation for the Mexican border. It worked out at either 16 B-52s or 38 F-16s. But he was going to need every last one of his B-52s and his F-16s for China and Russia. He checked aircraft availability on the spreadsheets that his smart new assistant Brett had printed off, and saw that he had plenty of A-10 Warthogs to spare. Another quick calculation revealed that he'd need around forty of them. He checked the location on his computer and found there was a wing of Warthogs stationed at Barksdale Air Force base, Louisiana. That was within easy each of the Mexican border. Good. Now he had to find some of them A-10 Warthogs stationed up north. Unfortunately, he couldn't find any stationed close to the Canadian border. Maybe he wasn't looking in the right document. The Air Force kept installing new software, which the General found very confusing. That's why he'd brought in young Brett. Brett was brilliant with computers. He also had high standards of personal hygiene. Yes, Brett would track down the Warthogs for the Canadian end of the operation. Anyhow, the Mexican end was more vital; the General felt sure that dead Mexicans smelled worse than dead Canadians.

46

The Rheinländischer Serumwerk GmbH in Cologne was the only facility in the world capable of producing flu vaccine by means of mammalian tissue cultures. This was still an experimental technology, unsuited to producing vaccine in large quantities. Each dose of vaccine took several days and many thousands of euros to produce. The head of research at the Rheinländischer Serumwerk was confident that the traditional egg-based method of production would soon be superseded by the new process, a confidence not always shared by the board of directors. So far, some 28 million euros had been invested in the process, without any indication of a commercial return. It was therefore a source of some relief when a mysterious client from America made a discreet approach with a view to purchasing a single dose of a new vaccine against a new strain of flu known as Flaxil-4. The client explained that he would provide, in conditions of strict secrecy, a sample of the live virus that the German company would need in order to manufacture this small amount of vaccine. In return for complete confidentiality and direct supervision of security, the client was willing to pay a total of $10 million. The directors of the company were delighted, if a little puzzled, and quickly agreed. Three days later, an American doctor, accompanied by six very large and scary men in dark suits, arrived in Cologne and handed over a small refrigerated box containing a sample of the live virus. They said they'd be back in six months to get the precious dose of vaccine.

In America meanwhile, manufacture of the normal egg-based vaccine had been put in the hands of the vast multinational conglomerate known as Arkan. Arkan's interests ranged from heavy engineering to hairsprays, from newspapers to toothpaste, from oil to education, from fertilisers to banking, from beef to insurance, from waste disposal to dental implants, from baby wipes to construction, from logging to health clubs, from armaments to underwear, from boutique hotels to pharmaceuticals, from garlic sausage to Christmas cake.

For many years, Arkan had been a good friend to Ritchie. And in return, Ritchie had been a good friend to Arkan. The deal was unwritten and mostly unspoken. Without Arkan, Ritchie would not have had the money to buy hundreds of prime-time spots on television during two devastatingly successful election campaigns. Without Ritchie, Arkan would never have been able to dispose of two million gallons of toxic waste in the Gulf of Mexico, build three chemical plants in a bird sanctuary, lay waste to a sizeable part of Alaska, reduce the holiday entitlement of its workforce by four days annually, cheat 80,000 former employees out of their pensions, save 900 million dollars a year on taxes, and get the monopoly on electricity generation for large slabs of the Middle East. In fact, you could argue that Arkan had got a pretty good deal for its money.

Of course, in theory, once elected for a second time, the President had no further need for his corporate friends. In theory he could turn round and screw anyone he felt like screwing. But just as there is said to be honour among thieves, so there is something approaching honour on that wild frontier between politics and big business. Ritchie would no more throw Arkan to the wolves than he would suggest a peace conference with Al Qaeda. The only limit was self-preservation. If Arkan's questionable accounting procedures were to be exposed, or its chief executive revealed in public to be the crook he was, or Arkan's murky sponsorship of political murders in Central America brought to light, Ritchie would distance himself at great speed. That was okay. That was understood.

Just to be sure that such a thing didn't happen too easily, though, Arkan's directors had taken a few precautions. Not long before Ritchie was elected for the first time, a dozen or so key people around Ritchie, the people who seemed most likely to become members of his administration, were taken out for a series of meals in private rooms in some of Washington's finest – and most discreet – hotels and restaurants. There they found themselves being offered incredibly attractive share option schemes. Frequently they would be nudged towards buying shares in certain obscure companies, shortly before Arkan made a takeover bid for these companies. Those who'd been smart enough to take the hint soon found themselves very rich indeed.

All this was a kind of insurance policy for Arkan. It was a comfort to the board of directors to know that when crucial decisions were being reached in the White House, several of the decision-makers were likely to have a personal stake in the well-being of Arkan. That's how, even midway through Ritchie's second term, Arkan found that the tap had not been turned off.

And that's how around eight hundred obscure ordinances regulating the production by private companies of pharmaceuticals were quietly done away with in an Act that hardly anyone even noticed. Well, why should anyone worry about it? Nowadays everyone knew that the market was best left to its own devices; they knew that private capital would always behave fairly and wisely and in the best long-term interests of the citizen.

Among the eight hundred ordinances was one that specified a minimum duration for the filtration and centrifugation processes used in the manufacture of vaccines. Nobody gave the removal of this specification a second thought.

PART ★ FOUR

47

A standing ovation at the General Assembly of the United Nations was a rare event. A standing ovation for the representative of the United States of America was unheard of. Even the most cynical delegates were moved to put their hands together. In a speech of stunning honesty, the American ambassador confessed that the United States had been dragging its feet on the issue of climate change. He agreed that the United States had not been sufficiently internationalist in outlook. He conceded that existing pollution controls were inadequate, and that as the most powerful nation on Earth, the United States had a solemn duty to lead the way on environmental issues. To demonstrate her new-found commitment to saving the planet, the United States of America proposed that a new holiday be proclaimed. To be called International Day of the Planet, this holiday would be a festival of hope for humanity.

Proving that their commitment was more than symbolic, the United States proposed to put at the disposal of the world its entire air force for one whole day, entirely for peaceful purposes. In order to combat the degradation of the atmosphere, the ambassador explained, it was essential to have a global snapshot of the levels of pollution throughout the world, not piecemeal, not a nation here and a nation there, but the entire planet simultaneously. Only the United States had the means to coordinate and carry out such a vast undertaking. For the sake of humanity, for the sake of a better future for all our children, the President of the United States had ordered that the results of this unprecedented global survey would immediately be made available to every nation on Earth, entirely free of charge. It was with pride that the ambassador was able to announce that the Defense Forces of the United States of America were in a position to launch this survey in just four months' time. He therefore proposed that the very first International Day of the Planet should take place on March 20th, the first day of spring, the vernal equinox, a time of 'hope and renewal'. This was, of course, only a time of hope and renewal if you lived in the northern hemisphere; for the rest of mankind it marked the onset of autumn, but then the ambassador had never given very much thought to people living in the southern hemisphere, so why start now?

Normally the United Nations takes ages to make a decision of this kind. This time it was different. Dramatically different. Overwhelmed by the power of the moment, the ambassador of Iran had taken the floor. Everybody waited for him to denounce the American plan as an act of treacherous imperialism. Instead, he welcomed the proposals, and then, in an act of unparalleled emotional power, crossed the vast floor of the General Assembly and embraced the American ambassador. As one, the entire gathering rose to its feet, roaring its approval. It was more like a ball game than an international gathering of diplomats. As the applause finally faded away, the French ambassador walked unbidden to the rostrum. Despite the pleas from the chair to observe the normal protocol, the French ambassador insisted on making an unscheduled speech. Waving one elegant hand high in the air, he said he took back everything nasty he'd ever said about America (which was quite a lot) and proposed that an immediate vote be taken to accept the American proposal and declare next March 20th the very first International Day of the Planet. The proposal was carried *nem con* (North Korea abstained, just on principle).

It was probably the happiest day in the ambassador's life. His speech had sounded sincere because it *was* sincere. Long suspected of harbouring liberal sentiments, he had been carefully excluded from all planning for Operation Deliverance. The poor man really believed that his country was at last facing up to the challenge of environmental degradation. He really believed in the International Day of the Planet. He really believed that the tens of thousands of American warplanes in the skies that day would be measuring levels of air pollution particles. True, he was a little surprised at the suddenness of the President's conversion, but to be picky about details was to look a gift horse in the mouth. That evening, he did an apparently endless tour of the television studios. It ought to have been exhausting, but it wasn't. He was on a high. He talked about America finding itself again. He talked about America being at a crossroads. He talked about America walking down new roads. And then, forgetting that it was the name of a Marxist guerrilla group in Peru, he talked about America walking down a shining path. He was definitely getting carried away.

48

'So isn't there enough vaccine, or what?'

'No, there's enough vaccine, sir. The manufacturing side has gone well. They had to skip a few of the clinical trials, that's all. No, the vaccine supply's no longer the problem. The problem is not enough people taking it.'

'Why's that?'

'People don't believe us any more, sir.'

'Oh?' The President shot Vince a surprised glance as they strode down one of the ground-floor corridors in the White House. 'And why's that?'

Vince considered saying, 'Because we lied to them too often,' but thought better of it. 'I think there have been too many unfounded terrorist alerts.'

'Better than being caught with our pants down.'

'That's right, sir. But we have a problem. Most people don't think there's anything to worry about. They're not scared.'

'Well, maybe we gotta do something to *make* 'em scared.'

'How would we do that, sir?' said Vince.

Ritchie didn't answer. They reached the stairs. Without warning, the President bounded up them two at a time, leaving Vince behind. By the time Vince caught up with him on the third floor of the White House, Ritchie was standing on the landing, smirking at him. 'You're not as fit as you could be, Vincey-boy.'

Vince forced a smile. 'You're right, sir.'

Ritchie led the way down the corridor to the White House gym. He called it the White House gym, but really it was his personal gym, and nobody dared use it without his permission. In a display of mock courtesy, he held the door open for Vince, bowing low and making flowery obeisance with one hand. Embarrassed, Vince walked in. The President followed, chuckling with delight at the sharpness of his wit.

The President's personal trainer, who was a qualified paramedic (just in case the President keeled over during a workout), leapt up from a bench against the far wall. 'Good morning, Mr President.'

'Morning, Karl. I brought young Vince along.'

'Good morning, sir.'

'Hi.' Vince dropped his sports bag down on the bench.

The President grinned at him, then turned to Karl, 190 pounds of perfect body. 'I think it's time Vince met Mr Spunky.'

'Yes, sir!' said Karl with enthusiasm. Mr Spunky was Ritchie's pet name for his new elliptical fitness cross-trainer, a fearsome device somewhere between a treadmill and a cycling machine, with huge footrests and moving handlebars. There were thousands of other elliptical fitness cross-trainers in top-end gyms across America, but none like this one. This one had been designed specially for Ritchie by the makers. Tailored to the President's height and weight, it had all kinds of extra features; Ritchie's favourite was the display that came up showing moving images of himself jogging right around the globe. The faster he worked Mr Spunky, the faster the little figure jogged. With the push of another button he could activate the 'splat' device in chosen countries. Ritchie thought it was neat to watch himself jogging across his least favourite countries in the Middle East, with big 'Splat!' signs exploding out from under his feet.

Vince had worked out with the President a few times, not an experience he relished, but it was considered an honour to be invited to work out with the President, and there was no real prospect of refusing. Since the arrival of the new machine a few weeks before, he'd managed to avoid the invitation to 'meet Mr Spunky'. This time it looked like there was no way out.

They went through to the little changing room where the President kept his gym clothes. Vince closed the door behind him, in case Karl heard anything that he ought not to hear, then hurried to choose a spot on the other side of a thin partition. Vince believed in modesty, but unfortunately the President did not. The real crunch would come later, when Ritchie would expect his guest to share the shower room with him. True, it was a pretty big shower room, but it was still an experience that Vince dreaded. It just didn't seem right to see the President of the United States stark naked.

As he changed into a tracksuit, Vince wondered if the President was going to come back to the issue of 'scaring people'. Probably not. One of Ritchie's techniques was to raise some difficult issue, half-suggest some brutal solution to it, then never mention it again. Normally some keen staffer would pick up the cue and come back a few weeks later with the brutal solution fully thought through, at which point Ritchie would act surprised, as if the idea had been nothing to do with him. Well, Vince had no intention of playing that game.

From the other side of the partition Vince could hear little muted grunts as Ritchie pulled his clothes off.

'Vince?'

'Yes, sir?'

'I'm worried about my burgers.'

Vince tried to figure out some kind of context, and gave up. 'In what way, sir?'

'What I mean is, there will still be burgers, right? You know, AOD.'

AOD was a recently coined White House acronym for After Operation Deliverance.

'I assume there will still be burgers, yes, sir.'

'So cattle can't come down with this virus, right?'

'That's correct, sir. My understanding is that no animals will be infected.'

'That's good. A life without cheeseburgers ain't worth living, right?' Ritchie gave a little chortle.

Vince thought a life without cheeseburgers a very attractive prospect. 'Right,' he said.

'Hey, Vince, I just thought of something. If this Flaxil-4 stuff doesn't kill animals, that means I'll have saved the animal kingdom too, not just humanity, right? All those threatened species, you know, bald eagles and whales and butterflies and shit like that, all saved by me.'

'That's right, sir.'

'Holy shit, that's some achievement, that makes me feel proud.' Ritchie appeared round the end of the partition. He was in a pale blue sweatshirt with long silvery-grey tracksuit bottoms. 'You not ready yet, son?'

'Be right there, sir.' Vince was sitting on a bench, struggling with the laces on his gym shoes. Ever since he was a little kid, he'd had a terrible relationship with shoelaces.

The President tugged at his pants. 'Sorry. My damned jock keeps riding up.' Ritchie wiped the end of his nose with the back of his hand. 'Come on, son, time to meet Mr Spunky.'

Vince was lying flat out on the floor of his office, still aching from his meeting with Mr Spunky, when the phone rang. It was Ritchie, summoning him to the Oval Office. Vince glanced at his watch. It was four in the afternoon. Ritchie didn't normally consult him around that time of day. It must be something urgent. Mind you, thought Vince as he left his office and walked down the blue-carpeted corridor towards the Oval Office, the nearer it got to Operation Deliverance, the jumpier Ritchie was becoming. He was also spending more and more time 'alone with his God' in the presidential study. But Vince had begun to notice the drinking.

As Vince entered the room, Ritchie looked up from behind his desk and barked, 'Canada!'

Vince closed the door behind him and approached the desk.

The President looked angry. 'What the fuck are we going to do about Canada?'

'Nothing, as far as I understand.'

'Mrs Ritchie's getting very upset about Canada.'

Vince gave the President a long, hard look. 'Mrs Ritchie knows about Operation Deliverance?'

'Sure she does. Okay, okay, so I broke the rules. Sorry.' The President threw his hands into the air. 'Presidential privilege.' He suddenly stabbed a finger in Vince's direction. 'Don't you go telling Lucy.'

'I wouldn't dream of it, sir.' Oh God, thought Vince, now that Ritchie had mentioned Lucy he'd feel obliged to ask after her health, then he'd deliver the married life homily.

'How is Lucy, by the way?'

'She's in great form, sir.' Vince reflected that he'd hardly seen her for about a week.

'Good, good, give her my best, Vince, will you?'

'Yes, I will.'

'A good marriage is like a good leather belt, Vince. Treat it right and it'll last you all your life.'

'I agree. About Canada, sir?'

'Yes, well, Mrs Ritchie has a bit of a soft spot for Canadians. I know that's weird, but in many ways, Mrs Ritchie *is* weird, Vince. For example, she thinks homosexuality is not evil. Don't mention that to anyone, Vince, I don't want people sneering at her behind her back. Well, anyhow, she just loves Canada. As a kid, she used to spend her summers staying with an uncle and aunt on some farm in Winnipeg. So she thinks we ought to inoculate all Canadians. I'm against. Well, I think I'm against. I mean, Canada is a pain in the ass, no question. I'd be thrilled to get rid of it. But on the other hand . . . Canadians don't feel completely foreign, not 100 per cent foreign. It's not the same as getting rid of, say, Pakistan, is it? Or even Mexico. I mean, Mexico's pretty damn close too, but they're definitely foreign. It feels okay to get rid of them. Well most of them. Seeing how we're going to inoculate about a couple of million wetbacks. Which I think is fucking nice of us.'

'We could maybe arrange to have the uncle and aunt vaccinated.'

'Oh, they're long dead, Vince.'

'Well, sir, I think it wouldn't be a bad idea to consider letting Canada have the vaccine.'

'Yeah, that's what I was thinking. Do we have enough?'

'I'd have to check that out, sir.'

'Yeah, right. No way do we want to delay just for the sake of ten million moose-hunters.'

'The population's actually thirty-two million, sir.'

'You're kidding. Who'd have thought there were that many?'

'It would make things a lot easier, sir. A lot of Americans are married to Canadians, a lot of them have close work colleagues there. It would have a lot going for it.' Vince suspected that by trying to save one nation he was merely salving his conscience.

'Right. On the other hand, when other countries find out we're dishing out vaccine to the Canucks, well, that's really going to get them mad. Like the Brits. The Brits'll go crazy. They think they got a special relationship with us.' The President mused for a few moments, then reached out for a sheet of paper. 'Tell you what, let's do for and against.'

Using a marker pen, Ritchie wrote 'ELLIMINATING CANADA' in big black letters across the top and drew a line under it. The President was getting careless. Vince didn't think it was a very good idea to put stuff like that on paper. Especially headed paper. Especially with 'eliminating' misspelt like that. Anyone who saw it would know it had been written by Ritchie. A few weeks before, Ritchie had been caught on camera writing 'Elliminating Waste' on a blackboard during a school visit. The press had had a field day. Vince watched as Ritchie drew a vertical line down the middle of the page. On one side he wrote FOR and on the other, AGAINST. 'Okay. For: One: No more Canadians.' Ritchie chuckled. 'I kinda like that.' He held up the paper for Vince to see. Vince managed a faint smile.

Ritchie ploughed on. 'Against: Mrs Ritchie won't like it.' He wrote that down. 'Okay, let's do another FOR. For: We get all their space.'

Vince chipped in. 'Against. A lot of our people are married to Canadians.'

'Okay, okay, let me write that down . . . got it.'

The phone rang. Ritchie scrutinised the computer screen that told him who the call was from. 'Sorry, Vince, I got to take this.'

'No problem, sir. Do you want me to . . . ?' Vince rose from his chair.

Ritchie waved him back down into his seat. 'Hi, Edward,' he said into the phone. 'How're you doin' son?'

Vince wished he were somewhere else. Ritchie was trying so hard to be nice to his son that it was painful.

'Great . . .' The President's face lit up. 'That's great news, son. Your mother will be very happy . . . No, no, I'll be happy too, I promise you . . . Yeah, that's terrific. I'll take a long weekend off.' Ritchie covered the mouthpiece and beamed at Vince. 'Edward's coming to the ranch next weekend after all.'

'That's good news, sir.'

'You bet it is.' Ritchie turned back to the phone. 'What time you expect to arrive? . . . That's great. Maybe we can go riding together. It's a long time since we went riding together . . . Excuse me? . . . Well . . . I don't know, son . . .' Ritchie's face clouded. 'What . . . what *kind* of friend, son? . . . No, sure, sure, that's right, I always said you could bring friends, but that was before I knew you were – um, anyhow, that was a while back . . . What's that, son? . . . Well, I'm sorry, I think I have a right to ask that question . . .' Now the President's face was turning red. 'What? . . . Because I have a responsibility to protect your mother, that's why. All I'm asking is whether your friend is . . . like, well, like you . . . What's that? . . . He'd got the same colour eyes? I expect you think that's funny, do you? Well come to think of it, son, if you're noticing the colour of another man's eyes, that's really pretty damn worrying.' The President dropped his voice. 'Just come on your own, Edward. Please. Please. For the sake of your mother.' There was obviously a silence at the other end.

Then Edward must have asked why he couldn't bring a friend. 'Why?!' roared the President. 'Why?! I'll tell you why, son. Because I'm not having some fag you picked up in a restroom somewhere cornholing my own son under my own roof!' Ritchie slammed down the phone. He was gasping for breath.

Vince remained silent.

Ritchie stood up. He grabbed the 'Elliminating Canada' document, crumpled it up and threw it into the waste-basket. 'I'll see you later, Vince.' The President got up and half-walked, half-ran to the door. He turned to Vince. 'Sorry. I just got to be alone with my God.'

After Ritchie had left, Vince stood up. It wasn't considered acceptable for anyone to be alone in the Oval Office in the absence of the President. He was about to leave when he thought about the sheet of paper lying in the waste-basket. He took it out and put it in his pocket. Was this the proof he needed?

49

Vince and Lucy were having sex. The clothes scattered across the bedroom floor were proof that passion had not entirely disappeared from their lives.

Vince lay back and enjoyed the sensation of Lucy's mouth on him. But he wanted to do something for her. Lifting her head gently from him, he kissed her. Then he licked his way down the side of her neck to her breasts. Her nipples sprang obediently to attention. She made little moaning noises as he tongued them. Finally he gestured to her to turn over.

She turned and lay on her stomach, her head just over the side of the bed, her ass invitingly pert. Vince kneeled above her for a moment and caressed her with his fingers. She was as ready as he was. He slowly entered her from behind. He knew she liked it this way. He paused for a moment, now all the way inside her. He began to move. His strokes gradually grew firmer and faster. Lucy found herself staring at the carpet, about a foot away from where Vince's pants lay in a crumpled heap. On the carpet beside his pants was a sheet of white paper, half unfolded. She wasn't particularly interested in it. She loved being fucked this way, especially when it got a little rough. Vince was driving fiercely into her now. With each stroke, the bold lettering across the top of the sheet of paper seemed to go in and out of focus. Vince was making his grunting noises. This was the moment she would normally lose all control, but this time something else was fighting for her attention.

'Oh, God . . .' shouted Vince.

'ELLIMINATING CANADA' shouted the piece of paper.

Lucy reached out a hand and unfolded it.

What the hell was she doing?

Lucy saw two columns, headed FOR and AGAINST.

'Oh yes, YES!' Vince roared.

'Bloody hell!' Lucy muttered.

Vince came, collapsing over her back. He was vaguely aware that Lucy was holding something in her hand. It looked like paper.

'Luce? You all right? What are you doing?'

'Reading this.'

Reading? Reading what? The words on the paper swam into focus. He stared at them for quite a long time. 'Oh shit,' he said.

50

'It's a *game?*'

'That's right.' Vince realised it didn't sound too convincing.

'Let me get this straight.' Lucy was sitting at the kitchen table in her dressing gown. In one hand she held the sheet of paper, in the other a large glass of white wine. 'You and the President of the United States sit alone in the Oval Office and play a game called *Elimination?* Is that right?'

Vince was pacing moodily around the kitchen in a pair of boxers, beer bottle in his hand. 'Yup. That's right. Now can I have that sheet of paper back, please?'

'So how does this game work, exactly? I mean, what are the rules?'

'Um, one of us has to come up with all the arguments for. Then he folds the paper over – you can see it was folded – and the other one has to come up with all the arguments against. And then each has to guess what the other wrote.'

'So how come it's all in Ritchie's handwriting?'

Shit, thought Vince. He threw his empty bottle into the trashcan and opened another beer. 'It was a kind of dummy run. Ritchie was trying it out. We were just fooling around, that's all. It wasn't really a game.'

'Oh, so it's *not* a game. I'm sorry, I thought it was a game.'

'Just give me the paper, will you Lucy?'

'I'm glad it's not a game. Because it would be a very sick game, wouldn't it?'

Sicker than you know, thought Vince. 'Lucy, I think it's crazy to let this spoil things. We were having a great evening. Let's just forget the piece of paper, will you? Give it to me and I'll burn it right now. Then we can get dressed and go out to eat some place.'

'You know something, Vince? I hate your job.'

'I hate it myself sometimes.'

Lucy gave him a look of contempt. 'No, you don't. Not deep down. Deep down you love it. Because you love being close to power. It gives you a hard-on, Vince. More often than I do.'

'I'm sorry, I think I just gave you a lot of pleasure.'

'I didn't realise it was an act of selfless giving.'

'You know what I mean.'

'Okay, yes, Actually I do know what you mean. And yes, you did give me a lot of pleasure. But I think what really turns you on is lying at the feet of Ritchie L. Ritchie with your tongue hanging out. Do you lick his shoes clean, Vince? Or is it something more intimate than that?'

'I can make a difference. There are still things worth fighting for. Like I said, I can make a difference.'

'That's complete bollocks, Vince, and you know it.'

Vince normally laughed when he heard that word *bollocks*. Somehow it was so quintessentially English. But he didn't laugh this time. 'I'm fed up being sneered at, Lucy. What's so great about your job? What are you doing to make society a better place? Oh, and where's that sheet of paper?'

'Not telling you.'

51

'So, how many people have taken the vaccine so far?'

'Around 48% of the population, said Harriet Knibbs.

'What?! That's no good at all!' shouted the Defense Secretary. 'Listen people, we're 120 days away from Operation Deliverance and half of America hasn't been vaccinated. This is bad. This is very, very bad!' Skidelski paced around behind a sofa in the Oval Office, furiously excavating wax from his ear.

Vince took advantage of the silence. 'Mr Secretary. I think we should wait for the President before having this discussion.'

'So go get him,' said Skidelski with casual rudeness. When Ritchie wasn't around he didn't see the need to be polite to Vince.

'I can't do that,' said Vince.

Dolores Delgado said, 'Why not?'

'Because the President is alone with his God,' Skidelski said, with a sneer. A frisson of suppressed laughter ran around the room. 'The President is alone with his God' was rapidly becoming the standard White House euphemism for 'The President is locked in his study drinking bourbon.'

The number of people in on Operation Deliverance had grown. Skidelski kept on telling everyone that access to the plan should be strictly on a need-to-know basis, but the problem with a need-to-know basis is that sometimes an awful lot of people need to know. Vince looked around the room and counted twelve people present, some of them new, some of them members of the original inner group. There was Jimmy Lombok, the President's born-again National Security Adviser, looking supremely calm and unruffled, his vast bald cranium completely free of the usual sheen of sweat. It was easy for him. He believed in the Rapture, that curiously literal version of the Day of Judgement, when all non-believers will be toast and all believers hoovered up to Heaven.

For him, Operation Deliverance was merely a prelude to the main event, and therefore nothing to get excited about. There was Secretary of Defense Skidelski of course, and his faithful recruit, General Barry B. Steinberger III, who was keeping a wary eye on Al Boyd.

It was clear that Boyd had finally been persuaded to buy a decent suit, but he still looked grubby, and General Steinberger was planning on keeping his distance. Vince actually wondered whether Boyd had put on weight and decided he probably had, hard as that was to believe.

Something odd had happened to Dolores Delgado: she looked happy. Had her personal life picked up or was she just getting off on the prospect of killing a lot of people? Over by the window stood Vice President Murdo Robertson. He was quietly whistling some obscure Scottish jig whilst jingling the loose change in his pockets. On a sofa, two men in their late forties sat side by side. One was Ed Garoufalas, Director of the CIA, the other was Hickie Langshite, Director of the FBI. It struck Vince that Garoufalas and Langshite were remarkably similar, almost like twins. It was more than just their closeness in age; both were lean and tanned and had swept-back hair greying at the temples, both were wearing virtually the same discreet dark suits. They could have been television anchormen. Vince had noticed that the FBI and the CIA were full of men like that. Maybe it was something to do with being conformist; maybe doing secretive work meant you had to blend in and not be noticed.

Garoufalas and Langshite might be like twins, but they hated each other. The FBI and the CIA had a history of mutual enmity, which had grown dramatically in virulence over the previous few years. Although in theory the FBI was responsible for security at home and the CIA for operations abroad, the old divisions had partly dissolved as a result of the war against terrorism, sharpening the sense of competition and the struggle for power. Add to that the National Security Agency, the office of Homeland Security and Delgado's recently created post of Homeland Futures, and the possibilities for rivalry and confusion were endless.

Standing behind one of the straight-backed chairs, with a silver-coloured notepad in her hand, was media chief Anna Prascilowicz. She'd only been brought into the plot about a week before. Vince had been there when she was told, and had been amazed at the casual way she'd reacted. She'd nodded, made notes, and asked a few intelligent questions in a matter-of-fact voice. She might have been planning the press launch of a minor policy initiative. Primly perched nearby was Health Secretary Harriet Knibbs. The decision to bring her in on the secret had surprised Vince, because he thought she might raise objections to Operation Deliverance. But, like everyone else in the room, she seemed to find it easy to think the unthinkable.

Vince couldn't decide whether power had corrupted them, or whether they actually all bought into the key argument used to justify Operation Deliverance. At times Vince himself was half convinced. There was, after all, a horrible simplicity about it: we're running out of planet, we've passed the point of no return, what we're about to do is ghastly but the long-term alternative is the extinction of the human race. And long-term didn't seem to be that long any more; only the other day a respected scientist had predicted that by the end of the century only the Arctic would be able to sustain human life. Vince shook his head. He didn't want to be drawn in and seduced by the argument. He cast a glance of contempt at Larry Dodge, sprawled loose-limbed and horribly at ease on one of the sofas, a smug expression on his face. Anna Prascilowicz had persuaded Ritchie they needed Larry on board. Vince sometimes thought Anna had the hots for Larry. Good luck to her if she did. Vince noted with satisfaction that Larry had the same festering zit on the side of his nose that he'd had since Vince first knew him.

General Steinberger had also noticed the zit and was considering whether to give the young man some advice on matters of personal hygiene when the door of the Oval Office opened and the President entered. With the focused determination of a man who doesn't want to reveal that he's had a drink, Ritchie walked over to his desk and sat down. Behind him came Rascal. Anyone who'd been seated had jumped to their feet for the President's entrance. Now Ritchie waved them back down. 'Relax, people. It's only Ritchie.' He chuckled.

At least three shots of bourbon, thought Vince.

To everyone's relief, Rascal was tired, and immediately settled down to sleep under the President's desk.

'Okay guys, what's to decide?' said Ritchie.

Skidelski seized centre stage. 'Mr President. The numbers vaccinated are still very poor. Forty-eight per cent, right, Harriet?'

'That's correct. But we do have a new initiative planned.'

'Which is?' asked Skidelski rudely.

'A massive billboard campaign featuring Cheech Lingaard. He's been very popular ever since the Great Californian Fire. We've costed it out and it won't be cheap, but—'

'Cost doesn't matter,' said the President.

'. . . And we can launch it within days.'

'That's great, Harriet. Do it.'

'Thank you, Mr President.'

Skidelski tugged at his scrawny neck, as if his neck were to blame for the unpopularity of the vaccine. 'Okay, okay, let's do the billboard campaign, no problem. But that's not enough on its own. We can't rely on that. People aren't scared. I think maybe we got to scare them some more.'

Vince remembered the conversation with Ritchie on the way to the gym. It looked like the same provocative thought had been dragged casually past Skidelski's hideous nose. Skidelski would of course have figured out a way of scaring people.

The Vice President was frowning. 'Why do we want to scare them?'

'Oh for Christ's sake, Murdo, why do you think?!' said Skidelski.

Jimmy Lombok raised a hand, for all the world like a kid in school. 'Can we have this discussion without anyone blaspheming? Please?'

'I agree,' said the President.

Skidelski didn't bother to hide his irritation. Dismissively he waved his spotted hand in the air. 'Okay, okay, no blaspheming. The fact is, Mr President, we have a problem.'

The VP said, 'I heard the percentage is increasing all the time.'

'Yeah,' said Skidelski, 'but not fast enough. I believe there is a solution, though.' He looked significantly in the direction of the CIA, but the FBI guy got in first.

'Let's just look at what people have been told,' said Hickie Langshite. 'They've been told that there's the threat of an attack on America by terrorists armed with a terrifying new biological weapon. They've been told that thanks to the vigilance of our security services, we know the exact nature of this weapon, and we have been able to develop a vaccine against it. This vaccine is now available to all Americans. We have told them the threat of this specific kind of bio-attack is credible and serious. We have put whole-page advertisements into the newspapers. We have taken hundreds of advertising spots on national television. We have allocated 2.4 billion dollars to health agencies at the state and county level for them to conduct their own publicity campaigns. We have upped our state of terrorist alert from yellow to orange. On selected days we've even gone to red. And what's the result of this campaign, unprecedented in its size and its efficiency? Less than half the nation comes forward.'

'Why?' said Ritchie.

'Because they think we're a bunch of lying bastards, Mr President,' the FBI man replied.

Skidelski picked up the thread. 'There have been so many terrorist alerts that people don't take them seriously any more. They're not scared. They think we're bullshitting. You've been doing some work on this at The American Way, right, Al?'

Al Boyd nodded, each nod rippled downwards through his chins.

Jeez, thought General Steinberger, that man is so gross. No way should that man be given the vaccine.

Boyd said, 'We found a widespread belief that terrorist alerts are being used for political purposes. Earlier today I spoke about this with our media unit at The American Way. They're having trouble getting the right people on to radio and TV shows. There's resistance out there, a new scepticism about the motives of government.'

'That's so depressing,' said Jimmy Lombok, shaking his head.

'In other words,' said Skidelski, 'they ain't scared. So let's ask ourselves, what would scare 'em? I'll tell you what'd scare 'em. Another terrorist attack.'

Ed Garoufalas nodded.

'I think we can be pretty sure that a major terrorist attack will take place in the near future,' Garoufalas said, hoping he was spelling it out clearly enough.

'Good,' said Delgado.

'Leave it to us.' Garoufalas leaned back in the sofa.

Harriet Knibbs gave the CIA chief a beady look. 'Why don't we wait till we see what impact the Lingaard campaign has?'

'We can't risk that,' said Garoufalas. 'The timetable's too tight.'

The Vice President jingled the loose change in his pocket and said, 'Could it be abroad?'

'Why would we want it to be abroad?' Skidelski asked. His head was on one side as he used his pinkie to dig a little ball of wax out of his other ear.

'Well, let's say there was a warning of an attack in some other country, say Britain. And the Brits do almost nothing about it, which could be more or less guaranteed, because the Brits basically never do anything right, then a lot of Brits would die, instead of a lot of Americans, but it would have the same effect here, you know, to scare people.'

Boyd sniffed. 'That won't work. Nobody in America cares what happens to a bunch of Brits. Sorry, guys, this terrorist incident is going to have to be done properly. And that means doing it in America.'

'That's right,' said Skidelski, checking out the results of his aural excavation. 'It's going to have to be in America. And it's going to have to be high-impact. In other words, people are going to have to die. Possibly in considerable numbers.'

A gleam had come into Boyd's eye. He shifted on his feet.

Oh no, thought Skidelski, as he realised Al Boyd was getting excited.

Boyd was now bouncing up and down on the balls of his feet. 'Yeah, that's right. People are going to have to die. A lot of people are going to have to die.' With that, Al Boyd farted. He farted with a volume and a duration and a fricative sonority that could only be generated by a man weighing 260 pounds.

'Jesus Christ!' said General Barry B. Steinberger III.

'General! Please! I said no blaspheming!' Jimmy Lombok's face was red with indignation. At that point, the odour of corruption reached him. 'Oh, God almighty,' he muttered, and sat down on the nearest chair.

'Sorry guys,' said Boyd, wondering why everyone was making such a big deal out of it. It wasn't as if he'd meant it, was it?

General Steinberger turned to the President. 'Permission to open a window, sir!'

'Denied,' snapped Skidelski, who feared the whole meeting was losing the thread.

Steinberger said, 'Basic standards of propriety and personal hygiene are not being observed by certain people present. And I mean you, Mr Boyd. Yes, sir, it is time you paid attention to your person, sir, yes, sir, yes, indeed.'

'Fuck you,' said Boyd.

Skidelski blanched. 'That's enough, Al! Apologise to the General. Now!'

Boyd muttered, 'Sorry,' and shifted uneasily on his feet. General Steinberger pointedly crossed the room so as to be further away from him.

'Okay,' said the President. His eyelids felt heavy. He'd had big swigs of bourbon and was longing for an afternoon nap. 'I'm happy to stop at this point and leave the CIA to work out the details. So, if there are no further contributions ...'

Vince stepped forward. 'Sir, I have an alternative proposal.'

Ritchie's mouth turned down. He didn't need this. 'I'm okay with the proposal we got, Vince.'

In terms of White House protocol, this was equivalent to the President saying, 'Shut your mouth', so the whole room became suddenly tense as Vince continued. 'Sir, I think you should at least hear this other proposal.'

Skidelski was pulling in his thin lips in a fury of disapproval. His mouth was no longer visible.

Ed Garoufalas was sitting forward in the sofa again, staring with open malevolence at Vince. Who did that smart-ass punk think he was? 'We already got a proposal, son. And it's been accepted.'

Vince was angry now. 'Oh, I see. Leaving it to you is the same as accepting a proposal, is it?'

'Don't talk to me like that, Mr Lennox.' Garoufalas suddenly sounded like a Mafia hit man.

Vince appealed to Ritchie. 'Sir, let's just realise what it is we're agreeing to here.'

Skidelski's mouth returned. 'The President wants to close the meeting, Vince.'

Everybody in the room turned to look at the President. His eyelids were drooping. He opened his mouth to speak.

Vince got in first. 'We're agreeing to a plan which will involve the deaths of many Americans.'

'For the greater good of America,' said Skidelski.

'Yeah, okay, but what if there was a way of getting the same result without anyone dying?' As he spoke, Vince realised that he was merely postponing his own moment of truth. Saving a few hundred or a few thousand Americans didn't weigh much in the moral scales against the destruction of most of the human race. Still. 'I believe there is an alternative, sir. And I believe it's better.'

Ed Garoufalas said, 'But we don't want to hear it, pal.'

Harriet Knibbs leaned forward on her chair. 'Why not? Where's the harm in hearing a proposal that would avoid the loss of American lives?'

'Because it's a dumb plan,' said Garoufalas.

Knibbs looked at him severely over the top of her eyeglasses, and in a steely voice said, 'And how would you know that, Mr Garoufalas, since you haven't even heard what it is yet?'

'I don't need to hear it, I just know, okay?'

'Oh,' said Knibbs. 'Does running the CIA give you powers of telepathy?'

Garoufalas gave her a look of unalloyed hatred.

The President raised a hand. 'Hold it. Hold it right there.' He turned to Vince and looked at him through sleepy eyes. 'Let's hear the alternative.'

Vince said, 'You haven't had your shot yet, have you, sir?'

'No, that's right. I haven't. I believe it was flown in from Germany a few days back. Is that right?'

'That's right, Mr President,' said Vice President Robertson. 'It's in refrigerated storage in a secure facility, with an armed guard 24/7.'

'So,' continued Vince, 'you get your shot, live on television. That would have a massive impact, sir.' Vince thought he saw a glimmer of interest. 'I mean, obviously we don't mention that it's slightly different from everyone else's shot, because the principle's the same, right? I mean, sir, you are the role model for millions of Americans. If they see you doing it, sir, I promise you, the very next day, they'll be lining up round the block for their vaccinations. And not a single American will have died.'

A furious Defense Secretary stepped forward. 'Mr President, this is crazy, we—'

But the President had raised a hand to stop him. Ritchie didn't much care which plan they went for, he just needed to get that nap in, and soon. Vince's plan seemed simpler and more wholesome. He liked the idea that he was the role model for millions of Americans. And it seemed kinda sick to set about killing fellow Americans, even if it was for a higher cause. He stood up. 'We go with Vince's plan,.. If it doesn't work, we go for the other plan.'

There was an audible gasp of fury from Skidelski. 'We'll be losing time, sir!'

Ritchie ignored him. As he made for the door, he pointed at Prascilowicz. 'Anna. Get in touch with the networks. Set up a date.' He clicked his fingers and said, 'Come on, Rascal!' The presidential spaniel leapt up, barked, and followed his master out of the Oval Office.

The President gone, Vince found both Skidelski and Garoufalas staring malevolently at him.

52

Two hundred miles south of San Francisco, on the outskirts of the small town of Parlier, lived Maria Melissa Menendez. In better times, Maria had made an almost comfortable living as a maid to the famous actor Cheech Lingaard, but after his Malibu house burned down, she'd heard nothing more from him. She'd written twice, asked him to pay the two weeks' wages he owed her, but he hadn't replied. Unable to find work in the area, Maria had taken her three young kids and gone to live with an aged aunt in Parlier. She'd regretted the decision almost immediately. Parlier, with an unemployment rate of 35 per cent, was one of the poorest places in America, and the end station for Hispanic families abandoned by the American dream. Half of the businesses in town were closed and boarded up, and the only patches of green to be seen anywhere were the sad attempts at lawns around the cinder-block housing projects. Each day, Maria would get up at 5.30 am, wash in the grim little kitchen (there was no proper bathroom) and take the bus to Fresno, where she worked in a fast-food restaurant for a cash-in-hand wage fifty cents below the hourly national minimum. Each day she would come home to three needy children and a complaining aunt.

One evening, Maria returned to find a giant billboard erected on the site of the failed auto parts shop opposite. The following evening, she came home to find the handsome face of Cheech Lingaard staring down at her. NOW AMERICA'S CALLING THE SHOTS! screamed the slogan. Beneath it, a tough, tanned, heroic Cheech Lingaard was portrayed, with one sleeve rolled up as he prepared to get his shot of vaccine. Beside him was a very cute nurse poised with a hypodermic.

Following his heroic behaviour in the Great Californian Fire, the Hollywood actor's fame and popularity had grown and grown, until he'd become an icon of American manhood. Cheech Lingaard, being a patriot, had agreed immediately to the request for help from the

Department of Health and Human Services, pausing only to get his agent to up the fee from $5m to $7m. He wasn't entirely surprised to have been asked. He still saw himself as a friend of the President, even though the friendship had cooled a little when young Eddie quit Harvard and moved to LA to take up film studies, a career move which Ritchie suspected had been influenced by Cheech. Still, if Cheech Lingaard was able to assist in the enormous task of persuading every American to get vaccinated, then Ritchie wasn't going to hold that against him. Ritchie knew his priorities. To cement the friendship, he had invited Cheech to launch Faith Opportunities Week at a ceremony on the South Lawn.

Maria stood in front of the billboard for quite some time, just staring up at Lingaard. She'd not yet had time to get herself or her children or her aunt vaccinated, and wondered whether it really was necessary. But there was another thing on Maria's mind. Somewhere, in a plastic suitcase behind a ragged curtain in her aunt's house, was a DVD that she'd almost forgotten about. She detested the idea of making money out of somebody else's private degradation, but the instincts of a survivor had made her hang on to the disk, just in case the day came when her children's needs would be greater than her sense of honour.

As she wearily prepared yet another bean stew for her children that evening, Maria decided that maybe the day had come.

53

'Well, fuck you!' said the President of the United States to the Prime Minister of Canada and slammed the phone down. He turned to Vince. 'Asshole says somebody sent him a piece of White House paper headed *Elliminating Canada* ... Says it must be mine because eliminating is spelt wrong.'

Vince felt his stomach turn over. Oh, God. Now he understood. Lucy must have mailed the sheet of paper to the Canadian PM ... Oh, shit ...

Then Ritchie remembered. 'Hey, didn't I write out a sheet of paper with something like that on it?'

'Not that I recall, sir,' lied Vince.

Ritchie shrugged. 'Hell, who cares? We don't need anyone any more. Fuck Canada. That's it. No way are we going to make an exception for those bastards.' He checked the computer screen on his desk. 'I got Harriet Knibbs coming to see me in a couple of minutes. She claims it's urgent. Any idea what she wants?'

'Afraid not, sir,' said Vince. 'I'll get back to my office.'

'No. Stay here.' There was an urgency about the President's tone.

'As you wish, sir.'

Ritchie eyed Vince. 'So. The big vaccination moment is tomorrow, right?'

'Yes, sir. It's scheduled for 8 pm, sir. The networks have cleared their schedules.'

The President pulled a face. 'Maybe it ought to be a pre-record.'

'Won't have the same impact, sir.'

'This vaccine from Germany. It is one hundred per cent safe, right?'

'Absolutely, sir. In fact, I'm informed that the tissue culture method is even more reliable than the one we use in the States.'

'You make sure there's no mix-up, okay? If I get injected with eggs I could be a goner. It will be Dr Briggs, won't it?'

'No, sir. For security reasons, we don't want your regular doctor to appear on television.'

'Okay, well you get me a top doctor, okay? I don't want some asshole stabbing around in my arm, OK?'

'Don't worry, sir. You'll have the best possible care.'

'Good.'

There came a knock at the door and a steward ushered in the Secretary of State for Health and Human Services. This time Ritchie was gracious with her. He came round the desk and took her warmly by the hand. 'Harriet. Great to see you. Let's make ourselves comfortable.' He indicated the two sofas.

Knibbs looked at Vince. 'I'd like this to be a private meeting.'

Ritchie quickly said, 'I have no secrets from Vince.'

Knibbs hesitated, then sat down. Ritchie sat beside her. Vince sat opposite.

'What's on your mind, Harriet?' asked the President.

Again, she hesitated, then finally spoke. 'I think we should stop Operation Deliverance.'

'Why?' asked Ritchie, apparently full of concern.

'Because it's horrible? Because it's wrong? Because no good can come of it?' Harriet Knibbs was suddenly close to tears.

'Ah.' Ritchie looked over to Vince as if to say, 'She's gone insane.'

Knibbs clenched her fists. 'I was with my two grandchildren yesterday, and I looked at them and I thought, well, I thought, I don't want you to grow up in a world where your parents and grandparents have the blood of millions and millions of people on their hands.'

Ritchie gently stroked the back of her hand. 'Harriet. That's exactly why we're doing it. For your grandchildren. Because if we don't take action now, there will be no world for them to grow up in. What we're doing seems brutal, but it's right, it's the right thing to do, and in your heart of hearts I think you know that.'

Harriet Knibbs pushed him violently in the chest. 'Don't you tell me what I know in my heart of hearts. How dare you!' She got up and walked towards the door. 'I will have nothing more to do with this . . . this mass murder. This . . . this second Holocaust. And I'm going to make sure it's stopped.' She walked to the door, threw it open, and left.

'Look after her, Vince.'

Vince leapt up and followed her.

Ritchie waited until a steward had closed the door, then went over to his desk and picked up a phone. 'Get me Ed Garoufalas. Quick.'

54

Vince persuaded Harriet Knibbs to leave her car at the White House. He then drove her the ten or twelve miles to her son's home in Rockville. She'd promised to baby-sit her two grandchildren that evening while her son and daughter-in-law went to the movies; she didn't want to let them down.

She noticed that Vince kept checking the rear-view mirror. 'Do you think we're being followed?'

'No, but I'm glad you're not at home tonight.'

'Why?'

'It's just not a good time to be on your own.'

'Why?'

'I think you ought to go away for a couple of days.'

'Are you trying to say I'm in danger?'

'I'm saying you need to be careful. I'm saying you need to think things through.'

In the driveway, he cut the engine.

She gave him a long hard look. 'Vince. You need to decide what side you're on.'

Vince didn't return her look. 'Want me to come in?'

'No,' she said. 'No. Thank you. I'll be fine.'

'Take care,' said Vince.

55

Unable to face going back to the White House, Vince had driven straight home from Rockville. At last together at home with a couple of hours to relax, he and Lucy were sitting watching some dumb-ass game show, a bottle of wine open in front of them, when the news flash came through. The Secretary of State for Health had been slain by an unknown gunman while looking after her grandchildren. Both of the children had also been shot dead. Police were working on the assumption that the children had been killed because they would have been witnesses to the slaying of their grandmother.

That evening, Vince told Lucy everything. For over two hours she sat and listened in silence.

Then she asked a lot of questions. And he answered them. And they discussed everything calmly and rationally.

Then she said, 'You should have told me sooner.'

And he said, 'You should have told me about the book you're writing.'

And then they argued for most of the night.

56

Deep in the windowless basement of the CIA headquarters in Langley, Virginia, sat Jay Positano, half-listening to a conversation he was bugging, while at the same time leafing through the gay magazine he had found on a bus. Nobody had been looking, so he'd taken it. He needed to see for himself just how disgusting it was. It was the first time he'd seen pictures of two men having sex together – well, apart from that time in New York when he'd gone into a multi-screen porn cinema off Times Square and found himself by mistake in the gay cinema. A guy standing in the shadows had tried to touch him and Jay had punched him in the stomach and run out of the cinema.

Turning the pages, Jay discovered a special feature on Edward, the President's gay son, who was due to appear at some book-signing event in Washington DC the following day.

As Jay read, he became aware that the conversation he was recording was pretty dramatic. Some guy was telling his wife or girlfriend or something about some plot to murder billions of people. The guy was obviously a lunatic, but a dangerous lunatic, because to judge from the way he was talking, he seemed to have access to the White House. Jay looked at his watch. It didn't matter how late it was, he would stay on and check that the auto-transcript all made sense, and then he'd hand it over to Desiree Greene, even if he did hate her guts, because Jay was a patriot and it was his duty to let people know about this guy and his wife who were obviously plotting against the President.

Jay felt sorry for the President, not only because he had a real tough job defending freedom all over the world, but because he had a gay son. A decent President like Ritchie did not deserve to have a gay son. And what support was the President getting from his son? Zero support, because his son had no morals, no decency. Tomorrow was Jay's day off. Hell, maybe he'd go to that bookstore and do something about that

Edward. If Jay had a real gun he'd shoot the pervert down, but he didn't. So maybe he'd just take his paintball gun and humiliate the guy a little. The President would probably be grateful.

57

Half an hour to go till the live televised vaccination, and the President of the United States was learning his lines. Larry Dodge had just handed him a card with several spontaneous quips on it, all of them pretty good. Ritchie wanted to be relaxed and manly, without coming over as heartless, because it was so soon after the brutal slaying of his Secretary of State for Health and her two innocent grandchildren. In his opening remarks, Ritchie intended to say he was doing this in memory of Harriet who, in her determination to provide enough vaccine for the people of America, had put herself in the forefront of the war against terror, without regard for her own safety.

With ten minutes to go, Ritchie cast his eyes towards the doctor who was going to administer the injection. The guy looked pleasant enough, indeed his pleasant, fatherly appearance was the main reason for choosing him, but Ritchie thought he saw something steely in his eyes. It wasn't that Ritchie was afraid of needles or anything like that, but, well, it had been a long time since he'd had a shot and this one was pretty special and maybe the German-manufactured vaccine would hurt more than the old-fashioned American vaccine.

In the background, Anna Prascilowicz hovered. She was alarmed at how nervous the President was. She couldn't decide whether or not to cancel the live transmission. It had been heavily trailed. Cancellation now would look very bad.

With only ten minutes to go, six armed guards appeared, escorting a refrigerated box. It was carried over to the doctor, who opened it and prepared to fill his syringe. The armed guards remained in place.

The floor manager requested the President and the doctor to take their places on the set, which was built to resemble a very ordinary treatment room in some very ordinary hospital. Larry Dodge came down on to the floor and checked through the President's lines with him. Larry was happy that for once he didn't have Vince getting in his way. Nobody seemed to know where Vince was, not that Larry cared.

The floor manager called for silence and counted down. As he came on air, the President was rolling up his sleeve and joshing, while the doctor tested the syringe. Ritchie turned to camera and said a few heartfelt words about Harriet Knibbs. He then spoke briefly about the vital importance of getting every American vaccinated. Finally, he delivered a couple of Larry's wry gags, and turning to the doctor, said, 'Okay doc, do your worst.'

The doctor smiled, while a pretty nurse sponged anaesthetic on to the President's upper arm. Ritchie winked to camera. The doctor administered the injection.

Ritchie turned to camera and said, 'There you go, folks, there's nothing to it.' He then smiled, rolled down his sleeve, and fainted in front of forty million viewers.

Watching at home, Joe Skidelski exploded in rage and picked up the phone. So much for Vince's stupid vaccination plan. Skidelski had always known there was a better way. Now they were going to do it.

58

'Don't use your cell phone, okay?'

'Okay,' said Lucy.

'Find a payphone somewhere, call your parents in England, tell them to call here in half an hour. They've got to say that your mother is gravely ill.'

'She's going to ask why.'

'Just fucking tell her to do it, all right?'

'My mother's not like that, Vince. It doesn't work telling her to just fucking do something. It doesn't actually work with me, either.'

Vince groaned. It was past midnight. They'd been talking and arguing for several hours now. He knew that if their phone records got checked, the emergency call from England would need to have come before they booked the flight to London.

'All right,' said Lucy grudgingly. 'I'll do my best.'

'You'd better do better than that,' said Vince grimly.

59

Had Jay Positano not become quite so agitated about the gay mag, he might have been more careful with the transcript he left on Desiree Greene's desk. For once, he'd left the building later than Desiree. Seeing she wasn't there, he'd hurriedly slapped the transcript down on the corner of her desk and rushed out again, slamming the door behind him. The impact was enough to send the papers sliding neatly into the waste-paper basket, from where a cleaner would later that night take them for shredding.

60

Lieutenant General Lydia Abramovich, the preternaturally blonde Senior Media and Communications Officer at Barksdale Air Force base in Louisiana, was well into her Powerpoint presentation about International Day of the Planet and the role that Barksdale Air Force base was to play in that historic event. Barksdale Air Force Base ('home of the 2nd Bomb Wing and the Mighty 8th Air Force and one of the biggest employers in the Shreveport/Bossier City area') was proud to put its entire force of B-52 bombers and A-10 Warthogs at the service of the international community and the global environment, she explained. Barksdale Air Force Base had always believed in peace and cooperation. Barksdale Air Force Base was a family-oriented community asset. All in all, Lieutenant General Abramovich made it sound like Barksdale Air Force Base had been founded primarily in order to help old ladies with their knitting.

The twenty or so local journalists in the base's press centre made desultory notes. Right at the back of the briefing room was a small, battered guy with a squint. At forty-nine, Bob Bloom looked like a loser. What's more he felt like a loser. Some people have setbacks in their lives and get over them. Others nurse their grievances, fanning the flames of outrage for years after the event. Bob Bloom belonged in the second category. Drowning in self-pity and alcohol, Bob would never forgive the President of the United States for the wrong he'd inflicted on him all those years ago in the Red Rooster Roadhouse in Boise, Idaho. Somewhere Bob sensed that it was a little more complicated than that. But it was easier to blame Ritchie for all his ills. Easier, too, to blame Ritchie for the slow slide from committed and passionate young journalist to middle-aged hack, from investigative reporter on a decent paper in Idaho to 'community correspondent' for the *Bossier City Enquirer.*

The *Bossier City Enquirer* did not, on the whole, do a lot of enquiring. The big stories that Bob Bloom had covered in the previous twelve months included Farmerville's Watermelon Festival, the Louisiana Peach Festival, Bernice's Corney Creek Porkfest (featuring the Louisiana Producers' State Cookoff), the opening of a new exhibit at Hamel's Amusement Park and Sci-Port Discovery Center, and a mysterious illness killing off the Louisiana pine snake. The recent extreme weather conditions in the area could well have had an impact on the sudden decline of the Louisiana pine snake, but Bob Bloom knew he wouldn't be allowed to make the connection. The *Bossier City Enquirer* did not like to alarm its readers.

Lieutenant General Abramovich was explaining the exact procedure that would be followed on International Day of the Planet, or IDP as she liked to call it. 'Each plane will be fitted with a Lidar system. That's L-I-D-A-R.' She always made a point of spelling out difficult words for the press, which they appreciated, because some of them were so Spellcheck-dependent that if you took them away from their computers they couldn't spell piss. 'Lidar,' she went on helpfully, 'stands for laser radar. It uses a series of laser pulses to measure atmospheric constituents. Profiles of these atmospheric components as a function of altitude or location are necessary for environmental monitoring.'

By now, Bob Bloom was not the only one yawning. Most of the journalists there would simply quote big chunks of the press release more or less verbatim anyhow; it was easier that way. Nowadays, you could be a journalist without actually having to do much in the way of writing. During a visit like this it was routine for every hack to be given a press pack containing a disk with all the copy and all the images that might be needed to file a report. Basically, unless you wanted to rock the boat (and thus guarantee that you'd never be invited back) it was more a cut-and-paste operation than anything resembling what used to be called 'reporting'.

'On International Day of the Planet each plane will simultaneously release a vapour containing marker particles that will help us to highlight and observe the behaviour of aerosol particulates,' said Lieutenant General Abramovich. She saw that she was now losing her audience completely. Guessing correctly that most of them thought of an aerosol as something connected with under-arm deodorant, she added a line from the material she'd been given by the Defense Department. 'A simple example of aerosol particles' (she was a little unclear as to the difference between particles and particulates) 'is the smog you see above a polluted city. This is composed mainly of sulphate, carbon, dust, salt, nitrate and trace gases such as ozone. Most aerosol particles are not visible in this way, but the global behaviour of such particles influences climate as well as human health, and by tracking the movements of such aerosols and their constituent parts, we are helping the world community understand potential threats to our environment.'

Bob had drunk too much the night before. He decided he had time to get to the bathroom, take a leak, swallow a couple of aspirin, and get back before the bus departed for a tour of the base. He might even find a quiet corner to sneak a smoke, if Abramovich was still droning on. The tour would end with lunch, he didn't want to miss lunch. He slid out of his seat and snuck towards the exit.

Lieutenant General Abramovich ignored the departing journalist. It would be his fault if he missed the bus. She regarded all press and media people as low life and was never surprised or shocked by their discourteous behaviour. 'At the conclusion of the operation,' she explained, 'the data collected in-flight will be stored and processed digitally and sent to a central computer for evaluation before being made available worldwide.' She looked round the room. 'Are there any questions?' She didn't think there would be, so she only left a very small gap before saying, 'Okay. So let's move on and I will show you around the facility and the IDP-related planning areas. There will be an opportunity to inspect a B-52 fitted with the IDP equipment and to talk briefly to an air crew. You will be accompanied by Barksdale's own PR photographer, who will record still images during the visit. While you are having lunch,' (she detected the first flicker of interest) 'while you are having lunch, we'll burn a disk for each of you, with a wide selection of stills for you or your editors to choose from. This is a security zone and no photography on your part will be permitted. All visitors must remain in the designated areas. Anyone found filming or taking photographs will have their equipment confiscated and will have rendered him or herself liable to prosecution and imprisonment. Please follow me. Thank you.'

Pleased at the thought of seeing planes and military stuff, but most of all stirred by the thought of lunch (Barksdale Air Force Base had a reputation for serving pretty good food), the press shook themselves into action, put away their unused notebooks, and followed the Lieutenant General out to the bus that would take them round the base.

Bob Bloom missed the bus, of course. Maybe this revealed a deep need in him. Bob Bloom hated buses. They always made him feel sick. International Day of the Planet also made him feel sick. He was not a believer in the goodness of America. Quite why the United States should be putting tens of thousands of warplanes at the disposal of the 'global community' was beyond him, but he refused to believe there was no element of self-interest involved. (This was not, of course, a point of view he could express in the pages of the *Bossier City Enquirer*.)

Emerging from the bathroom, Bob Bloom made his way back to the briefing room and found it empty. He then set off in the general direction of the bus, but it had gone. He was thinking about giving up on lunch and going back to the office to do a quick cut-and-paste job with the press release when he spotted something very odd. Something that made him recall a phone call he'd had a while back from his old girlfriend Marina, in San Diego. A phone call about a very strange order for millions of gallons of Buffalo deodorant. He hadn't done anything about it then. Now he was thinking maybe he should have.

61

For a long time now, Vince had been aware of a small but significant gap in White House security. Having shown their ID, staff entering the building had to pass through a metal detector arch. Many of those staff would be carrying a takeaway coffee hurriedly purchased on their way in. The container of coffee would routinely be placed on a little ledge by the side of the detector and then picked up again from the other side. It never seemed to occur to the security personnel to put the container of coffee through the metal detector.

Vince walked in with his big cardboard container of latte, said 'Good morning' to the guys, placed his latte casually on the little shelf, went through the metal detector, and picked up the container on the other side. Nobody looked twice at him.

Once in his office, he opened the container and pulled out a tiny digital video camera, the best he could buy: fuel-cell-powered, and with two-channel digital audio, 3 CCDs and image stabilisation. He then carefully taped the camera to the inside of the big file that he always had under his arm when he gave the President his morning briefing. He checked that the microphone was pointing in the right direction. He looked at the file from each side. If he was really careful, he reckoned Ritchie would never spot the lens. It probably wouldn't be possible to switch it on and off during the meeting. The total recording time was just ten minutes, so he would have only one chance.

He checked his watch: 08.25. He put the file under his arm and set off down the corridor to the Oval Office.

62

The next day, the killing of Health Secretary Knibbs was fighting with the fainting President for supremacy on the networks when news came through of the slaughter in the gay bookshop.

Poor Jay Positano had foolishly failed to reckon with the presence of Secret Servicemen in the vicinity of the President's son. He'd assumed that fag sons didn't get protection.

Jay had burst into the gay bookshop with the simple intention of causing maximum paintball mayhem. He'd scraped together every last dollar to buy a Dragon Intimidator specially for the occasion. Yes, he'd sure as hell scare the shit out of those fags. As he burst through the doors, Edward was just stepping up to have a book signed by the handsome Latino author he'd recently fallen in love with. The handsome Latino author wasn't in love with Edward but was enough of a businessman to know that a photo-op of the President's son buying his new novel was going to be worth a lot of sales.

'Die, faggots!' screamed Jay Positano as he advanced on the group, firing off paintballs at fifteen rounds a second. The room filled with the sound of screaming. Jay had loaded his Timmy with all-red paintballs, so within a very few seconds it looked as if dozens of people were being slaughtered. The Secret Servicemen drew their guns and began firing wildly. Jay got real close to the President's son and was pumping paintballs into the sicko bastard when he went down in a hail of bullets.

The final death toll was one handsome Latino author, one junior CIA employee with a paint gun, and four innocent bystanders.

63

Al Boyd pulled up in the parking lot of the American Way building, cut the engine, and clambered out of his dark-green Lincoln Navigator. He was in a hurry. Joe Skidelski's plan to scare people into getting the vaccine was about to be executed, and Boyd wanted to be at his desk when it happened.

Lumbering across the parking lot, he as usual cast an apprehensive glance at the swivelling CCTV cameras, and prayed that today wouldn't be a day when the gait recognition system malfunctioned. To his relief, the system recognised him and he got to the lobby without incident. As he approached the security gate, he noticed the giant panda in the bamboo grove in the atrium was looking restless. A few people had stopped to watch. God almighty, thought Boyd, it was time they got rid of the fucking beast. Nodding to the four security guards, he reached into his wallet for his ID. 'Hi, guys,' he said, swiping his card through the scanner.

'Morning, Mr Boyd,' they replied cheerfully, each of them watching the revolving security gate. Recently, the betting on when Boyd would become too fat to get through the gate had grown fevered; everyone could see that Boyd was still putting on weight. The security team that happened to be on duty when Boyd got stuck now stood to pull a jackpot of nine hundred and forty bucks. Boyd pushed at the revolving gate and nothing happened. He pushed again. No result. Shit. He tried to back out, but couldn't. Fuck. Boyd realised he was firmly wedged in the security gate. He turned to the staring security guards. 'Hey, you guys, can you give me a hand here?'

'YEAH!' roared the security guards, leaping in the air, grabbing one another and whooping with joy.

Alarmed by the sudden noise, the giant panda panicked and began to crash around in the bamboo grove. While two of the celebrating security men went to extricate Boyd, another reluctantly went to check out the panicking panda. As he opened the little gate in the compound, the panda lumbered straight at him, knocking him off his feet.

An escaped panda is definitely less worrying than an escaped lion or an escaped tiger, but still a *bit* worrying. As Boyd cursed and sweated and two cheerful security men pushed and pulled at him, the giant panda made a bid for freedom. Several employees tried to divert it from crossing the marble-floored lobby. Puzzled by all these people waving their arms, the panda padded into an open lift. The lift doors closed. From the atrium, dozens of American Way staff stared up at the glass lift gliding up the side of the atrium. The giant panda looked surprisingly happy.

Hot and sweaty, Al Boyd finally made it to his office. To his disappointment, the panda had been recaptured rather than shot. Stuffing a cream donut into his mouth, Boyd switched on the television and waited for the news flash.

64

The vast hangar contained more than twenty A-10 Thunderbolts. As Bob Bloom walked slowly past them, he was reminded of why they were known as 'Warthogs'. With their fat tailfins and their two huge GE-100 Turbofan engines mounted high on the rear fuselage they were every bit as ugly and ungainly as the animal they'd been named after. Bob Bloom didn't know a whole lot about military aircraft, but he knew a bit about the A-10 Warthog. The A-10 happened to be the primary aircraft of the 124th Wing of the Idaho Air National Guard, based at Gowen Field, Boise. When he'd still been a serious journalist in Boise, before Ritchie and his friends had wrecked his life, Bob Bloom had written a few pieces about the environmental impact of the military in Idaho, including the polluting effects of a wing of Warthogs taking off and landing several times a week. He clambered under one of the Warthogs and looked up at some kind of frame that had been attached to the underside of the fuselage. He examined it for a few minutes, peering at it in the gloom. He stood still for a moment, listening, to make sure nobody was around. He took out his lighter and flicked the flame on. Now he really would be in trouble if he were caught; they'd probably think he was trying to set the planes on fire. Examining the metal frame, he could see that the bolts attaching it to the fuselage were all brand-new. The frame had runners where some kind of equipment was obviously meant to be slotted in. He assumed this was to hold the spraying and monitoring equipment for International Day of the Planet. But he couldn't help thinking that the shape of the runners was more suited to the containers that had first caught his attention outside. Containers that appeared to hold male deodorant.

A loud rumbling sound filled the air. Voices were shouting over the noise. Bob realised the huge hangar doors were being raised. Over the roar of the motor that was raising the doors, three or four men seemed to be arguing about who had left the side-door unsecured. Seconds later they were walking right past his aircraft. He ducked out from under the Warthog and walked crisply towards the main doors of the hangar, hesitated for a second, and then dived into a narrow passage between two rows of huts. As he'd hoped, he came out where he'd started from. He was facing a stack of metal cylinders. As he stared at them, he knew for sure they were designed to fit on to the frames that he'd seen under the Warthogs. He went nearer, and saw that on each of the cylinders was a printed label:

USAF: Buffalo deodorant
Defense Logistics Agency
Order # 217665A/CA/8766623/0-20/ BBSIII-01

Bob Bloom went up to the nearest cylinder and began carefully to peel off the label.

65

The chemical attack on the Supreme Court killed every single judge, more than forty members of staff, and some ninety people who happened to be in the area at the time. The agent used was a gaseous form of a substance identified as Carfentanil, a drug 10,000 times more powerful than morphine.

That same day, the President went on air to confirm that this had been a terrorist attack.

Within twenty-four hours, there were lines outside every single vaccination centre in the United States. True, the victims of the latest outrage had been killed by a chemical, not a virus, but that didn't matter the least bit: people now realised that when their government talked of a terrorist threat, it was to be taken seriously.

The President was sure it had been the right thing to do, and anyhow, he'd never much cared for those Supreme Court judges. His only problem was a kind of catastrophe fatigue. There were so many disasters hitting the American people that he was finding it hard to go on television and find something new to say, especially since Vince wasn't there to help him. Vince was in England, where his mother-in-law was apparently at death's door. Ritchie was not pleased that Vince's mother-in-law had chosen such a bad time to shuffle off the mortal coil. It showed lack of judgement. And it also showed a poor sense of priorities on Vince's part.

66

The minute Vince and Lucy saw the enormous line of people waiting for cabs outside Heathrow's Terminal 3 they doubled back. Heathrow was always overcrowded, but on a Saturday it was especially bad.

'We'll take the Heathrow Express to Paddington,' said Lucy. That would be good for her anyhow; she could catch her train to Oxford from there. She had a lot of explaining to do to her parents. She also had two vials of vaccine to give them, vaccine brazenly stolen from under the noses of staff at the vaccination centre in Annapolis where, at Lucy's insistence, she and Vince had gone to get inoculated just before setting out. As she'd said to Vince, what if Operation Deliverance were suddenly brought forward?

They'd both been worried that the vials, carefully packed in a chilled container, would be picked up by security or customs at the airport, but nobody had shown the slightest bit of interest in the two travellers from Washington.

As they followed the signs to the train platforms, they became aware of an announcement being repeated over and over again on the public address system. They stopped to listen. The sound was horribly distorted, but by the time they'd listened carefully twice over, Lucy was able to deduce that the rail link into Paddington had just been closed 'due to operational difficulties'. There was no indication of when it would reopen.

'Let's take the tube,' said Lucy. A few minutes later, they found hundreds of confused people milling around near the ticket office, so it took them a while to spot the warning scrawled in chalk on a blackboard near the ticket machines. PICCADILLY LINE SERVICE TO CENTRAL LONDON SUSPENDED DUE TO PERSON UNDER TRAIN. Oh, great, thought Vince, with only the merest flicker of regret for the person under train.

'You know something, Luce?' said Vince as they trudged back towards the cab rank. 'I understand why you left this country.'

A full two and a half hours later, he was dropping her off at Paddington Station.

As she got out of the cab, he said, 'I'll call you at your parents' when it feels safe to do that. But be careful what you say. And don't use your cell phone. Oh, and Lucy . . .'

'What?'

'The vaccine for your parents. The minute you arrive, get it into the refrigerator. Not in the door, okay? In the middle of the refrigerator, away from the freezer compartment.'

'Yes, yes, I know.' They kissed, and a moment later she was gone. Vince told the driver to take him on to Marylebone Station. There he got on a train to Aylesbury.

67

Three thousand miles away, General Barry B. Steinberger III was finishing a thirty-minute shower. The General believed that a shower lasting less than thirty minutes was a shower not worth taking. It was mid-afternoon and it was only his second shower of the day. He'd have to keep an eye on that. In the run-up to Operation Deliverance he was working an eighteen-hour day seven days a week, and the pressure to cut back on personal hygiene was very great. He rinsed off the last of the Buffalo shower gel, stepped from the shower, and took a huge, freshly laundered white towel from a pile.

OpDel was a big job, but so far, nothing big had gone wrong. With only nineteen days to go, over 31,000 warplanes had been fitted with the necessary equipment. This still left several thousand planes over, many of them freshly delivered from the factory as part of the new consignment the General had said he'd need to carry out the operation. It was a reassuring feeling to know they were there. It was good to have a strong America. A good feeling, yes, sir.

The General carefully sprinkled some Buffalo talc into his clean underwear before pulling it on. He made a mental note to ask his orderly for another delivery of fresh boxers; he was down to his last ten. He walked over to the mirror to check whether he needed a shave, enjoying the generous space of the bathroom. He thought of this as his Deliverance Bathroom. He'd had it installed alongside his Control Room at the National Military Command Center in the Pentagon. It had cost $200,000, but in the mind of General Barry B. Steinberger III this was money well spent. A clean general was an efficient general.

The logistics of getting 31,000 warplanes fitted with the right equipment and flown out to over 900 bases, airfields and carriers around the globe had not scared the General in the least. So far, it had worked pretty smoothly. Sure, a couple of planes had crashed, but hell, those things happened.

68

Installed in his hotel room in Aylesbury, Vince poured himself a whisky. Then he sat down at the little table (which was too low for his knees) and for the third time checked over James Halstead's timetable for the next twenty-four hours. This information hadn't been hard to come by: Washington was routinely informed about the movements of the British Prime Minister.

Vince's plan was simple, but had only been arrived at after a lot of hard thinking. His objective was a meeting with Halstead. He was sure that Halstead would agree to see him, even at short notice; the special assistant of the most powerful man on Earth had to be taken seriously. But Vince didn't want news of such a meeting getting back to Washington. Over there they thought he was in England because of his mother-in-law's health. This meant Vince couldn't risk making contact via a Downing Street intermediary, who would almost certainly check back with the White House. Vince needed somehow to come face to face with Halstead, and he thought he'd worked out how to do it. The hotel near Aylesbury was five miles from Chequers, the Prime Minister's country residence. At 11 o'clock that morning, Halstead, his wife and his teenage daughter would be in the local church for the traditional Sunday morning service of worship, along with several dozen local people. Of course, there would be security, but it would be discreet, and Vince thought he would be able to deal with it. He'd met Halstead before. Halstead would recognise him. At least, he *hoped* Halstead would recognise him.

He wished he could phone Lucy. It wasn't just the late hour that stopped him. He didn't want any record of calls from Aylesbury to the home of Lucy's parents. He couldn't rule out that Garoufalas or Langshite had put some kind of tap on that line. A call from Vince in a location only five miles from where the Prime Minister was spending the weekend, that would definitely set alarm bells ringing. So far he'd been lucky – this was one of those old-fashioned English hotels where nobody insisted on seeing your passport as you checked in. He wasn't going to blow it all now for the sake of one phone call.

He drained the glass of whisky.

69

The launch of Faith Opportunities Week was one of those events that Ritchie would normally have enjoyed. But as Operation Deliverance came closer and closer, he was finding it increasingly difficult to keep up an appearance of normality.

Never mind, thought Ritchie, at least the weather was good. By the beginning of March, afternoon temperatures in Washington DC were reaching 88 degrees. As usual, climatologists were claiming this was evidence of climate change, but Ritchie had long since stopped even pretending to listen to those assholes. Nice warm weather was nice warm weather, right?

Thanks to this nice warm weather, Ritchie was reasonably relaxed as he and Cheech Lingaard strolled out into the Rose Garden to have a word with the assembled press. Media chief Anna Prascilowicz was pleased at the breadth of turn-out; of late she'd been trying to open up this kind of event to smaller newspapers and new media outlets, rather than just the usual Beltway crowd of tired old hacks.

Ritchie planned to let Cheech do most of the talking. The press liked Cheech. The churches liked Cheech. Everybody liked Cheech. Even the President's son liked Cheech, and was flying in to Washington that afternoon to join them both for the Faith Opportunities Charity Dinner. A faint flame of hope glimmered in Ritchie's soul, a hope that maybe his son was about to realise the error of his ways, commit himself to Jesus, and settle down with a nice girl.

Anna Prascilowicz hovered discreetly to one side as Ritchie and Lingaard cracked a few jokes and prepared to take questions from the press.

The first question came from the *New York Times* and was about the importance of faith in the life of Cheech Lingaard. Cheech replied with a simple, moving eloquence.

The second question came from a cable station in Oklahoma, and was about Cheech helping young people to discover faith. Ritchie nodded as Cheech explained how he tried in his own small way to be a role model for young people.

The third question was put by a young female reporter from an LA newspaper. 'Mr Lingaard, tomorrow my paper will be running pictures of you engaging in a variety of sexual acts with both young women and young men. Would you like to take this opportunity to comment on how you feel this relates to your view of yourself as a role model?'

Cheech Lingaard froze for a second, then turned and walked off.

Anna Prascilowicz moved in immediately. She bore down on the young female reporter. 'Okay. I'm sorry. That's completely irresponsible. That's an abuse of White House hospitality. We're not taking questions like that.'

Ritchie hesitated, then said to the press, 'Hey, you guys, let's have a nice old-fashioned question about politics, okay?'

The press laughed. They liked it when Ritchie joshed with them like this. But they were also quite interested in the new sex allegation.

'Okay,' said a small guy with a squint. 'Here's a nice old-fashioned question about politics.'

Prascilowicz didn't remember seeing the little guy with the squint before. She was getting very jumpy. 'Who are you?' she barked.

'Bob Bloom, *Bossier City Enquirer*,' replied the small guy with the squint.

The reporters from the major papers sniggered.

'You invited us, remember?' said Bob Bloom.

'Oh, yeah. Right.' So she had. Prascilowicz was having a bad day. 'Go right ahead.'

'Mr President,' said Bob Bloom. 'I guess you don't remember me.'

Overacting madly, Ritchie put a hand over his eyes and stared at the little guy with the squint. 'I guess I don't,' said Ritchie, winking at the press corps and getting another laugh.

'That's okay, Mr President. I remember you.'

'Just ask the question, please,' snapped Prascilowicz.

'Okay. Mr President. Why are A-10 Warthog Aircraft at Barksdale Air Force Base, Louisiana, being loaded up with Buffalo male deodorant?'

Loud laughter filled the air.

Bob Bloom held up a label. 'I have here a label with a USAF serial number confirming that containers of male deodorant are being held at the base. I have established that they were ordered by General Steinberger. And I have reason to believe that this deodorant will be sprayed from the air on International Day of the Planet. Could you explain that to us, sir? I mean, why should that be necessary, sir?'

The laughter was fading now. The other journalists were looking vaguely interested. Anna Prascilowicz had gone very tight-lipped. She didn't want to overreact in case it lent credibility to what the little guy was saying.

'Hey,' said Ritchie, beginning to feel he had met the little guy some place before. 'Hey, does the *Bossier City Enquirer* have any more like you?!'

Again he got a laugh, but not much of a laugh.

Loud and decisive, Prascilowicz said, 'That's it for today. Thank you, everybody, and goodbye.'

70

Vince got out of a taxi a few hundred yards away from the parish church and wandered casually up the village street, looking in the windows of the many antique shops. He felt horribly out of place and wished he'd stopped to pack something other than a dark suit and raincoat. In one hand he carried the Gideon Bible he'd taken from the Aylesbury hotel room, in the hope that this would confer an air of piety upon him. He recalled that back in Washington it was Faith Opportunities Week, so somehow it was appropriate.

As he approached the church, his heart sank. There were at least twenty police officers, in bright yellow jackets, making sure that nobody parked within a hundred yards around. Little groups of local people were already making their way into the church, past a knot of bulky young men with watchful eyes. Vince assumed that probably the Prime Minister waited until everyone else was seated before arriving.

Vince took a deep breath and walked up the gravel path towards the church doors. He could feel the watchful eyes upon him. As he got to the porch, one of the bulky young men touched him on the arm.

'Excuse me, sir.' He indicated that Vince should step to one side.

Vince did so.

'Sorry to trouble you, sir. Are you local?'

'No, I'm here on vacation.' Vince tried to make himself sound as earnest and geeky as possible. 'But no matter where I am, I always make sure I get to church of a Sunday.'

'I see. Would you mind very much if . . . ?' He indicated he could like to search Vince.

'No problem,' said Vince, opening his coat and holding out his arms. Shit, he thought. The digital video camera was in his coat pocket. Security wouldn't like that. They'd assume he wanted to sneak pictures of the Prime Minister. He kept his arms in the air, hoping they weren't trembling. The young man leant forward to search him. At that moment his eyes fell on the bible in Vince's hand. He hesitated. 'Oh, let's not worry about it, sir. Go on through.'

'Thanks.' Vince walked into the church. As his eyes adjusted to the gloom, he could see a pew with an empty space on the aisle. He sat down in it.

It was a good fifteen minutes before the Prime Minister and his family arrived. They went to a pew near the front of the church and sat down. Several of the bulky young men sat down in a row behind them.

At the end of the service, Halstead and his family were the first to leave, though as he moved up the nave there was a certain amount of hand-shaking and quiet greetings with the locals, most of whom were on their feet. The bulky young men with the watchful eyes kept close to the Prime Minister, their glances constantly raking the congregation. Vince slipped out a small folded piece of paper from inside his Gideon Bible and waited. James Halstead was only about a yard away when Vince said crisply and clearly, 'Good morning, Prime Minster.' Halstead paused and stared at Vince for a moment, then his big, beefy face broke into a smile. 'Vince ... Vince Lennox? Goodness, what a surprise.' The Prime Minister shook his hand and leaned close to his ear. 'Haven't brought your boss with you, have you? It's the poodle's day off, you know!' Halstead chortled at his own little joke. Vince laughed in response and in turn leaned close to Halstead's ear. He was aware that the security people were paying him a lot of attention. 'Sir,' he whispered, as he slipped a small piece of paper into the Prime Minister's hand. 'Please read this immediately. It can't wait.'

Halstead gave no response, but took the paper and moved on.

In the porch, the Prime Minister and his family paused to exchange a few words with the vicar before being escorted down the gravel path to the waiting car. As he settled down in his seat, the Prime Minister unfolded the piece of paper and read it. Then he read it again. The driver started the engine.

'Hold on just a moment, will you?' said the Prime Minister. Ignoring the questioning look from his wife, he opened the window and gestured to one of the uniformed policemen standing nearby. 'Officer, would you kindly go inside, find a Mr Vince Lennox, and ask him to join us? Thank you so much.'

'What's going on, Dad?' asked his fourteen-year-old daughter.

'We have an extra guest for lunch.'

'Oh, bo-ring!' said the daughter.

71

To Vince's relief, the journey to Chequers took only a few minutes. Inside the car, there was only small talk. Having been casually waved through at the main gate, the Prime Minister's car followed a narrow road through parkland lined with trees until the red-brick east front of Chequers came into view. The gates to the walled forecourt were open and unattended. Only the glint of spring sunlight off the lenses of the surveillance cameras set at close intervals along the high walls suggested that this was anything other than the residence of some local gentry. The vehicle crunched to a halt on the gravel driveway. An attendant appeared and opened the car doors. Vince stepped out and looked up at the house. The massive stone-mullioned windows with their leaded glass panes loomed over him, making him feel for a moment that he was in an Agatha Christie story. He followed the Halsteads through the entrance porch and into a small hall with a flagged stone floor.

'Why don't you wait in the Hawtrey Room, Vince? I'll join you in a couple of minutes.'

'Thank you, Prime Minister.'

The attendant opened a wide oak-panelled door leading off the hall. Vince entered. The door was pulled closed behind him. He looked around the panelled room with its jumble of chintz-covered chairs and sofas and wondered where to sit. He wandered over to the bay window and peered through the yellowing and murky glass panes. Two uniformed police officers carrying sub-machine guns were walking past. So the security wasn't quite as desultory as he'd first thought.

He wandered past a huge Chinese vase of fresh flowers and inspected a row of oil paintings along one wall, each one lit by a little brass wall-light above it. These sat oddly with the big plasma screen on the wall and the powerful desktop computer on an oak table in the corner. Vince sat down on a chair near the fireplace and gazed into the flickering log fire. He realised he was about to cross into new and dangerous territory. If the Prime Minister didn't believe him, one phone call to Washington would finish him.

The door opened and James Halstead came in, Vince's note in his hand. A big-boned, red-faced man, a little overweight, Halstead seemed to be a throwback to an earlier age. But after years of cool, modern, spin-obsessed leadership, the British people had taken old-fashioned, no-nonsense, true-blue Halstead entirely to their hearts.

'Bloody strange note, Vince, if you don't mind my saying so. Bloody strange way to behave, too,' said James Halstead as he sank into a big armchair by the fire.

'I'm sorry, sir. You didn't . . . you didn't make contact with Washington while you were . . . I mean, while I was waiting in here?'

'Haven't made contact with anyone. Your note asked me not to, and I had the courtesy to respect that. Now I hope you will have the courtesy to tell me what the hell is going on.'

Vince took out the little video camera. 'Prime Minister. I need to show you something.' He went over to the oak table, booted up the computer, and placed the camera alongside it. A few seconds later, the wireless connection kicked in. Some wobbly shots of the Oval Office appeared on the big plasma screen on the wall. The camera swung wildly up towards the ceiling for a few seconds, then down to the carpet, then went in very close on the left nostril of the President.

'Home movies?' said Halstead.

'Kind of,' said Vince. He wasn't sure whether Halstead was really paying attention.

The camera abruptly zoomed out then zoomed slowly back in before finally settling on a head-and-shoulder shot of the President.

Vince increased the volume.

'Forget it,' the President was saying, 'It's too late. OpDel is going ahead. I'm not changing my mind now.'

'OpDel?' Halstead enquired.

'Operation Deliverance,' explained Vince.

'Meaning?'

Vince pointed at the screen. His own voice could now be heard on the soundtrack. Being nearer the hidden microphone, he was much louder than the President. 'So, you're comfortable with the idea of killing around six billion people, is that right?'

'Yes, Vince,' said the President, 'that's right.'

'Christ,' said Halstead.

Now he was paying attention, thought Vince.

Vince's voice was heard again. 'What if it comes out? The biggest mass murderer in human history. Is that how you want to be remembered, sir?'

The President's face slid out of a shot for a couple of seconds and then returned. 'It's not going to come out, Vince. And anyhow, even if somebody went public, who's going to believe it?' He paused. 'You're not thinking of going public, are you Vince?'

'Of course not, sir,' was Vince's swift reply.

'That's good,' the President replied, 'because I'd be obliged to prevent you from trying.' He smiled a chilly smile. The camera remained still.

Ritchie's mouth was now wide open as he worried away at his molars with a toothpick. He finally put away the little silver box containing his toothpicks. Ritchie then said, 'Vince, three weeks from now, it'll be all over. And we'll wonder why we didn't think of it before. Sure, killing six billion people, said like that, it doesn't sound good, I know that. But it's like Dolores argued, long-term this is about saving humanity. I have prayed long and hard about this, Vince and I know that God will forgive us.'

Out of vision, Vince could be heard saying, 'I wish I believed that, sir.'

The President leaned forward, his face suddenly contorted with rage. 'Quit jerking me around, Vince! Are you in or are you out? Just make up your fucking mind!' The camera wobbled around the room for a bit, as if Vince had been sent reeling by the blast of anger.

After a short silence, Vince could be heard saying softly, 'I'm in, sir.'

The camera finally settled again on the face of the President as he sat back in his chair and chuckled. 'Hell, boy. If God had wanted them six billion people to survive, he'd have made them take out American citizenship!'

The video ended.

Without taking his eyes off the screen, Halstead said, 'Run it again.'

When it was over, the Prime Minister stood up and went over to a phone. 'Hello? Would you kindly tell Mrs Halstead that it may be necessary to delay lunch a little? Thank you.' He put down the phone and looked across the room at Vince. 'When was it shot?'

'Two days ago. The date's on the screen.'

Halstead went over to a desk and flipped through a diary. 'Three weeks from then would take us to . . .'

'International Day of the Planet.'

'I don't understand . . . You don't mean that the planes . . . all those aircraft, they're not actually . . . Christ. They're not going to be used for some other purpose, are they?'

'Yes. They'll be releasing an aerosol. It will contain a virus . . .'

Halstead froze. 'This isn't . . . I mean, it's not the virus that you've been busy inoculating everyone against?'

'Every American, yes.'

'Oh, hell.' He paused and rubbed his face. 'Why bring this to me?'

'Because I believe you can stop it.'

'How?'

'You are our most loyal ally. If you tell the world about this, people will believe it.'

'Give me a moment.' Halstead stared into the fire. 'I need to be sure that I've understood. The United States of America is planning to wipe out the entire population of the planet, with the exception of the population of the United States itself. Is that correct?'

'More or less, yes.'

'*Is it correct?*'

'Yes, sir.'

'Thank you. You'll forgive me for double-checking. It isn't every day of the week that one discusses the killing of six billion people.'

'I wish . . .' Vince shook his head in exasperation. 'I just wish you would believe me, sir.'

'Actually, I think I do believe you.'

'Thank God.'

'But it takes time to absorb it. Being told that our most powerful and important ally is three weeks away from wiping out most of the human race – including us presumably, I assume we're all for the chop too, are we?'

'Yes.'

'Right, well that's . . . that's, well, Vince, it's pretty much beyond words.'

271

'I understand.'

The Prime Minister threw a log on to the fire. 'I think I ought to fly to Washington right away.'

This wasn't what Vince had been hoping for. 'Why? Why do you plan to fly to Washington, sir?'

'I think I should talk Ritchie out of this.'

'I don't think that will work, sir, I really don't.'

'Why not? I have influence.'

'Not as much as you think, sir.'

'Ritchie's always listened to me.'

Vince wondered how to break through the self-serving illusion that all British prime ministers seemed to have about the extent of their influence in Washington. He stretched out his arms in an imploring gesture to Halstead. 'He won't listen to you. Nobody will. You need to go on television, sir, and tell the world the truth. You tell them that the United States is nineteen days away from slaughtering billions of people. You get the TV station to run the video I just showed you.'

'Why don't you just get a television station to do that anyway? I mean, without involving me?'

'Are you kidding, sir? There's no American TV station left that will even *criticise* the President, far less run a video of him planning mass murder. That's why you have to tell the world, tell them that International Day of the Planet is a fraud, a cover for a massive spraying operation around the globe, for the distribution of a deadly virus that will leave only Americans alive.'

'I think maybe that would be disloyal.'

'Disloyal?!'

'Yes. Going public with these things isn't necessarily the best way of dealing with them. The proper role for an ally is to have a discreet word in private. That's what I've always done before.'

Vince then made a very obvious point. 'You're about to be wiped out. That does not make you an ally.'

The Prime Minister pulled a face. 'Ritchie's probably been bounced into this by the hawks. Ritchie and I communicate well. I'm sure if we can spend some time together alone, I'll get through to him.'

'I think that's the wrong route. I think you need to go public. Immediately.'

272

'And how's that going to help?' asked the Prime Minister.

'People will believe you, sir. People trust you. You have international standing.'

'Let's suppose for a moment that they do believe me. What happens then?'

'The overflying rights that have been granted to our Air Force world-wide would be withdrawn. Any American warplane over the territory of a foreign power would be seen as a military threat and shot down.'

'Which would mean war.'

'Exactly. So America would have to back off, would have to abandon the plan.'

'Suppose America didn't abandon the plan? And then suppose China or some other nuclear power shot down a few American planes? In no time at all we'd be in the midst of a nuclear exchange. Is that what you want, Vince? No, I shall fly to Washington, and I shall dissuade him. Simple as that.'

'You'll dissuade him?'

'Yes. I'll talk him out of it. Don't worry. After all, it's absolute madness. But it'll be your job to keep Joe Skidelski out of he way. And Delgado. And any of the other hawks.'

Vince grimaced. Did this man really think he would be listened to? 'It won't work, sir.'

With an air of finality, James Halstead said, 'We disagree.'

Silence descended.

Vince's mind was racing. If the Prime Minister was determined to go to Washington, he couldn't very well stop him. And who knows, maybe he'd succeed. Maybe it was the only chance. But how would Halstead explain that he knew about Operation Deliverance without betraying Vince?

The Prime Minister seemed to have read his mind. 'We'll have to protect you, of course.'

'Yes,' said Vince abstractedly. He was torn between a need to ensure his own survival and a sense of certainty that the British plan could not succeed. For the moment, the former proved stronger. 'You'll have to come up with some explanation for knowing about OpDel.'

'Right,' said the Prime Minister.

Vince said, 'Okay. Here's what I propose. You say you intercepted

273

communications between Delgado and Skidelski, revealing the essential outlines of Operation Deliverance.'

'Is that likely?' asked James Halstead.

'Well, a few years back, you managed to bug about half the UN. Electronic surveillance is still one of the things you guys are good at.'

Halstead laughed. 'That's true, of course.'

Vince was thinking, if this fails, as I think it will, then the only hope is to make sure that the meeting takes place very quickly, so that after it fails, the Prime Minister will still have time to go public. Yes, that was just about the only hope.

The Prime Minister glanced at his watch. ' I have a lot to do. I need to talk to colleagues.' He saw the look of fear in Vince's face. 'Don't worry, I shall keep this within a very small circle. Thanks for coming, Vince. I'm grateful.'

Vince realised he was being dismissed. He stood up. 'Thank you for giving me the time, Prime Minister.'

'Oh, your little camera thingie ... how do we make a copy of the video?'

'Keep it. I already made a copy.'

'Fine.' Halstead stood up and rang the little brass bell. 'We'll order you a car.'

'One thing,' said Vince. 'You'll only bring up Operation Deliverance once you're there, right? I mean, you won't say in advance why you're coming, will you?'

Halstead smiled. 'Of course not. We'll just say it's a matter of extreme urgency concerning our national security. We rely on you to make sure the President accedes to our request and gives us a meeting in the next few days.'

'That might not be so easy ... But, yes, okay.'

An attendant opened the door.

The Prime Minister jumped to his feet and held his hand out to Vince. With his free hand he clapped Vince on the shoulder and flashed him a yellow-toothed smile. 'See you in Washington. Good luck.'

'Thank you, Prime Minister.'

Vince left the room. The attendant held the door open for him then followed him out.

The Prime Minister sat down again and waited till the footsteps in the stone-flagged hallway had receded. He stared into the fire for a few minutes, lost in thought. He thought his chances of dissuading Ritchie were not in fact very good. But the beginnings of a different plan were coming to him. A much better plan.

72

Vince rang from a call box in London. To his relief, Lucy answered the phone.

'Luce. Hi. How's your mom?'

'She's fine . . . oh, no, I mean, she's a little better. Well, actually quite a lot better.'

'Oh, good.'

'How was your meeting . . . I mean, how did things go with you?'

'Good and bad.'

'Where are you?'

'Um . . . London. I think we should meet back here. At the airport. As planned. That's assuming your mother has made a complete recovery.'

'Oh. Oh, yes. Yes, she has. A remarkable recovery.'

Christ, thought Vince, if anyone was listening in they wouldn't find any of this stuff very convincing.

Twenty-four hours later, Vince and Lucy were back in the States. Neither knew what would come next. Lucy cleared papers and packed bags. Vince headed for Camp David, where a final planning meeting had been called.

PART ★ FIVE

73

Heads were bowed around the long table that filled the conference room in Camp David's Laurel Lodge.

'Oh Lord, at this time of danger and challenge, grant us fortitude,' Jimmy Lombok intoned, his bald head gleaming in the fierce sunlight that was flooding in through the windows facing him. Outside the windows, flowers normally seen in early summer were already in bloom, and it was only early March. The air conditioning could be heard humming softly as Lombok paused. Everybody hoped he had finished, but he hadn't. He continued, 'Give us the courage to be bold in the pursuit of great endeavours, resolute in the defence of liberty, and yet humble in the knowledge that we are only doing Thy will. A great enterprise lies before us. As the time of trial draws near we ask Thee to look down upon us gathered here in this simple log cabin, and bestow Thy blessing upon us.'

Vince, his eyes firmly shut, thought the simple log cabin thing was pushing it a bit. The Laurel Lodge conference room was wood-panelled, but that was about as far as the simplicity went.

Jimmy Lombok's prayer was turning into a marathon. Ritchie shifted in his chair. It might be a plus to have a National Security Adviser with a direct line to God, but the long prayers were definitely a downside. Ritchie felt sure the Almighty would happily settle for something shorter. Ritchie wasn't feeling very patient. Too much stuff had been going wrong. Since the publication of the compromising pictures, Lingaard had been in hiding some place, which wouldn't have mattered that much, but Edward had publicly taken his side, giving an exclusive interview to *Gay America* in which he argued that Cheech Lingaard had a perfect right to have sex with men or women or both at once if he felt like it, and anything else was sheer hypocrisy.

'Lord, the struggle between this nation and her enemies is the struggle between good and evil,' prayed Lombok, and drew breath to continue.

'Amen,' said Ritchie quickly and loudly.

'Amen,' said everyone else at the table.

Lombok was irritated. He felt sure the President must have known he hadn't finished.

'Beautiful prayer, Jimmy,' said Ritchie. 'Very moving.'

'Thank you, Mr President,' said Lombok, a little stiffly.

Vince was pinning his few remaining hopes on the meeting between Ritchie and the British Prime Minister, planned for the day after tomorrow. This would leave only days to stop Operation Deliverance being launched. Several days had already been wasted arguing about whether or not to accede to the British request for an urgent meeting. Everyone was pissed at the Brits for refusing to state clearly in advance what the meeting was for. Skidelski was firmly of the opinion that the President had too much on his plate to take time out to meet James Halstead, and in any case, in a couple of weeks' time the Brits would all be dead so what did it matter if they were offended? But Ed Garoufalas had presented a typically cautious CIA approach: what if the Brits were on to OpDel in some way? True, the CIA wasn't able to find any evidence of that, but it would explain the British refusal to declare the purpose of the meeting. This argument had carried the day. Partly because it was a good argument; partly because most everyone was scared of Garoufalas.

'Okay,' the President said. 'Joe, the agenda's yours.'

'Good morning, folks,' said Skidelski and looked around the table, nodding, as if approving the choice of invitees. Effectively, this was a war cabinet. Vince had counted twenty-eight people present, three or four more than the room could comfortably seat. The idea of restricting the truth about Operation Deliverance to a tiny handful of people had long since been abandoned. Knocking off six billion people wasn't that straightforward. Despite Skidelski's relaxed, folksy performance, the atmosphere in the Laurel Lodge that morning was tense.

'There's only one item on my agenda, of course. But you could say it was a pretty big item.' Skidelski chuckled, but the sycophantic laughter that followed was uneasy. The reality of Operation Deliverance was beginning to weigh on people. You couldn't exactly say there was a crisis of conscience, merely an oppressive awareness of the scale of forthcoming events. Even Larry Dodge looked a little bit anxious, and he didn't really have anything to do with the planning of the operation, his job was just to gather notes and write the big speech that Ritchie would make to the nation immediately after OpDel. Larry Dodge was determined to write a speech commensurate with the greatness of the event. He'd been working on it for several months now, in addition to his normal work on speeches that the President had to make in order to keep up the appearance of normality. This meant even more late nights than usual, even more fast food than usual. As a result, Larry's acne had made spectacular advances, had left behind the bridgehead of his nose and sent legions of spots up across his forehead and laterally across both cheeks, with advance parties skirmishing along the frontiers of his chin. His entire face was a horrific battleground, the pustulant vermilion of the spots clashing horribly with the carroty red of his hair.

General Barry B. Steinberger III had been staring at Larry Dodge with revulsion, thinking how he would like to clean up the young man's face with a flamethrower, when he realised he was being called upon.

Skidelski was saying, 'I'm going to start by asking General Steinberger to summarise the state of preparations. General?'

'Good morning, gentlemen,' said Steinberger, ignoring the presence of Head of Homeland Futures Dolores Delgado and Head of Communications Anna Prascilowicz. Two women to twenty-six men was a pretty low ratio, even by the male-oriented standards of Ritchie's administration, but Joe Skidelski had been clear from the beginning that 'the ladies' were not to be trusted with mass murder, they might suddenly develop sentimental doubts, start worrying about killing other people's babies, stuff like that. Delgado and Prascilowicz were different. They were ladies only in the sense that Lady Macbeth was a lady.

Dolores Delgado wasn't going to let the General get away with his opening line. 'This is not exclusively a male gathering, General.' She smiled, her flawless makeup a reflection of the two hours spent every morning ensuring she looked good. Delgado saw no reason why a ballsy woman shouldn't be an elegant woman.

The General sighed. He hoped that the frontier spirit of the new global America would sweep away all the tedious political correctness that stalked his life. 'My apologies, girls,' said the General.

'Ha ha,' said Delgado.

The General grinned. He looked forward to a time, now not far off, when real men could express their masculinity again, and call women 'girls' and pat 'em on the rump without them getting all upset.

Skidelski waved a spotted, leathery hand in the air. 'Can we just get on, please?'

'Sure,' said the General. 'Only too happy to get on, yes, sir, getting on, that's what we're trained to do. All right. Here's where we stand. Lieutenant?'

Brett, his clean-cut handsome 25-year-old lieutenant, had been appointed the General's personal assistant for OpDel. Unquestioning and full of zeal, tireless in his dedication to the job, and possessing complete mastery of the computer technology that sometimes baffled the General, Brett was Steinberger's idea of how youth ought to be. Heck, the boy even showered twice a day, which was not quite often enough, but a damn sight better than most kids nowadays.

Brett flicked a button on a remote control and a curtain covering the end wall of the conference room slid silently back to reveal a plasma screen occupying the whole width of the wall. He flicked another button and a map of the world appeared.

The General popped a fresh stick of gum into his mouth. 'Okay. Brett's gonna take us on a little world tour. I think you'll find it self-explanatory, but I'll maybe throw in the occasional comment. Okay, kid, roll it.'

Brett said, 'I'll start with Australia and the Pacific.' Anna Prascilowicz tightened her lips. She'd been trying to shut out the subject of Australia. Her ex-husband was Australian. They'd split up three years earlier amidst great acrimony. They had no kids, so the bitterness was all focused on their $600,000 home in Virginia. He'd forced her to sell it so as to get his share, which she'd found mean, because he wasn't short of a buck. He'd said 'Tough shit' and gone back to Sydney to live with the 23-year-old air hostess-cum-airhead he'd met six months before. Ever since then, she'd dreamed of revenge. Now revenge could be hers more completely than she had ever imagined. Yet as the time drew near, Anna was feeling conflicted. She wondered whether she ought to warn him, but then she dare not let out the secret behind International Day of the Planet, she was too committed to President Ritchie to even think of doing that. Maybe she could call her ex-husband and tell him to fly to the States for a few days around the crucial time. But of course he'd ask why and she couldn't think of a pretext that he would believe. And he'd probably bring that air hostess bitch with him, and Anna Prascilowicz was far from sure that she wanted to save *her* life.

Brett was zooming in and out of the map of Australia. The displays showed overlapping swathes of infectivity in various colours, each based upon projections of wind speed and temperatures. A vast area at the centre of the country was free of colour. This pale grey zone denoted an area that the aerial spraying was not expected to reach. Even if General Steinberger had thrown in all his secretly spare aircraft, it just wasn't going to be possible to spray Flaxil-4 over every square foot of the planet. The assumption was, the disease was so infectious that people living in sparsely populated areas not directly sprayed would succumb to the deadly pathogen within a few days or at most a couple of weeks. It was an assumption that not everybody shared.

Brett turned to the Defense Secretary. 'With your permission, sir, I will move on now to South-East Asia and China.'

'China first, please,' said Delgado.

Young Brett looked questioningly at General Steinberger.

Steinberger shrugged. 'Sure.'

The map of China came up on the screen. Again there were some areas in pale grey.

'I have a question,' said Dolores Delgado.

'Go right ahead,' said Skidelski.

'The grey zones, the non-infective areas, some of them are pretty big. What if the infection takes longer to spread than your projections assume? I mean, what if there are survivors hanging on there for weeks, maybe months?'

Boyd intervened. 'Our assumptions are based on reliable and fully tested scientific hypotheses.'

'Yes, but let's allow a margin of error and—'

'We already allowed for a margin of error,' said Boyd dismissively.

Delgado wasn't about to be fobbed off. 'I'm interested in what happens to people who survive the first few days.'

Boyd beamed at her. 'There won't be many of *them*!'

General Barry B. Steinberger III experienced a twinge of anxiety. He had recently worked out that Boyd's uncontrollable flatulence was brought on by excitement, and there was nothing that excited Boyd more than the thought of killing lots of people. That's why the General had fought long and hard for Boyd to be excluded from the war cabinet, but he'd been overruled by Skidelski.

Skidelski intervened. 'Dolores, I promise you it's not a problem. Most of those grey areas you see on the map are desert. Population density almost too low to measure.'

'I can see it's not any kind of a problem in Australia. They don't have nuclear weapons in Australia. But what about China? Or Russia? What if there's a silo somewhere out there in the middle of nowhere with a dozen very angry Chinese survivors? And what if they learn from some radio station that there are no Americans dying? And what if they decide that this is no coincidence and just to make themselves feel a bit better before the virus reaches them they send a thermonuclear warhead in our direction?'

'Hell, lady,' said General Steinberger. 'You think we ain't thought of that? We thought of it, yes, sir, we did, so don't you worry your little head about that! Show her, Brett.'

Brett flicked the remote and up came a series of tiny red triangles scattered across the pale grey areas. 'The red triangles signify nuclear silos, Ma'am. We'll hit each of them individually with a designated spraying aircraft. The personnel will all be dead within twelve hours.'

Delgado was only partly mollified. 'Don't those silos have air-filtration equipment?'

'Yes, Ma'am,' said Brett. 'They surely do. But they won't be switched on. The filtration systems are only activated in times of high alert, our equivalent of Defcon One or Defcon Two. And they won't be on high alert. They think that International Day of the Planet is a peaceful undertaking.'

'In other words, lady, those guys won't know what hit 'em,' said the General. 'One minute they'll be drinking China tea or whatever the hell they drink in China and the next minute their lungs will be filling up with mucus and they'll be dropping like flies.'

'All right,' said Dolores Delgado, examining her nails and thinking maybe this shade of red wasn't right for Camp David. 'All right. But generally, won't it take longer to kill people who're in buildings?'

'It will. But the genius of the plan is that the whole world thinks the operation is peaceful. Remember, March 20 has been designated an international holiday. A lot of people will be out and about instead of in offices and factories.'

Ed Garoufalas chipped in. 'I have an update on this front, if it's all right with you, General.'

'Go right ahead,' said the General, flicking his gum from cheek to cheek.

'I'm pleased to be able to tell you that the CIA has made a significant breakthrough in the last twenty-four hours.'

Hickie Langshite sighed stagily and stared up at the ceiling. If only the CIA's gift for self-promotion, he thought, were equalled by its ability to deliver.

Garoufalas was used to FBI envy and ignored the loud sigh. 'I'm pleased to be able to tell you that no fewer than . . . ' He checked with his notes. 'No fewer than sixty-two countries have subscribed to our Kids Together for the Planet initiative. In those countries, the children will be taken to parks and other open areas to wave up at the planes as they pass overhead, thus ensuring an effective dispersal of the pathogen among the pre-teens. We believe this will be useful in the further spread of the infection, since parents are unlikely to be concerned for their own safety when looking after their young.'

A silence fell in the room. Vince's head was spinning. He thought he was going to be sick. President Ritchie pulled a face. He didn't like the idea of killing all those little kids. Little kids were cute. 'Let's move on,' he said firmly.

Al Boyd's bowels were boiling. 'I think it's a terrific idea, Ed,' he said, his voice suddenly husky. He pressed down deep into his soft leather chair to suppress the eructation that he knew was near.

'Yeah,' said the General, glancing in Boyd's direction. 'Let's move on.'

With occasional contributions from Steinberger and Skidelski, Brett spent the next hour and a half taking everyone through a visual presentation of Operation Deliverance. Not everyone's attention was focused on Brett and his sophisticated sequences. Operation Deliverance was no longer an abstraction, no longer some war plan that would kill people you'd never even heard of, far less met. This was getting personal, this was getting close to home. Every single player around the table that day had started to cheat. Hickie Langshite had secretly arranged for his Japanese daughter-in-law to be inoculated. What was the point of being head of the FBI if you couldn't make an exception for your own daughter-in-law? Of course, it hadn't turned out that easy. He'd ended up having to ship forty doses of the vaccine over to Japan so that her entire extended family could be protected. Ed Garoufalas had arranged for seven Turkish belly dancers to be invited to the US embassy in Ankara and offered inoculations. Ed Garoufalas was not an ungrateful man. He had once run the CIA station in Turkey and would never forget the special offerings laid on for him every Tuesday evening for four years. Larry Dodge had called an Estonian girl who'd been his hotel chambermaid at a conference in Tallinn three years before, urging her to bring her little girl over for inoculation, even offering to pay the fare as long as that wasn't taken as an admission of paternity. With stupid pride, the girl had refused, and Larry had given up.

Even President Ritchie was up for a little cheating. Afraid of what his wife would say about wiping out Canada, he'd arranged for every Canadian she knew and liked to cross over into the States and get vaccinated.

Everybody knew that making exceptions like this wasn't a good idea. The more exceptions that were made, the greater the chance of a leak. And even if the lucky recipients of the vaccine didn't know the real reason for being inoculated, some of them were bound to boast about having access to the vaccine, and that would of course contribute to the growing pressure on governments around the world to offer protection to their own citizens. But knowing is one thing, and acting on the knowledge is another. Dolores Delgado was the only one in that conference room who wasn't already cheating in some way. Dolores Delgado was what the Germans called *konsequent* – she saw things through in a logical manner and did not allow her judgement to be corrupted by sentiment.

Brett wrapped up his presentation and sat down. Ritchie felt restless. It was nearly lunchtime. He wanted a beer. Maybe he'd even have a quick shot of Wild Turkey. No harm in a man having a drop of bourbon before lunch. It steadied the nerves in difficult times. Look at Churchill, he'd gotten through World War Two with the help of a bottle of brandy a day, and he'd gone down as one of the great leaders of history. Ritchie was just about to suggest that they break early for lunch when Jimmy Lombok intervened. Goddamnit, that man was getting on his nerves.

'About the vaccination program,' said Lombok. 'I'm very concerned about the high number of American citizens who still haven't been inoculated. We're about to launch Operation Deliverance and our latest estimate is three-quarters of a million Americans unprotected. That's three-quarters of a million of our fellow citizens we're condemning to death. I would like to propose that we postpone Operation Deliverance for a month, until we do something about those poor people.'

General Barry B. Steinberger III narrowed his eyes and stared at the President's National Security Adviser. 'Are you crazy? Postpone? It's not that easy, Mr Lombok, no sir, not that easy at all. OpDel has been eighteen months in the planning, and if you want to postpone it now, then I'd say we have to postpone for at least six months, probably more.'

Skidelski nodded. 'That's pretty much how I see it, Jimmy.'

Ritchie was horrified. A sixth-month postponement would take him close to the end of his second term. No way was he going to allow a six-month postponement.

The Vice President, who'd been silent for the entire meeting, finally opened his mouth to speak. As usual, his rare contribution was designed (so he thought) to strike a sensible balance between opposing views. 'The way I see it, we ought to make one more big push to help those poor folks get vaccinated, but we ought to try not to postpone unless it's absolutely necessary.'

Al Boyd sighed. He couldn't bear this kind of woolly thinking. 'Listen, people, let's not even think about postponing.'

'Absolutely, Mr Boyd,' said the President firmly. 'Postponement is not on the agenda.'

'Right,' nodded the General. 'No postponing, no sir, not right, not right at all.'

'Anyhow,' said Boyd, watching Jimmy Lombok wipe the sweat from his shining dome of a head, 'I reckon most of those people are *choosing* not to be vaccinated, right? Because they're some kind of goddamn Jesus freaks who think vaccination is against God's rules. Am I right?'

Jimmy Lombok leapt to his feet. He pointed a quivering finger at Boyd. 'Do not, do not ever refer to believers as Jesus freaks! NEVER! Got that? You fat fruit!'

'Gentlemen, please,' said Skidelski.

Boyd laughed. 'I'm just saying, if people want to die, rather than get vaccinated, that's their God-given right as citizens of this great nation. Right?'

Lombok was still on his feet.

Ritchie sighed. He needed a drink. And soon. 'Sit down, Jimmy.'

Lombok sat down, his face still red with indignation. 'I just want believers to be treated with the respect they deserve, that's all, okay?'

'Sure, Jimmy,' said the Vice President reassuringly. 'We understand.'

'What's the problem?' sneered Boyd. 'They're all going to go straight to heaven right? This way they'll just arrive a little ahead of schedule.'

Jimmy Lombok was about to explode with renewed fury when Ritchie raised a hand. 'Shut up, both of you. We're breaking for lunch. Now.'

Vince felt relief. He'd spent the entire meeting fighting off waves of nausea. Ahead of the others, he walked out of the cabin into the fierce sunshine. He took out his cell phone and called Lucy. He didn't know why, he just needed to hear her voice. About thirty seconds after she answered, they started arguing.

74

Bob Bloom's funeral was a simple affair. Marina came all the way from San Diego to say goodbye to her one-time boyfriend. She was glad she'd spent almost a week's wages on flowers, because she and a very bored priest were the only mourners. Like millions of others, Marina had seen Bob Bloom on television, giving the President a hard time, and it somehow brought back a little of the love she'd once felt for him.

It was a tragedy that Bob had fallen asleep at the wheel on his way back from Washington to Louisiana. People said that a couple of hours earlier he'd been drinking with a couple of strangers he'd met in a bar, but the barman said Bob hadn't had any alcohol, just the coffee that the two strangers had bought for him.

For some reason, the police didn't want to investigate.

75

'He wants to meet you *alone*?'

'That's right,' said Ritchie.

Skidelski and Garoufalas were aghast. Even by the relaxed standards of Camp David, this was unheard of. Skidelski said, 'I'm sorry, Mr President, this is crazy. No way can we agree to that.'

'Why not?' said the President, in skittishly cheerful mood.

'It's . . . well, it's unacceptable. You can't meet foreign leaders without a proper team at your elbow.'

'Hell, Joe, in a few days' time we won't have to worry about foreign leaders. There won't *be* any foreign leaders. There won't be any for-eigners.' The President sniggered. Skidelski thought he caught a whiff of bourbon on the President's breath. That could be a worry. It was only six in the evening, and normally Ritchie only ever drank beer at Camp David, and never to excess.

The three men were sitting in rocking chairs on the porch of the President's cabin, enjoying the last of the day's warmth.

'I agree with Joe,' growled Ed Garoufalas.

'Well, do you know what, Ed? I don't give a damn.' Ritchie punched the Director of the CIA on the arm. It was halfway between being a guy sort of thing and a straightforward assault.

Garoufalas winced and was furious. 'If you want to ignore the advice of the CIA, you go ahead and do that, sir.'

The President stood up and gave a little mock bow. 'How kind of you to give me your permission. I accept your offer.'

Garoufalas stood up, stomped down the little flight of steps leading from the porch, and walked away.

Walking away in anger from the President of the United States was not generally seen as a good career move.

Ritchie stared after him. 'He's finished,' said Ritchie. 'He's out.

Day after OpDel, he's out. Motherfucker.'

'Right,' said Skidelski. 'I never trusted the guy.'

'Exactly. Let's have a beer, Joe. And some pretzels.'

'Sure.'

'Aw to hell, I need a bourbon.'

'Is that wise, sir?'

Ritchie fixed Skidelski with a cold eye. 'Hey, Joe. One Mrs Ritchie is enough. Okay?'

'Sure,' said Skidelski quickly. 'Sorry.'

'Oh, and tomorrow I'm meeting James Halstead the way I want, okay?

'I just don't think it's a good idea for you to meet him all on your own. I don't trust the British. Never did, never will.'

'Okay. I'll take Vince along.'

'Just you and Vince?!'

'You heard. I trust Vince.'

'Are you sure that's a good judgement call, sir?'

'Yes.' The President walked into his cabin and came out with a bottle of Wild Turkey and two glasses.

Skidelski looked around. This wasn't good. Anyone wandering past (like any one of the eighty secret servicemen on duty) would see the President drinking.

Ritchie poured two generous shots of bourbon and passed one to Skidelski.

'Here.'

'I'll just have a beer, Mr President.'

'You're having a bourbon.'

Skidelski took the glass. 'Maybe we should go inside, sir.'

'Maybe we should stay here.' Ritchie sat down and drained his glass.

'I think I ought to be with you tomorrow, sir. I don't understand why Halstead isn't bringing anyone along. He brought people with him on his plane, didn't he?'

'No. Only his wife and daughter.'

'That is weird, sir. I don't understand it.'

'Me neither,' said Ritchie, pouring himself another shot of Wild Turkey. 'But to tell you the truth, I'm feeling sorry for James Halstead. He's been a good and faithful ally to this country and I'm going to feel bad when we wipe him out. Don't worry, I know it has to be done. But, you know, there are some decencies that have to be observed in this

291

world. I'm treating this meeting with James like a condemned prisoner's last request. I'm not a hard man, you know, Joe.'

Joe Skidelski thought he saw a tear in the President's eye. 'I know that, sir. But—'

'Joe,' said the President. 'Shut up.'

'Yes, sir.'

Early the following afternoon, two Americans and one Brit strolled in the unseasonably warm sunshine through the grounds of Camp David and chatted. The reason the British Prime Minister had wanted a meeting on his own was quite simple: he hadn't told a single one of his colleagues about Operation Deliverance. He had a reason for that, a good reason. James Halstead believed that if he played his cards right, he would shortly be in a position of enormous power.

For the first few minutes, Ritchie and Halstead chatted about the weather, while Vince walked silently alongside. Ritchie, being an out-doors kind of guy, pointed out oak, hickory and tulip poplars. The Prime Minister was too polite to mention that this was exactly what Ritchie had done on his very first visit to Camp David several years before.

In the distance, sometimes visible through the trees and sometimes not, heavily armed Secret Servicemen strolled along at the same pace.

Without warning, the British Prime Minister said, 'Ritchie. I know all about Operation Deliverance.'

The President stopped in his tracks, as did Vince. A hundred yards away, a young Secret Serviceman stopped. He turned slightly so that the concealed directional microphone he was carrying would be better aligned to pick up their conversation. Under his shirt, the long, thin microphone was strapped to his forearm from wrist to elbow. Provided the wind wasn't too strong, he could pick up a conversation at two hundred yards either by pointing his hand in the direction of the subjects or by pointing his elbow. Neither pose looked entirely natural, so he kept switching between the two.

'I don't know what you're talking about,' said Ritchie, with surprising conviction.

James Halstead smiled. 'I know you have to say that. It's under-standable. But really, I know all about it, I really do. I know about the flu virus. I know about the spraying operation on International Day of

292

the Planet. I know you plan to wipe out most of the world's population. I know everything. Don't ask me how I found out, but I found out.'

The President remained silent for a very long time, then said, 'How did you find out?'

The Prime Minister laughed, and said, 'British technology's rather good you know. Especially surveillance technology. We picked up a couple of conversations that Mr Skidelski was having.'

'Just a couple?'

'Well, quite a few, actually.'

'The guy's an idiot.' Ritchie turned to Vince. 'So. Vince. They know all about it.'

Vince hoped that he looked shocked. 'I'm just . . . just kind of absorbing the news, sir.'

'Yeah, takes a bit of absorbing, don't it?'

'It certainly does, sir.'

The three men stood in silence for a few more seconds. Vince wondered when the Prime Minister would launch into his impassioned plea to cancel Operation Deliverance.

James Halstead said, 'Look, Ritchie. I think it's a terrific idea.'

What? thought Vince. *What?!*

Ritchie said, 'You think it's a terrific idea?'

'Yes. The logic is inescapable. An overcrowded planet. The environment in a state of terminal decline. Species loss. Climate change. Global warming. You've made a bold, imaginative decision. It must have been hard. But it was right.'

Suddenly, Vince knew what was coming.

Sure enough, the Prime Minister made his move. 'Of course, we want to be part of this. We want our population vaccinated. To be quite frank, I'm upset that I have to ask. I thought there might be a quid pro quo for all our support over the years.'

Ritchie grunted non-committally. He needed to buy thinking time. He needed to buy *a lot* of thinking time. He took a little silver box out of his shirt pocket, selected a toothpick, and got to work on his molars.

The Prime Minister continued. 'Look, we're willing to let bygones be bygones. Provided you put the vaccine at our disposal, enough for the entire British population.'

To Ritchie, this sounded a bit like a threat. He wondered what, if any, evidence Halstead had obtained. Maybe he was bluffing. Maybe not.

Maybe he had recordings of Skidelski talking. From his lower incisors Ritchie flicked out a little sliver of bacon left over from breakfast. It landed on the Prime Minister's shirt. 'Sorry,' said the President, and picked the bacon off the shoulder of his most loyal ally. He then turned to Vince. 'Have we got that much vaccine to spare, Vince, you happen to know?'

Vince was struggling to hold focus. He fought off waves of rage against the Brits. The bastards, he thought, the bastards have shafted me. Duplicitous to the end, just like the Brits had always been. Bastards. But he couldn't do anything about it. If he tried to do anything about it, he'd give himself away.

'Vince. Vince? You okay?' The President was squeezing his arm.

Vince jumped. 'Yeah. Yeah, I'm fine. Sorry, sir. I . . . look, I don't know whether there's enough vaccine or not.'

'Let's find out.' He turned to the Prime Minister. 'James, I am so sorry. I feel real bad about this. I said to my people, I said to them, we have to let our friends in Britain have the vaccine, I fought long and hard for you, I truly did, but you know how it is, a President doesn't win all the arguments.'

James Halstead looked sceptical.

Vince tried to recall a single moment when Ritchie had argued in favour of letting Britain have the vaccine and decided there hadn't been any.

In the distance, the Secret Serviceman with the concealed microphone was having to adopt increasingly contorted poses to keep his microphone lined up on the President and the Prime Minister. Halstead noticed him and was puzzled why a security chap was doing tai chi.

The President took the Prime Minister's hand and stared deep into his eyes. 'James. We have done you a terrible wrong. And I'm going to right it. I swear to you now, your nation will be given the vaccine. Even if we have to postpone Operation Deliverance.'

The emotional power of Ritchie's little speech was so enormous that Halstead really, really wanted to believe him. But it was sort of hard to believe in the sincerity of a person who has spent the previous couple of years planning the annihilation of your entire population.

The Prime Minister said, 'I suggest we confer separately and meet up again some time this evening.'

'Good idea,' said Ritchie. 'Yeah, you go to your cabins, we go to ours, we noodle this thing out, and we meet up again later on.'

As the three of them strolled back, they passed a Secret Serviceman leaning against a tree, his elbow cocked in a very camp manner. Ritchie frowned. It wasn't good if even the Secret Service was turning gay.

76

Ritchie and Halstead and their two aides were not the only ones wandering through the grounds of Camp David that afternoon. Far away from the cabins, almost on the perimeter of the estate, Joe Skidelski and General Barry B Steinberger III were deep in conversation.

'In other words,' said Skidelski, 'once OpDel has been completed, is Ritchie necessarily the right man to rule the planet?'

'That's a good question, yes sir, that is a good question. But I can't say I've given it much thought.'

'Then it's time you did, General.' Skidelski laid a withered hand on the General's shoulder. The General immediately jumped back. He didn't like being touched by other men; you never knew where their hands had been. True, you didn't know where women's hands had been either, but there was a statistical chance they'd been somewhere more pleasant.

'There's a drink problem,' said Skidelski. 'And it's growing. How can we trust the judgement of an alcoholic President?'

The General shook his head grimly. 'That's bad. Alcohol's a terrible thing.'

Skidelski said, 'After OpDel, we will have two needs. One is clarity of purpose. That is what I can supply. The other is the means to implement that clarity of purpose. And that, General, is what you can supply.'

The General stopped. 'What are you saying here, Joe?'

'I'm saying, let's rule the planet together. Just you and me.'

Skidelski did not see this as an attempted coup. In fact, he felt he was making a sacrifice. It would mean giving up Europe. But what the hell. He could use Europe as his holiday home. Yes, Versailles for the summer would be just fine.

At exactly the same time, a few hundred yards behind the cabins, Dolores Delgado and Ed Garoufalas sat side by side in a set of swings.

The swings had been installed a few years previously by a family-loving President who wanted his staff to be able to bring their kids with them at weekends.

Delgado swung back and forward rather daintily, making sure she didn't scuff her shoes. She was only on the swings because it kept Garoufalas sweet, and keeping Garoufalas sweet meant keeping the CIA sweet, and keeping the CIA sweet was important.

'Ritchie's planning to bring the Brits in on OpDel,' said Garoufalas, as casually as he could. In his experience, casual usually had a bigger impact.

'No!' said Delgado, genuinely shocked. 'How do you know?'

'I'll let you have the transcript,' said Garoufalas.

'If it's true . . .' said Delgado. 'If it's true, he has to be stopped.'

'It's true.'

'If we start making exceptions, there will be no end to it. And there will be leaks, bound to be leaks. It could endanger the whole procedure. No, we have to be tough.'

'I agree.'

The two swung back and forward in silence for a few moments. Garoufalas looked over at her. 'I gather you've been offered Asia.'

'Who told you that?'

'I wouldn't settle for Asia if I were you, Dolores. You're worth so much more than Asia.'

'Thank you. And what do you think I'm worth?'

'The whole goddamn planet.'

Dolores Delgado leapt off her swing. 'Are you out of your mind?!'

Garoufalas kept swinging. 'Think about it. With the CIA behind you, we could make it work. Ritchie's not up to running the entire planet. You know that. I know that. We all know that. We've been in denial. We need someone hard, decisive, clear-headed. Someone like you.'

'I see. And what would be in it for *you*?'

'Well,' said Garoufalas, 'we'd have to deal with Steinberger, I don't trust Steinberger.'

'And who would replace General Steinberger?'

'I would.'

'You'd run the military?'

'Sure. Why not? In a few days from now it'll be the only military in the world. Running it is too important to leave to some dumbfuck general.'

Garoufalas was sitting motionless on his swing. Delgado was standing nearby like a nervous mother. Neither spoke for a few moments. Then Delgado said, 'What are we going to do about the British?'

'Don't worry,' said Garoufalas. 'I'm on the case.'

77

The President was alone in his cabin with Skidelski, trying to figure out what to do with the Brits. The Defense Secretary was furious. He wished he'd been at the meeting; he'd have poked that English asshole right in the eye.

Ritchie wished Vince were around, but a couple of hours after the walkabout summit with Halstead, Vince had gone down with a bad tummy bug and retired to his cabin. Or so he'd said. Ritchie didn't think Vince had looked all that ill. But if a guy's got the shits, you don't want to run the risk of making him stay in the room with you.

Ritchie poured another bourbon. 'When are we planning to put the amendment through Congress, Joe? You know, giving me a third and fourth term? Should we do it say, a week after OpDel? Or should we let the dust settle for a couple of months? I think we need to decide.'

'It's not the priority, Mr President,' said Skidelski. 'Right now, our problem is the Brits. What are we going to do about the Brits?'

'Okay, let's decide about the Brits. But then let's talk about that damned constitutional amendment. I'm not planning to go through all the stress and strain of killing six billion people just to find myself with only a few more months left in power.'

'Sure, sure,' said Skidelski. 'The Brits.'

'I say, what the hell, let 'em have the vaccine. James Halstead's been a good ally to America. Done just about everything I asked him. Seems kinda mean to wipe out his country.'

'This is not the time to get sentimental, sir.'

'Yeah, I know, but—'

'I checked. We'd need more time to manufacture the extra vaccine. We'd probably have to postpone.'

Ritchie screwed up his face. 'That's no good.' His face brightened suddenly. 'I got it! I got it, Joe. I just thought of a compromise. The

British like compromises, right? So, here's what we do. We offer the vaccine to Halstead and his family and a few of his inner circle. We fly them out here to Camp David and install them in a compound. Under lock and key, you understand? Oh and maybe we invite a few of their royals at the same time. It'd be kinda cute to have a royal compound, wouldn't it? People could come and see the British royals and the British Prime Minister, just like they were in olden times. Kids could come along and throw bread to 'em. And if we got bored having them around, heck, we'd sell the lot to Disneyland.'

'Mr President. How much have you had to drink?'

'Not enough.' Ritchie cackled, and went over to the bourbon bottle.

'I think we need to tell the British that we agree to their proposal.'

'Okay. Whatever. Gee, I'm hungry. Wouldn't mind a cheeseburger. That's the only downside to Camp David. The cheeseburgers. They're no good.'

'What I'm saying is, Mr President, we ought to tell them we agree to all their demands. Even if . . . well, regardless of what we finally decide.'

'You mean, like, keep our options open?'

'Exactly, sir.'

'Sounds okay to me.'

'You see, we can't risk them going back thinking we're going to refuse.'

'Why's that?'

Skidelski cast a glance at the half-empty bourbon bottle. This was getting hard. 'Because they might go and tell the whole world.'

'Shit. You're right. Tell you what, Joe, I'd settle for a T-bone steak instead. Call the kitchen for me, willya?'

78

Vince drove hell for leather towards Annapolis. He was afraid that Halstead might tell Ritchie about the visit to Chequers. Every ten minutes or so he called Lucy on his cell phone, but couldn't raise her. Now that the Brits had betrayed him, he sensed the only small glimmer of hope was to try to get the killer video of the President aired on some TV station. But which one? Would *any* of them agree to run it? And would it be believed?

Turning south on I-70, Vince checked his rearview mirror. He had no doubt that once his disappearance from Camp David was noticed his life would be at risk. And Lucy's. He began to think that heading home was a dumb thing to do. It would be better to meet some place. But he daren't say where over his cellphone. He called Lucy one more time, and she answered.

'Where are you?' she said.

'Listen, Luce. Things are bad. Pack a suitcase and meet me at—'

'Why should I do that?'

Vince groaned. 'This is really important, just trust me, Lucy, okay?'

'And why should I do that?'

'JUST SHUT THE FUCK UP AND LISTEN, OKAY?!'

A pause. 'Okay.'

'Now don't say the name of the place. I'll meet you in an hour outside the restaurant where we had our biggest fight ever.'

There was another pause. 'Okay.' Again a pause. 'Is that the one where you called me a stuck-up English bitch or the one where I poured the dessert wine over you?'

'The one where you poured the dessert wine over me.'

79

For about twenty-four hours it was generally agreed to have been the most audacious and best-coordinated terrorist attack for many years. The F-22 hijacked from Langley Air Force Base caught up with the Prime Minister's plane just south of Delaware Bay. Thanks to its advanced stealth technology the F-22 didn't show up on the radar of the Boeing Business Jet taking James Halstead and his family back to London. Halstead had only acquired the jet six months before. For years he'd been embarrassed at not having his own Prime Ministerial aircraft. He'd finally persuaded the Treasury to let him lease his own plane, at a cost of £20m a year. This, however, was substantially offset by sponsorship. Halstead was a great proselytiser for business; he saw no shame in having a few corporate logos on the outside of his plane.

The first missile slammed into the fuselage just below the McDonald's Golden Arches, and exploded in the luggage hold. The second entered cleanly through the Nike swoop, exploding beneath the cockpit floor and killing the flight crew instantly. The F-22 pulled away, turned steeply and came back to make sure the job was done. The pilot had four more AIM-120c air-to-air missiles to play with, but decided he wouldn't need them. Just for the hell of it, he squeezed off a two-second burst of 20mm cannon. What was left of the fuselage of the Boeing Business Jet unpeeled, the fuel tanks exploded, and the Boeing disintegrated.

Many thousands of feet below, 82-year old Abe Grandage was strolling along the boardwalk in Atlantic City. He was feeling happy. He'd just won $4,000 at blackjack. It made him so happy that he'd decided to quit smoking. Hell, there were years of life still ahead of him if only he started taking better care of himself. He stood on the boardwalk and pulled on a cigarette. People passing gave him disapproving looks. Taking the cigarette out of his mouth, he looked at it for a moment and then tossed it over the side of the boardwalk. Turning to the people walking past, some of whom were looking up at the sky in a strange manner, he shouted, 'Hey! That was my last cigarette, ever!'

A moment later the battered remains of the British Prime Minister's red box hit Abe Grandage at a terminal velocity of 204.3 miles per hour.

Some people found it odd that the terrorists safely returned the plane to its base, before disappearing completely.

80

'Very interesting,' said the senior news editor and switched off the DVD. 'Can we hold on to this?'

'No,' said Vince.

'Uh, I'd like to show this to my boss before we decide to transmit it or not.'

'Then your boss comes here and we all look at it together.'

'I don't think I can do that.'

Vince shrugged. 'Okay, then I'll take the DVD and go.'

'You're being unreasonable,' said the editor. 'Look, we're one of the world's biggest cable news stations and this story is dynamite. Hell, it's not dynamite. In news terms, it's a hundred Hiroshimas. You seriously want me to run a story saying the President of the United States is planning to knock off six billion people the day after tomorrow without consulting my boss?'

Vince kind of saw his point. Equally, he knew he daren't leave the DVD behind. This was the third TV station he'd been to. It was getting dangerous. If there wasn't an alert out for him there would be soon. He crossed to the DVD player and removed the disk. 'Thanks, anyway.'

'Sit down and have a coffee. Let's chat some more about it.' Vince was immediately suspicious. News editors didn't have time to sit around and chat. They either ran a story or they didn't. He headed for the door.

The news editor picked up the phone and said, 'Get me security.'

Vince ran for it. Lucy was waiting outside in the car. Vince leapt in. 'Go!' he shouted.

'Why?' said Lucy.

'Just fucking go!'

81

'I told you before. No way am I going down to the bunker, okay?!'

International Day of the Planet had dawned, and President Ritchie's advisers were again telling him he'd be safer in the bunker beneath the White House.

But Ritchie wasn't having it. 'I'm doing this for the American people. I want the American people to know that I was at my desk throughout. I want them to know that I'm no coward.'

Of course, Ritchie also wanted them to support the Constitutional Amendment that would soon give him a third and fourth term in office. Hell, maybe the American people would be so grateful that they'd want to go even further, and allow Ritchie to stay in office till the end of his life. Like the Pope got to do. So forget all that bullshit about spending the next twenty-four hours in a goddamn bunker.

A giant screen had been set up at one end of the Oval Office, carrying a direct feed from the Command and Control Center underneath the Pentagon, where General Steinberger was supervising the operation. Joe Skidelski and Vice President Murdo Robertson and Jimmy Lombok and Dolores Delgado and Anna Prascilowicz and Larry Dodge and most important of all, Rascal the spaniel, were all gathered in the Oval Office with him. Nobody wanted Al Boyd in the room, because they knew how excited he would likely get, so Al Boyd had been exiled to his office in the American Way building.

As Ritchie put his feet up on his desk and opened another bottle of beer with his teeth, he felt a warm glow inside. This was fun. This was like the Super Bowl, only better. Yeah, Ritchie felt pretty good. The only cloud on the horizon (apart from his goddamn son) was Vince, who'd been going round TV news stations trying to get them to transmit a damning film of Ritchie talking cheerfully about the deaths of six billion people. Ritchie felt hurt. After all that he'd done for Vince . . . Well, the bastard would pay the price. CIA and FBI agents were combing America in search of him and Lucy. They were authorised to use lethal force.

Several hours later, Ritchie was getting bored and had moved on from beer to bourbon. The steady flow of information about planes taking off and returning to base with missions safely accomplished was exciting at first, but quickly palled. Ritchie wondered if his team in the Oval Office would be upset if he suggested they watch a movie instead, just until something started happening, but decided it wouldn't make him look like much of a leader.

Ritchie remained behind his desk. Larry Dodge had settled down in front of a computer. Everyone else was pacing up and down, watching the big screen and taking phone calls. Then Ritchie was told that his son Edward was in the building, 'with a friend'. Ritchie felt a bit anxious about the friend, but hell, this was a big day for the human race, and it would be right and proper to have his own son at his side after several weeks of separation. 'Send 'em in,' said the President.

A couple of minutes later, Edward came into the Oval Office, with Cheech Lingaard close behind. Ritchie's joy turned to rage. 'What the hell are you doing here, Lingaard? This is a great day for mankind. No way do I want a pornographer in the White House on a day like this.'

'Dad. We're partners.'

'Huh?'

'Me and Cheech. We're partners.'

Ritchie took his feet off the desk. 'Now you listen here, son. If you want to go into business you can go into business with just about whoever the hell you want to, but I am not allowing you to go into business with a pornographer! GOT THAT?!'

Edward shook his head. 'Not that kind of partner, Dad. I mean, Cheech and I are lovers.'

Cheech Lingaard took Edward's hand. 'It's the truth.'

Ritchie struggled to speak. 'You're . . . you're at least twice his age, you filthy fucking pervert!'

'That's right,' said Cheech. 'Eddie needs a father figure.'

Ritchie hit Cheech Lingaard in the face. Lingaard fell to his knees and burst into tears. 'Well, hit him back, for Chrissake!' screamed Edward.

At this point the violence might have escalated had Skidelski not intervened. 'Mr President . . . Sir, can I have your attention? This is pretty serious.'

'What?' asked Ritchie, his fists still balled. 'What is it? Can't you see I have a situation here?'

'Sir, we just had a call from our embassy in Beijing. They report several of the staff unwell.'

Ritchie was still staring with hatred at Cheech Lingaard, who was holding a handkerchief over his bleeding nose.

'*American* staff, sir.'

'Yeah, well, so they're unwell. Fuck 'em. Stop bothering me, willya?'

Skidelski took the President by the elbow. 'Four of them already died.'

Ritchie wasn't listening. 'Get those two cocksuckers out of here!' he shouted.

'Don't worry, Dad, we're going. Come on, Cheech.' Edward helped a dazed and bloodied Cheech Lingaard to his feet and together they left the Oval Office.

'I want that man killed, okay?' shouted the President. 'Call Ed Garoufalas and tell him I want Cheech Lingaard killed.'

'You can't do that, sir,' said Anna Prascilowicz, deeply shocked.

'Why the hell not? Things are going to change around here, you know. This is my planet now, okay? I can do what I like!'

'Mr President!' shouted Dolores Delgado, phone in hand. 'General Steinberger reports outbreaks of illness at one of our bases in Asia.'

'What are the symptoms?' snapped Skidelski.

'What are the symptoms, General?' Delgado nodded as she listened. 'He says, chest pains, dizziness and nausea.'

A chill descended on the Oval Office. Chest pains, dizziness and nausea were the first symptoms of the deadly new strain of flu being released upon the world.

'Sounds a bit like Flaxil-4,' said the Vice President unhelpfully.

'Some of our people must have missed out on their vaccinations,' said Skidelski, taking the phone from Delgado. 'General, what the hell's going on?'

From his place in front of the computer screen, Larry Dodge was reading messages coming in from other American embassies around the world. 'Ten of our people dead in Tokyo!' he shouted out.

Delgado picked up another phone. 'Get me our embassy in Japan!'

Skidelski had gone pale. His leathery hand was clutching the phone so hard the knuckles were turning white. 'What? All of them? . . . What are you trying to tell me, General? . . . Jesus Christ.'

'Please,' said Jimmy Lombok. 'No blaspheming.'

Skidelski put the phone down. 'Mr President. All the flight crews who've returned from the first missions over Japan are showing symptoms.'

'I don't understand,' said Ritchie.

'Quiet, everybody!' hollered Delgado, and resumed her phone call. 'Can you say that again? I can't hear you very well . . . All right, I'm sorry you're not well, but . . . Look, give me the ambassador, will you? . . . He's dead . . . What? . . . They're . . . you're . . . you're the only one still alive . . .'

'Oh Jesus,' said Skidelski softly.

Jimmy Lombok clapped his hands. 'I said, no blaspheming.'

'Shut the fuck up, will you, Jimmy?' roared Skidelski.

'Where's Rascal?' said the President. 'I need Rascal.'

Rascal obligingly trotted out from beneath a chair, tail wagging.

'Good boy,' said the President.

The news agencies were now carrying early, unconfirmed reports from various countries of a massive and mysterious outbreak of illness. Many people were already dead, many more dying. All over the world, TV stations were breaking the news of some terrible new plague that was sweeping all before it. And then, very soon, the TV stations started going off air. For the people in the Oval Office, all this was of course good news. But Americans abroad were also dying, and that wasn't good news, because Americans everywhere had been vaccinated.

Vice President Robertson had been thinking hard. 'Do you know, I suspect this isn't going according to plan.'

Skidelski narrowed his eyes. 'You are one useless motherfucker. Did I ever tell you that?'

Delgado put down the phone. 'OK. Let's be calm. There's clearly something wrong with the vaccine we used for our people in Asia. It's giving no protection at all. Was it a different batch from what we used here at home?'

'No,' said Skidelski.

There was a long silence.

'Shit,' said Delgado.

'It's the end of the world,' said Jimmy Lombok. 'The Lord be praised.'

The President didn't like the sound of things and ordered in cheese-burgers.

A human being's ability to go into denial is very great. For most of the next twelve hours, every single person in the Oval Office managed to believe that the reports coming in of American deaths around the world meant only some minor glitch in the operation. The deaths of hundreds of millions of non-Americans was hardly discussed – that was the successful part of the operation.

It was twenty-two hours into Operation Deliverance before anyone could bring themselves to say what they were all beginning to think.

'I think we're fucked,' said Skidelski.

82

The free market made America and the free market destroyed America.

If President Ritchie's administration hadn't swept away several thousand 'petty regulations', then the Flaxil-4 vaccine would have worked just fine. But thanks to a reduction in the minimum time specified for filtration and centrifugation, impurities had been left behind.

These impurities caused a massive deterioration in the potency of the vaccine. Normally this would have been picked up during clinical trials. But clinical trials take time, and the manufacturers had been told that what counted was speed. And this was a very lucrative contract. And the customer didn't mind that corners were being cut. And everyone knows that the customer is king.

83

The Flaxil-4 virus only took a few days to spread right across the United States. Within a week, half the population had died. Within three weeks, everyone had died.

Everyone, that is, except the President. The vaccine manufactured in Cologne by the cell-tissue method was the only one that proved efficacious against the new Terror Flu. It was just a pity that only one person in the world had been given it.

Dolores Delgado died worrying about her appearance.

Murdo Robertson died putting on his kilt.

Al Boyd died eating a cream donut.

Joe Skidelski died during sex with his much younger wife, something he'd often worried about.

Anna Prascilowicz died wondering what spin to put on the story.

Larry Dodge died drafting a speech in which the President gracefully accepted the offer of a third and fourth term of office.

Hickie Langshite and Ed Garoufalas died blaming each other.

Edward and Cheech died while co-hosting a chic 'goodbye mankind' party in California.

General Barry B. Steinberger III died in the shower. It was how he would have wanted it.

Vince and Lucy died arguing.

Only a few weeks after Operation Deliverance, Ritchie gave up trying to find signs of human life anywhere on the planet.

84

The President lived on in the White House for several years. It was a lonely existence, but he still had Rascal and sometimes they would go out among the high grass that had once been the South Lawn and Ritchie would throw a ball for Rascal to fetch, and in his imagination Ritchie would hear military bands playing for him and see limousines drawing up with foreign leaders coming to pay obeisance.

One day, in what had once been the Rose Garden, but was now a haven for wildlife, Ritchie saw something that definitely wasn't imagined. He saw a bald eagle. It made him very happy. He realised that he was the President who'd saved God's creation. That evening, he went into the Oval Office and lit all his remaining candles. By the flickering light he looked up and stared at the picture on the east wall, that huge colour photograph of himself dressed as a cowboy, astride the planet, riding it like a bucking bronco.

The President finally had what he wanted. The President had a planet. All to himself.